Unbreakable

Blood and Bond Series • Book One

L. M. ROCKERS

EmberMantel Productions

Contents

Courage isn't the absence of fear—it's choosing to move forward anyway.
Thank you to everyone who believed in this story along the way.

Prologue

Meaty hands wrap around my face and body pulling me into a janitor's closet, as usual. But, instead of getting smacked or punched, my hands and feet are bound with rope, a gag covers my mouth, and something covers my head. I truly think I am going to die, this is going to be the last memory I have. Once I'm bound, we just stand there, and I have no idea why. I try to struggle, testing my restraints, but that earns me a punch to the face, breaking my nose. Blood splatters over the cloth covering my face, and I lose my sense of smell. We stand in silence until I hear the faint sound of the bell. They timed this so I will miss the last class of the day and since I don't talk to anyone, no one will miss me, including the teacher. They wait another few minutes or maybe it's an hour after the shuffle of feet died down; my head hurts and keeping track of time is hard. Without warning, I am shoved forward into the door as it opens moving more slowly than my captors want me to. A large, painful hand is on each upper arm dragging me forward. The black cloth doesn't let any light in, and I can't keep track of which turns we are making as we go. Something I make note of later, beat myself up for, and prompts me to really start working on individual senses and tracking. I will never be captured like this again. if I make it out alive. We do go outside and tromp around in the woods. I keep tripping over branches and plants, and my captors grumble their annoyance, but they are the idiots who are dragging me blindly.

When we get to our destination, I am thrown to the ground hitting my shoulder and head on stone or concrete since my hands are bound behind me. Little white stars are popping behind my eyelids. I hear whispering, which means these kids don't have their wolves yet to mindlink.

The Alpha, Beta, Gamma, and Delta have the power to push a mindlink through to anyone in our pack. It makes giving directions in a crisis easier. But, until you have your wolf you cannot link back or talk to anyone else. That's all I have to work with, though. Male and around my age.

They are talking too low to recognize a voice and without a scent I can't identify them. I just get myself to a sitting position after threading my arms over my legs so they rest in front of me, when my arms are yanked over my head and hooked to something, holding me off the ground so my toes barely touch and my shoulders are screaming. I am doing everything I can to not make a sound, they don't deserve my fear or cries of pain. That's what they want. My shirt is ripped open in the back, and I let out a strangled grunt through the gag. The first sharp sting registers as I hear the loud crack echo in the air. I try to hold back my scream, I'm not sure what I was expecting, but it wasn't the white hot pain of a whip. My whole body flexes involuntarily. The first time they whipped me I was held down on a bench in the girls' locker room and the five lashes came quickly. They wanted it done before my attackers could be caught. This time, there is more bite in the whip and there are several moments between the first and the second. The second one doesn't disappoint. This time I do scream and hear an amused huff behind me, sick fucks. As the third and fourth strike tear through my flesh and I can feel blood trickle from my back, I start to go to my happy place, counting the lashes, but hiding in my mind trying to turn the pain off, go numb, don't feel, control my breathing, stay awake. By number seven I am panting heavily but no longer make noise, which pisses my attackers off. The last three come in quick succession from either side of my body, telling me two people wield whips this time. Then my legs are lifted behind me, but not to take weight off my arms, just to put me in more of a horizontal position. I think this is one of the worst feelings ever, like both shoulders are trying to dislocate while the raw skin on my back is puckering with the movement. I am so wrong. A blinding, searing pain hits me like a rocket blasting its engine across my back. I instantly lose vision and can't even breathe to scream. I can feel my skin bubbling and burning away. Then the sensation hits me again and my body convulses and bucks up in my captor's grip, my stomach tries to empty its contents into the gag and I start choking.

"Take that fucking thing out of her mouth, I want her to suffer, not die. Not yet anyway. She needs to suffer over and over again for all the shit she keeps causing me." This voice I know.

I'm still gagging as one of my legs is dropped and I'm hanging awkwardly sideways. The tie is undone behind my head, roughly, taking some hair with it and thrown to the ground as I cough out everything from my stomach, lungs, and wherever else the vomit is. My dangling leg is lifted back up and the blinding white hot pain resumes. This time, the pain is accompanied by the smell of burning flesh—my burning flesh. My sense of smell telling me my nose has healed just in time. I convulse and try to wretch again with the added sensation. I am struggling to take air in, my lungs don't want to function, and I am pretty sure my bladder has relieved itself too. Tears are streaming from my eyes and I mumble incoherently in between the burning sensation, retching and screaming. The grips on my ankles are getting tighter, I'm either getting hard to hold or they are having trouble with the different putrid smells now in the room. I hope it's both. The pain is always physical, leaving my mind intact to know exactly what is going on. This is her specialty.

I hear the high nasally giggle, she is enjoying herself. How does someone enjoy watching another person go through pain like this? I still don't know what I did to her this time to earn a punishment, let alone one that is in the form of torture.

"Remember this, you little bitch. Stay away from my men and stop trying to prevent me from disciplining the lowlifes in this school. Stop trying to suck up to all the adults. You aren't wanted and aren't good enough for anyone's attention. I am your future Luna, and you will all bow to me. Fall in line and follow orders or next time you will beg me to kill you." Kaley says from across the room. "Now clean this shit up and dump her in the woods, let's see if she's worthy of surviving." She says right before the door closes.

Chapter 1
3 Years Later

I walk up to the school building, and it feels like I'm willingly walking into a prison. I tug at the baggy shirt that's shifted beneath my backpack, lower my chin, and slip inside, trying to blend in with as many kids as possible. With enough bodies shuffling, no one notices my small frame jostling with them. Kaley, Jeanie, and Marnie still find some way to torture me every single day. The longer I can avoid them in the morning the better. They prefer to deliver punishments in the public eye of school, but I have to put just as much effort avoiding them during breaks and holidays too. Some days it's small things like taking a book out of my hands and lobbing it down the hallway while kids just stand around and watch hoping to not be the next victim, or in our freshman year when they pulled my ten-page essay out of the pile we were handing forward in English and tearing it into small pieces. It was handed back to me with a 'whoops.' I saved it on my laptop, so I was able to reprint it, but the teacher marked it late and gave me only half credit even though she watched the whole thing happen. She's just as afraid of Kaley and her dad as everyone else in our pack. I spent that weekend locked in my room, with no meals for being lazy.

When my father found out about my tardy homework, it was another reason for him to lash out at me. He avoids being in any room I am in at the best of times and pretends I'm not there when it can't be helped. And because Mr. Cunningham, Kaley's dad, will make sure my father knows if any misconduct happens again, my punishment will be worse next time. My father never wants to hear my side of the story, I'm not allowed to speak to defend myself... ever.

Yelling and degrading comments are the only way my father will communicate with me. It's times like that when I really miss Mary, she would have removed me from my father's sight and sneaked me something, even a granola bar later. My brother was nowhere in sight when my father berated me in the kitchen after school that day. He's never really around much anymore. Since Mary left, he no longer has to pretend to watch out for me, even with our father. He spends as little time at home as possible. He's always with his friends 'training' or 'working' or whatever it is they do when they hide away from everyone.

Kaley has a propensity to get physical with anyone that displeases her. I can see the satisfaction in her eyes when she inflicts pain on anyone, but she has a certain look reserved just for me. Pulling my hair and shoving me into doors and walls is a common favorite amongst her followers too. An overly full backpack manages to knock me in the head at least once every class on her orders, which is why I try to be the last in and the first out when I can help it. She makes sure no one ever hits me where marks can be easily seen since my dad keeps me from school if he sees marks. 'I cannot make him look weak in front of the pack.' Kaley realized they can't torture me if I'm not in school.

I'm pretty sure I have a couple ribs that have broken so many times, a good sneeze would re-break them. I won't let my wolf waste energy on healing the small stuff, it's not worth it, and it keeps Kaley content to think I can't heal. The illusion that she's stronger than me keeps everyone safer. My wolf does make sure that I'm not in pain for long, though. She really is great; her running commentary on the three Barbie wannabes helps lift my mood, especially after some of the more harsh beat downs. Kaley knows I won't let her harm kids in the school, especially the younger ones, she uses this as a way to get to me daily. This has been my entire high school existence. And, how I am going to start my morning as I see the group of raging Barbies huddled over something.

"You little fucking bitch! Do you have any idea how expensive these shoes are?" Marnie is holding the ponytail of a girl about my size, but a lot younger, while Kaley screeches in her face. "These are brand-new, limited-edition Vey-onne Luxe heels imported from Italy, and you spilled coffee all over them!"

"I d-d-didn't, though. I was just s-s-standing here. Sh-sh-she bumped into me with her co…" SMACK! I hear the crack of skin on skin. The red handprint is instant on her cheek. She silently sobs, knowing if she cries out, there will be hell to pay.

"Hey!" I shout. All three bobble heads snap to me, "I'm sure Jeanie didn't mean to trip, but walking and thinking are tricky." The result is instant, all three turn and start walking to me, the little girl, forgotten altogether, runs away.

"Who said you could talk to us?" Kaley asks, I don't respond. She doesn't want an answer, and we have done this dance long enough. She shoves me and I let her, falling back into a set of lockers and letting out an 'OHMPF' for effect. I keep my eyes down in submission as she pushes me again and again letting out small insults. She's not on her game this morning. She isn't actually strong or does any real damage herself. But her words are her best weapon, and her tongue is usually sharp as a blade. Maybe it's too early for her true viciousness, but I'm saved by the warning bell. Even she won't be overly late on the first day back.

My wolf and I have both decided this is for the best. Even when she has the strongest kids beat on me, my beta lineage can handle it, and we heal faster than Kaley thinks. It seems to keep her and her friends pacified to take their frustrations out on me and less likely to target other kids. As long as she thinks I'm isolated from everyone and she is in control of that fact, her pawns target only me. We are both content with the situation, which means her friends are happy and there is peace in the school. If you can call a calm raving lunatic 'peace.'

+)❯●❮(+

One of the best decisions I ever made is taking extra classes over the summers, I have no friends, so I have tons of free time and there's no way the Barbies would be caught dead in school over the summer. I am now a full grade ahead of them. So, while I am a technical junior, I am a senior based on my classes and credits. That means that this year I might have a rare class with Kaley, Marnie, or Jeanie since they are in all the standard junior classes. Now I just have to stay hidden in the back of the room in any combined Junior-Senior classes and this year might be uneventful, which is better than anything I have experienced in the last three years.

Having my wolf makes things less lonely. We figured out how to get out of my room without my father knowing a few summers ago. We hunt for food when he keeps it from me, go on runs around the border almost daily, and have picked up many survival skills along the way. I know that I can survive on my own and in the wild, which sounds nice some days. This year is set up to be pleasant and boring and I am looking forward to it. I can't wait to be done so I can leave this hell hole. I don't want to be a rogue, I just need to keep my head down, graduate, and do my obligatory college years outside of this pack. With so many jobs unique to our species, all students are required to attend college training for their intended profession. Some will continue on to University for higher level training after college, some go straight to work. I want to be a warrior, a pack protector. Most packs have a college course for that and encourage learning from other pack's systems.

Everything was going to plan until a new girl showed up mid-November. She joined us at our mandatory 5 a.m. pack training. All kids in high school are required to attend every morning before classes to learn to protect themselves, even if you don't have aspirations to become a warrior. As we get older the training is divided up into three parts. Basic training for all adult pack members. This is self-defense to allow weaker members to get to safety in the event of an attack. Intermediate training for patrols. These warriors have a greater knowledge of the borders and pack scents. They keep track of the rogue population outside our lands on the mainland side and the comings and goings of boats and ships on the waterfront sides of our territory. Advanced training is for our Elite Warriors, Alpha, Beta, Gamma, Delta, and their mates and kids. The ranked members are the most targeted so they train the hardest. They are also our strongest, so they tend to be on the frontlines of any attack.

I love training and go to every one I am allowed to attend. Much to my father and brother's irritation, I am allowed to go to everything, being a Beta by blood. My brother always has a scowl on his face when I make eye contact with him, which I try very hard not to do. I don't know why it bothers him, and I don't really care. I keep my distance from him and the rest of the future leadership and just do my own thing. I am only one of two high school females who come to the extra training. Carra is a senior and is only here because her father, one of our Elite Warriors, makes her. She comes, trains, doesn't talk to anyone, and leaves. Typically, as ranked members, we follow in the line of work our parents do. The Alpha's kid becomes the next Alpha. The Beta's kid, the next Beta and so on. But, every now and then, someone deviates. I think Carra is one who is going to deviate. She is super interested in science, always has been, and that is what she is studying in college next year. She'll probably end up at the pack hospital.

The rest of the females are mates of our current leadership or warriors. The Luna is very nice and a great fighter, she always keeps me on my toes and she and the other females share stories and insights while we spar. I feel almost normal during these sessions. I don't get to spar with the males during elite training. The dads, including mine, are more interested in teaching their proteges. My dad, actually, does not acknowledge I am there. But, the Luna and the female warriors have some great tips on how to use my size to my advantage, because many guys underestimate a woman in a fight, and I am abnormally small. It amazes me how short-sighted guys can be. They cherish their mates, praise our female warriors, even pray to a female Goddess, and are fiercely protective, but in the end, their actions show they think their ideas and strength are better than a female's and that they are the true protectors of the pack.

Intermediate training is, hands down, my favorite. The border patrol is fascinating because our pack sits on a peninsula. We have a unique way of protecting our minimal land borders and still run the ocean sides of the pack. These times are the only times I don't have to worry about Kaley, Jeanie, and Marnie or any of their other minions messing with me. They aren't dumb enough to cause their usual kind of scenes with me when the future Alphas, my brother, and the rest of the future leaders are here participating. I can be free and be myself, hiding in the back where no one pays me any attention. I have often thought about doing Elite Warrior training following school. It is done at the Alpha King's facility near his castle, far away from this pack. I even started running the patrol route around the territory in the mornings before regular training sessions or after school if I need to avoid people or my house. We don't have a lot of rogue attacks, but they do happen, and our border patrol keeps us in close contact with neighboring packs in times of need. I enjoy getting to know the patrol warriors and learning what they do as the first line of defense for our pack.

I am a good student, but that is more due to the pressure my dad puts on me to act like my high rank and not embarrass him, then actually being smart or caring about school. I also have a ton of free time since I don't hang out with anyone. Kaley has made sure that no one will associate with me on pain of social suicide. I am a good fighter and have completed all the things that look good on paper, so I should be able to apply and get accepted for Elite Warrior Training Camp. I just need to survive one more year of torture for teenagers.

I am pulled from my thoughts as Delta Kyle brings us all in and explains what we are going to do today, then casually throws in that we have a new member joining us. "She is staying with her uncle and aunt while her parents are working for the Alpha King," he calls out to the group at large.

That gets everyone's attention, including Kaley, who somehow manages to sit on the sidelines in her short dress and heels, clearly not participating, like every other day, but she showed up, which is a hit or miss with her. I still haven't figured out how she gets out of *mandatory* training without a consequence.

My attention is snatched as this tall girl walks in like she owns the place; her confident stature is what catches my eye first. Her youthful, carefree face, long dark brown hair and bright golden honey eyes tell me she can't be much older than me, but the way she holds herself and how the eyes of every guy at training follow her very developed and toned body makes me smile at the thought of how the Barbies are going to react to having competition. I must have made a noise out loud, because the new girl turns around and looks right at me. Her stare is piercing, but not hostile. Delta Kyle tells her she can join the group, and we will get her up to speed on what we are working on.

She takes a step in my direction, not breaking eye contact. Oh no! She's coming this way. No. No. No, no, no, no, no! She cannot talk to me, that will mean a world of hurt for both of us. I look everywhere but at the intimidating female making a beeline in this direction. She walks right up to me and holds her hand out. "Sierra, nice to meet you."

I look up, I can't help it, and stare at her blinking. It takes me a second to register what I am supposed to do. She raises her eyebrow at me, not backing down at my hesitation or complete lack of manners, so I stutter. "Oh, sorry, Skylar." I shake her hand quickly once, then drop it, "I'm not used to people talking to me," I mutter out awkwardly, turning back to face the front where Delta Kyle and the lead trainers are giving a few more instructions, mentally smacking myself for sounding like an idiot. I see her look at me questioningly in my peripherals, but before she can ask, a trainer divides us into pairs and has us start our warm-up and sparring. He must have decided I am as good a person as any to work with her. She chose me to talk to first and he knows I attend all the training we have. These trainers are some of the few people who know that I'm working to get out of here, so they let me come to the gym and training grounds whenever I want. Delta Kyle even gave me a key to the gate when I started showing up before him.

I like to stay as invisible as possible, but I love sparring. I typically stick to the back of the training group and only work with warriors that are here to help Delta Kyle teach. He has seen my separation from the group and, I'm sure, can guess why, so he makes sure there is a warrior there to partner with me. Today the help isn't needed. Sierra sets up to work with me. I guess I'm doing this.

Chapter 2

Sierra is a really good fighter, but so am I. She is tall compared to me. She has to be like 5'7" and my 5'1" stature can't compare, but we are built similarly which helps with learning the new movements. Her black sports bra and leggings accentuate all the tan and defined muscles in her body, she could be a supermodel with those curves. I have muscles too, and actually pretty defined. I prefer to not show much skin, if any, it helps hide the injuries and scars, so I tend to appear overweight in my too big clothes. Today I have baggy sweatpants and a T-shirt on. I also have two tank tops under the T-shirt. I learned the hard way my scars and bruising can be found in the heat of a match if I don't have layers. I don't want anyone to see them and pity me or pretend to try to help, or worse, report to my dad. It sounds stupid and my wolf and I have gone around and around, but I don't want help from people who can't be bothered to help me when I am receiving the injuries in the first place. It's easy to make themselves feel better by offering help or assistance here at training, saying I 'just have to ask,' but in reality, they are the same people who turn a blind eye at school or laugh along with my bullies because their own self-preservation is more important than doing what's right. So, I keep my pain hidden.

I don't know if it's me or my Beta blood, but the thrill and adrenaline rush of a good fight always makes my day better. I am a really skilled fighter, the fact that I let Kaley and her minions beat me up makes my wolf cringe. It's just better that she targets only me and not someone else who can't take the abuse. If I don't fight back, things end quicker because they get bored. And I don't get in trouble if I don't throw any hits at all, since those *do* seem to show up on videos and leave marks for a long time. Kaley had a black eye for a week once, not long after I got my wolf, it was chalked up to my Beta blood and a lucky swing, I didn't argue, because I'm not allowed to. But the punishment was terrible. I was suspended from school for the week, relegated to helping the Omegas who clean the locker rooms, and my dad locked me in my room at night and told Mary she wasn't allowed to talk to me or feed me. She did neither of those things, and made sure I had all of my schoolwork. She went as far as taking my assignments to my teachers, so nothing was late. I wasn't giving anyone any more reasons to punish me and no one questioned her actions if they thought it was weird. I knew how much she helped me, but I didn't realize until she was gone how much she really made this situation the best she could. Now that I do this all alone, I'm sure there was so much more she shielded me from.

I shake my head, I can't get distracted. Sierra is a beast, and she is good at finding my weak points. I have never enjoyed going up against one of my peers before. I have to fight the smile that is trying to creep up on my face as we move.

Delta Kyle and a few of the advanced pack warriors are walking around correcting form and giving feedback. "Nice job, ladies, you both seem to be the first to grasp the concept I was trying to teach today. A quick submission is always the best one," Delta Kyle says then leans a little closer, "Even the young Alphas and Beta didn't catch on as quickly and they are still struggling," he whispers and winks at us. "But don't tell them I said that." We both giggle, setting up to run the move again.

"You got it, Delta," I say. He knew the jab to my brother would make me smile. He's seen me work my tail off, but doesn't make a big deal about my accomplishments because I don't like it. And he's not able to work directly with me outside of the group training we do here. I think that is my father's doing; making my brother and the other future leaders the priority, but I'm not actually sure.

Delta Kyle acts more like my older brother than my actual older brother does. He helps me hide a few of the more severe injuries I've gotten from the constant bullying. And he doesn't judge or ask too many questions. He and Luna Ava are the only people who know I got my wolf too. It's rare to get your wolf as young as I did. Sometimes ranked wolves will show up early if they are really strong. I think the Moon Goddess gave her to me to help me handle the trauma. As much as I love my wolf and appreciate her help, I wish the Moon Goddess would just make the bullying stop.

Luna Ava has been helping me with shifting and working on the pack link too. There is something to be said for being invisible. None of my peers have any idea I have my wolf, they are nowhere near getting their own and can't sense my aura yet. Kaley has them avoiding being in my presence, so they also give me no focus. And just as I think that, Kyle smashes my thought process and completely ignores my need to stay unnoticed with a loud clap and his next words.

"LISTEN UP!" He yells as he claims the attention of the entire arena. "I think a demonstration is in order. Sierra, Skylar, why don't you two show us how the new defensive move is supposed to look." He smiles at me and winks, and I just want to punch him in his pearly white teeth. He gestures towards the center sparring ring. I stall.

"I really don't like you," I say through the mindlink.

"I know, but someone other than me has to see what kind of fighter you are, and your brother and the guys need a lesson in humility."

"Why do I have to do it?!"

"They have been left alone for far too long. Humor me for five minutes."

"You get two." I huff and move to face Sierra. She is smiling like I just brought her to her favorite store and told her she can have anything she wants. Oh, goody...she enjoys the attention.

"Even better!" Kyle laughs.

"Asshole," I grumble.

"Ready." Delta Kyle's deep authoritative voice booms over the crowd now circling around us. We take our positions. "Sierra, you are on the attack, Skylar, use the new defensive move and let's see if you can pin her in less than thirty seconds this time."

I hear mumbles of 'what?' '30 seconds, no way,' along with other mumbled insults and giggles. That sets me and my wolf off.

"Screw trying to be invisible," I say to my wolf, her irritation rolls through me and my temper flares in a way it never has before. I don't normally care about proving myself to these idiots, but they won't make fun of me here...in the one place that makes me feel whole.

"Arrogant fuckers think they are so great, when they can't even submit each other with basic moves." She grumbles.

"Shall we?" I ask my wolf.

"Oh, kiddo, I thought you'd never ask," she replies. I can feel the smallest hint of her energy seeping into my muscles. She knows I don't want to hurt Sierra, but if the boys need a lesson, they are going to get one.

I hear laughter and skeptical murmurs from somewhere in the crowd, but I am too focused on Sierra, my warrior instinct has kicked in and the laughing jackass isn't a priority.

"No one could complete that move in under thirty seconds, let alone her," a snarky high pitched male voice says loud enough for everyone to hear, causing a low chorus of agreement. Now my blood is boiling, along with my wolf's.

"We are taking her down in less than ten and I better not find out which pansy ass insulted us or he's going down too." She clips out. I can feel my muscles vibrate with anticipation now.

"Just watch," is Delta Kyle's only, very dry, response. "Set...GO!"

I move immediately on the word 'go.' I don't even give Sierra time to come at me. She responds quickly to my movements though and tries to feign to the left then duck down to catch me with her shoulder. I'm too quick for her and as she starts to duck down, I send a knee up toward her chest and face, knocking the wind out of her. As her body comes up from the momentum, I make an elbow strike to her back, and she reaches out to wrap her arms around my waist trying to force me down. Instead of fighting the momentum, I allow it, but twist so she is under me face down, then shift to pin her throat to the ground with one of my knees and have her arm in a lock she can't get out of.

My eyes are locked on the one of Sierra's I can see. Hers are wide in amazement, surprise maybe, I'm not really sure. The first thing I notice when my breathing starts to return to normal is silence, not even breathing can be heard. The next is a hand patting me on the back. I look up and see Delta Kyle beaming at me, looking like he is fighting off laughter. What's funny? I don't understand.

"Less than ten seconds, damn, sorry Sam, she beat your best take down time... by a lot!" He laughs out. "Dismissed!" Delta Kyle says loud and clear while he shrugs his shoulders at his son, laughing harder now, not being able to hold it back. The crowd around us dissipates reluctantly with low conversation all around.

I stand up and help Sierra to her feet. "Shit, you're fast. You're going to have to help me learn how to react like that," she says with a mischievous look in her eyes. I just nod, because what else is there to do? When she finds out where I fall in the high school pecking order, she will not want anything to do with me. I notice the crowd is more subdued than usual at the end of training, but I also don't care so much, I took her down in under ten seconds. I am riding high after that! I have to fight a smile, that is something that would for sure get me beat up, I'm not supposed to be good at or happy about anything. I walk past Delta Kyle in serious conversation with Sam, my brother, and the other future leaders, and head back to the bench where my things are. I can't take the looks I can feel burning holes in my back from all the kids still milling around. I don't like the staring at all. Now that my adrenaline is fading, I want to go back to being invisible. I can't let my temper get the better of me again. I need to stay in control and invisible so I can get out of here. I grab my things trying to ignore the dominating presence beside me, Sierra is just following my lead, without a word. It's kind of weird, but I don't say anything, I just turn around and start walking. Maybe she'll take the hint to leave me alone. I head towards the locker room, her hot on my heels. It's so strange to have someone walking next to me by choice.

Chapter 3

"I really do want to know how you got that fast. And your moves are better than I have seen at some of the warrior camps back home." My eyes snap to hers, eyebrows furrowed, she's just being nice now. And why is she still talking to me?

"Umm, okay. I really just train a lot, that's all." I don't know her enough to tell her about getting my wolf so early, which is part of the reason I am so fast.

Most kids get their wolf sometime between junior and senior years. Around seventeen or eighteen years old. The young Alphas, my brother, and the rest of the guys all got theirs in the middle of their freshman year, which is early, but not unheard of for powerful high-ranking wolves.

I got mine at the end of my 8th grade year though, which is rare even for a ranked wolf. I was freaking out, since it wasn't that long after the guys and even though I have Beta blood, I'm not really a ranked member, I'm the second born. Nor am I likely to be one. Delta Kyle was the first person I could think of to go to. He brought me straight to Luna Ava and they have been helping me ever since.

"Hey, Sky, here." I look over to see Delta Kyle slow jogging toward us with something small in his hand. "Your shirts rode up a bit in the back, I think you opened up one of your more recent injuries." He looks at me expectantly, crossing his arms after I take the jar. I give him the same look back. I'm not having this conversation in front of the first non-adult to talk to me in years. The new girl doesn't know me, and I don't want to freak her out.

I appreciate the offering though. It is another vital piece to keeping my secret. "Thank you, Delta, is there anything else?" His raised eyebrow tells me he doesn't appreciate my attitude and yes, he has plenty more he wants to say. He flexes his massive arms crossed over his chest trying to look intimidating. The problem is, it works on everyone but me.

"Not now, okay? I promise I will explain later." I mindlink. I have to give him something or he will keep hounding me.

"Fine, when I figure out who is doing this, there will be hell to pay."

"Which is why you won't find out. You have bigger things to worry about than petty school bullies who are so weak they have to resort to silver powder to actually cause pain."

He lets out an audible growl that shakes the ground around me and I can feel his Delta aura surge out from him. Everyone stops and looks at us. I should not have let that bit of information out. Everyone that is not an Alpha, Beta, Gamma, or Delta rank tilts their heads down and to the side in submission. My wolf feels the power and recognizes that he, as an adult with full rank, is more powerful than me, but my Beta blood allows me to fight it. I do not break eye contact. He has no idea how strong my wolf makes me, but I can't submit. My wolf and my pride won't let me. I do notice that Sierra is also able to fight the full submission. Her chin is still raised, but her eyes are lowered in respect. I wonder what rank she is in her pack?

"What are high schoolers doing with silver powder?! That is used as an interrogation tactic and torture. You need to tell me who this is, Sky. <u>NOW!</u> This is no longer a game." He is seething, I can feel it radiating off of him in waves.

"No! I handled it and I won't have you causing more trouble by stepping in. It makes me look weak and I am already a target, you'll just make it worse. Every time someone tries to help, it only makes things worse."

Before he can respond I turn around and head into the locker rooms to shower and get ready for school. Sierra just follows me and says nothing about the staring contest I had with our head trainer.

I head to my locker and grab my shower stuff. I take all of my things to the furthest cubicle and close the outside curtain. I set my clothes and towel on the bench in the little changing area just outside the shower stall before turning on the water as warm as my body can handle it and step in closing the shower curtain. I like having the double barrier, I never change out in the open, I don't want anyone seeing the bruises and cuts on my body, especially now with the lashes on my back that are taking forever to heal because Kaley rubbed silver powder in them after they whipped me. It's been almost four years and they scab and grow new skin, but never heal completely. Kyle was right though, I can feel the sting of the hot water on the open wound and watch the blood flow down the drain tinting the water pink.

Once I'm done showering, I reach my hand out of the curtain to grab my towel, not taking any chances at being seen and wrap myself up nice and tight. Once I feel like I am completely covered, I open the curtain only to jump and yell. "Oh, damn!" Slipping and tangling up in the wet curtain. "Don't do that!"

Sierra just laughs at me, leaning against the wall like it is the most normal thing to invade someone's privacy in stealth mode.

"You forgot this, and you may need help putting it on, some of those cuts are in hard to reach places," she whispers at me and then twirls her finger, motioning me to turn around as if the discussion is over. I don't move, just stare at her. "I am going to help you whether you cooperate or not, so it would save us some time, if you willingly let me help you." She stares unblinkingly. "I am not going to ask questions... yet." Her determined look doesn't waver.

Okay, help it is then. I loosen my towel and expose my back where there are fifteen lashes. The oldest five are from the fifteen minutes of time I wasted asking a question in history class, causing us to take extra notes and have a pop quiz. Even though our teacher mentioned the quiz the day before making it a 'known' quiz. There was no negotiating with a fuming Kaley. The newest ten happened at the end of 8th grade, right after the guys got their wolves. I guess that upped their celebrity factor and me asking my brother a question while standing next to the rest of them was too close a proximity for her liking. Apparently, it is a punishable crime to be in the personal space of people that are better than you.

If Sierra is surprised or grossed out, she doesn't say anything. She is super gentle, applying the cream to every cut on my back. "There are a few here that are older, but the cream might help get rid of some of the scar tissue. I'm sure my parents could give us something more powerful fo–"

"No!" I jump and turn around. "I am handling it, I promise. You don't need to tell your parents. Thank you, though." I don't want to be rude, she is just trying to help, but I am not going to give Kaley the idea that I am too weak to take her so-called punishments. If I let Sierra talk to her parents about this, the possibility is high of it getting back to the Alpha and Luna and who knows who else. The less people who know the better it is for me.

"If you say so. Anyway, I need someone to show me around the school, you up for it?" She changes the subject so abruptly that I almost get whiplash.

"Uh sure, let me get dressed then we can head over and get your schedule." She doesn't take the hint to step out, and I am forced to awkwardly get dressed under my towel. I'm pretty sure she knows she's making me uncomfortable and doesn't care or is enjoying it.

We head to the school which is just a block away from the training grounds. I take Sierra to the main office and introduce her to the secretary who gets her all set up with her schedule, locker, and combination, then we head out to tour the school since we are still about 45 minutes early. Most of the kids go home after training. I just find hanging with Delta Kyle or in the locker room keeps me safe from Kaley for a little while longer. The peace is nice.

I find out Sierra and I are in a few classes together. She's a year older than me, like the my brother, but I am taking some advanced classes, which in my school just means 'the next grade up.'

"So our first two classes are together at least, that will make things way more fun," she says with a little happy chirp in her voice. "You'll have to point out all of the people to know and who to stay away from."

"Uh, I don't think I'm the person to do that. I tend to keep to myself and blend into the background as much as possible. I am not popular at all and avoid the social scene like it is my job," I say as we make it to the first class of the day, and I walk to the back of the room to take my usual seat. She just huffs in response, but doesn't say anything and follows.

The day actually goes pretty smoothly, meaning I didn't have any run-ins with Kaley and her crew. I'm not sure if that is because of the display this morning at training or the new friend I seem to have acquired. No one talks to me or really looks at me normally, but no one actively tried to do anything to me either. Whatever, the break was nice and I find myself smiling as I walk down the hallway to put my things in my locker at the end of the day. Of course good things only come in small moments for me.

"You think you're so tough, being Delta Kyle's favorite suck up. I bet that's not the only thing you suck, it's the only explanation for how you manage to gain his attention." I ignore Kaley even though I am completely disgusted by her insinuation. Gross. I take a deep breath and continue shuffling things in my locker, hoping she will get bored and walk away, now that she has thrown her insult. She slams my locker shut and steps right up to my left ear. I'm lucky my reflexes are fast, otherwise I would have lost fingers.

Before she can spit whatever venom she has at me, Sierra walks up. "Hey, girl, I am so hungry, and you promised to hang out with me after school." Sierra completely ignores Kaley's presence, and I catch the look of death Kaley is throwing her way. I have to stifle a laugh.

I am not stupid and take the out she's giving me. "I almost forgot, sorry." I turn my back on Kaley, and we take about two steps before she shouts.

"Hey, new girl, you'll want to watch who you hang out with. Some people in this school will give you a bad reputation and only cause you problems." We both look back at her.

"Thanks for the tip." Sierra links her arm into mine and starts to turn us away again.

I hear clicks of heels approaching us. "Listen here, you little... Hey, guys!" Kaley's voice goes from venom to bubble gum in a flash and I notice she is looking over our shoulders.

A general bored mumble of 'hey' comes from the group of guys walking our way. Seriously? Can't I just catch a break? They are all staring and I want to melt into a wall.

"Damn, they are even hotter up close," Sierra says quietly to me, turning us around to face my brother and his friends as they walk up to us. I roll my eyes at her and say nothing. They have never approached me in school before, like ever. So I can only assume they are here for the beautiful brunette friend that has attached herself to my arm. I stand with dread pooling in my stomach, waiting for her attention to shift to them and to be dismissed from the group so I don't embarrass her in front of these people.

I can't deny these guys are gorgeous and unfortunately they all know it too. My brother, Mateo, and I look almost identical, with sandy blonde hair and gray blue eyes, getting most of our looks from our mother. The only difference is his build is exactly like my fathers', wide at the shoulders and narrow at the waist and so freaking tall. He keeps his stick straight hair military short on the sides and in the back and longer on top. It looks like he ran his fingers through it a couple times to make it stick straight up, but somehow the look works for him.

The future Delta, Sam, is Kyle's son. And he looks like he just stepped out of a Hurley surfing ad with wavy sun-kissed light blonde hair that hangs just below his ears, dark blue eyes, and lean muscles. He's tall but not as wide set as the other guys. He is no less ripped and one of the fastest warriors I have ever seen.

Oliver, our future Gamma, looks like your stereotypical biker. Medium length, dark brown, almost black hair falling in a mess on his forehead, and piercing brown eyes that are almost as dark give off a 'don't mess with me' vibe. He has tattoos on both forearms and one just peeking out of the collar of his shirt. He is the most quiet of the group, lending to the mysteriousness. His expression is regularly bordering on resting bitch face and fuck around and find out.

Our future Alphas are twins that could melt you with one glance, or maybe that is just me. They both have black hair with a gentle wave to it. It's short on the sides and back like my brother. Cameron is always perfectly groomed, no curl on top of his head is out of place. His light green eyes soften his severely sharp features. Dakota lets his curls do whatever they want on the top of his head. Dakota's baby blue eyes are more playful than his brother's, he is definitely the troublemaker of the two.

Somebody must have said something, because Sierra elbows me in the ribs. Oh, Goddess, please let me not be drooling. I mentally facepalm myself and look around. "I'm sorry, what?" I have no idea what we are supposed to be talking about.

"I was just saying, nice moves at training today. Hopefully we'll get a chance to work on those again at advanced training and you can give us some tips. Sam needs to redeem his top take down time," Cameron says to me, smiling, and Dakota laughs, slapping Sam on the back.

I try to smile and nod, feeling a little dumbfounded. I have no idea how to respond. These guys have rarely talked to me more than a 'hey' in passing at my house before, and never at school. Even though they have been friends with my brother for their whole lives and spend a ridiculous amount of time at my house. This is the longest interaction I have ever had with any of them.

"He, he, he." A weird, forced, high-pitched giggle comes from my left. I look over, not realizing Kaley was standing next to me. She reaches out and puts her hand on Cameron's chest. "You're so funny, babe. Sam is one of the best warriors we have, I bet he could do that move with one hand tied behind his back. His dad was just being nice to Sierra and S-Sk-Sk... Mateo's sister." Did she just choke on my name? I guess she's never really used it before. I'm normally just the b-word to her. "It's not fair to compare lower wolves to you, guys."

"Who is she calling a lower wolf?" I can feel my muscles shake with my wolf's irritation. I look down at the ground and blink a few times to make sure my eyes aren't changing color, giving away that I have her.

Cameron takes a slow breath in and takes an almost imperceptible step back as his twin chimes in. "Nope, I'm pretty sure Sam sucks and needs to start from the basics again. Maybe we should send him to train with the pups for the week." Dakota laughs out, and my brother joins him this time. So does Sierra, and I allow myself a giggle. I can't help it, their laughs are infectious, but it doesn't last long. This is the first time I have felt comfortable around my brother and his friends and probably the first time ever in a public setting like school. I break eye contact and look away, taking a few deep breaths to settle my mind around that. I look back up at my brother. A sort of pained look flashes in my brother's eyes, one I can't quite read, but isn't unfamiliar. Does he not want to be over here talking to me? Probably not, but the rest of the guys are here to talk to Sierra, so...

The thought that he doesn't want me shouldn't sting this bad, since it's really the only solid emotion I ever get from him, but my heart sinks into my stomach. I look at the floor again. I don't want to earn more slaps for someone's weird fetish over my brother.

"As much as I enjoy making fun of your boy Sam here," she pats Sam's arm, "Skylar promised me some food, we were just heading out to eat, if you will excuse us, gentlemen." Sierra basically pushes us through the wall of six foot tall guys like it was no big deal and leads me toward the parking lot of the training grounds where she left her car this morning. I hear a huff behind us, but I'm not sure who it was and can't wait to get out of here as soon as possible. My skin is crawling from being so uncomfortable around so many people who usually avoid me like the plague.

"How do you already have a car here?" I ask, momentarily distracted.

"With special permission from the Alpha of course." She winks at me. "My parents were always so busy researching and working for the Alpha King that I needed a way to get around. My aunt and uncle thought it would be a good idea for me to have it here too." She shrugs like that is a totally normal thing. I have a feeling she can talk anyone into just about anything without putting much effort into it.

"Hey!" A shout from behind us has us both turning around just before we get in her car. "I almost forgot, are you guys coming to the bonfire tonight?" Sam comes jogging up to us.

Chapter 4

"What bonfire?" Sierra looks at me accusingly.

I shrug my shoulders. "I don't do parties because I don't have friends. So I don't usually pay attention to the social scene." I look down at the ground after that word vomit confession. Taking a deep breath, I look back up at Sierra. I wonder when she is going to figure out I am not someone to know and she moves on like everyone else.

Sam looks at me and chuckles a bit but then quickly turns confused when I don't join in laughing then and looks between the two of us when he realizes I'm not kidding. "We have a bonfire for Samhin, to celebrate the start of fall. Which happens to be tonight, you should both come. It's in the clearing in the woods behind the packhouse, nothing too crazy, but it is tradition. Will you come? Please say you'll be there." He's looking at Sierra with big puppy dog eyes and his hands praying under his chin. Is he pouting?!

"Of course! We can't break tradition!" Her cheery personality shines through. "Is there a dress code for this particular get-together or is it come as you are?" She smiles up at him, taking a step closer and I swear his whole body shivers. So, this is what flirting looks like up close, interesting. She definitely does it better than Kaley, I think I get the appeal now.

He looks a little lost for a second before blinking and coming back to his senses. Yep, she could sell water to a whale. "Come as you are, but I would dress warm, it's already starting to cool off and the clearing is in a bit of a valley that holds the cooler air. For those who don't have their wolves yet it can get chilly." He smiles at her and it's like I'm not even here. I feel like I am trespassing.

"We'll do our best. We might just have to find someone to cuddle with. What time?" I am cuddling with no one, this girl is insane!

"We are going to start setting everything up now, so you can come whenever, but the bonfire is lit when it officially gets dark, so like seven or eight. But, really, you can come whenever." He smiles at Sierra. It's really cute to watch him flirt. I don't even know if he realizes that's what he's doing. She seems to have him under a spell.

"Well then, we will see you later, Sam." She smiles at him again and she gets into her car, I follow suit. Once we are both in and the doors are closed, she looks over at me. "Okay, I was just trying to get us away from the bitch and the hot brigade, but after all of that I really am hungry, where's the best burger place here?"

"The hot brigade? Really?" I question her, shaking my head. She just laughs as she starts the car.

I laugh with her after a minute and start giving her directions. We eat at the local diner. All eyes stare at us as I make her sit in the back corner, but no one approaches or tries to talk to us. We head to her place after, which just so happens to be at the end of my block.

"I didn't realize your aunt and uncle were some of our lead warriors. That would explain your fighting skills. I guess I never really asked about you today, sorry about that." I look down at my lap sitting on her bed as she digs through her closet. My awkwardness around people has been very apparent today.

"Don't worry about it, we have plenty of time to get to know each other. And what I want to know right now is what do you mean 'you don't do parties because you don't have friends?' You're not going to just slide that into conversation and hope no one heard it." I cringe. After I said it, I felt like I was whining like a brat and really hoping she didn't hear.

I scrub my face with my hands and huff out. "Exactly that, I do not have friends. I don't go to parties, no one chooses to hang out with me. They mostly choose to avoid me. It's been like that for a long time. You are the first person I have had more than one conversation in a row that wasn't in school about an assignment or at training." I shrug. It's strange though. Thinking those things used to hurt, but now I feel nothing. It's like I've become numb to the fact that my peers avoid me unless it's absolutely necessary. That can't be a good sign. It's weird though, when I used to think that stuff to myself it hurt, but now, I feel nothing, like I am numb to the fact that I am avoided unless absolutely necessary by my peers. That can't be good.

"That's a lot to unpack and I have a feeling the silver laced whip marks on your back fall into this same story too, right?" She peeks around the closet door, pinning me with her stare.

"Wait, what? How did you know they were silver laced whip marks?" I'm stunned, that's oddly specific knowledge to just guess based on one look. I have kept that secret for years and I only told Delta Kyle by accident over mindlink today. No one else knows.

"I will allow the topic to change. Only because it is relevant, but we are going to circle back to the friends thing." She waggles her finger at me, "My parents are scientists. I already told you they work for our Alpha King. Many of the things they work on are chemical weapons and antidotes for war." I flinch at the thought that her parents make things to harm other wolves, things like the silver powder that was rubbed into my wounds. "Don't look at me like that. They aren't bad people, but they have seen bad things. It's their job to know the worst things that could be done to our Alphas and the Alpha King and be able to stop it or reverse it. Sometimes they have had to reverse engineer some of the things used in battles. That's one of the reasons I am here, my parents are on some mission I don't even have details about. It wasn't safe for me to be alone, but it would be odd if I stayed with people in my pack for too long since I normally stay by myself when they travel. So staying with family was the best cover for my protection. Something very serious is going on and someone very powerful is using more than just everyday poisons to harm leaders. My parents are well known, and I can be used as a target if they get on the wrong side of these bad people." She leans back out of her closet and attempts to glare at me, but her happy features don't really do that look. "This goes without saying, but keep all of this to yourself."

"You just met me, why would you trust me with that information?" I am almost appalled at her easy confession.

She shrugs, stepping in front of the mirror admiring her reflection. "Because, you have been taking beatings for something you didn't do and clearly no one knows, meaning you can keep a secret. And those who suspect can't get the truth out of you. You have integrity and loyalty, though your lack of self-interest concerns me a bit." She giggles. "So tell me, why is someone using some of the worst forms of torture on you? You don't strike me as a boyfriend stealer, a cheater, or a liar. Which means you are a threat, and I think you don't even know it." She scrunches her nose and heads back into her closet.

"I'm not sure what I did to gain the constant negative attention, but the 'who' isn't important. It started to get bad when I stepped in to protect another, younger, student from some bullying and it has just escalated over time." I shrug.

"Is that the same line Delta Kyle let you get away with too?" She raises an eyebrow, but she is still smiling at me, trying on clothes like this is everyday normal conversation.

"Maybe." I shrug again, looking at my lap. I feel like she is just warming up her line of questioning and I am really going to have to choose my words carefully with her. She could be an interrogator.

"So, back to the no friends thing. Care to explain?" She tries on her third coat and is twirling in front of her full-length mirror. "From what I have seen you are great and genuine, and I am an excellent judge of character." She huffs and throws the coat into a pile on the chair of her vanity and goes back in her closet. How many coats can she possibly have?

"It's complicated. And it's just easier to not get close to people, with every-thing going on. I don't want anyone else as a target just because they decided to be friends with me. My brother will take the next Beta title, and I will take whatever rank my mate gives me. I'm nothing special and don't have anything to offer. You'll see, the only reason you lasted this long is because you are new and haven't figured out the teen hierarchy here. You are gorgeous and have already gotten the attention of my brother and his friends..." I let the 'and you'll move on and forget me' thought hang in the air.

"You have not met any real friends then. This bitch, whoever *she* is, won't scare me away and the way I saw you fight today, I'm surprised you let anyone treat you poorly, let alone physically harm you." She grabs a hat that matches the bright red pea coat she chose and does another twirl in the mirror. She looks fresh out of a French fall magazine. "I can't believe that your Alphas or even your brother haven't stepped in."

"I told you, it's complicated. They don't know about stuff like the whipping and anything else is not worth their time. If I can't fight my own simple battles, I'm not worth the time or the effort. I'm a Beta by blood and should be strong enough to handle my problems without running to them with every little problem. Some levels of minor bullying are tolerated by my brother and his friends. It's a survival of the fittest mentality."

"Then they are all dicks and not worthy of leading in my opinion. But, they probably don't know half of what you put up with based on the scars you carry on the outside. If they did, I'm sure their opinion would be different. The inside scars, though, they wouldn't have a clue, they're guys, that's just stupid territory for them. I can't help but laugh, long and hard. She's not wrong. The emotional turmoil in my head is worse than anything that has been done to me physically. "So let's make you look and feel as hot as you are tonight and see what we can find out from these boys."

"Wait, what are you talking about? I am not hot and what do you want to find out from which boys?" Now I am scared. She's looking at me like a predator looks at its prey.

"I saw how each of those boys looked at you today at training, even in classes and again after school. You are not as invisible as you may think, and I am going to prove it to you. Even your brother was impressed at training."

I freeze in my spot. I wish she were right about my brother being impressed. That would be amazing, to show him I'm not a waste of time and space. But who am I kidding, my brother doesn't look at me, let alone pay any attention.

"I doubt that. My brother, like my dad, only focuses on the position and job and I do not fall into that category, so I am not noticeable or worth the time. But, you are cute for thinking that."

"I'm still dressing you up hot tonight, there's no getting out of it." She points a painted fingernail at me. I roll my eyes, this might be the worst of the torture yet.

"How hot can you make me look wearing a coat and hat? You are ridiculous." I giggle at her as she drags me in her closet.

Two hours later, we are walking from Sierra's place down our 'U' shaped block. I have a bright blue coat on, a T-shirt, and dark washed jeans, my blonde hair tied on my head in a ponytail and my black combat boots. She added light make-up and insisted on this pale pink lip gloss.

The block houses all of the ranked members of the pack. Our driveways all make the center of the 'U' and our well-manicured backyards fan out to a forest line all the way around. It is great if you want to go for a quick run and part of the reason I have been able to hide my shifting from my brother and my dad. At the center is the main packhouse where Alpha Lucas, Luna Ava, Cameron, and Dakota live. To the right of them is the Beta house where Dad, Mateo, and I live. To the left of the packhouse is the Gamma house where Gamma Brett and Oliver live. Next to the Gamma house is the Delta house where Delta Kyle, Gwen, and Sam live. There is a house next to the Delta's, housing an Elite warrior named Ben and his young family and two houses next to mine also housing Elite warriors. One of which I now know is Sierra's aunt and uncle. I know them all on sight, but we don't interact much outside of training. I basically keep myself from everyone, just in case. Kaley has shown more than once that she will harm a pack member in some way to get me punished, and it tends to be the pups, and I just can't have that. No one's children need to get hurt because she is mad at me for whatever reason.

Before I got my wolf and my fast reflexes, she was trying to get me to give her the answers to a history test she couldn't be bothered to study for because she was too busy chasing Cameron and Dakota. I refused and she told me I would pay. I don't know if she chose Ben's daughter on purpose or at random, but Kaley, her two friends, and some random Omega guy grabbed the girl, covered her head with some kind of bag and dragged her to the side of the school and the guy stomped on her leg and broke it. They sent me the video anonymously with the message 'next time choose better'. They covered their tracks pretty well, no one spoke and nothing but the guy's lower leg, hands, and Ben's daughter was in the video. I took it to my dad, but when he went to look at it, the message and video was gone. He accused me of wanting to be mixed up in the drama and jealous of the attention the popular girls were getting with the boys. Which had nothing to do with what I was telling him. But someone managed to let our principal know the girl's injury was my fault. I was suspended for two days, no questions asked. That's when I stopped going to him for my troubles or advice altogether. He only pretends to listen to me most of the time anyway, more focused on his files and paperwork and whatever else he did for the Alpha. I don't even eat in the dining room with him and my brother for meals, I'm not allowed. When I had a nanny, I would eat with her in her suite unless we had company. It was always that way and I didn't question it until after 7th grade she was dismissed, and I was deemed old enough to look after myself.

Unfortunately, no one told me.

I went to the suite to have dinner, but it was empty. All furniture, her belongings, everything was gone, like she never existed. Confused, I searched the house and found my father and brother in the formal dining room with a full spread of food. The only thing my father said was that she was needed for a more important child, and I shouldn't interrupt dinner again. Neither said anything or came to check on me after I ran from the room crying. I eat in the kitchen with our cook now and help her with the clean up when we are done. She doesn't question it, but I can see the pity in her eyes when she looks at me. I hate the pity more than I hate being alone.

I didn't realize how lost in my thoughts I am until Sierra nudged me. "Hey, where have you been the last ten minutes?"

I blink, trying to shake the memory from my head and wrap it around what I'm about to do. "I don't know if I can do this," I finally blurt out, looking at her. "I wasn't lying before, I really have no friends and none of the people here like me. I am not wanted. I should just go, you will have a better time without me."

"Not a chance. And you are wrong, you do have a friend— me." She places her hand dramatically on her chest. "And I would have a terrible time fighting Kaley without you. You deserve to put that bitch in her place or at least witness someone doing it secretly on your behalf." She winks at me.

I just raise my eyebrows at her. How did she know Kaley was my problem? Not even Kyle has figured it out and he knows most of the stuff she's done to me.

"Uh, I don't know what you— –."

"Mean? Really? You're going to try and lie to me? You don't have to confirm it out loud, but I already told you I am an excellent judge of character, and she is a social climbing parasite wannabe who couldn't fight her way out of a paper bag, with a map and GPS. I could give two shits about her pretend status and influence. I'm an exchange student only here for a year. What is she going to do, get me expelled? I'd like to see her try. Technically speaking, I'm the Alpha King's Gamma's only child, no one here but the Alpha outranks me, she can kiss my ass."

My eyes go wide, and I try to open my mouth to say something, but nothing comes out. How do you respond to something like that? Her confidence is a little scary.

I pull her to a stop. "Okay, you win, just know her dad is on the school board and several kids have gotten in trouble or suspended just for accusing her of things or being in my vicinity when things happen. People have also been hurt because of her hatred of me. I don't want you risking anything just to prove a point. I'm not worth that, and I can handle what she throws at me, it keeps her attention away from harming anyone else in the pack and protecting them is the most important thing." I look her straight in the eyes to make sure she knows that I am serious.

She grabs my shoulders. "You are worth it. I don't know where you got that idea from, but for being as smart as you are, that is the dumbest thing you have said all day. Now let's go! We have hot boys to flirt with and a bitch to taunt."

I have a feeling I am going to regret this night so much while Sierra looks like she is about to enter her favorite place in the whole world. I take a deep breath in and let it out slowly. "Fine, let's do this, but you cannot let me make a fool out of myself. That's all I need. This is not my scene at all. I have no idea what I am doing."

"Don't worry, I've got you. And from the looks your brother's friends were giving you, I don't think you could make a fool out of yourself." She winks at me. "Now lead the way, the sun is starting to go down. Boys playing with fire all man-like is something I can't miss."

I couldn't help the eye roll this time. Sierra was legitimately crazy, boy crazy and there is no stopping this train now that I am on it.

I lead her along the path around the packhouse into the back yard. The Luna does such a great job making her garden so pretty. I wish we had flowers like this, but my dad thinks it is impractical and refuses to let me do it or pay someone to do it, but the Luna lets me sneak over and read in one of the many secluded areas back here whenever I want. She even keeps some of my favorite wild flowers in the planters and a hammock in one of the nooks. It's a great escape from my house when it feels too big and empty or overly hostile.

"Skylar! It's so nice to see you! Are you joining the boys for their bonfire?" Speak of the devil.

"Hi, Luna Ava, how are you? The guys did invite us if that's okay." I am suddenly unsure of how all of this works. I've never been invited to a party and certainly didn't expect the Luna to be sitting on her back patio when we got here. "This is my friend Sierra, she is staying with warriors Robert and Stephanie for the year. She's in the same grade as Mateo and the twins."

Now I can't seem to stop talking, why am I nervous? This woman has been the closest thing to a mom I have ever known. She probably knows all of this too. I'm sure she was the one who arranged for Sierra to be here in the first place. Now, I really feel stupid.

"Hello, Sierra, it's nice to meet you I heard that you sparred with our Skylar here this morning. You both are the talk of the warriors today, isn't that right, dear?" She looks over her shoulder, with a smile that lets me know she is implying something, but I'm not sure what.

I didn't even realize that the Alpha was out here too, man, what happened to my observation skills all of a sudden?!

"You got that right." He sits up from his reclined position, his gruff laugh contrasts with his thick eyebrows and naturally stern look. "None of my warriors have been able to beat your take down time, including Delta Kyle and Gamma Brett." He laughed to himself again. "Trust me, they tried for a solid three hours, changing up who they each fought and everything. We have a few bruised egos being nursed tonight." He smiles as he relaxes back in his chair like he is savoring the joke.

Sierra laughs next to me. "That is amazing! And thank you again Alpha and Luna for letting me spend the school year here. I really do appreciate it."

"Not a problem, dear. Clearly it was the right choice." The Luna winks at us. "You had better be on your way or all the good seats next to the fire will be gone." She wiggles her eyebrows at us, and I have no idea what that is supposed to mean, but Sierra clearly did as she grabs my arm and starts to drag me away.

We follow the path of little twinkling lights through the woods and walk about 10 minutes before we can hear voices and see the warm glow of the fire. We walk through a small crowd of people. I'm not sure if it is invite only or just upperclassmen or what, but there are only about 30 people milling about. Maybe it is still early. I have no idea what to expect or what I am doing, so I just follow Sierra, clinging to her arm, since she seems to have a destination in mind. When we walk a little further around the very large fire I can see where she is leading us. My brother and his friends are posted up on the far side of the clearing guarding what looks like coolers. We barely step around the fire. As soon as we are visible, Sam shouts, "You made it! Finally, we have been waiting forever." The other four guys snapped their heads our way. That earns us some looks from the surrounding crowd. I am for sure out of place here based on the looks we are getting, and Sierra either doesn't notice or doesn't care. I'm guessing, does not care.

"Hello boys, we are right on time. Don't be dramatic, Sam." She smiles and waves him off as we walk closer.

"Wow! You both look great! Do you want a drink? We have water, soda, beer, take your pick." He is far too eager and it's kind of cute.

"I'll start with water, Skylar?" Sierra looks back at me. I think she took the safe option for me so I wouldn't feel so out of place and I am grateful for it. She must know what I'm thinking because she winks at me.

"Water for me too, please." I look at Sam as he trots away and kicks some kid off the furthest cooler he was using as a seat and grabs two bottles of water. We keep walking towards my brother and his friends, reaching them the same time Sam does with our bottles.

"Seriously though, what took so long? Your car was back the same time we were with supplies." Neither of you live that far." Is he pouting again? That little wounded boy act must work for him if he keeps trying it with us.

We both laugh at him, but Sierra, in all her glory, cups his face and runs her thumb along his lower lip. And if he were a cartoon, hearts would be shooting out of his eyeballs and his tongue would have dropped on the floor and rolled away into the forest. "Tuck that lip in, sugar, save it for girls who fall for it. Perfection like this is not free, nor is it easy. It takes time and cannot be rushed." She looks back at me and winks again, she definitely knows what she is doing. I feel like I should be taking notes.

I giggle with her and take a sip of water, which draws the attention of Cameron and Dakota. "She is right, it was definitely worth the wait," Dakota says, not taking his eyes off of me and I'm not sure what to make of that, but my whole body heats up. So I look away only to lock eyes with Cameron who is nodding and then Oliver who is hiding a smile behind his beer bottle. I don't know if I have ever seen him smile, but I don't have time to ponder that as Cameron draws my attention again.

"I don't know if I have ever seen your hair up like that, it looks nice, Sky," He he says, looking puzzled, like he's trying to figure something out.

"Yeah, Tiny, who'd you get all dressed up for?" Dakota winks at me.

"Who are you calling Tiny?" I scoff at him. "I had no control over this." I gesture to myself. "My look is that of a hostage situation by a very demanding friend." I smile over at Sierra who is laughing at something Sam is saying. Before Dakota could reply to me, Sierra jumps in.

"It was not a hostage situation, I was just being a good friend and highlighting all of your amazing assets." I roll my eyes at her. She's not wrong, though. She found this amazing blue coat that accentuates the gray of my eyes and the eye make-up she did made my eyes glow almost silver. She then pulled my blonde hair into a high ponytail and added soft curls to it making me look taller and more confident. I still have my jeans, T-shirt, and black combat boots on from school today. She didn't do a lot, but what she did makes me look like a different person.

I don't know how long we stand there talking to the guys, but we seem to have their undivided attention. My brother and even Oliver joined in the conversation after a while. I found out Oliver is actually really smart and takes a ton of extra math classes. He and I had a long discussion that went over the heads of everyone else, at least one of them likes school, it makes me feel less weird since it's the only thing I can talk about. Cameron and Dakota are discussing a few of the things their dad wants them to consider since they are becoming co-Alphas and some of the other pressures they have to think about. My brother even talks about the pressure Dad puts on him to be the best Beta. We find out all five of them are into sports and training. They have all tried almost every outdoor sport there is to try, several I would love to join them on. I think Sierra just has that charm about her, it draws you in, and if she chooses to pull you into her orbit you can't resist. These guys have never had these kinds of conversations around me let alone with me.

Dakota walks by me after getting another beer, stops right next to me and looks straight down into my face. "You really are tiny, Tiny. What happened? Was Mateo given all the height and nothing was left over for you?" He stands towering over me, his six foot and growing frame requires me to tilt my head all the way back to look at his face. It should intimidate or frighten me to have him this close, but I don't feel anything but safe around any of these guys.

"I guess I never realized how small you are, Smalls," Cameron adds. My head is so far back, I only have to shift my gaze slightly to notice he is right behind me. Not touching me, like Dakota, but close enough to feel the body heat radiating off of them. I am very warm, and yet I can't seem to move.

Still not intimidated, I respond the only way I can think of, like Sierra. "I guess some of us needed less time to reach perfection. Some of you are still working out the rough edges." They both give me a slow, sexy smile that has me taking deep breaths in to control my rapid heart rate. I'm suddenly dizzy.

"Like a fine wine, Little Bit, we are only getting better with age," Sam chimes in, his arm firmly grasped around Sierra where it's been for the last hour or so since she switched to beer. We all laugh at him.

Chapter 5

"Do either of you have a variation on short you would like to throw in for good measure?" I look at Oliver and my brother. They both chuckle and I attempt to use the moment to get out of the twin sandwich I am in. I need some breathing room.

But they just move as I move, so I stop trying to get away and look around Dakota's chest to Oliver as he says, "Let me get back to you, Bite Size, I'll come up with something clever." I roll my eyes at him and Sierra just laughs.

"And you?" I look at Mateo.

"Right now, Shorty, the only thing I get to call you is the take down champ. Dad is never gonna let any of us live that down." Everyone chuckles at the memory. He reaches for me between the twins and wraps an arm around my neck, effectively pulling me away from them in a gentle headlock type hug, a gesture he has never done before. I don't know if it is the beer slowing down his uptight faculties, although I didn't think beer really did much to werewolves, and he hasn't had a ton, but who knows, I've never had any and he stopped the guys from giving me any tonight. They all offered multiple times as we mingled. Or is he uncomfortable with how close the twins were to me? He's never been protective before, but I guess I haven't given him a reason to be, we don't hang out. Hell, I don't hang out, with anyone, ever. This is all new for me and he probably knows it. I just can't place if he does or doesn't care about that.

The moment seems to go unnoticed by the others as they start discussing this morning's training. We all move closer to the fire, finding seats on logs or the ground. Mateo doesn't remove his arm from my shoulder until I sit down and lean against one of the logs. Sierra sits by me, Sam sits on the log behind her, placing her in between his legs. My brother sits on my other side, leaving Oliver, Cameron, and Dakota on the next log that is angled towards us.

"Don't remind me. I was on the receiving end of that particular beat down," Sierra mumbles. I am worried for a minute that maybe she is irritated with me for the way I beat her during training, but when I look at her, she doesn't look upset or embarrassed. She actually looks amused. They all laugh again, and I take a deep breath and join them. These social interactions are an emotional roller coaster.

Man, was that training only this morning? I feel like so much has happened since then. I do notice as we changed our location many more people have shown up too. I am so caught up in our own group, I didn't notice before. I guess Sam was right, everyone comes whenever and just hangs out as long as they want. The fire is really nice. It is more chilly than I anticipated. I'm not cold, but I will take warmth over cold weather any time.

"The Alpha told us that all the warriors tried to match or better her time using the take down today and no one could do it." Sierra supplies to our group. "Including all your dads," she adds like an afterthought taking a pull from her beer, but I think she is rubbing salt in the wound.

"Really?! Damn! Well, I don't feel so bad then, if none of our dads could beat it either," Sam says.

"How many training sessions do you go to?" Oliver asks in his low growl. I can see his brain doing some kind of calculation. "I know you're at all the mandatory pack training and you train with Luna Ava at advanced training, but what else?" He seems genuinely curious as he takes a slow drink of his beer, not breaking eye contact.

"All of them." I shrug, keeping my focus on the fire. I don't know why, but I feel uneasy saying that out loud. Until today I didn't hang out with anyone, so outside of getting my homework done I train. It is the only time I leave the house and Kaley leaves me alone. I am not going to explain that to them, though. I am just starting to feel a little normal.

Oliver chokes on his beer. "All of them, what do you mean 'all of them'?" He he asks, wiping his face and wide jaw.

I'm not sure how that was unclear, but whatever, maybe the beer is getting to him too. "I attend all of the morning mandatory training for the high schoolers, the advance training for the warriors and ranked members three times a week, and I help and work with Delta Kyle and the warriors who do the basic training, patrol training and work with the pups during beginner training." I shrug again like it's no big deal, because to me it isn't, never has been. I look forward to working with the pups and with all of the crap Kaley pulls, I like knowing they are learning to deal with people like her so no one else has to go through what I am when I finally leave. It keeps my head clear too, the effort makes me happy. I also think that basics are undervalued, and people don't focus on them enough. It's the best way to warm up and stay sharp. In the middle of a fight, your muscle memory is what takes over and it's not the fancy shit these guys like to mess around with that saves you.

"That's almost 30 hours of combat training a week. You do that on top of school and everything else?" He's looking at me like he's never seen me before, and I look around at the rest of the group and their looks aren't much different. Yep, I am a freak. I sigh.

"I've never done the math before, so I'll take your word for it, but yeah, I guess," I stammer out, looking back to the fire and feeling uncomfortable with all of the attention. I shift a bit and try to look smaller, if that's even possible. Like it will stop all their staring.

"Aren't you like the top student in your grade?" Cameron asks me.

"And in advanced classes and stuff too, right? I know you're in my English class for sure," Dakota adds, finishing his twin's thoughts.

"I'm in all your standard classes," I mumble. "I have been for a couple years." I scrub my hands over my face, partly to hide from their incredulous looks and partly to rub off the flush of embarrassment that I know is burning in my cheeks right now.

Silence.

"Okay, we get it, she's amazing. Now stop making it weird." Sierra jumps to my aid after coming out of her own shock and pulling me in for a hug, knocking my hands from my face in the process. I let her pull me to her side, as weird as it is to be smashed against Sam's leg, but I keep my focus on the fire or the ground. I was doing so well fitting in, but now my oddities are starting to be revealed, and I don't really want to talk about why I avoid people or I am a year ahead in school.

"I think we all just got an ego smack down, and are feeling a bit inadequate right now, that's all," Sam says, wrapping his arms around my friend, sliding down behind her and pulling her back to his chest, but still staring at me.

"Speak for yourself, no inadequacies here." Oliver laughs and we all join in.

"Yeah right, you're so competitive, I'd put money on you attempting to hit 30 hours of training next week." Sam laughs back at him. Oliver doesn't respond but takes a large gulp of beer, telling me Sam is probably right, and I will see more of Oliver in the coming week. I can't decide if I like the idea or not. Training is my oasis from all of the crap going on behind the scenes at school and home, which they are a part of, even if they seem to have no idea. I am not going to pretend like this little show of friendship is going to last. They have never acknowledged me before today and Kaley makes sure everyone at school stays clear of me on the threat of physical punishment. My dad makes sure I'm not involved in any leadership training that he is aware of. The only reason I get to train with Luna Ava is because she requested me specifically as the only daughter of a ranked member and my dad isn't going to deny his Luna. I think she and Delta Kyle said whatever they had to say to get me permission to work with her, especially after I got my wolf.

We are sitting in comfortable silence after that. Small conversations here and there, but nothing major. I just listen in, mostly staring at the fire, enjoying the warmth and the calm. This is not what I pictured a high school party to be like.

I expected wild kids trashing the place and loud music. Kids dancing on tables, super drunk, stuff like that. I'm sure there are parties like that, but this is very nice.

I should have known things were going too well and something bad was due to happen. My luck just isn't good enough to have a whole day of peace. Just as I have the thought 'I can't remember the last time I had this much fun' the sound of a fake high-pitched voice cut through the crowd.

"OMG! Babes! Your favorite girls are here, now the real party can start!" Kaley squeals from the entrance to the clearing with Jeanie and Marnie in tow.

The mood around me dropped palpably. I can actually feel the tension in the air from every person present pushing against my skin, it is not pleasant. Each of the guys takes a breath and blows it out, like they are preparing for battle as the trio walks over smiling like royalty. They each have on miniskirts that barely cover anything and cropped long sleeved shirts that look to be a few sizes too small. Jeanie's boobs look like they might fall out of the bottom and the top at the same time. To top it all off, they're all wearing tall, pointy black heels. It's cold, and we're in the woods. Sure, wolves feel the cold less than humans, but these are definitely not the outfits for the forest. They probably arrived the same time Sierra and I did, and it just took them hours to navigate the soft forest floor in those ridiculous shoes. I fight to keep my smile in check at the thought, but I don't succeed. I let out an involuntary giggle, which earns a death glare from Kaley, before she turns back to the guys.

"I brought your favorite tequila. I thought we could do some shots to celebrate the new school year and another year closer to you both being Alphas!" She she squeals again, trotting, is that a thing girls do, over to Cameron and Dakota. "But I forgot shot glasses." She pouts and it is nothing like the endearing pout Sam uses. It kind of makes her look constipated.

"Just drink straight from the bottle, the alcohol actually makes it pretty hygienic," Sierra supplies dryly.

Kaley's lip curls as she slowly looks over at Sierra. I'm sure noting how Sam has her wrapped up in his lap. "Um, thanks, new girl, but I figured my men could just take shots off of me. That would be more fun anyway, right? A little warm-up for later." She flips her hair looking at Cameron and Dakota expectantly. My stomach flutters, and not in a good way. Why does she keep calling them her men? On second thought, why do I care?

"I'll do one off, Sierra. Sam volunteers." Wiggling his eyebrows at her. She just rolls her eyes. I am clearly the only person who has no idea what is going on right now. I hope my face is as neutral as I am trying to keep it.

"You can take one off me, Matty." Jeanie looks at my brother and wiggles her fingers. Matty? Since when is that a nickname? My brother hesitates, but doesn't outwardly disagree as she walks over and wraps both arms around his waist from behind, in what I'm sure was supposed to be a loving gesture, but looks uncomfortable.

"That leaves you and me, Oliver." Marnie strides over and sits on the ground between his legs, right as he stands up and she tips back awkwardly through his legs and falls against the log, I'm sure flashing someone with the right angle.

"What about Bite Size? We can't leave one out," Oliver exclaims looking at me, taking a large step over Marnie's head and away from her.

"Who?" Kaley pretends not to notice the odd number since she seems to have claimed both the twins.

"Bite Size, needs a shot partner." He gestures his head towards me and my cheeks flame again.

Now that she is forced to acknowledge my presence, an ugly scowl forms on Kaley's face. This is her true face. She schools it quickly. "I'm sure she doesn't mind being the odd man out, or we could grab one of the other guys for her." Kaley flips her hand in the air dismissively like it's a minor inconvenience.

"NO!" All all five guys state together. I flinch a little at the aggression in their tones and Kaley, Jeanie, and Marnie jump at the outburst.

"Well, that was impressive." I smile, trying to defuse some of the tension. "It's okay, I do not feel left out. Do whatever." I try to match Kaley's tone, hoping I got it right. I'm still lost, but I don't want to stop any of them from enjoying things they usually do when they get together. This is clearly not something new for Sierra either based on her reaction. She gives me a sympathetic look. "It's fine," I mouth to her.

She jumps up and grabs my hand. "I have an idea." Her smile does not give me a good feeling.

"She is not taking a shot, Sierra." My brother looks at her with his best 'I mean business look.' It doesn't work.

"Of course not." She rolls her eyes and pulls me to sit on the log next to Sam. Then she sits across Sam's lap, and lays back, adjusting so that she ends up lying across my lap too. Her shirt has pulled up, exposing her torso. "All right, Mateo, set us up." She giggles as Sam catches on.

"Yes! This is so much hotter!" Sam basically growls and it makes me really uncomfortable, but I hope it doesn't show on my face since most eyes are on us now. He wraps his arm around my waist making sure every inch of my side is in contact with him.

My brother takes the bottle of tequila from Kaley's hands and brings it over to Sierra, then meticulously pours it into her belly button. She squeals a bit and then giggles again. Sam leans down and drags his tongue across the waistband of her jeans and then up her stomach and around her belly button. He wraps his big hand further around my backside and settles it on one of my butt cheeks with a firm grip as he trails his other hand up my friend's side and settles it on my knee before latching his whole mouth on her belly button and taking a very long time to get such a small amount of liquid off of her. He never once takes his eyes off my friend and I begin to relax in the situation considering how new this territory is for me. Sam and Sierra found another way to include me without my having to drink or be embarrassed. I smile and let out a giggle as Sam squeezes my knee and finds that perfect spot that tickles enough to make me squirm.

"Alright, asshole, you made your point. Stop giving Sierra a hickey and groping my sister." Mateo sounds stern, but also amused at his friends' antics. The rest of the guys just laugh along at his annoyance. I think he would have ripped Sam's arms off if he felt like I was in any kind of actual danger, so that makes me feel better. He looks at Sierra and gives her a little head nod. I know he is thanking her for once again allowing me to be a part of this without feeling stupid or inexperienced.

The rest of the guys take their shot off the girl that claimed them, but none were as entertaining or excited about it as Sam. I now know how my brother felt watching me sit there. It is not pleasant and yet it is comical to watch him take a shot off of Jeanie, who insists on grabbing his hair and keeping his lips on her at least as long as Sam did on Sierra making weird gasping sounds and moans. Marnie is a little more gracious, but by force. Oliver holds her wrists together over her head, so she can't grab him. But she appears to like the show of dominance, mentioning letting him tie her up later. Kaley of course insists both twins take a shot off of her. It just feels ridiculous and forced now. She goes over the top, grinding her butt in their laps, flipping her hair around, and arching her back as she lays down. I'm sure she thinks it's enticing to them, but if she actually looked at everyone's faces, they are more grimaced than smiling or lust filled. Our whole group dynamic changed after they arrived, and Sierra and I are ignored by the trio, clearly trying to maintain all of the attention, even though the guys refuse to leave us out of conversation.

After about an hour I look at Sierra. "I think I'm going to head out, you can stay if you want to."

She jumps up faster than I thought possible in her former sleepy state leaning on Sam's shoulder. "Nope, I was actually thinking the same thing. We were both up early and some of us, non-slackers, have training in the morning." She says the last words loud enough to be heard over the trio's squabble of which couples are most likely to be mates after we all turned 21.

"Seriously? Saturdays too?" Oliver said, completely walking away from the Barbie trio's conversation. I just stare at him, was he listening in?

"I'll still put money on it," Sam chimes in with a big old smile on his face.

You can see the clear confusion on Kaley, Jeanie, and Marnie's faces at the attention diverting from them so easily and having no idea what the guys are talking about.

Oliver groans. "I guess that means I'm out too. I'll walk you guys home."

"Called it." Sam stands up too, laughing. "But, I'll walk with you. I have to see you in action early on a Saturday, man." He pats Oliver on the chest as he walks by.

"I guess we should all be there, shouldn't we?" My brother stands up, having a harder time extricating himself from Jeanie's tentacle-like grip.

"You're right, we should all go. Delta Kyle will appreciate that we are all there," Cameron says as both he and Dakota stand up from the log they occupy with Kaley.

"But we just got here, and we haven't even started having fun yet," Kaley whines. She grabs the twins' hands, stumbling a bit. "I was hoping we could end with a little two on one time. It's been forever." She looks up at them through her heavily mascaraed eyelashes. Gross, is she talking about what I think she's talking about? Who does that in public?

"Sorry ladies, we got called into the weekend training, so it's a light and early night for us. Maybe next time," Dakota says as the five of them turn around like a unit and start ushering us up the lit pathway before anyone else can argue.

"Damn, that was brutal," Sam lets out under his breath before we even make it through the path opening. "Don't get me wrong, I loved the two-female body shot, we will definitely be revisiting that situation, but did anyone else feel the whole night just tanked as soon as the party got too big?"

"First, over my dead body are taking a shot off my sister and second, yes, I don't think it's ever been like that before," Mateo says.

I realize they're speaking in code, and I'm smart enough to know who the reason for it is, but at the same time, I don't understand why. Does it matter if she hears them? They are the future leaders of the pack and have never been shy about sharing their opinions before.

The twins say goodbye to us from the back patio and say they will drive us all to training in the morning. Also a new situation, because I'm pretty sure I might have been included in that invitation, but we will see come morning. Once we get to the front Mateo, Sam, Sierra, and I split off toward our side of the packhouse and Oliver starts walking to the other side towards his house. He shouts over his shoulder that we will leave at 6 a.m. sharp so none of us should be late, no matter how long it takes some of us to say goodnight.

I openly laugh at the insinuation and then again at the look on Sam's face. It isn't shocked or defensive, it's hopeful. I hug Sierra goodnight at the end of our sidewalk and she and Sam keep on walking to her house.

When we finally get home, Mateo stops to take his jacket off at the door, I just continue into the kitchen looking for a snack. All I had was soda and water at the party and I am starving. I walk into the dimly lit kitchen, the light over the sink the only illumination in the room.

"Where the hell have you been?!" I jump about a mile into the air and scream at the growling words. Mateo comes running in, grabs my shoulders and pulls me behind him protectively looking around for what scared me. He relaxes a little when he notices my dad sitting at our rectangular kitchen table, a short empty glass in front of him.

When my heart rate starts to go back to a normal rhythm, I have to force down an eye roll. I step around my brother to fully face my dad. "After school I showed the new girl, Sierra, around and then we hung out with Mateo and the guys. I'm sorry, I didn't realize how late it was. When we noticed the time and that we have training in the morning, we all left to get some sleep."

"Is that true, son?" I can barely hold back the growl from my wolf at my brother being questioned to see if I was lying. My hands ball into fists at my sides to curb the anger. I never do anything out of line, always his perfect little Beta daughter, but worth nothing to him other than an image he presents to the outside world.

"Yes, sir. She's been with us the whole time. It was the annual bonfire." Simple explanation that would have gotten me a smack to the face and grounded.

"And are you really going to the training in the morning?" My brother nods. "I'm impressed with the initiative. Keep up the good work." He looks at my brother only, as if I'm not even here. I am fuming, my anger burns across my skin.

I take another step forward and away from my brother's protection. I snap at him with my own growl, "I go to training Every. Single. Day. Delta Kyle reports my progress weekly to you, sir," My whole body is shaking as I walk out of the kitchen to the stairs, and up towards my room. I know he gets regular updates, because the Delta asked if I minded at all. I figure, the more I do and the more my dad hears about it, the better. I guess I am wrong. I hear the loud scrape of the chair, knowing my father will rush to punish me for my back talk, little girls don't back talk, they do what they are told and stay silent. I don't get far when I hear my brother.

"Leave her alone. She convinced us all that we should invest more time into training, especially after her display this morning. All the guys and I decided she's the best person to learn from. Sky is going to show us the ropes since she is the most familiar with the set up."

"We have been asking you boys to go to weekend trainings for years. Why the change now?" My my dad asks sarcastically.

"I guess she's just more persuasive than you. Now, it's late and I need to sleep if I am going to be able to function that early." Then I hear Mateo's boots clomping up the stairs behind me. I let him catch up and he swings his arm around my shoulder and kisses my temple. "I'm sorry, I can't pretend like the way he treats you is okay anymore, it was never okay. I never should have let it get this far. I know why you work and train as hard as you do. You don't have to do it alone anymore." He walks me to my door and kisses my forehead before turning around and walking to the door across the hall from mine.

"Thank you, Mateo," I whisper, but I know he can hear me.

Chapter 6

That was the first night in a long time that I cried. I never cried after getting beaten by Kaley and her friends, I wouldn't give them the satisfaction and I have never been close to my dad so there has never been an emotional connection to feel sad about. But Mateo. Mateo was a loss that I didn't know hurt me until now, when I have a glimpse of what we had before he started focusing on his duties as the next Beta. I fall asleep hoping he and I can have the close relationship we did when we were little. Today is just one day though, and they only noticed me after they found out I am better at something than they are. And they only had a reason to notice because Sierra happened to partner with me. It's all chance and coincidence. So, we'll see how long this lasts.

The morning comes quickly after that. I am actually too antsy to sleep much. At four, I finally decide I need to go for a jog, my wolf agrees. A run in the forest really early helps clear my mind and settle conflicting thoughts. It's like everything falls into place out here. I am trying to gather my thoughts on my emotions. Am I more excited or scared that they are going to join me? I was planning to ask Sierra if she wanted to come anyway, but adding the guys is something I never thought of. They always have their own things going on and are too busy to look in on how the rest of the pack fares or trains. I walk back into my house at 5, after running half the patrol border route and go to start breakfast. It's the one thing I do on the weekends for my brother and dad. It's the only morning our housekeeper gets off too, and she has always been good to me, it's the least I can do. Neither acknowledge or thank me, but there is never anything left, so it must be at least decent. I plate everything and leave it on the island then I go to knock on Mateo's door to make sure he is up and getting ready. This is their idea, not mine, and I won't wait for them if they decide to sleep in.

"Hey, sleeping beauty, you up?" I sing in at him, opening the door. "We have to get moving or we will be late, and I don't actually know what Oliver does to people who are late, nor do I want to find out the hard way."

"I think I actually hate you. Why do you sound so chipper already?" He he grumbles with his face still firmly planted in his pillow.

"Lies, you love me. Get in the shower, it helps, and I made breakfast and coffee." I smack him on the back, and he groans again.

"How long have you been up exactly?" He peaks out from under his pillow and looks rough.

"Little while, I went for a run and made breakfast, no big deal. I do it every weekend. This is my normal."

"Wait." He pushes up to look at me. "You run and make breakfast...before you go to training?! Since when do you make breakfast?"

"I always make breakfast on the weekends, it's the only time Gretchen takes off."

"Does Dad know it's you and not her? Cause, I had no idea. I just thought she came in and made quick stuff before spending the day with her family. I am feeling more and more inferior the longer I talk to you." He groans, finally climbing out of his bed to head toward the bathroom.

"Whatever, Beta, get ready fast, you only have 15 minutes before we have to meet the guys."

I walk out of his room smiling. His subtle compliment gives me a little more hope that we can be friends. It's a bit strange to have that thought. I haven't had this much conversation with my brother in years. My dad has had him so busy training for becoming the next Beta that he hasn't had any time for me since he was about 10. But, as strange as it is right now, I would be lying if I said that I didn't enjoy it. Even if it is only temporary. I know they are all only coming today because Oliver felt a slight to his fragile male ego knowing that I train more than he does, even with the extra time they put in with their dads. He needs to know if he could handle it. The rest of the guys are coming to either cheer him on when he does it, or have proof when he fails. What he doesn't know is that I don't do half the things they do. I don't go to parties, or hang out with friends. I don't go to study groups or hold meetings with our current leaders to understand how the pack functions. Physical training is my only escape from the hell that Kaley and her friends bring me.

She has gone as far as searching for kids misbehaving, and letting me know what the punishment for those deeds are. The punishments are always way over the top and far more sadistic than they should be. No person, let alone a peer should be able to inflict pain on another peer. I'm not sure how she has gained so much power, but if I don't step in and take the punishment, she really will harm these kids.

I found out at the end of last year her father appointed her and a few other 'select students' to monitor the school for minor infractions that are beneath the administration's interference, but need to be handled. It has all been approved by the Alpha supposedly. Things like being late, littering or vandalizing the school, and fighting in the hallways are all subject to her scrutiny; then she hands out and fulfills punishments accordingly. A few victims have gone to the principal about the abusive tactics she uses, but our administrators either agree with what she is doing or something else is allowing her to continue. It doesn't matter, I won't let her torture our pack members and she knows it, so I am her personal punching bag.

I don't talk about it and neither do the students I am taking the torture for. We have all decided that nothing will be done to her and I refuse to look weak and keep tattling when she comes up with stories for her actions and every adult has been led to not believe me or fears siding with me because of who my father is and how he feels about me. As long as other pups are not getting hurt or, more likely, don't report getting hurt by her, all the adults are perfectly fine turning a blind eye. I do know the kids I take punishments for appreciate it, even if they can't say anything directly to me. It's in their eyes, when we pass in the halls. I know they would approach me if they could, and that is part of the reason I endure this, it doesn't go unnoticed by everyone. I just wish the people who could do something to stop it would open their eyes. Kids shouldn't be afraid of going to school.

But training is where I am free. I will never complain about her not being at training, the peace is divine.

Another reason I don't retaliate and fight back is my father. The one time I did fight back our freshman year, I punched her in the nose. I was still learning how to control my emotions with my wolf and we lashed out physically. I hit her so hard that I not only broke her nose but also fractured the bone around her right eye. She went straight to her dad with some sob story about me hurting her since I am a higher rank and therefore stronger than her. My father was called in and the verbal lashing I received in front of Kaley, the principal, and her father is one I will never forget. I was called worthless, a slacker, deviant, spoiled and so difficult that my mother's body couldn't survive having me. He said I should not be alive to cause so much stress and trouble for innocent people. If I am going to force my presence on the pack, I should be working with other ranked members to make the pack better, not beating up on weaker members.

That was the day I stopped talking to my father altogether. If he doesn't directly talk to me, I no longer make the effort. My only problem is I thought if I just did better, became stronger, tried harder and was able to hide the bullying, he would see that I am worthy. So, like a crazy person I threw myself into everything he made me believe is important, like being the top student. I'm sure he knows, he has to know, but he will never say anything to me about it. I also have made myself the best warrior in the pack. Just because I won't be the Beta, doesn't mean I can't be a warrior here or better yet, in a different pack if my mate happens to be from somewhere else. That is my dream, to meet my mate and get to leave. I will miss Luna Ava and Delta Kyle, maybe even my brother a little bit, but being free to walk around and have friends, to not be looking over my shoulder all of the time or feel like a waste of someone's space. That will be heaven.

Mateo pulls me from my thoughts, walking by to put his plate in the sink. "Let's get this over with. I am already regretting agreeing to this insanity."

He gestures and we walk out the door together, I start to turn left out of habit, walking away from the houses to my usual shortcut to get to the training grounds.

"Where are you going? The packhouse is this way," he calls over to me.

"Training, where else? It's faster to cut through the woods behind Oliver's house."

"We are not walking." He scoffs at me. "Cam and Kota are going to drive us, remember?"

"Oh, I figured that was a you guys thing," I mumble out, looking down at my shoes. "I didn't think I was included in that." When he doesn't answer, I look up at him and his eyes are closed. He takes a breath just deep enough for me to notice before he schools his face.

Maybe it's mean of me, but I can't help the little jab. Since the twins started driving all five of the guys have been riding to school together, and I was left to my own devices. It's not actually that far, but there was never even an offer, like I was invisible to them. Which I guess I was… until yesterday. That thought is the little reality check I need to remember things will not be like this once we are back at school Monday. They will go back to being the popular guys at school that everyone fights to talk to, and I will go back to being invisible, unless Kaley says otherwise.

"Come on, you are not walking either," he wraps me in that headlock hug thing and starts to drag me towards the massive truck in the packhouse driveway.

"It's about time, I was worried you were making up all that extra training crap last night." Sam laughs before removing his arm from around Sierra's shoulder and jumping in the truck's backseat. My brother climbs in and slides to the middle of the back, and Oliver sits on his other side. I move to stand beside

Sierra, the twins are in the front looking over at us, unreadable expressions on their faces.

"She's already been on a run and made breakfast." Mateo laughs out to the group, patting his stomach then elbowing Oliver. Oliver groans and rolls his eyes.

Sierra and I just look at each other. "Do you expect us to sit in the truck bed?" She laughs at them as they look around and realize we are not a normal part of their entourage, and they take up every inch of available space with their ever-growing size. They really don't spend much time outside their bro bubble.

"We can just do laps, it's not that far. Sierra, you can join me." Sam pats his thigh and wiggles his eyebrows at her. "Little Bit, you can ride on Oliver." I did not miss the sexual innuendo this time and my cheeks flame instantly.

"Tiny can ride up here in the front, she'll fit in between us," Cameron says a little clipped from the driver's seat.

Dakota nods, but instead of getting out like I thought he would, he just says, "Climb on up." With an evil smirk on his face. He must know how uncomfortable and weird this is for me, I'm sure my face is going an even brighter shade of red.

I take a deep breath and slowly climb up the truck sideboard. I must be going too slow for Dakota, because he grabs my waist and plants me on his lap before closing the door. I start to slide off his lap to sit in between the twins as Cameron pulls out of the driveway. Dakota's arm stays behind my back as I move and slowly drags his fingers across the back of my T-shirt. I gasp a bit as he nudges on of the fresh wounds from Kaley's latest punishment, and I also realize my shirt is still a bit damp from my early morning run. I hope a cut isn't open again and bleeding. My black tank top and black T-shirt should hide it, but if I bled enough, it will show on Dakota's hand and then they will ask questions.

"How are you already sweaty, Smalls. We haven't done anything yet." Dakota looks over at me again with that crooked grin.

"I told you, Miss Shorty Overachiever here has already gotten in a run this morning along with cooking up a feast. That's why we were right on time, I was not letting any of that go to waste." My brother spouts behind me. I can hear the smile in his voice though, so I think he's teasing me.

"Wait, you made food and didn't bring us any?!" Sam asked. I can't help but laugh at his expression when I look over my shoulder. "I would have complained less if I knew there was food involved." Now everyone laughs.

"There wasn't any extra to bring. I'll remember you are all easily bribed with food next time." I laugh as we pull up to the training grounds barely five minutes later.

"I can't believe you can cook too on top of everything else. Do you wanna get married?" Sam asks me, still holding Sierra in his arms.

"What about me?" Sierra asks, laughing. "Am I just a plaything?"

Sam growls a little in his chest and nuzzles into her neck. "Is it so bad to be my plaything? Besides, if you can cook too, I'll marry both of you and we can start a harem."

"No!"

"Gross."

"Seriously?" All of the guys protest together.

"I don't share. No offense, Sky." She and I laugh at all the guys' faces.

Cam parks right outside the gates to the practice arena and we all pile out of the truck like it is our own personal clown car. Much to the surprise of Delta Kyle who is checking the pups in. He definitely did not expect to see us this morning. Did Sam not tell him they were joining me?

"Hey, Delta, I brought some help, hope you don't mind." I skip up to him. Training with the pups is one of my favorite things to do.

"Mind?! How in the hell did you manage that?" He points behind me, eyes wide, chin basically on the ground. "I couldn't even get my son to come to work with me by force and he shows up with you looking kind of awake and happy about it. You need to teach me your secret ways." He bows mockingly.

I just laugh at him and roll my eyes. "No secret, Oliver asked how often I trained, and I told them, now they are here." I shrug my shoulders. It didn't seem that big a deal to me, but clearly it is based on his reaction.

Chapter 7

"Will you get the pups warmed up? I have a couple more things to wrap up here," he says to me but not looking at me. He is genuinely confused about the guy's' presence here.

I grab Sierra's hand. "Come on, you can help with warm-up." We walk in the smaller arena. We have three so we can run multiple training sessions or training styles at a time. Each arena is essentially the same, with different capacities. Our largest is for big group training or when we have events with neighboring packs. The mid-range one is where most of our training happens. This arena is the smallest, designed specifically for the pups. It has an obstacle course at one end that we let the kids run on at the end of class. All the pups start shouting their hello's to me, and then I watch their eyes pop as they realize who is following behind me. It is really cute to see them starstruck with the future Alphas, Beta, Gamma, and Delta. They are celebrities at school, but I don't think the guys understand what these little kids think of them.

"Why do they all look terrified?" Oliver asks in my ear. I jump, not realizing how close he was to me. He's a ninja.

"You guys are idols to them. They've never seen you up close before since you spend very little time with pack members younger than you." All their heads snap to me. Was that mean? The way the guys are looking at me makes me feel like I said something wrong. Sierra nudges me with a huge smile on her face, I shake off the thought and get started. "These are our youngest pups, they range from five to seven. They are learning basic movements and body control, really."

I introduce the guys and explain that they are joining us today to see what we have been teaching and that they better make me look good in front of our future leaders. That earns a small laugh from the pups and breaks the tension a bit.

We go through our usual warm-ups; Sierra and the guys follow my lead walking around and giving corrections. The kids must have thought this was the best day ever, based on their faces every time someone stopped to talk to them. The pups are working harder to get noticed. After about an hour, I look around and realize Delta Kyle never came back, so I just keep going. The pups are putting in more effort to get noticed. I look around after an hour and notice Delta Kyle never came back, so I just keep on going. I have been helping with this class for so long, I could probably teach it in my sleep. We do a lot of games to motivate the pups. It keeps them engaged and they do the conditioning with less groaning if it seems fun, and they know we will do something exciting if they get done quickly. Today is tag, but I have an idea to make it more interesting for them and for me.

"Okay, today's game is tag!" An eruption of cheers follows. I wave my hands. "Wait though, we are going to play a little differently than normal." A chorus of Aww's has me rolling my eyes. "You didn't even hear how we are changing it up." I put my hands on my hips and look at them sternly. "We are going to see which leader you can catch the fastest. You are all going to be chasers against one of our future leaders, work as a team to tag them. Let's see what you can do. Get together to make your strategy." I turn around to the guys and they are looking at me like I have lost my mind. Sierra is openly laughing. "What? All you have to do is not get tagged." I shrug my shoulders. "It's not that difficult."

"But there's like a thousand of them." Sam whines.

"It's only 50. You'll be fine. You can use any means, except leaving the arena, to steer clear of them for as long as possible. And just so you know... they take this game very seriously. Don't let their little cuteness distract you." I wink at them. "Who wants to go first?!"

"I'll go. It can't be that hard, can it?" Oliver volunteers.

I turn around. "Alright, we have our first victim...I mean volunteer." I laugh. "Future Gamma Oliver is up. Remember, he is going to try and evade you at all costs for as long as possible. Ready? Go!" I shout with zero warning.

The kids all charge at us and the momentary panic in Oliver's eyes has Sierra and I almost crying with laughter. I don't think he expected them to be that fast and they work really well together due to the team building games we play. At two minutes and 40 seconds they finally corner him. He walks back to the group panting.

"...Should maybe work a bit on that cardio, less on the weights, big guy." Sierra pats him on the back.

"I really don't like you," he says to the ground, but he could be talking to either Sierra or me at this point.

"Who's next?" I ask, ignoring him.

"Let's get this over with," Mateo grumbles good-naturedly.

"We have Future Beta Mateo. Ready? GO!" I don't give him a second to get his bearings.

Mateo has a better strategy at least, he runs a couple circles around the obstacle course and when they catch on, he runs under it to cut off the two groups they formed, jumping to the rope climb, I'm sure he's hoping they don't know how to use, but he underestimates my training or their abilities or both. A kid follows him up his rope and two jump on the ropes on either side of him, effectively blocking him in.

"That was done in two minutes thirty-five seconds." The kids scream at their accomplishment.

"Damn, they are fast. What kind of training do you put them through?" Mateo asks, going to grab a bottle of water then stands next to Oliver. I ignore both of them, beaming at the kids surrounding us.

"Let's do this. All I have to do is make it longer than two forty." Sam chuckles.

"Willing to make a bet?" Oliver asks. Seriously, these two and making bets?! I'm sure they bet on who can hold their pee the longest. I roll my eyes.

"You're on. Winner buys lunch... for all seven of us." Sam wiggles his eyebrows. This must be a very good wager, because they all seem to have gained a newfound energy. I'm not sure if I will ever understand the dynamic of boys.

"Okay, Ready for Future Delta Sam?" I don't even wait for their response before shouting, "GO!" trying not to laugh at their antics. Sam is really fast and seems to be just as sporadic in his movements as the kids. I hate to doubt Oliver, but Sam might actually win this bet. He's laughing and dodging, spinning, and jumping over the kids' heads. He clearly has the movements of a natural born warrior. He's leaner than the rest of the guys, like a runner who happens to lift a ton of weight. The kids eventually break into 5 groups, 4 of them covering the entrances to the obstacle course Sam decided to climb and the rest have made a perimeter around in case he decides to jump from somewhere random. Which of course he did. He made a running jump to the rope climb, but did not anticipate the kids being able to shimmy up and tag him.

He climbs down laughing with the kids, looking at me expectantly. "Sorry..." I hesitate, enjoying the suspense, "Oliver, he made it, two minutes and 43 seconds." I look at Oliver apologetically, while Sam is hooting and hollering, doing the do-see-do with some of the pups.

"Ugh! I'm never going to hear the end of it now." Oliver rolls his eyes, but has a small half smile on his face.

Both the twins take their turns, but they are less serious about it. Opting to tease and taunt the kids before letting themselves be caught after only a minute or so. I'm not sure if they were trying to give the kids a break or if they didn't want the added pressure of having to beat Sam. He would definitely gloat.

"Alright cadets, now it's time to see if you can finally stop your biggest nemesis," Delta Kyle calls from the seats near the center of the arena, only he isn't alone. For the first time in a long time, he is accompanied by the Alpha, Luna, Beta, Gamma, and a couple of our Elite Warriors.

Some of the kids groaned and some cheered. I get why, though. This is the only challenge they haven't won yet.

"What's he talking about?" Sierra asks.

"They have to play capture the flag against me." I wink at her.

"Wait, you're their biggest nemesis?" Dakota asks.

"I guess, you could call it that. I think Delta Kyle is being dramatic, but they haven't beaten me yet." I shrug my shoulders.

"What do you have to do?" Cameron asks.

"I have to capture the flag." I point to the flag one of the pups is attaching to the top of the forty foot rope climb. "And get back to this side of the stadium without being tagged in under a minute."

"WHAT?! And they haven't beaten you? How many times have you played this? Once or twice?" Oliver asks.

"We have played this at the end of every Saturday training for almost a year." I say, walking to my end of the field, not looking over my shoulder. I don't want to look at them and I also have to get my head in the game. I've never had an audience before, and the current and future leaders are here, including my dad. It's a little bit nerve wracking.

Chapter 8

"You ready, Sky?" Delta Kyle calls out to me. I nod my head without looking away from my target. "Ready? GO!"

A torrent of sound comes from the kids. Several charge my way as I run towards them. Just before they reach me, I break left towards the side walls of the arena and jump to the ledge, continuing to run without a missed step. I go as far as I can and make a large broad jump landing on the tips of my toes on the top of the curved climbing bars leading up to the main platform of the obstacle course. I continue running and make the same leap to the ropes that Sam did. The only thing I do differently is jump from the side collecting 2 of the three ropes in my legs while reaching for the third. I climb up using my arms, pulling the extra ropes with my legs so they can't follow. I get to the top, secure the ropes out of their reach, and grab the flag, stuffing it carefully in my sports bra. I look around to assess where the kids are. For the most part they are starting to swarm the ground where the ropes would land if I let them go. I walk across the support structure like a gymnast. Making it to the cargo net before any of them can make it around, climbing only as low as I need to jump to the arena wall on the other side, almost missing my footing. I hear a bunch of gasps from somewhere in the arena, but I can't place the voices. As soon as I'm sure, I take off as fast as I can. I know I have to be close to time. They made me run more than in the past. They are starting to learn to trust their instincts and learn my habits, weaknesses, and strengths. Kyle and I decided to not let them win this without a fight to make them build their long-term observation skills, anticipation, tracking and learning from past mistakes. I jump from the wall, the kids hot on my tail and run like my life depends on it over the finish line. I don't get tagged, which sucks for the kids, but I want to know if I maintained my time. I am just as competitive as Oliver, but I will never say that out loud to him.

I look expectantly at Delta Kyle, my hands on my knees while I am bent over panting, trying desperately to ignore the looks on the faces surrounding him. He just stares at me blank faced. I am ready to cry from anticipation. He looks down at the stopwatch and back up at me a couple times before taking a deep breath in. He's trying to kill me with suspense now.

"52 seconds." His face breaks out into the biggest smile I have ever seen. I let out the breath I didn't realize I am holding and match his smile and then it's like someone turned the volume on full blast. Cheers and yelling surround me with all of the pups coming up to congratulate me, tugging my arms and hugging my legs.

Sierra wades through the crowd of kids and gives me a hug. "Why are they so excited, they lost?"!"

"That was my fastest time yet and they put the flag as high as it could go. Today was hard, they put up a good fight." ," I say, patting a little boy on the back, while one of the girls is trying to push through for her own hug.

There is a commotion of words. I catch bits and pieces, but you would have thought the kids won the challenge the way they are retelling it. "Did you see that jump? It was at least 20 feet." "No way, it was more like 30, we could totally do that."

"I'm going to remember that rope trick, it was crazy good."

"I think she's part cat, not wolf, the way she ran on those walls."

"I bet she's faster than a cheetah."

"Nice work today." A deep booming voice comes up from behind me.

"Alpha Lucas! Hi! Thank you." I take a step back from his very close posture. "It's a game we have been working on for a while, so I've had some practice," I say, blushing again and looking at the ground. I don't think my cheeks are ever going to be normal color again.

"I wasn't talking about the game, although that was impressive." He laughs and I look back up confused. "I will have you show us some of the training you do to be able to move like that. I think you should join the trainers and help them plan." My face goes slack. He did not just say that. "No, I was talking about the fact that you got the entire future leadership team out of bed *voluntarily*, before 6 a.m., on a Saturday, to teach a class with you and they participated fully. That, my dear, is pretty close to a miracle." My eyes go wider, and I am speechless as the rest of our leaders collectively laugh at their sons. "You are also a very skilled teacher for someone so young, you are a natural with these kids. No wonder Delta Kyle praises you so highly." And there goes my cheeks again, and I'm pretty sure the blush is creeping down my neck too.

"Well, thank you for the absolute destruction of our fragile male egos. Now, we have a date after all of that to eat our sorrows away and Oliver is buying." Sam walks up and puts his arm around my shoulder, trying to steer me away.

"Actually, there's another class," I say biting my lip, looking as apologetic as I can. "But you guys can go, I'll catch up later." I wave off, having no intention of chasing them down at all. I feel like this little friend bubble we have been in for the last 12 hours is about to break, and I should be the one to pop it before something really bad happens.

"How many more classes are we talking about?" Sam leans back to look at me. "I am slowly dying from lack of food here, Little Bit." He crumbles to the ground dramatically, making all the kids laugh.

"You should have eaten before we came, like a normal person." Sierra laughs at him, kicking his leg for good measure.

He's gesturing wildly from the ground on his back. "I was unaware of the team breakfast at the Beta House to satisfy the ridiculous amount of exercise I would be subjected to today." He covers his eyes like it will soften the blow. "How many more, Little Bit? If you're here, then we're here so you can stop making us look pathetic." He laughs.

"The next class is a basics class for beginners and non-warriors just to stay sharp and in shape. It's less intense than the rest of the training, but I think it's super important. It runs for 2 hours. Then we're done for the day."

"Remind me to never, ever, ever rise to your challenge again. I'm going to die. Does anyone have a snack for the hangry Delta?" Sam scrambles off to grab his water bottle as the rest of the guys, the Luna, and Sierra all laugh at him.

"I didn't challenge you!" I yell at his back, receiving more laughs.

Basic training goes better and as we all walk through correcting form and technique, I can see the current leaders watching us again with curious and hopeful expressions on their faces. They even come down to do some of the exercises with us, which is a rare thing. They don't normally have time to intermingle casually like this. I think it's great for the pack members that are here. If anything, the looks on the pack members' faces are totally worth the full interruption and distraction of having more than a dozen extra people here.

The slow stretching and body weight exercises are great for our newer, younger fighters and our older fighters who want to stay in shape. We work on dynamic and functional movement, building up muscle memory so they don't hesitate in an unfriendly situation.

Even though the training is light for us, we are all still a sweaty mess when we are walking out of the arena. "Should we go home and change before we eat?" I ask, noting I probably look something close to a drowned rat that's been run over a couple of times.

"Not a chance, Little Bit, get your sweaty ass in the truck, and for the love of my sanity somebody feed me!" Sam growls out. "Martha won't care, when she hands Oliver the bill. I'm going to eat one of everything on that menu. You guys are going to have to roll me out the door like Violet Beauregard." Everyone is laughing now.

Mateo, Oliver, and Sam jump in the back. Sam basically hauls Sierra in and onto his lap with a lot of protesting on her part. Dakota picks me up from behind and slides me into the center of the front seat like I weigh nothing, as Cameron jumps in and fires up the truck. It is weird that after all of that working out and sweating, I am not at all bothered by the smell of these boys. Collectively, it's a musky scent that is all male, but not bad by any means. I, however, am sure that I wreak.

Another five minutes later we are pulling into the local diner. The guys must be regulars because they didn't even wait to be seated, they walk straight back to an extra-large corner booth. I somehow end up between Cameron and Oliver making me notice my small size. I look like a toddler next to all these guys and I can't help but laugh.

"What?" Cameron asks gently next to me.

"Some situations make my lack of size very apparent." I laugh again, pointedly turning my natural line of sight to the middle of his bicep then looking up at his face, then doing the same to Oliver. Everyone else joins in.

"Would you like a booster seat, I'm sure they have one around here somewhere?" Sam asks.

"Nope, I'm good. It would be my luck to fall out of it." I blush. Everyone chuckles at me again.

An older woman comes out with a tray full of drinks. "Oh! You boys brought company. How did you manage to get these lovely ladies to even come near you like this? You smell like a locker room that hasn't been cleaned in a year." Oh, Goddess, I love her already.

"Hey! I smell sexy!" Sam looks a little offended. "All man here." He pats his chest.

"Martha, if you must know it was actually her fault we are like this, she is a ruthless trainer who made us train for four hours straight, early, on a Saturday morning. So if you're going to complain, talk to Tiny here." Dakota laughs and points at me.

She looks at me and smiles like the rat that got the cheese. "You did this, deary?" She points to our group. I nod my head at her, slowly, not sure where this is going. "You eat for free. Keep these boys on their toes. They have never once come to see me on a Saturday after training, nor have they ever looked this ragged after their usual training. Keep up the good work." She winks at me. Sierra and I just giggle at her description.

"Martha, babe. We have been coming here forever, and you have never let any of us eat for free. I thought we had something special." Sam pouts at her tapping the spot over his heart.

"You are something special, sweetheart." She pats his cheek. "But us girls have to stick together, and she's probably the first girl, in your lives, that hasn't had her pants charmed off by one or more of the five of you. And, you certainly never bring those...bed warmers here." I spit my drink out and began choking. Super attractive, I'm sure. WHAT?! I can't decide if I love this woman or am scared of her. Maybe a little of both. She just says it how it is without any regard to who's around and listening in. Cameron and Oliver are both patting my back as I cough up the rest of the water that went down my windpipe and up my nose.

When I finally calm down, Martha looks at me pointedly. "Oh, did you not know? They don't bring girls in here to me, this is a known fact, so you two must be special." My eyes are wide, but not as wide as the guys, and are they blushing? Like she just gave away their greatest secret.

"We bring girls in here, Martha," Oliver says, looking confused.

"Yeah, all the time." Sam agrees, sits up straight eyes wide, and then looks at Sierra whose eyebrows shoot up in question. He then sits back looking a little sheepish at the confession.

"We are always in here with groups of people, both guys and girls." Cameron tries to calm the tension while contributing to the point.

"Yeah, but how many sit here... at this booth... with you? Hmmm? None, that's how many. Think about that while I grab your food. Ladies, are you just going to pick off the guys' plates or do you want to see the menu?" She abruptly changes the subject.

"Oh, I am definitely going to need a menu," I say far too quickly.

"Same," Says says Sierra.

She smiles brightly at us. "Girls who eat and make decisions for themselves. See, special," She she says, pointing and winking at us then walks away.

Sierra and I order and once our food comes out, it looks like we are feeding a small army. I did not even hesitate to smash the plate of waffles and fruit in front of me. Sierra follows suit and the guys look at us with surprise in their eyes before coming to their senses and digging into their food. We are all enjoying a great time and most of the food is gone when, again, the moment is ruined by the condescendingly chipper voice of Kaley.

"Oh wow! We didn't know you boys would be here today, you should have called us and we would have come to keep you company. We were just out doing some shopping. We have to look good for our future Alphas and company." She giggles and it sounds strained as she moves close to Cameron, as if he would move to make a space for her on the bench seat. When he doesn't, she gives him a pointed look he ignores.

"Our table is full, but thanks." Oliver points out and I want to melt into the seat. He has no idea what kind of target he just put on us. Although Sierra doesn't give a shit based on her expression.

"Oh?" She pretends to just notice us sitting here. She looks daggers at me then at Sierra and there's nothing I can do or say. I'm stuck between these two giant guys, and I just stuffed a large bite of burger into my mouth. "You never have extras at your table. We are with you all the time and have never sat with you. Are you guys changing it up?" She almost whines. "I can't wait to come here with you next time." Her eyes light up at the thought. The guys stay quiet.

It takes me several minutes to chew and swallow without choking again. I don't need to embarrass myself in front of these guys any more than I already have. She takes the time to assess the plate in front of me and gets a large grin on her face while her over-done eyebrow raises to her hairline.

"I hope you have more sense than to eat that whole plate of calories at least, you wouldn't catch me eating any of this." She twiddles her fingers over the table. "It will destroy your figure more than it already is and then not even your mate will glance your way." She looks straight at me, and I place the burger back on my plate, feeling ashamed of the amount of food I have put down before she even got here. I have never cared before, I have always just eaten when I'm hungry and when food is available because for me, that's not always the case. But she is the most popular girl in our school and always has boys looking at and talking to her, no one talks to me. She's a terrible person and I should just ignore her. I know I'm not fat, by any means, but the words don't sting any less. She's also got the attention of most of the people in the diner now, with her loud rambling, which is more embarrassing. They will spread those rumors like wildfire.

"Are you kidding?" Oliver asks, is he upset? He places his arm across the chair back behind me as he turns toward her, pressing his chest to my shoulder. It feels almost protective. "After the amount of calories we all burned training, I'm surprised she hasn't eaten more. She worked harder than the rest of us today." He wraps his bulky, tattooed arm around me, pulling me even closer. Marnie's eyes flash.

"Yeah, I like my girl with an appetite, it means she can hang with the big boys. Not trying to keep up with some stupid fad," Sam says, putting his arm around Sierra's shoulder who is still happily eating her fries. He winks over at me, knowing I just smashed an omelet and hash browns before digging into the burger and fries. I smile appreciatively at him and the rest of the guys mumble that they agree with him.

"You all trained together? Is that like the new guy code for getting laid? Is that why you left early last night and haven't called me, because you're cheating?" Her hand goes to her hip, but she looks hurt, actually hurt by the thought, looking between the twins.

"NO! NO! Not at all. They really did come to training this morning. I teach with Delta——"

She put her hand up at me to stop me talking. "Don't speak, you little homewrecker, don't defend them. They can explain it for themselves, and I will decide if I want to forgive them or not. You will be dealt with later," Kaley snaps at me and I close my mouth and look down at my lap. This week is going to be one of the worst of my life if she thinks I am trying to steal the twins from her.

"First, we aren't dating so there is no cheating..." Cameron starts, motioning between himself and Kaley.

"Second, who we hang out with is none of your concern," Dakota finishes.

"It is when we are going to be mated," She she screams. If she didn't have everyone's attention before, she has it now. "And you better figure that out quickly and stop trying to take mates that aren't yours," She snarls, pointing at me before she flips her platinum blonde hair and struts out of the diner, her friends close behind before any of us can say a thing.

"What the hell was that mate stuff all about?" Sam asks. "Please tell me she isn't going to be our Luna, I might shoot myself. We're only 19, she's younger, like Little Bits' age, right? How would she know if you guys are mates or not?" He's rambling now, almost panicky.

Chapter 9

"There's no way! Just wishful thinking on her part probably. That's what you get for giving into the crazy ones. Now that she's had you two in the sheets, she thinks she's got her claws in you permanently," Mateo supplies. My face goes beet red again. All this open, nonchalant sex talk is new for me.

"You two actually slept with her?" Sierra sounds appalled. "I thought that was just another rumor she spread."

"It was a very drunk and terrible mistake," Kota says.

"One she hopes you both will repeat. That's why she keeps bringing the tequila," Oliver mumbles next to me.

I'm not completely stupid when it comes to sex, but by what it sounds like these guys get up to, I am less than an amateur by comparison. And this is not the group I want to learn from, I am going to permanently be red from all the blushing. I sit up straight, my breath picking up, she is going to try and kill me after this, I need to get home quickly and hide. I will not get away with just simple beat downs after these guys defended me and rejected her so publicly.

"I just realized, I need to go. I have a big project I need to start on." I am ready to climb over Dakota and Cameron's laps if I have to. I am seriously about to have a full-blown panic attack and need to go before I make a complete scene. "Please let me out." I try to keep my voice calm as I look at Cam. I don't know what he sees in my eyes, but he doesn't argue, just starts to shift and pushes Kota. I can feel my heart rate pick up. It's beating so hard I'm sure they can hear it.

"Wait just a couple minutes and we can drop you at home." Cameron looks at me worriedly.

"No, it's okay, you guys are still eating. I was done anyway," I say as Cameron shifts to put his hand on me. I dodge to the side, far enough out of his reach. "I'm just going to walk. It will help my food settle." I turn quickly and head out before anyone can argue with me.

Once out the door, I look around to see if she is waiting for me before darting behind the diner to take my shortcut through the woods. She doesn't seem to ever want to look for me there, but she will corner me if I'm walking down the sidewalk, been there, done that, no thank you. I've gotten good at avoiding main roads as much as possible. Once I get to my backyard, I look everywhere, and my wolf and I sniff for anyone hiding out before dashing to my backdoor. Once I am safely inside, I lock the back door and lean on it for a minute, taking deep breaths. Once I feel calm, I go straight to my room where I stay the rest of the weekend. Mateo tried knocking once, but I ignored him completely. He doesn't try to bother me after that. I do every bit of homework I can and take a risk running at 4 a.m. Sunday morning. I figure I will be safe from Kaley and her minions and the guys this early. The trio will be working on their beauty sleep, and I don't think even they have the power to make someone watch me 24/7. It's not that I'm afraid of them, I think. I just don't want any more trouble than I usually have.

She leaves me alone for two whole weeks. Which is weird, but that doesn't stop me from jumping every time I hear my name or when someone taps me on the shoulder. I know something is coming and it's just a matter of time. It's too much to hope that she will leave me alone for good because the guys have decided I am a part of their friend group and she wants that status. I do think having one or more of them around in between classes has kept her away, for now.

I do my best to stay away from all the guys too, but as they all slowly discovered, I'm in several of their classes and they insist that I sit near them and work with them. I'm not allowed to disappear into the background. Thank the goddess that Kaley isn't in any of them with us. I'm just not sure which people she has spying for her, and I always make excuses to not walk with any of them for too long, so she rarely sees us together in the hallway. I even avoid my brother, who shouldn't be an issue at all, but I don't know with her level of crazy, she may not have put together that we are related and therefore he isn't a romantic option for me. I'm sure Marnie and Jeanie see me as a complication for Mateo and that would be enough for Kaley to retaliate.

After two weeks, I am pulled into a dark closet following school, a large hand covers my mouth and part of my nose making it hard to breathe, another gripping the back of my neck, squeezing the muscles tight enough to render me motionless. Then I feel punches to both sides of my ribs from the back. It's over almost before it began and no threats are made, but the message is clear. I'm a target again. I am shoved out of the closet quickly and trip over myself hitting the ground. The sound of footsteps running away hit my ears as I sit there struggling to breathe and sit up straight. I don't even try to look to see who grabbed me, I just know they are huge, and I am for sure going to have bruises for a few hours. No one cares who hurts who in this school anyway, so knowing your attacker doesn't matter.

The mandatory trainings have become hell as well. With the display Sierra and I put on when she first got here, many people want to train with us to genuinely get better, but several are trying to hurt me for Kaley or they are upset that I make them look bad. It is hard to tell some days, but I am a punching bag and can do nothing about it. I set myself up for this. I never should have let Delta Kyle force me to show off. I fight all of them off, but having twice the amount of opponents wears on anyone and when your body is physically exhausted, mistakes are made. That's when I take the most hits. Under watch, my opponents can only come at me one at a time, which is the silver lining.

Now that I have shown off my skills, the pool of people who hate me has expanded from Kaley to anyone who is trying to climb the ladder and get noticed by our leaders. I am the one to knock down a peg and if I show any weakness they all will eat it up, so I show nothing and take everything they can give without making a sound.

There is a system now. The weaker fighters find me first so by the time I'm starting to get gassed out, it's the bigger, rougher guys that become my opponents. But, I won't let Delta Kyle or any of the guys step in to help. I can't look like the favorite or like they are spoiling me, or that I can't handle it. It'll just make everything worse.

I can guarantee Kaley is fueling that fire too, I just can't prove it. It's the little comments that are made when I'm close enough for these idiots to whisper in my ear. Some say I cheat or that I found a way to use magic to enhance my skills.

The other problem is, because I won't let any of the guys do anything, which pisses them off, they try to stick closer to me. They did finally catch on to the fact that my sparring partners are more than just training rough. The discussion of them stepping in is shut down quickly, but has to be done daily. If they step in, it makes me look weak, like I can't actually defend myself, which turns me into a bigger target. They do help though, in their own way. They all manage to be 'randomly' paired, later with some of the people who are exceptionally aggressive, by Delta Kyle and they return the aggressiveness in kind. None of them challenge me in front of the group either.

Sierra tries to get me to talk about my sudden introverted tendencies at school, when she knows I am not based on what she saw in her first weekend here. I do my best to dodge the questions, but eventually, I'll have to give her something. She's not going to let my lame excuses slide for much longer, getting pretty creative with her lines of questioning. Throwing in the oddball comment while we are talking about homework or when she joins me on early morning runs, which she thinks is ridiculous, but we can be alone, which allows her to interrogate me. The guys all flat out refuse when she asks them to join so the torture can be shared among the group.

I have never been more thankful than when they say no. I don't want to have to stop running or find another thing to avoid doing. The early morning run and teaching the pups are all I have left that bring me any kind of joy, and I can't avoid talking to them at the pups training. We seem to always have a future leader's fan group of teenage girls at extra training, they don't train however, they sit in the stands and cheer. Even the one we have with the current leaders is starting to gain an audience, much to the Alpha's annoyance, so hopefully he will ban spectators. I can't be myself with all of these people watching and I'm sure the guys notice even though none of them bring it up.

About a month after the diner incident, Sierra pulls me into an empty classroom. She looks around to make sure we are alone. "Talk, or I am going to Delta Kyle and Luna Ava. They clearly know more than the rest of us. I saw the marks on your back and you have more and more bruises all the time. You can't tell me it's just from training. You don't take that many bad hits, you're too fast for that. You walk around this school like a paranoid nervous kitten, which you are not. So start talking or I'll go to someone who *will* give me answers." She looks angry, and I know her threat is not an empty one.

I huff, knowing there's no way out of this, but I have to make her understand that she can't step in. It just gets worse when people do. "Fine, I will tell you what you need to know and that is all. First, you need to understand that what is going on is *actually* a controlled version of the situation." She snorts at me, but doesn't interrupt. "No, we cannot go to anyone. No adults, no teachers, and I will not explain why." I look around the room. I am convinced listening devices or cameras are planted. "There is one student who wants control of the school, and for the most part has it. I have gotten in the way on more than one occasion, mostly unintended, and I am seen as a problem to be handled. This person has converted several people to that line of thinking. They clearly take their dislike out on me physically. But better me than any of our younger students, who used to be the main focus. I have made myself the target, *on purpose*." I emphasize the words. "This is my choice, and it is not so bad that I can't handle it." I rush all of this out in a whisper, just loud enough for her to hear me.

"What about the guys? They would be pissed if they knew what was going on. You are one of their favorite people and, in case you haven't noticed, they are a little on the protective side. It's kind of weird to watch you with them from the outside. They each show their protective streak differently, but it's there and unmistakable. They would rip someone's arms off for laying a hand on you." She, at least, caught on to the whispering, but her voice is rising in a sort of panic.

"NO!" I hiss, "Do not tell them anything. They know bullying happens in the school, it has for years, and they have never done anything to help control it."

"But, it's not just anyone getting hurt, it's YOU getting hurt. They would lose their minds!"

"Why does the fact that it is happening to *me* make the situation different?" My temper is rising. "I am not more important than anyone else. Anyone getting bullied is a problem, not just me because I'm the Beta's little sister and friends with the rest of the guys. That is absolute bullshit!" I growl out, then pause to take a few deep breaths to calm myself. Sierra goes to argue some more, but I hold up my hand to stop her. "Besides, I will not look like a weakling that has to run to her big strong guy friends to protect her. No, absolutely not. And trust me, that friendship hasn't gone unnoticed, and is a current problem. I received a couple more love taps and a reminder to keep my distance very recently. Say nothing to them, I am trying to figure out how to make it stop, without putting anyone else in the cross hairs of my bully, but right now I have nothing, and no one else could handle the level of brutality they dish out."

"Huh," Sierra says, looking at me like it's a big decision. I don't break eye contact, though. She's not going to win this argument. I was dealing with this long before she got here. "Fine, I will keep this quiet, for now, but on one condition."

"What?" I grumble, knowing I'm going to regret this, but it feels good to be able to tell someone other than Delta Kyle. I give him even fewer details, I thought his wolf was going to force itself out when I confided in him the first time he noticed whip lashes on my back. His reaction was on par with what I think my brother's and possibly the rest of the guys' reactions would be if they saw.

"I want to know every time it happens."

"Wait, what? No way! Didn't I just say I wasn't running to anyone for help?"

"Not for help. You don't have to give me details, I want to know so I can help you heal quickly. You won't let anyone step in to stop it or help, but you at least let Delta Kyle give you stuff to treat the really bad injuries. Let me be a part of that, but I want to know immediately. The first time I see a new cut or bruise or whatever and you haven't told me, I'm going to the guys."

My eyes widened in shock. "You wouldn't?"

"I will. Starting with your brother." She crosses her arms and stands to her full 5'7" height. Daring me to object.

I roll my eyes, she knows I'm caught now, I can't do anything but accept. If I don't, she'll just go to the guys anyway. "Fine," I grumble out.

"Fine, what?" She raises her eyebrows, not wavering from her demanding stance.

"Fine. I will tell you anytime bullying happens so you can help me heal."

"Great!" She she chirps, her mood changing instantly and wraps me in a tight hug. "I, sort of, understand why you are doing this, but you don't have to be alone, okay? And we need to get the guys on board with opening their minds and observation skills. They do suck at noticing things happening right under their noses."

I just nod and let her hold me while I force the tears down. I will not cry here, not at school, not when anyone could be watching. They will not get to me. I only have a little bit more time here and then hopefully we can all grow up.

This is how the rest of my junior year goes. The winter is brutal, but I keep to the same training schedule I always have, no matter the weather or how much my friends complain. Sierra, finally, convinces me that it is okay to let the guys in a little bit as friends, but I keep it to training and school as much as possible. No matter how many times they invite me to parties and the diner again, I always find a way to get out of it.

I may be a little crazy for allowing the bullying to continue, but I'm not suicidal. I am not trying to earn jealousy punishments too. Other girls give me dirty looks when I am with the guys, they just don't go to the extremes that Kaley and her friends do.

As the school year goes on, more and more rumors start flying about Kaley being the next Luna. No matter what Cam and Kota say or do to squash them, the rumors just keep coming as we get closer to graduating high school and moving towards college and job training. I'm sure most of it has to do with Kaley cornering one or both of the twins at every possible chance in and out of school with hands all over them. Social media pictures have started popping up too. From what the guys say, the Alpha isn't going to do anything right now since everyone is underage and it's 'harmless teenagers practicing marking their territory.' What he doesn't know is there is nothing 'harmless' about Kaley. She shoots any girl who looks at the twins a death glare, giving the universal girl sign for back the 'F' up off my men. I don't know how much of her crazy behavior the guys see though. She can turn it on and off like a switch. I'm sure the rumors are all started by her through Marnie and Jeanie.

At least hanging out with all five guys together, she can't accuse me of going after the ones she wants and what is she going to say about me hanging out with my brother? We are less than a year apart in age, making us almost as close as Cam and Kota. At least that is what I keep telling myself.

I am true to my word and go to Sierra every time an injury happens. She does a decent job of holding in her anger and never asks me questions, but she is right, I'm not alone and her knowledge of healing solutions, powders, and creams are seemingly endless. I recover in no time with her help, and my wolf doesn't have to work as hard to heal me, allowing me to get stronger. I am also becoming more comfortable in the crazy ass clothing she insists on. I'm no longer allowed to wear all baggy long clothing that allows me to hide. According to her, I have to show off the figure I have earned with all my over-training.

Chapter 10

Crap really hits the fan in the spring when our annual mating ball happens. It was originally designed for any wolves who are 21 or older and are unmated to try and find their mate if they are in the pack. We can't find our mate until the first full moon following our twenty-first birthday. If your mate is older or younger, you just have to wait to find out.

About a decade ago or so, the school council decided that any of the high schoolers could attend the ball too. This basically took the place of our spring dance. I think it is a way for them to get out of having to host and chaperone a high school dance, but that's just me. Either way, it has become the event of the year and come April, is all the girls can talk about.

I honestly could care less. I never had any friends to go to things like this with and I really don't like dressing up. My dad is to thank for that. Any time we have to dress up for some event he's required to take both Mateo and I, he has me dress a little closer to the Queen of England on a business trip than a teenage girl. The skirt suit feels like a straight jacket and is not comfortable in any form. So now when I hear 'formal' that is all I can think of.

Since I want nothing to do with it, naturally, my best friend is obsessed. Sierra has drawings upon drawings of dresses she imagines for this dance. It doesn't even matter, we can't find our mates yet anyway. She does not like or care for my logic and ignores my lack of enthusiasm at the idea of dressing to impress.

One day at advanced training she throws me under the bus with Luna Ava, hoping to get an ally. "What color do you think would look best on Sky, Luna?"

All the women had been casually talking about past mating balls and regaling us with their stories between rounds. The question is innocent enough, but it shocks me and I freeze, allowing the female warrior I'm sparring with to take me down.

At least the Alpha finally made these training sessions private. No one saw me take the distracted hit or can eavesdrop on this conversation.

"She could actually get away with several colors, I think. Blue in any shade would bring out her eyes and make her hair glow. But deep jewel tones would look amazing on her skin tone. What were you thinking?" Luna Ava throws over without slowing her movements down. It's as if conversation is a part of the sparring she's doing.

"I'm not sure, really. She refuses to dress shop with me and says she isn't going to the dance, leaving me all alone with these crazy boys. And we *have* to go, this will be my only year here. I leave this summer to go back home and we can't miss the 'biggest event of the year.'" She air quotes the overused tagline, making a pathetic pouty face to go right along with it. I close my eyes and take a deep breath through my nose, adjusting the shoulder that took the brunt of the hit.

Luna Ava stops to look at me now. "Oh, sweetheart, you have to go. You will have so much fun, we have so many things planned. I normally wouldn't push a junior to go, but you can't miss going with your best friend, and who would keep the boys out of trouble?" Her pout matches Sierra's.

"Let's get something straight. No one keeps the boys out of trouble." All the females on our end of the training arena laugh loudly. "And I don't really see the point in prancing around in uncomfortable clothes and shoes like a slave for auction when I can't even sense my mate, therefore getting nothing out of the torture." I rest my hands on my hips, we are clearly done training for the moment.

Luna Ava and the other females just laugh again, they know I'm not wrong, but at the same time, I'm wavering. They are right too, I can't miss Sierra's only dance here in the pack. Ugh, I can't believe I am considering this. I rub my temples with my fingertips.

"It's not all bad and depending on the dress, some remarkably comfortable undergarments help you feel like you're wearing regular clothes. How do you think I get through all the formal events with the Alpha? If you don't want to buy a new dress, I'm sure I, or any of the ladies here, have several things you could look at and we can have them altered. We could always do a dress day at the packhouse, it would be so much fun!" She claps her hands and is getting too excited. I can see the wheels turning. Oh Goddess help me!

"Fine, fine, I'll go." They all squeal, getting the full attention of the guys. "But I have conditions," I say to no one listening to me at all anymore. They all sound like a flock of birds chittering away.

"What's got you all excited, Love?" Alpha Lucas walks up and asks, wrapping an arm around Luna Ava and kissing her softly. He can't seem *not* to touch her when he is within ten feet. It's really cute.

"We just talked Skylar into going to the mating ball," she says happily as I wince and shield my eyes trying to hide as best I can from watching eyes, waiting for someone to make fun of me.

"Wait, you weren't planning on going?" Oliver asks, taking his usual defensive stance and crossing his massive tattooed arms over his chest. Why would he care if I go? He's got Marnie to entertain him anyway. There's no way I'm going to be able to hang out with the guys much with the Barbie trio around.

"Uh, no. Where have you been the last couple weeks? I hate all of this dress up stuff and I'm not old enough to find my mate, so it's kind of pointless. But it's Sierra's only time to go, I can't miss it according to her and the Luna." Dripping my last words with sarcasm just for her.

"We have to go shopping this weekend." Sierra claps her hands like the Luna, skipping right over my last comment.

"We are totally joining you, you know, for professional opinions," Sam adds, stepping comfortably close behind Sierra and trying to wrap his sweaty arms around her shoulders. She squeals and jumps out of his grasp.

"Gross, you are exceptionally nasty today, go shower before you touch me." She wipes her shoulders off with her own towel scowling at him as we laugh.

"You just want to watch me make a fool of myself trying on stupid dresses." I roll my eyes at him and laugh at my friend.

"It will actually be a nice change from your usual choice of baggy and comfortable or workout clothes." He laughs and jumps out of the way as I aim a swift kick to his butt. "It will be interesting to see what you're hiding under all of those layers. I'm sure you're fit enough to make all the girls jealous." He wiggles his eyebrows at me.

I take a deep breath, fighting the heat in my cheeks. "Fine, you can come, but you are buying me food," I snap back, missing another kick as he dodges around my brother to hide from me.

"Deal, Little Bit." He stays behind my brother, intelligently anticipating another attack from my foot, but he reaches around Mateo to shake on it and then he's looking at me funny.

"What?" I ask slowly, questioning if I really want to know.

"I was just wondering if they made dresses in hobbit sizes." He laughs along with everyone else and takes off as I chase him across the field. I easily catch up to him and jump on his back. He jogs back to the group like I'm not even there, both of us laughing.

"Hey, Sam, let me help you out, you have a tiny little something on your back," Oliver chimes in and lifts me off Sam by my armpits and holds me out away from his body like someone who's never held a baby before. His large hands have a firm grip on my rib cage, and I am painfully aware of how close he is to touching my boobs with his massive hands, and I'm not sure what to think about that. My feet dangling off the ground.

"Put me down, asshole." I kicked my legs backward, trying to divert my embarrassment, earning more chuckles from everyone since it did absolutely nothing.

"Let me help you with your baggage." I'm still squirming as Dakota grabs me bridal style. At least I feel less like a little kid now. I wrap my arms around his neck naturally to try and hold some of my own weight. My brain kicks in at how close I am to him, and I feel embarrassed all over again. Before my cheeks can even flame up, Cam steps up to us.

"That's not how you carry her properly." Cameron quickly scoops me up with one arm and throws me over his shoulder. I squeal and then laugh at the abrupt change in direction. His hand rests just above my knees, in between my legs. He gives me a playful squeeze while all the guys continue to laugh.

"Is she the new toy you're all trying to play with now?" Sierra laughs at them and smacks my butt while I'm in a compromising position and can't do anything to stop her. The smack was hard enough that I could feel my butt wiggle with the impact, and I let out a little squeak.

"Oww! That's going to leave a hand print on my ass!" I shout at her, trying to reach back and rub the sore spot. She and I are still laughing as I'm trying to look around Cam's back to see where she went when, suddenly, Cam stops, puts me down slowly, and Sierra and I realize they are no longer laughing.

"We have to run. See you guys at training tomorrow morning," Oliver says a little strained, before they all take off. Sam looks amused, Mateo angry, and Oliver, Cam, and Kota are, I don't know, uncomfortable and blushing maybe. Weird.

"What the hell was that all about?" I ask, watching the guys leave the large training grounds like they couldn't move fast enough.

"You're kidding, right?" Sierra asks, hands on her hips. I just stare blankly at her. Even for them, that was weird, but she is looking at me, eyebrows raised, like I missed a punchline. "They all just realized you're a girl, a hot girl, that's what."

"What does that even mean? When have I ever not 'been a girl?'" Sarcasm dripping in my words. I skip right over that last bit.

"I have my suspicions, but let's just wait until we shop this weekend. You know they are all going to come to 'give opinions' since you don't normally dress up, and your brother is probably going to try and smack at least one of them for making inappropriately accurate comments."

"No way, my brother would never fight any of them. They all make inappropriate comments all the time. Why would shopping make it any different?"

"Wanna bet?"

"You sound like Oliver and Sam." I laugh. "But sure, I think you're effing crazy. There is nothing different about me now versus this morning or in training gear versus a dress and they are not going to want to dress shop with us, that would be torture. I know it will be for me. Sam is just coming to hang out with you and give me a hard time about being awkward as hell."

"Well, you sound like all of them with your new colorful language." She winks. "And if they all show up *and* if your brother argues with any of them, in any way, you owe me lunch at a place of my choosing." She laughs at me flipping her still sweaty dark hair.

"Deal. What is it with me and making bets with everyone all of a sudden?" I shake my head and laugh as we start to make our way out of the arena too. It's just the two of us now. I'm not sure when the adults left, maybe when the guys took off randomly.

"Another product of hanging out with very competitive and idiotic guy friends." She stops and looks around the parking lot. "Those jackasses left us. Man, you really messed them up, they must be more scared of you now." She cackles as we both start walking towards our street. I roll my eyes again. This is also becoming a new habit.

She is speaking in riddles, and I normally think of myself as a pretty smart person, but I can't figure out what in the 'F' she is going on about. I wave her off when we finally make it back to her house 20 minutes later then continue to mine. The twins' truck is in the packhouse driveway, but there is no sign of any of the guys. I shake my head and keep on walking to my house and head straight for my room once I'm inside.

The silence used to comfort me. It let me know I am safe and no one is around to find something to correct or criticize, but now that I have been spending so much time with such loud people, the silence is almost suffocating. I can hear soft music from my brother's room, letting me know he's home. I'd love to talk to him about what Sierra was saying. He'll usually give me a straight answer when I don't understand people's behavior; then again, he left us high and dry with the rest of them, which is just as weird. I'm afraid to knock on his door, music can mean one of two things. He's doing homework or a girl.

I really don't want to interrupt in case it's a girl. My brother doing the horizontal tango is not something I want to imagine, let alone get a live picture of. Those boys seem to get around and I guess I understand the appeal. They are all tall, hot, and completely muscled out and I don't even think they have hit their prime of good looks yet. They know how good-looking they are, their egos are a testament to that. Combine that with the fact that they are future leaders of the pack; they are heavily sought celebrities.

I keep this train of thought running as I head straight to the shower. I have never understood the complete lack of self-respect it takes to throw yourself at someone with status just for a little bit of attention. If you aren't noticed without having to, sometimes literally, throw yourselves in their path, why bother? They aren't worth the time. If the rumors are true, they have been with all of the sophomore and junior girls and are making their way through the seniors now. Which also surprises me. Kaley doesn't seem to make a big deal about them sleeping around with most of the female population of our school. She just has a problem with Sierra and I.

It's kind of nasty if you think about it too much. Thank the Goddess wolves don't get STD's or they would be in trouble. I'm not a prude, well not really. I get the appeal of sex and have even done some self-exploration, but I am one hundred percent inexperienced when it comes to being with a guy. And yet, I have no desire to jump some rando strictly to say I did, that is less appealing than having zero game in the sex department.

I am a little jealous of how easy it is for Sierra to flirt with any of the guys. She seems to only have eyes for Sam, but is playful with all of them and it is so natural. The thought of trying to flirt makes me sweat bullets. I am just that awkward, so I figure I will wait for my mate who will love my crazy, inexperienced awkwardness no matter what. On that note, I step out of the shower and wrap up in a towel. As I brush out my sandy blonde hair, I look at myself and really analyze my reflection for the first time.

I don't think I am ugly by any means, I just don't think I am anything special either. My hair is mostly straight with a slight wave at the end and it is so long it goes past the middle of my back. I like it full and long, I think I would look like a baby doll if I ever cut it. My muscles are defined in my arms and legs and I know my back and abs have definition. I am putting on muscle now that I eat most of my meals with the guys and get the calories I need for all the training that I do.

I wear sports bras and layered tank tops and sleeveless T-shirts for training all the time, still covering the scars on my back, but being more comfortable in my skin. My figure is still on the smaller side with no real curves to speak of, even with the muscle definition. I'm only seventeen and I don't really know what my mom looked like, so I don't have a clue what to expect my body to do in adulthood. My dad only keeps one picture of her in his office, and I'm not allowed in there. I saw it once when I was little, but I don't remember any details. According to everyone else who knew her, I look exactly like her, but that doesn't help me predict what kind of woman bits I may end up with. I sigh and get dressed in some pajamas and get started on my homework. I have a feeling there will be no room for homework this weekend if Sierra has any say, so I need to get ahead now.

Nothing out of the ordinary happens the rest of the week at school which is only saying I didn't bleed from my attackers. It's almost like they know what I am doing this weekend and are being courteous with their torture.

Saturday morning comes and I find I can't sleep, so I take my very early run alone today. I decide to take a chance and let my wolf out too. We run the full border patrol route around the pack territory. I'm not on patrols, so I don't have to really pay attention and can run as fast as I want to. The whole thing only takes me a couple hours. I usually wait until it's dark so it's easier to hide with her thick jet-black fur if we do come across someone. It is dark and peaceful right now and allows me time to wrap my brain around all the crazy I am about to be subjected to.

When I get home, I start breakfast, getting out ingredients to make enough to feed everyone, since our house has been the new Saturday hangout before training. Even the Alpha and Luna join us sometimes too. I was worried the first time Mateo brought the guys over so early that dad would have a fit. But I guess when it comes to my brother and the future Alphas, he doesn't really care what goes on. Dad went as far as to ask Mateo what needed to be on the grocery list specifically for the Saturday morning breakfasts the third time it happened. That conversation got tense really fast when Mateo said he didn't know and to ask me, which earned me a disapproving look and the reply, "I'll have Gretchen follow up with you kids and make sure the kitchen is stocked." Before he abruptly walked out of the kitchen.

His avoidance of me shouldn't hurt, it's been like this my whole life. He only talks to me when he absolutely has to in front of other high ranking wolves for appearance's sake. But, every time he outwardly and blatantly rejects me, I feel that familiar jab in my heart and all of my insecurities haunt me for days after. I got more obsessed with training and schoolwork, avoiding people, including Sierra and my brother after that interaction shortly after the Christmas holiday. Something they both noticed and questioned immediately, and I expertly avoid talking about.

My room and anything I use in the house has to be spotless and meticulously put away. The behavior is manic and the sad part is I am fully aware of what I'm doing and why, but I can't help myself and I can't go to anyone for help. How would that make my dad look in the eyes of his peers? The peers he's been putting on a show for my whole existence. Ruining his reputation will make the emotional hell I have been going through worse and I don't need to feel anymore like an unwanted problem. And as much as I should be mad at him or hate him for treating me like this; I can't bring myself to make him look bad, hoping one day he will wake up and notice all the hard work and effort I put in to please him, to make him happy and proud of me. As long as there is that scrap of a chance,

I will hold onto that hope. It takes several days for Sierra to pull me, mostly, out of the obsessive behavior. Really, I think I got better at hiding it from her.

I shake my head out of the dark memories and keep working on the breakfast spread. I really do like having Sierra and all the guys here. I find I enjoy caring for the group as a whole. They make me laugh and forget about all the things I normally focus on every day. I actually feel like a teenager during this time, and I find I have relaxed into the friendships the longer I am around all of them. My dad's demands don't exist, Kaley and her bully patrol doesn't exist, schoolwork doesn't exist. It's almost magical.

The front door slams, I jump and I look at the time. It's not quite 5 a.m. and I'm not even halfway into prepping all the food. What the hell is going on? The commotion in the hallway tells me it's at least a few of the guys. Their sounds are pretty distinct. I walk out to tell them to be quiet, I haven't even gotten Mateo up yet, and my dad will actually be pissed at the ruckus this early. I slowly make my way down the hall into the entryway.

"Guys? What ar—-"

"SURPRISE!" A whole group of people shout at me.

"Oh Shit!!!!" I yell and then clap my hand over my mouth as I'm trying not to fall on my butt in front of everyone.

Chapter 11

Sierra runs up to me first, catching me in a hug. "A little birdie told me it is your birthday today and we thought we would surprise you. We brought breakfast, I hope you haven't already started cooking." She steps back and takes in my running clothes. I don't usually shower or change since we go and workout with the pups, which leaves us disgusting.

"Um...uh...I just started getting things together." I am super confused and disoriented. We don't celebrate my birthday, never have. It's the day my mom died, the day I killed her, and that is the only part my dad remembers about today. Mateo used to make me cards when we were little. At least I think it was him, there's no one else. He would never sign them or say anything about it. Once we hit about eleven though, those stopped.

"Um, come on in, we can set it up on the island." I lead the group down the hall and stand off to the side watching the parade file into the kitchen.

Mateo comes strolling in with the rest of the guys. He was a part of this? Did he tell them? I can feel my heart tighten at the thought. Then all the adults come through and my shock has my brain stuttering. Alpha Lucas and Luna Ava have two large platters of fruit and pastries. Cam and Dakota are each carrying a tray of food. Gamma Brett follows Oliver in with a very large pan that is steaming. Delta Kyle and Gwen come in ahead of Sam and they are all carrying balloons and a vase of flowers. Sierra's Aunt Stephanie, and Uncle Robert bring up the rear with another steaming pan.

All my friends are carrying gift bags too. I am so overwhelmed, but I can't help myself and look at Mateo. He knows my question without me having to ask. He shakes his head once, almost imperceptibly. The wave of sadness that rolls over me makes my heart break. My hands are numb and my breathing is shallow.

I close my eyes and take a deep breath. I am not going to let his absence detract from this amazing thing my friends and their families have done for me. They don't have any idea what this means to me. The first birthday I will celebrate outside of my bedroom and with other people is my 18th birthday. Even my nanny wasn't allowed to celebrate my birthday. She always acknowledged me, but we couldn't do more than that. She tried once to bring me a cupcake and my father punched her in front of me, then kept her away from me for a week.

This will be one of the most special memories I have. But, I cannot cry, I won't cry. I take another deep breath. Not happy tears, not sad tears. Today is going to be an amazing day, even if it has to include dress shopping.

I come out of my daze and walk around to hug and thank everyone. Luna Ava hugs me longer than necessary, telling me she probably has a pretty good idea what is going on in my head right now. Like always, she lets me have my silent moment and then moves on like it's nothing, not drawing attention where I don't want it. She has always just understood me without explanation.

"What about training?!" I suddenly ask, looking at Delta Kyle and noticing the time. Panic washes through me at the thought of the pups running a muck by themselves.

"We canceled it today and told the pups you are not allowed to workout with anyone today on pain of having to play capture the flag against you, solo, after completing your entire, personal, daily workout. I can guarantee none of them are going to even look in your direction today." Delta Kyle laughs along with everyone else. I don't know if I should be offended or smug.

"I guess it's good I already went for my run today then, jeez," I mutter, and they all just laugh again.

Luna Ava helps me get dishes out, stack them on the island and we all dig in. The food is amazing. Along with all of the fruit and pastries, the hot dishes have eggs, sausages, and fried potatoes. We go through most of it, these boys can put down some food. Sierra and I eat almost as much as the guys do, and Delta Kyle is quick to mention it.

"I like that you girls eat a healthy amount. I am always worried about some of the girls who don't eat enough getting hurt at training. They are worried about gaining weight, but it's really hard to do even if they train the bare minimum." This launches a whole load of conversations about girls and eating and picky eaters. Which turns into a competition of the worst dinner dates they have all had. These boys spend far too much time on high maintenance girls from the sounds of it, but who am I to judge. Until I met Sierra, I did the exact opposite and avoided people like it was my job.

I'm standing at the center of the island, Cam, Kota, and Mateo to my left. Oliver, Sierra and Sam to my right and their respective adults across from them. It is kind of a neat image, the current and future generation of leaders all at the table. The Beta is the only person missing. It makes me sad for a moment, not for myself, but for Mateo. Because of me, our dad refuses to share this moment with him. I take another deep breath. I have to remember not to let myself cry, I can't look weak here.

"Okay!" Sierra sings. "You have to open your presents."

"What? Now? I thought I would just open them later. We are all having fun just hanging out and I really need to go shower, I probably smell." I grimace, stepping back from the group, as I come to that realization.

"You smell fine to me." Choruses from all of the boys, except my brother who lets out a little growl and looks at his friends with his eyebrows smashed together.

"What?!" Asks Oliver, looking around. "She smells fine; like the forest." He shrugs. "I assume that's where she was running this morning."

"Yeah, Tiny, you smell good, now open your presents." Cam smiles at me.

The look that Luna Ava gives Alpha Lucas does not go unnoticed by me. What is going on?

Naturally breaking the tension, Sam shoves a bag in my face. "These should help, Little Bit." His Cheshire Cat smile makes me a bit nervous to open this in front of the adults for some reason.

"Should I be afraid?" I peek in the bag slowly. It's heavy. When I get through the tissue paper, I find a pair of black platform converse high tops. "Awe, thank you. I was actually expecting something to embarrass me."

"Nope, but now you will at least be taller than our elbows." He laughs along with everyone else, me included.

Cam and Kota got me black skinny jeans with a few rips in them to look worn, but not trashy, and a black belt with metallic thread woven into it.

Oliver got me a cornflower blue cropped peasant top, that sits off the shoulder and has puffy long sleeves.

Mateo got me a delicate white gold chain with a crescent moon pendant that has two little stars on the end.

"Mine comes later, so you just have to be patient." Sierra wiggles her eyebrows at me, and I am instantly afraid.

"This is all great guys. Thank you! I really am going to go shower and change now. I'll be right back." I grab all my stuff and turn to race out of the room. I am becoming uncomfortable with all of the attention on me, and I can't hide it much longer.

"If you didn't catch on, that's the outfit you are wearing today," Sierra yells at my back followed by a boom of laughter. I roll my eyes, of course she picked this out and I can't not wear what the guys gave me. I have to watch out for her sneaky tactics.

I have never showered so quickly in my life. I debate on having Sierra come up and help me do my hair and makeup. I've never cared before, but for some reason, having my birthday recognized by all of them makes me want to care a little bit, at least today. Wrapped in my towel, I race out to my room to grab my phone, and get a shock from seeing her on my bed.

"Oh Shit! Stop doing that." I place a hand on my forehead, the other is still keeping my towel secure. She just laughs. I should have noticed her scent right away, but I am too distracted to pay attention. "Will you help me do my hair and make-up, please?" I'm still trying to steady my racing heart.

"Oh, girl! I thought you would never ask! Let's do this!" Way too excited, she looks *way* too excited about something as simple as hair and make-up.

Thirty minutes later, I have been brushed, curled, styled, mascaraed, and lip glossed. She didn't actually put a ton of makeup on my face, but what she did brought out the blue gray of my eyes, making them stand out. My lips are just average in size, but now they look full and fit my face better. My hair is up in a high ponytail with big beach waves. I feel confident like this.

"Do you like it?" She sounds unsure.

"Yes! I'm sorry. This is great. I've never really worn make-up before. I train too much to put the effort in and have it all sweat off. But, this is just right. Thank you, this really means a lot to me." I hug her tightly, hoping to put all of the emotions I am feeling into the hug. I can't explain why to her now, I will just get sad and cry. But she needs to know, this is not some little thing she did for me today.

"Okay, okay. Get dressed before these boys kill us. And I told you they would all go shopping with us." She giggles as she shoos me out of the bathroom. "Now for your brother to hit one of them."

I put the outfit on and do a little twirl in my full-length mirror. The outfit she picked was perfect. The pants hug me in all the right places, but I don't feel restricted and even though the top is cropped, it still skims the waistband of my high waisted jeans and covers the worst of the bruises and scars on my torso. What isn't covered, she applies a layer of tattoo concealer. She really did think of everything. She is trying to push me out of my comfort zone, but knows what I need to do that. I don't know what I did to deserve a friend like her.

"Oh, my necklace!" I search the bathroom counter. "I must have left it down in the kitchen. I think we are ready, right?" I do one more twirl for her approval.

"Seriously, you look amazing. I need to make a bet on who says something first. They won't last ten seconds," she mumbles to herself.

"What are you talking about? Let's go get this over with." I open the door and we both head back down following the voices still in the kitchen, although it sounds like less than earlier.

"Oh perfect," Luna Ava stops us in the hallway and, hugs me once more. "I wanted to see you before you all head off. You look beautiful, sweetheart. Have a fun day." Then winks at us as she heads out the front door. The rest of the adults must have cleaned up and left while I was getting ready. Sierra and I head back into the kitchen so I can find my necklace and we can get going.

"Damn, Little Bit, you clean up good. We are going to have our hands full today looking out for both of you, beauties. Mmm!" Sam rubs his hands conspiratorially.

"I knew it was going to be you." Sierra rolls her eyes at Sam. I ignore it, he is always telling us we look good in some way or another. Sometimes it comes out creepy, sometimes sexual to make me blush, and other times it's sweet, like now.

"Did I leave my necklace on the island?" I ask the room at large.

"I have it here." Oliver dangles the thin chain from one finger to show me and gives me shy half-smile.

"Oh, thank you." I reach out, but before I can get it, Dakota has it in his hands.

"Let me help."

"Oh, okay." Why did that come out as a whisper?

These guys are acting strange and it's starting to rub off on me. I hope something isn't wrong. I am finally starting to let them in, I don't think I can handle losing friendships with any of them. I turn my back to him and pull the end of my ponytail out of the way. His hands are very gentle as they clasp the chain.

"Perfect, Smalls," Kota says quietly close to my ear, and he lets a fingertip graze down the exposed part of my spine from my shoulder to the hem of my shirt before dropping his hand. My whole body breaks out in goosebumps at the sensation.

"Alright, alright. She's hot, we all just figured it out, let's go before I throw up," Mateo grumbles out, and Sam starts laughing loudly as we all head to the packhouse driveway, but we don't stop at the truck like I thought.

"We aren't taking your truck?"

"Nope, the mall is a little too far for Sierra to sit on Sam's lap or for you to be front and center. It's not safe and we can't have that." Cam places his hand on the small of my back and guides me to the third garage door and types the code in to open it up, not once taking his hand off of me. "We are taking Dad's Denali. It has the third row."

A sleek, black monster-sized truck is what I see when the door is fully open. I know nothing about cars or trucks, but this thing is beautiful. Super shiny, no dirt anywhere, even the tires and the rims are shiny. The Alpha is particular about his truck. We all walk up to open doors, the twins get in the driver and passenger seats. Mateo and Sam climb back to the third row, this thing must be custom sized, because they don't seem to struggle at all. Sierra goes back to sandwich herself in between them and Oliver and I take the second row seats. Once everyone is in, we are off. So far, 18 is looking pretty good.

Walking the mall is the worst possible torture that anyone could have ever designed, ever! I would rather condition for ten hours straight with no food or water than spend the whole day shopping. Anyone who enjoys this is certifiably insane. We got here when the place opened and have been slowly making our way to each and every store all morning. I will admit though, Sierra has good taste. I now have several outfits that fit me better and really make me feel good, without pushing too far out of my comfort zone or exposing my scars. We stop at a couple places where the guys insist on buying me little things. I do have to stop them when we get to the lingerie store. I am not modeling anything for Sierra, let alone the guys. Mateo quickly seconds my opinion and ushers us away.

My feet are killing me, and I am dying to go outside to breathe clean air. The recycled mall air and fluorescent lights make me feel kind of claustrophobic.

I don't know what Mateo told them about my birthday, but it feels like he is personally trying to make up for the last 18 years all in one shot. I quickly realize I have to be careful about what I show interest in. If he thinks for even a second I like something, he'll ask if I want him to buy it for me. I am worried our father is going to be mad at him for spending unnecessary money on me.

He finds a little kiosk that sells customizable bracelets and picks a design that has several layered straps, some leather, some chain links, some thread. He chooses one in black leather and stainless steel and pairs it with a tiny charm that the lady engraves 'sis' on. Not to be outdone, Cam chooses one that had sea glass green leather, like his eyes. His charm says 'Tiny.' Kota's is sky blue, his charm saying 'Smalls.' Oliver's is orange, which I thought was odd at first, because he always just seems to be in varying shades of black like a biker, but the more I think about it, when he does wear a color, it is orange, like construction worker neon. His charm says 'Bite Size.' Sam makes a big show of choosing his, but by this point I have figured out they are all choosing their favorite color and adding the nickname they gave me. Almost like they are marking me, without marking me. It makes me smile. He brings me the red leather bracelet and drops to one knee dramatically, holding his hands out in front of him displaying the bracelet in his upturned palms, really causing a scene.

"Little Bit, will you accept this humble gift and wear my friendship bracelet for ever and ever?" I think he's going for Romeo, but he's not subtle enough for that.

I just laugh and reply, "I would love to, good sir." With a curtsy for added effect and hold out my wrist to him. He jumps up squealing like a girl, clapping his hands before finally placing it on my wrist.

"Show off." I heard someone grumble behind me. Making all of us laugh.

"You're just jealous, you didn't think of it," Sam responds

Then Sierra walks up. "Let's finish your arm rainbow." She wraps her own yellow bracelet around my wrist, the charm having runes inscribed. One for warrior that looks like an arrow pointing up and next to it a three-pronged pitchfork with a small circle just above the hilt, two squiggly lines across the handle, and a semicircle at the top of the handle looking like a bowl.

"It means warrior friend," she says before hugging me.

I look at my arm and a sense of warmth washes over me as I take in the six inches of multicolored leather and metal wrapped halfway up my forearm. I realize I wasn't lying when I told Sam I would wear them 'forever and ever.' I don't think I could part with them.

"Okay, sentimental stuff is all over, let's feed the birthday girl so she cooperates while I dress her up like my own personal doll. Sam, go find your Little Bit some food," she commands like a dog trainer.

"At your service, madam." He bows at us not even looking offended, just turns and walks off, with all of us trailing behind laughing.

Once we are all good and fed, we start our second round of shopping. We hit the formal section of our third trendy shop. All of my bags are collected and stored next to the five chairs the guys have arranged in front of the three-way viewing mirror set up on a little platform. They each pull out their phones settling in for the long wait, this is clearly not a new thing for them. Sierra is rushing around the store grabbing things off the rack, without even seeming to look at them properly. I don't know if she is grabbing the right size, but, with clothes, I have come to trust her judgment today, so whatever, this is her show right now. I stand patiently next to the guys and watch the tornado that is my friend running around the store. She seems to like things here at least. The last two stores only got about five minutes of her browsing time. When her hands are full, she ushers me, followed by a sales lady with equally full arms to the dressing room.

She went all out for the first dress. It is full length and huge, I have never seen so much material before. The top is strapless and cut straight across, it also has a bunch of sparkles on it and the skirt is miles and miles of layered sheer fabric. It's a pretty gray/blue color that matches my eyes, not too deep or too bright but I'm not sure about it. This one is guaranteed to make me trip or get caught on something and I have to put my platform converse back on just to be able to not get caught up in the skirt when I walk.

I shuffle out, step up onto the platform and all the guys look up from their phones and just stare at me, frozen in their movements each with a different emotion on their face. I can't tell if the looks are good ones or bad ones, though.

"Yes! This is a great color on you," Sierra cries. "Spin, slowly, please," she indicates by twirling her finger. "I like it, but you don't look super excited. Next!" She doesn't even hesitate to move on. I would've felt bad for not liking something someone else spent so much time designing, even if they had no idea I rejected it. Sierra has no such qualms.

I jump at her exclamation to 'GO!' and head back. She throws another dress at me when I give her the poofy one. This one is a bit more reserved on the excess skirt material. It has the same straight cut along my chest that extends to one-inch-wide straps hanging off my shoulders. I have a feeling they are more for fashion than for actually holding up the dress. This one is a deep teal color and the satiny fabric feels great on my skin. The slightly less poofy skirt also drags on the ground. I step out to the mirror and my waiting audience.

"The Luna was right, jewel tones are great on you. Spin." She twirls her finger again. "Better, but there's more, so much more." She taps the tips of her fingers together in front of her mouth like a cartoon villain. Oh Goddess, what have I gotten myself into? She did plan everything to a T, though. My ponytail is long and full enough that none of my scars can be seen over the top of the dresses and the tattoo concealer doesn't seem to be rubbing off at all.

By the fifth dress I do catch on to a theme. She started with the most conservative dresses. Plenty of coverage and material to get me, and I'm sure my brother, comfortable with the real dresses she wants me in. The more I try on, the more daring the necklines and skirt slits are. They also get shorter too. She made sure to take pictures of all the dresses she deemed worthy of contention, so I won't have to keep going back and forth when we finally have to decide.

By dress, I have lost effing count, I am in a short black dress with a corseted lace top with a sweetheart neckline that laces up the back with a thick black satin ribbon. Sierra has to help me with this one. She has me tied so tight, this bitch isn't going anywhere. The lace corset is lined with a thick, soft, nude material so I am completely comfortable and covered while at the same time I look sexy. My shoulders and arms are tan and on full display. My muscle definition looks great with the fit of this top. There is a wide satin panel that goes around my torso, just above my hips dividing the top from the skirt. The black satin skater skirt is long enough to touch the middle of my thighs, and I can bend over without showing off the goods. I totally tested it before leaving the dressing room too. In front of the guys is not the time to realize that mistake. It makes my legs appear longer paired with my high top platforms and I love the illusion.

"There it is," she says in a low voice next to me. "That's the look I have been waiting for."

We both walk out smiling. The reactions come all at once when I get in front of the guys.

"Oh, shit."

"Damn!"

"Holy Hell."

"Fuck!"

"NOPE! Not happening. Absolutely out of the question," Mateo growls out, standing. "Next!" He points back at the dressing room.

Sierra just laughs, ignores him, and moves me to the three-way mirror and has me twirl. I can't tell if she's taking a photo or a video, but at this point I am having fun modeling all these stupid dresses.

Chapter 12

"I think we have found it, my friends." She claps her hands. "Go change so we can buy it and get shoes to match!" Her voice has gone a few octaves higher in her excitement.

"Wait a minute. I said not happening. And stop drooling you fuckers." Mateo looks over to his friends. Sam is the first to recover and laugh.

"Sorry bro, you said it before, she's hot. You are going to have to learn to deal with that. She's about to be very popular! You will have every single guy banging down your door after the ball. There are about to be some very pissed and jealous girls." He shrugs, there are growls surrounding all the guys, and Mateo walks over and slaps Sam up the back side of his head.

"Told you. You owe me lunch!" Sierra whispers to me and pushes me into the dressing room while Mateo is playfully shoving the rest of his friends. At least, I think it's playful as they all continue to laugh at him.

I roll my eyes. It's like they have never seen a girl before. Which I know isn't true. They are all well versed in the female species and anatomy on a pretty extensive level, if the rumors are to be believed. They have all been attending the ball as future leaders for a couple years now. This isn't new to them. I wonder if they are making a big deal to mess with my brother. That seems more likely.

Sierra unceremoniously slams the door to my dressing room, I quickly get out of my dress and hand it to her. She takes it and heads back out to the guys while I put my clothes back on. Once I have everything and do a double and triple check to make sure I am fully covered, I follow her out of the dressing room to find everyone at the store entrance.

"Where's the dress? I need to go check out," I ask Sierra.

"It's all done. Happy Birthday, Skylar." She hands the bags she's holding to Sam, one is a garment bag with this store's logo on it, and hugs me. "Now let's go get some sexy shoes to go with that sexy dress." She makes a pointed look at my brother before hooking her arm in mine and dragging me away. We start walking toward a massive shoe store, but before we can get too far our little bubble is broken by a high-pitched screech.

"BABES! What are you doing here? I thought you hated the mall. You never want to come shopping with me." Kaley's voice echoes across the large expanse of the stone mall hallways. Many people stop to stare at her frantically, and not super gracefully, trotting toward us in her dangerously high heels. I am kind of afraid of her hot pink tube skirt snapping off if she takes too big of steps.

The twins are in the middle of our group. So she has to push past Oliver, Sam, and Mateo to get to them. They don't willingly get out of her way either.

"Move, you big fuckers." She doesn't bother to keep her voice down with the insult. She has been getting more bold with her distaste of most people in front of the twins. All their facial expressions are shocked at how she just spoke to them and is attempting to shove them out of her way. One by one they lock eyes with the twins. The look, a cross between outrage and annoyance, at being ordered around and then ignored by this plastic Barbie.

"You should have called me. I totally would have come with you instead of them." She rolls her eyes and hooks her thumb over her shoulder at her friends who look like they are struggling to manage all the bags they have in hand with the teeny, form fitting outfits and high heels that coordinated with hers. She must be using them as her pack mules. "I was going to stop by later. I got something special for the both of you." She tries for a giggle again, but it sounds forced and painful. I can't see her face, but can imagine the psychotic smile and wide eyes she uses towards them regularly.

Cam and Kota just look at each other like they are having a silent conversation about how best to navigate this situation and get rid of her without her throwing a tantrum. Sierra and I are a few feet behind the twins, hidden. Kaley hasn't noticed us yet. I'm afraid to move for fear of gaining her attention. That is the last thing that I want, to add fuel to her already large fire of hatred for me.

"We are actually on our way out, sorry." Kota shrugs his shoulders, the bags in his hands shuffling as he tries to turn away from her, I'm sure hoping that is enough to end the conversation. On cue, the rest of the guys start to move too, hoping to make a quick exit, their bags also making a rustling noise. The movement allows Sierra and I to just barely see her around the twins' elbows.

"What did you get? Anything special for a special person, maybe?" She points to the very feminine shopping bags the twins hold then clasps her hands in front of her, twisting back and forth at the waist like an excited little kid. Maybe she thinks it's cute and innocent looking. She really just looks a little unhinged.

"Just some birthday gifts, no big deal," Cam says again, trying to turn. She grabs his elbow, she seems to only touch him. At least when I see them interact. Interesting. I wonder if it's on purpose.

"But my birthday was months ago, silly..." She pats his arm with her other hand then reaches for Dakota, but he moves away, giving me a direct line of sight to her. She trails off finally noticing Sierra and I behind him. "WHAT THE HELL IS SHE DOING HERE WITH YOU?" Her fakely sweet voice changes to a growl of angry menace in a flash. Her manicured claws fly to her hips. Her perfectly shaped eyebrows looked strange, smashed down in a scowl, her whole face going red.

The guys all move faster than I thought possible surrounding me, which to an outsider might look strange, but it is a clear defensive warrior move. Cam and Kota are in front, between Kaley and the rest of the group. Oliver stands directly in front of me, Sierra stays at my side, her arm still linked with mine, and Mateo is on the other. Sam steps behind me, sandwiching me between him and Oliver, giving me only inches of space to breathe.

On instinct, I place the palm of my free hand lightly on Oliver's back at the same time Sam places his on my right shoulder and Mateo touches my left shoulder, the contact makes us all instantly relax. I feel the taught muscles in Oliver's back melt under my touch.

It takes me a minute to realize what they did, though, and I don't know how I feel about it. I can protect myself and fight, but at the same time she is a different kind of threat. We all recognize it and they naturally go into a protective stance. What I find interesting is there was no hesitation on whether it was me or Sierra that Kaley referred to. That is something Sierra and I will have to talk about later. Now, I have to focus. I'm too short to see her around them, but I don't miss the rest of the conversation.

"She has no business being anywhere with the two of you, ever. I am your girlfriend. I demand that you leave with me, you are just embarrassing yourselves with her," Kaley screams. Does she not understand she is the one causing a scene right now? This mall is not just werewolves, it has witches, warlocks, other shifters, and humans too. And the humans don't know about us, what the hell is she thinking having her meltdown here? I hope she can't shift yet, we will be in trouble if she does out in public with humans. It takes a lot to modify memories and the casters who can do it are not cheap.

I feel the air change around the twins. Normally, they come off as calm and uninterested, but now she seems to have crossed some sort of line.

"Understand this, You do not demand anything from us, are we clear?" Dakota asks with a hard edge to his voice, it's a warning. That's a new sound to me. His usual casual demeanor is only outdone by Sam's.

"But——" she squeals, feigning innocence.

"No! What we do is our business. Who we choose to spend time with is our business. And where we choose to spend time is our business, not yours. You are not our girlfriend. Change your tone and watch how you address *all of us*. Disrespect will not be tolerated," Cameron finishes, the same harsh demand in his voice. "Let's go," He commands our group, I assume, I still can't see shit. Wow, Sierra's right, being around the guys has made my language more colorful.

She spins me around, keeping me in the center of the group and I notice the guys don't break formation around me although they spread out enough for me to move comfortably, Sam leading us out. Sierra still has my arm, playing with all of the straps of my new bracelets absentmindedly. It must relax her.

"You got her?" Cam asks from behind me. It's the first time any of them have spoken on the ten-minute walk back to the truck. Before I can ask what he means, someone steps close to me.

"Yep." Oliver slides an arm around my waist from the back and pulls me close to him. My back is touching his stomach and I'm leaning against one of his legs. It's kind of weird and personal, but oddly I don't feel uncomfortable. Just another thing to unpack with Sierra later. At least his arm around me is some kind of signal that everyone can move away from me. The bags are loaded in the back. Sam, Mateo, and Sierra jump in the third row. Oliver opens my door, lifts me and buckles me in my seat. When he closes my door, Dakota stands by it until Oliver gets in on his own side. The twins get in last, all while looking around as if there is a threat lurking in the shadows. It is natural movement from all five of them, like a well-oiled machine that has done this thousands of times before. I wonder if this is something they do at the summer training they attend each year. It is fascinating if you sit back, really break it down and analyze it.

We drive in silence, but I think the guys are talking over the mindlink. Oliver isn't looking at me, but he is turned in my direction and has his extremely long leg stretched out across the center of the truck and his calf touching my shin. I try to move to give him more space, but his leg follows my movements, keeping contact. I can see him making eye contact with Dakota, but I think they are trying to be subtle. I wish Sierra was in the pack and could link with me. I have so many questions about the guy's' behavior today and I don't think we can get away with texting right now. My thoughts are cut short as we pull into the packhouse garage and start silently unloading all the bags from today.

I break the weird silence. "Thank you for today. It was so much fun." I look at all the guys in turn. "Sierra, will you help me get these to my room?" I want to get her alone so we can talk. This seems like the best excuse.

"Oh, we aren't even close to being done, Shorty." My brother takes the bags I am holding, grabs my hand, and starts dragging me into the packhouse following the twins, the rest of the crew behind us leaving all the shopping behind. Once we take off our shoes at the front door, we head straight for the kitchen where I can hear and smell the most delicious food cooking.

"The day must end with a tradition," Sam begins pompously, walking up next to me. "We always celebrate birthdays with a poolside barbeque, no matter the time of year. Now you must adhere to the tradition. No complaining or whining allowed." His loud voice echoes off the long, beautifully decorated, cream-colored hallway. Family pictures going back generations hang, galley style, on the walls. Little side tables have vases with fresh flowers that smell amazing and are understated, not too perfumey and overwhelming. She always has fresh flowers everywhere.

"But, you already did breakfast, lunch, and shopping with me," I start, Dakota turns and puts his finger on my lips to stop me from talking. Another weird gesture. They have all been very touchy today.

He keeps his finger there and walks backwards. "Breakfast is also a part of the tradition, now don't break the rules, protesting falls under the category of complaining and whining." He smiles a devilish smile at me as he turns around and I can't force my smile to go away.

Sierra is openly laughing at me. "Did you know about all of this?" I wave my hand in the air looking at her like the secret keeping traitor I know she is.

"Of course. It isn't a surprise if you are told what is going to happen." She links her arm in mine again as Mateo lets me go. Come to think of it, someone had had physical contact with me since Kaley showed up. Man, my list of 'needs explaining' is getting dangerously long.

We step into the industrial sized open concept kitchen. It is all stainless steel, black countertops, and white cabinets. Very masculine compared to the rest of the house. But it is designed to be able to host large pack functions so fashion doesn't really play a role here. Although the Luna has more vases full of flowers to tie it to the rest of the main level. The wall that attaches to the hallway we came out of is full of cabinets and storage. To the left of us is the large island that can probably sit twenty grown wolves comfortably. The gray granite countertop here is covered in platters of snacks and appetizers. The wall behind it houses two sets of dual wall ovens that are separated by a ten-foot-long gas range. To the right of the hallway we exited are the industrial sized refrigerators and more storage wrapping around the third wall. The wall overlooking the back patio is mostly glass and the view is amazing. The patio and pool are lit up with string lights and just beyond that you can see the woods as it takes on the late afternoon glow. It is perfect.

"Come on." Cam grabs my hand this time and drags me out back.

Luna Ava and Delta Gwen are on lounge chairs, each with a glass of wine. Alpha Lucas is manning the grill where I can smell burgers. My mouth starts to water. Delta Kyle and Gamma Brett come walking out with coolers.

"Underage cooler on the right, Legal's on the left," Gamma Brett shouts out to everyone

"Seriously?" Oliver looks at his dad. "You aren't going to share?"

"Nope, what you do when not in my presence is what you do, and I don't care as long as you don't do anything stupid that harms someone or makes me a grandpa before you find your mate. But in my presence, you are an underage teenager with rules that apply." We all laugh, and I think it's the first time I have seen Oliver embarrassed. That's three whole emotions out of him today.

"I hope you like burgers, sweetheart," Alpha Lucas calls over to me as I am getting a soda out of the 'underage' cooler.

"They are actually my favorite, how did you know?" I walk over and give him a kiss on the cheek. He just stares at me for a minute with a goofy smile on his face before he clears his throat, "Warriors tend to be burger fans, and from what I've heard and seen you are one of our best." I smile again and I turn to walk away.

"Wait, are you blushing, Dad?" Dakota teases, making me smile a bit more. I try to hide it. The Alpha is cute when he is in dad mode.

"I don't know what you're talking about. If my face is red, it's due to the heat from the grill." Alpha Lucas clears his throat again. Cam walks over and both twins are laughing at him and talking too low for me to hear.

"Skylar, did you find a dress?" Luna Ava calls out, diverting my attention from the Alphas. And that was all the invitation Sierra needed to launch into descriptions of every dress I put on and showing her and Delta Gwen the carousel of photos she has. I didn't realize how many she actually took.

She eventually gets to the dress we finally chose. "So this is the one and you will be able to see we all agreed unanimously." She slides to the next picture, only it's not a picture, it's a video of me walking out. I don't recognize myself at first. I look happy and healthy. My high curled ponytail, crescent necklace, and even my shoes complete the look in the corseted dress. You can hear the guys' exclamations, but I'm stuck on the way their faces look when I first walk out. Eyes wide, mouths open, just in shock. But, it doesn't look like a bad kind of shock. Another warm feeling washes over me, their looks are of appreciation not scandal or even fake interest. I don't think I have ever seen them look at me like that before and we have been hanging out for months. She even caught the exchange between my brother and Sam and the four of us had a good laugh.

"I am going to need a copy of that video, the boy's' reactions are priceless." Both women laugh as they are wiping tears from their faces.

Chapter 13

"Alright, burgers are all done, everyone go and fill a plate," Alpha Lucas calls and ushers everyone into the kitchen with the large platter of grilled meat. We all fill up plates and move back out to take seats at an oversized table off to one side of the pool.

Everything is so delicious. We are all laughing and eating at the large patio table, conversation is effortless as the sun sets completely. The guys are talking about birthdays in the past and regaling Sierra and I with some of their antics. The adults fill in some more embarrassing details the guys 'forgot.' I know my stomach is going to hurt tomorrow from laughing so hard.

As we all finish up and plates are all but licked clean, Mateo gets up and grabs my empty plate. Sam does the same for Sierra. The rest of the boys get up and take plates from all the adults wordlessly. That's strange. The confusion must show on Sierra's and my face.

"These boys eat well and have it easy when they are in the house, so it's their job to clean up dinner when we all get together like this," Luna Ava explains. "They have done it their whole lives. They aren't too important to help out with basic things around the house." She winks at us.

Sierra and I look back over into the full glass windows showing the whole of the kitchen. Again, I think of a well-oiled machine. They move in sync with each other, all communicating without saying words, getting the job done quickly. The whole kitchen is cleaned and put back to normal in less than thirty minutes. It really is a sight to see, and I can't help the big smile that crosses my face.

"What has you looking like that?" Sierra whispers as she bumps me in the ribs.

"The way the boys move together, it's fun to watch. I noticed it at the mall today too. They don't even have to look at each other or say anything, like all the cogs in a well-tuned clock." I shrug.

A large cake is set in front of me with eighteen burning candles. Where did that come from? I really have to get better at reading Sierra's distraction techniques. I didn't even notice them bringing it out.

Singing starts as I look at the beautiful round cake with light blue frosting and dark blue piping spelling out 'Happy 18th, Skylar.' I blow out the candles and everyone claps and cheers. The beautiful moment sets me off and tears I have been holding back since this morning just spill over uncontrollably. A warm arm wraps around the back of my shoulders and pulls me sideways into a tight hug. I wrap my arms under his, bury my head into his neck and breathe in the familiar calming scent, letting my tears go.

Mateo shifts and pulls me onto his lap and snuggles me closer as I sob. "This is how it will always be from now on, baby sis. This is how it should have always been. Can you forgive me?" he's whispering in my ear. I can feel his chest heaving, smell the unshed tears. "I didn't know, or really didn't pay enough attention to notice that you never got anything on your birthday. No party, no presents, we didn't acknowledge it, and you never once complained. I can't imagine what that must have been like." He sniffles, squeezing me tighter. "I am so sorry," he whispers through his own strangled sob.

Mateo pulls back and looks in my eyes, his are filled with unshed tears. I just nod, I'm not sure if I can speak without crying again. "I don't know if Dad will ever be able to be around. He also lost his mate today and that breaks something inside of you, but I have made my choice and I choose to spend it with the person still here, alive and kicking. Instead of spending it six feet above a person I don't even remember." We both start crying again. He pulls me in for another hug. I let it all out and squeeze him as hard as I can. I don't know how long we sit like this, but the rest of our friends leave us in peace. When he pulls back, he rubs his thumbs under my eyes, drying the tears and wiping away the raccoon smudges that I'm sure are there.

I look at my lap. "Did you tell them? The guys and Sierra. Do they know this is a first for me?"

"Yes, I had to explain a bit. They know you've never had a party before and that I think you usually spend it alone because Dad takes me with him to visit mom. I don't think the Luna knew about that part. I think she assumed he took both of us. I have never seen her so pissed before. She had some choice words to say about Dad's and my behavior, straight to our faces. I thought Alpha Lucas was going to have to step in to calm her down." He grimaced at the memory.

I tense up in Mateo's hold. "But what about Dad, and his reputation?" I rub my temples, trying to get out of his hold. He doesn't let me go. "He's going to be so angry at me when he finds out people know that he doesn't really want me, and he blames me for Mom's death. He's going to lock me in my room for a week after this. Maybe worse if the Luna yelled at him." I'm rambling and can feel the panic rise, shallow breaths coming in fast but providing no oxygen, and I start to really try and get off my brother's lap so I can go back to the house and hide, waiting for the storm to hit.

"Don't you dare leave, and he won't be mad at you. He's not allowed to be. He already knows what we have been doing all day. Luna Ava set him straight pretty fast, I have actually never seen her use her Luna aura before, but it's impressive. I am more scared of her than of the Alpha, I think. Dad was told if he can't behave like a parent grateful for an amazing child, then he can make himself scarce for the day."

"But——" He got in trouble with the Luna, *and* she used her aura on him. I am going to be in really big trouble, he might actually harm me this time. My whole body starts to shake. I don't fear much, but my dad's wrath is something I never want to experience.

Mateo grabs my shoulders and gives me a small shake. "No buts, this knowledge changes nothing. He has known for three days that we were going to do this. I thought Sierra was going to rip my arms off when I told her today was your birthday and we had nothing planned. She is also very scary, you have some fierce women who care about you." He gives me a little sideways smile, that I'm sure gets him his way with any girl he wants, but it's not making me feel better. "You are going to enjoy the rest of the night with us. Like we told you, it's tradition and you are a part of the crew now."

I huff. "You guys really do breakfast, shopping, and a barbecue for all of your birthdays?" I ask skeptically. There is no way they do this with just each other. They are all attention whores. They probably have raging parties that they invite the entire school to. I wouldn't actually know, I've never been included in Mateo's birthday before.

"On our actual birthdays, yes, this is exactly what we do. We don't get up nearly as early as we did for you...that was brutal by the way. But, with your training schedule it was hard to beat you out of the house this morning. I am going to sleep the whole day tomorrow to make up for the lack of sleep last night." He laughs at me.

"Don't act like you don't stay up all night with your extracurricular females and get up and function the next day." I scoff at him playfully.

"They don't stay all night, we take care of needs and they leave."

"AH! La La La La La! I don't need details." I jump up and cover my ears.

He pulls my hands down, laughing. "But I still get more sleep having sex than I did planning and executing your party with that crazy friend of yours and the Luna." I scrunch my nose, but at least he said his conquests leave when he's done with them. I don't know if I could handle facing any of his bed buddies the morning after. Bleh!

"Okay, enough is enough. You are done with sibling bonding. He's a dick and he's sorry. The rest of us are stupid and we are sorry. You, being the gracious person you are, forgive us wholeheartedly. Now eat your damn cake, I slaved for minutes choosing it at the bakery and getting the icing to match your eyes just right." Sam saunters through the back door with the largest slice of cake I have ever seen and sets it in front of me. It's a two-layered cake with chocolate on the bottom and vanilla on the top and some kind of caramel in between the two. I take a small bite, it is heaven on a fork. I close my eyes and moan a little bit as the flavor explodes on my tongue.

"If that's all it takes, Little Bit, we can continue this— –"

"Don't you finish that sentence or you will be searching for missing teeth," Mateo growls out. I try to hide a laugh, but Sierra and the rest of the guys just roll their eyes and laugh along with Sam's antics as they join us. I shift to sit next to Mateo on the bench and finish my cake.

The parents must have decided to leave us alone after my emotional display. I can still hear them talking somewhere inside the house, though.

It's Sierra, the guys, and I sitting at the patio table now, enjoying dessert.

"So, you get to pick my birthday cake every year, Sam! This is so great!" I laugh at his smug expression as he starts to preen himself like the male peacock he is.

"Okay, one more tradition before the night is over," Cam says, standing up and taking his shirt off.

I immediately look away, but I am met with the rest of the guys taking off their clothes too. What the hell is going on? I am surrounded by the sexiest guys I know, who are now down to their boxer briefs. There is nowhere safe to look. I can feel my face burn with embarrassment at the idea of being caught ogling them.

They don't need that ego boost, but damn, it's hard to look away. They are all 19-year-old gods chiseled from head to toe. Every muscle is defined, no area receives more attention than another. Arms corded and ripped, moving with every small twist of the wrist and flex of fingers. Biceps and shoulders taught, abs flexing as they pull the shirts over their heads and those devilish 'V' muscles dipping into their barely hanging on shorts. Oh boy, did the temperature just go up?

"Like what you see, Tiny?" My eyes go wide at Cam catching me staring at all of them.

"Umm....." I sputter out not knowing where to look, but trying to avoid him as he smiles, which renders me stupid and speechless while also wanting the ground to swallow me whole.

"It's okay, you can always share too, if it would make you feel more comfortable." Sam winks at me and I feel my face burn brighter.

"Knock it off, Sam, I'm serious." Mateo slaps him upside the head again. "Who gets to do the honors? *NOT* Sam!" My brother points aggressively at his friend.

"What are you talking about?" I ask, standing up from my seat looking at each of them. I stop on Sierra trying to catch a hint of what's going on. She just shrugs, no ideas, but she's willing to go with whatever the guys are going to do to me. I can't decide if that makes me fell betrayed or glad that she trusts them so implicitly. At least I'm not the only one in the dark. I don't feel unsafe though, and she's probably thinking the same thing. Of all the emotions I feel around them, fear has never been one.

After a minute of silent staring, Dakota shouts, "Me!" Before I know what's happening, I'm lifted up and instinctually wrap my legs around his waist and my arms around his neck, painfully aware of all the beautiful bare skin I am touching. Before I can ask again what is going on, we are air born then hit the warm water of the pool. My muscles involuntarily tighten around him as the bubbles from our plunge swirl around us. Kota swims for the surface and as we break free, I can hear Sierra's scream as I assume she is being thrown in as well. Then a torrent of splashes and noise happen around us.

"What is this all about?" I question, wiping water and hair from my face.

"Tradition," He he breathes in my ear. "Once we finish eating and celebrating, we swim until midnight when the birthday is officially over." He moves a lock of hair off my shoulder.

"You really could have just said that. Was the aggessive dunk really necessary?" I giggle.

He looks down between us at my legs wrapped around him and then at my arms wrapped around his neck. "Absolutely." The little twitch of his lips, fighting his smile, makes me feel all warm again.

"Thank you for today, Kota. It was fun." I hug him again.

Cam swims up close behind me, wrapping an arm around my waist, effectively pulling me off of Kota. "Did you have fun?"

"I did. Thank you." I lean back, tucking my face into his neck and smile up at him as he hugs me from behind.

"My turn." Oliver swims over and I don't even hesitate to wrap my arms around his neck, laughing. Cam and Kota release me slowly.

"Thank you for today, you guys really made it special for me." The smile he gives me when I pull back from the hug, lights up his whole face. He really is a handsome guy.

Not one to be outdone by anybody. Sam swims over and scoops me bridal style from Oliver's arms. "What about me, Little Bit? You have to spread the sugar all the way around." He tilts his face away from me to give me better access to his cheek, clearly expecting a kiss like the Alpha.

I know it will start a whole new competition if I do, but I can't help instigating his troublemaker tendencies. I slide a hand in his hair at the nape of his neck and place the other on his opposite cheek and pull him to me, pressing my lips softly against his stubbly cheek. I barely touched him with my lips when he gasped.

His fingers flex into my side and leg where he's holding me. "Fuck! Little Bit. That was hot! Now I get why Alpha was blushing." His voice is deeper than normal and he's not quite looking at me.

"Does that mean the rest of us get one too?" Kota asks expectantly moving closer.

I pretend to think for a moment. "Of course." I wiggle out of Sam's grip and swim to his waiting arms. He grabs my waist gently and I wrap both hands into his curly black hair and pull his cheek to my lips. Turning in his arms, I reach for Cam doing the same and then Oliver. I leave them all looking a little stunned and swim over to Sierra.

"Ooh! Is it my turn?" She bats her eyes at me. I grab her, wrap my legs around her waist like the guys, and kiss her slowly on both cheeks before looking over my shoulder at them, smiling. I don't know what made me so bold all of a sudden. Maybe having friends who actually want to know me. I feel light and really happy, off the training grounds, for the first time in a long time.

"I think you broke them. I love it when you break them!" She laughs at them standing in a line, mouths open, not blinking, staring at us. "They don't know how to handle the Skylar orgy, or the girl-on-girl action"

"Ew!" I cringe and try not to be embarrassed by her statement. I laugh as I hug her tightly. "Thank you for being here today, this means a lot," I say into her ear. "Now, what are we going to do until midnight? These boys are being weird, and we need to lighten the mood."

"Let's see how long it takes them to join a volleyball game." She looks at me and then over to them finally broken from their trance and milling about talking together at the opposite end of the pool.

The pool is a beautiful large rectangle edged in large flat stones so it resembles a natural lake rather than a modern pool. The concrete inside the pool is painted a light green with lights placed every few feet so it looks ethereal. It's all one depth across, making pool games more fun, although, it's designed for the average tall werewolf, so I can barely touch.

Now, knowing these guys better, everything gets turned into a competition, so this should be easy. We pull the net across, hook it to the support bar and start lazily hitting it back and forth. It takes all of three minutes for Sam to reach over Sierra's head and return a volley for her. Then Oliver joins my side, and we start playing two on two. Of course the twins and my brother can't stand to be left out for long. With the odd number we just keep rotating, the plays get more and more wild and aggressive as we go and who knows what kind of point system they're using. I eventually stop trying to figure it out and just have fun. We start splashing as a distraction and once when I was close to the net,

Kota grabs my legs from the other side and pulls me under to make me miss the ball. That turns into an all-out dunking match and somehow Sierra and I become the main targets. I keep getting caught and tossed. It's too hard to swim away while still being fully dressed. The guys try to talk me into going in my underwear, Sierra eventually concedes, but there is no way I am joining in. My brother doesn't seem bothered by my choice either.

"I need a break," I call out to them and swim to climb out of the side of the pool to grab a drink. I barely stand to my full height, when I hear my brother.

"WHAT THE FUCK IS THAT, SKYLAR?!"

Chapter 14

I spin quickly, thinking there is some kind of threat, I'm on high alert. "What?" My wet ponytail whips around wrapping around my neck, hands at the ready for a fight.

"What is on your back, Skylar?" It's barely a growl. He hasn't used my full name in months, since I started hanging out with him and the guys regularly. He climbs out of the pool looking like he is trying to hold in his temper, eye color is swirling, letting me know his wolf is pissed and close to the surface.

I reach back and realize my shirt has been pushed all the way up to my bra, exposing my whole torso. I didn't even feel it move in the water. My eyes widen and I know what he can see, the bruising around my ribs in various shades of healing and the pink and mottled scars along my back from the whip and silver. The make-up Sierra put on the exposed parts must have come off too, not helping the case.

"It's nothing, just training injuries, that's all," I ramble out a little too quickly to be believable, more concerned with getting my shirt down.

"You're lying. Why are you lying to us, Skylar?" Cam and Kota ask in the crazy twin unison that happens sometimes. Again using my full name, not the nicknames they gave me as they climb out of the pool and begin to move closer to me.

"It's not a big deal. Some people go a little rougher since they know I can fight now, that's all." That isn't a total lie. My attackers have gotten rougher now that they know I can fight and have been holding back. They want to bait me into defending myself so they can get me in trouble when I do damage. And when I don't, they try to get paired with me during training, so I have to engage.

I have abandoned the idea of getting a drink or righting my shirt and now just want to get out of here and lock myself in my room for a few days. I'm disappointed, they should have never seen this and I was careless enough to let my guard down. They won't let it go. Using my peripherals, I'm looking for the best way to escape.

"You don't fight anyone but us and Sierra at group training." I roll my eyes at their wrong assumption. "Only with the Luna and a few warriors during advanced training. None of us have sparred with you in a way to leave marks like that and some of these marks are older, before we started training with you. You wanna try again, Skylar?" Oliver's deep voice and menacing look stalls my breathing as he stalks towards me, the rest of the guys follow suit. He's built to be an interrogator. I look to Sierra, but she is skulking behind the guys. She's not going to help me now, she wanted me to tell them forever ago.

"It's nothing really, let it go," I'm pleading, not even trying to come up with another excuse. I move backward towards the side of the house closest to mine. I am just as fast as all of them, but getting into my house is what will slow me down. Think, Sky, think.

"Sky, we aren't going to let it go. Who put their hands on you? We need to handle this and deal with them. Let them know they can't mess with any of us and get away with it." The question from Sam comes out growly and he has that same look as when we were at the mall talking to Kaley. All traces of his good humor gone.

But, his statement is what pisses me off. It's like a switch is flipped and my whole body vibrates. Deal with them? What? I stop trying to walk away, stand to my full height, and look at all of them. These raging, fuming boys who have no idea what they are even mad at. They all of a sudden notice something is wrong and get protective. Well, they are too late, way too late.

A hot boiling builds inside me and something snaps. Now *I* am pissed, and my rage flares the minute Sam's words sink in. For years I have been dealing with this... years. Because they believe in survival of the fittest and looking the other way when kids are being roughed up or pushed around, saying we are werewolves and play rough. And my particular bully thinks she's untouchable because of her dad and the rumors she's spread about being the next Luna. Along with other threats, I'm sure. They have heard all of this and just ignore it, do nothing, or at the very best, not enough to stop it. Because in their world, when you ignore things, someone else makes them go away. I see red and my wolf is fired up too, she knows what I have gone through, but we have kept her a secret, I am already a freak for the fighting skills that 'came out of nowhere' and the grades and schedule I keep, I don't need 'weirdo early shifter' to be added to the list.

I give them my own death glare. "NO!" I roar, and they all stop wide eyed. "You. Will. Let. It. Go! You will let it go, because I said so." I stand taller, shifting from foot to foot, breathing heavy. "You will let it go because while all of this has been going on," I gesture to myself, "I still did everything that was ever asked of me. I showed up, did the work, became the best at everything. The perfect daughter, the perfect student, the perfect warrior and no one took notice then. You never gave a shit before I was a part of your friend group, until you deemed me good enough." I look at my brother pointedly. "Delta Kyle and the Luna noticed eventually," I look at Sam and the twins with my best glare, "and that was just as instructors. They respected my wishes and let it go." I point to my friend. "Sierra noticed the first day we met, she didn't even know me, and she respected my wishes and let it go. You five have known me MY WHOLE FUCKING LIFE," I scream, making my throat hurt, "and didn't notice or give two shits until right now. You don't get to be protective now, it's too late. I don't need you to step in now," I spit out, letting years of pent-up anger flow from my mouth, not caring who I hurt with my words. I want someone to hurt as bad as me for once. To understand the isolating and suffocating pain. My chest feels like it's caving in.

"A lot of this has gone on in your presence and you were too caught up in yourselves to notice. You nonverbally gave permission for this to happen to me and, more importantly, to others. So no, you don't get to "'handle this' or 'deal with it.'" I air quote. "I am handling it in my own way, and that's the way it's going to stay. LET. IT. GO!" I turn and start walking off before I get so angry I shift in front of them. My muscles are shaking, and my wolf is clawing to get out and beat all of them. They deserve the beatdown, but they don't deserve to meet her yet. Not like this. There are already too many questions they want to ask.

Choruses of 'Sky,' 'Skylar,' and my various nicknames are being shouted behind me, but they don't follow. I don't know if they are finally respecting what I want or if Sierra is keeping them back, but I just need to walk away and cool off. I walk into my back door and through the kitchen straight to my room. I glance at the clock as I go to the bathroom. It's after midnight, so at least the fight happened after my birthday, technically. I flip on the light and notice I look ridiculous in the mirror. All my make-up is gone, but streaks of black remain under my eyes from my crying fit earlier, my ponytail is loose and drooping to one side as the ends are still wrapped around my neck like a noose. My shirt and jeans are a darker color and plastered to my body, dripping from the pool. I quickly take everything off, dump my clothes in a pile to deal with later, my new jewelry is in a pile on the counter and jump into the shower, feeling really cold all of a sudden. I let the water get as hot as possible and once I have scrubbed my body until all of the skin is bright red, I just let the steam enter my lungs and soothe my muscles as I cry.

I let out everything I have left. I will lose them, just like I knew I would. They will hate me for being weak and letting all of this go on for so long. For lying to them about the whole situation and then yelling at them. I haven't been able to find a way to make the bullying stop and anyone who has tried to help by going through the right channels, to the 'right' people, have been removed from the school. Either they transferred or they were suspended then not seen or heard from for weeks and when they come back, if they came back, they are a completely different person treating me like the problem. It hurts and it sucks, it's why I stopped trying to befriend people in the first place, so they don't become collateral damage. The only place I allow myself to feel the pity is here in the shower. No one will ever know that they got to me. I'm not sure how much more I can take and all alone again. That's what hurts the most. It only took months, months for those guys to get close to me. To break down my emotional walls, the connections wrap a tight web around my heart and tangle to a point where it might kill me to remove it. I have to let them go, though. I do not want to tell this story and it will drive its wedge, secrets always do. They will walk away from me like every other person who has tried to help. And, I won't make Sierra choose. She is just as close to them as I am. It is easier for me to walk away, I have been doing it forever. I am just one person, easily replaced.

I climb out of the, now cold, stream of water, towel off and head to my room to find something to sleep in. Once I lay in bed, I just stare at the ceiling for hours. I can't sleep as my brain goes over the whole fight over and over again. How mad at me they all were, the look of disgust at the marks on me, the imperfections. I'm just a weak little girl to them, damaged and broken. I can't even take care of a simple bully or, I guess, bullies. I never know who it is that grabs me, but it is decidedly male. Their scent is masked somehow, even my wolf can't find it if I bring her forward. I am positive about who instigates it, but I can't prove anything, which is one of the main reasons I never go to anyone. It's just my gut feeling and I can usually place it with something she has said earlier in the day, or the previous day. She makes threats all the time, but nothing that would be considered more than teenage girl empty words trying to sound tough. She never trains, meaning most people probably think she's weak, which in a one-on-one fight, I probably could kill her in a matter of seconds. But, I have no obvious reason to challenge her. I have even gone as far as sneaking in and looking at the camera footage at school to try and find me getting pulled into a closet then leaving bloody and bruised or her and I interacting at all. But she is so good, the footage with the attacks on me are never there. They are either being erased or she is just that good at covering her tracks and knowing where the cameras are placed. The only time Kaley let herself be known was when she put the silver powder in the wounds from the whip. She wanted me to know it was her that time.

I roll over, I cannot go down that rabbit hole. Everything that happened that day is literally burned in my memories. All I hear is 'Is she worthy of surviving,' for days when I let it take hold. I can still smell the stench of my burning skin, feel the ropes binding my wrists. The feel of the forest as I was dumped.

That last part hit me the hardest. That stupid fucking motto my brother and his friends live by. They let people think that only the strongest should survive. It is actually the way that they play when they do drills together. Last man standing and all that. They taunt and tease each other for being the 'weakest' that day. The problem is they never explain to our peers that they are teasing and motivating each other. They just say the stupid line and go about their lives not realizing who's listening and following their lead. They are oblivious to the influence they have without even trying.

I throw my covers off, I can't sleep. The memory just brings on more nightmares. I rub my eyes forcefully and look at the clock, it's 3 a.m. The only thing is to run off the nervous energy now.

"You want out tonight?"

"I thought you would never ask. It's been a while. Hanging out with those boys hasn't given you as much free time since we are still hiding that you are special."

"You know why we do, and it was your idea in the first place. Let's get a couple miles out and then I will turn it over to you. Maybe I can get a bit of rest that way."

"Whatever you need, I'm here for you. We got this, kiddo."

My wolf feels like an old soul. Almost like a cool aunt that gives me advice when I ask, but also lets me totally figure things out the hard way after instigating less than intelligent ideas that used to result in the form of broken bones or other self-inflicted injuries when I was trying some new defensive move with no assistance. I can at least say I haven't injured myself in a long time.

I get my running gear on and tiptoe to the back door, hoping to not make a sound going out. I don't know if the guys went home or are still out partying. Maybe they each found a girl to entertain now that they don't have to babysit me. I spare one look at the twins' backyard as I run towards the forest. I don't hear any noises, but the garden lights are still on, who knows. I can't dwell on it though, I have already decided to let them go. I'm not allowed to wonder what they are doing or who they're with. I can't want to be with them and keep my secret, that's not fair to them. The pack members are more important, they need to stay safe. That's the mission.

I make it to the edge of the forest and sit to put on my shoes. I can't risk tearing up my own feet and I can't shift here, someone could see or hear me. The transformation is not pleasant to go through or to watch, especially for a new shifter. Once you get the hang of it, you and your wolf can interchange pretty easily and quickly, but it takes a lot of practice. We are pretty good, but the noise could still attract someone, and I can't take that risk.

I tie my shoes tightly, check my ponytail to make sure it's secure and wrap the straps of the little backpack I brought to store everything around my waist so it doesn't bounce around while it's empty. I start to jog, thinking, again, about everything that happened today.

How does Kaley always seem to find me with the guys? Even if it's not the twins, she manages to track me down and make things difficult and cause a scene, then I am attacked the next day. I wish they would at least get creative and find a way to hurt me more at training. Then again, I would have their faces and be able to identify and prove who is abusing their strength and assumed power. What is it about her dad that gives her so much power to not get in any kind of trouble? Just that thought makes me angry again. I run faster, pushing my legs. I need to feel the burn in my muscles before I turn over control. I start running the patrol route and allowing muscle memory to take over letting the heat burn off all of the anger I have towards that one person and incinerate the emotion.

I've been going for about an hour when my wolf lets me know there is another presence near us. I'm on alert now, letting her enhance my vision and hearing.

To my left I can hear labored breathing, someone is trying to flank me, but at a distance. Then a twig crack to the right and a huff. I sniff the air, they are down wind, but not making an effort to be stealthy. Whoever is following me should have known I would figure them out quickly, so they either want their presence known or they are stupid. I'm hoping it's the first one, I'm not close enough to the border's edge for a rogue or neighboring pack member to be following me without patrol picking it up, but as I have that thought, six faces pop into my head.

As if I manifested them, all of my friends appear from different places behind me. Even Sierra is with them, looking worried. I keep running. I can't stop. I don't want them to try and understand. I don't want them to talk me into working something out. It will hurt more than anything. I have to let them go, protect the pack at all costs, be worth the Beta blood running in my veins, prove myself a loyal pack member, and put my job as a warrior above all else. I can't be distracted by the drama that having them as friends brings.

I run harder, I can hear them all struggling to keep up, but they are there, just as stubborn as me. There's only one way to get away from them.

"Let's shift. Lets get a full throttle run away from them."

"Are you sure you don't want to talk to them? Maybe they could help if you explained a little bit more."

"No, you saw them before, they aren't going to be reasonable, and they don't get to step in like white knights when they haven't paid enough attention to notice when things are wrong. This isn't just about me, they don't notice when any kids come in with marks and injuries that didn't come from training. They don't know any of these kids, unless they are a popular female old enough to fuck. No, they don't get easy explanations, they can do the work and find out the hard way. Now shift."

I can feel she wants to talk to them and is coming up with reasons to stop running.

"But you will destroy your stuff, are you sure? We've never done it moving."

"There's only one way to find out. I can't keep this pace up forever, and they have been training with me long enough to know when my stamina will give. They are wearing us down and starting to corral us. There's a reason they waited until we were an hour into our run. Worst case we crash, and they catch up anyway. We have to try."

"Alright. You got it."

I let her come forward and just focus on my legs moving continuously. We are on a pretty clear path, one I take regularly, so I don't have to think very hard about where my feet need to go. I can feel my lungs starting to burn with the effort of maintaining the fast pace longer than usual. I put on a burst of speed anyway to give us some distance.

"I'm ready, on the count of three, jump and I will take over. Let's hope this works. One... Two... THREE!"

As she says three, I jump as high as I can go, giving her as much time to change and land as possible. We twist in the air, and I can feel my bones dislocating and reforming, the hair on my body is growing thick, my nose and mouth lengthening. I hear the ripping of clothes. It's too bad, those were some of my favorites, and I will for sure need new running shoes. We land on the ground on all fours. My jet-black fur is gleaming in the moonlight. But we don't stop moving. Picking up speed we start to create some distance.

"Nice job!"

"My pleasure kiddo. Let's go."

"What the fuck?! Since when can she shift?" Oliver, I think, yells.

"And how has she managed to learn how to shift on the fly?" Cameron, as the oldest, usually gets his panties in a wad when he isn't first at something, which is rare.

"I have no fucking idea. Clearly, she's good at hiding shit from all of us," Mateo blurts angrily. Is he mad at me? He does not get to be mad at me when he hasn't been there for me the last few years. Why would I tell him anything?

We put on another burst of speed.

Chapter 15

We have put some distance between them and us, but I can feel my wolf's hesitation. She doesn't agree with running from them. She spins once to get a look at my friends, then keeps moving forward, but more slowly. They all look shocked. At the fact that I can shift, how quickly I shifted, or at the realization that there is another thing they didn't know about me. I'm not sure. She looks back at them with sympathy coursing through us, slowing more, I have no control right now. She is going to force me to talk to them and isn't hearing my protests. She slows completely and turns in their direction, but doesn't let her guard down. I know she wants to go to them, and rely on them to help. Wolves are pack animals, we are designed to work together, but I won't budge on this. They need to act like leaders, not just wait for things to fall into their laps. They make a semicircle around us, breathing heavily, as we all come to a halt. Mateo tries to take a step forward and we bare our teeth to warn him not to come closer. At least she agrees with my decision to make them earn my trust fully. My wolf refuses to growl though, she will not show hostility or disrespect, just that we are upset and don't want them near.

"Hey, Little Bit. I know you can hear me. You can shift so you can mindlink. I don't know what's going on, but clearly there are things we don't know, and you seem to be really angry with us. We just want to help. Don't shut us out. We can't help if we don't understand."

As goofy and air-headed as Sam acts, he is the only one who even thought to mindlink me, unless the rest of the guys are just listening, trying to keep me calm now that I have stopped running. I hear movement to my right and see Dakota moving to circle me. We bare our teeth at him and he stops. I'm fighting the urge to yell at them through the mindlink. Once Sam gets me to talk, he'll be able to distract me long enough for the guys to catch me. We spread our front paws and lower our head just a little, looking like we are going to strike, but in reality, I see a break in their formation I can use to get back to the house before them. They will never catch me in my wolf form, she is fast, especially when I let her go full tilt. If she will run away from them that is.

"Hey! Quit trying to run, we just want to talk to you." Oliver jumps in my line of sight, he's quick to figure out my movements. Damn his observant ass. They must have all been listening.

I keep my head moving, I want all of them in my sights. I still refuse to talk. My wolf says she can communicate with their wolves, and they are terrified of what they saw last night and what I said. They really want to be here for me, but I just can't. I don't want to get any closer to them. It hurts too bad now just trying to keep my distance, and it's only been a couple hours. We are only going to get hurt more. Whether it's from Kaley, Jeanie, and Marnie, or any other mate that doesn't want them to be close to us. It's just better for all of us if this whole thing ends now.

"Please, just come back and talk to us. You can stay in your wolf form if that would make you feel better." Cam takes a small step forward and then sits on the ground. "Or we can stay right here. This seems to be your favorite spot anyway. It smells like you no matter what time of day I run through here." He smiles at me.

My head snaps to him. What? He follows my trails? Does he know my favorite spots? Wait. No, I can't let them distract me. I shake my head to clear it, look around and get a head count, keeping them all in my sights.

Sierra comes over slowly and lowers herself to the ground next to Cam. "Well, I assume you are all having a riveting conversation without me, but it looks like we may be staying outside to talk. Can we at least go to the fire pit so the rest of us, not wearing fur, can get a little more comfortable?"

My wolf stands up to her full height and starts to walk in the direction of the fire pit in the little valley behind the pack house. Clearly, we are entertaining being around them for now. She seems to trust that they won't do anything to us while we walk in front of them. I'm sure that has something to do with her secret communications with their wolves. I seem to be along for the ride right now.

"Just don't tell them what's going on. I know, it's stupid and petty, but they really have never cared before and I don't understand why they all of a sudden give a shit about me. I want them to fix things, and I know that giving them information would, ultimately, help. But I can't prove what's happening to me and the other kids or by whom and I don't need them going on a rampage and making things worse. I don't need any more pack members thinking I am weak and need protection. I was left out here to suffer and hopefully die, that is the leadership they have shown. Letting pack members harm and torture each other without punishment to try and gain power in the pack."

"You got it, kiddo. I understand your reasons, but you need to understand mine. We need our pack, and they want to know. Why they have taken notice now is only something they can answer, but in any case they do care. Give them something to work with."

"Fine, but the minute they start asking about my injuries, I'm out. I don't want to rehash those memories again."

"Deal."

We gather around the fire pit. My wolf sits on one side watching as the rest of them sit on the logs across from me, just staring. Dakota and Cam set up the fire pit and get it started. Now it is a waiting game. They followed me out here, they can break the silence.

"Okay, so are we just going to sit here and stare at each other?" Sierra asks. "Or can I just ask one of you to translate if you are talking to her already?" She rolls her eyes.

"When did you first shift?" My my brother asks quietly, looking sad, almost in pain and I can guess why.

Shifting for the first time is agony and it takes a really long time as our human body figures out how to accommodate the wolf form. He's probably worked it out that I did it all by myself, just me and my wolf to comfort me through it. The guys all had each other and their parents to encourage and be supportive and of course a party to celebrate with everyone after. I didn't have that, never had that. They are starting to put the lonely pieces together.

"About a week after all of you did. The night of the celebration for all five of you shifting." My wolf makes eye contact with each of them as their eyes all grow in astonishment. My answer is short and to the point. Sam relays the information to Sierra.

"By yourself?!" Mateo screeches. "Sky!? No..... wha.....uh....." My brother is stuttering, pulling at his hair. His brain can't compute that his experience is not what everyone has. "I mean why didn't you come to get me or anyone to help you? Do you know how dangerous it was to go by yourself?" Now he sounds panicked and... is he really offended right now?

My wolf snuffs out our annoyance, just barely. ***First, you were all at a party I wasn't invited to, or probably allowed to go to, and very occupied by all of your friends. Second, why would I come to people who have avoided me for the last five or six years. I was not worth any of your time or effort, or Dad's for that matter. Why would I come to people who made it very apparent that I was not wanted, just tolerated and who would be more than happy if I was no longer a nuisance? Besides, even if I wanted to, I wasn't in a position to come and get anyone! I barely had enough energy to survive the thing. The shift was unexpected but necessary, at sixteen I certainly didn't know what I needed to do.***

He looks hurt, and the rest of the guys are looking at him as if they were the ones treated poorly. Even in my head it sounds like I am being bitchy and asking for pity, which isn't completely true. I don't want pity, and I don't want them to tell me they would have been there for me when we all know that isn't the truth, not then. They were all too caught up in their own lives and their own first shifts and being another step closer to becoming the pack leaders.

Anything they say now to try and make me feel better is strictly to ease their own conscience. I didn't trust them to take care of me in a real moment of need when they didn't take care of me in day-to-day things. And now they know it too. I know my place, have always known it, and they are blurring those lines, making it hard to keep my distance and keep myself from getting hurt. I can handle the physical pain from my bullies and training, I know how to heal from that, but the emotional pain, I don't know how to deal with that, so I kept my distance. I want to continue to keep my distance, but my wolf is right, we need our pack, or *a* pack.

"Is that why you ran? You run away every time the focus is on you," Oliver asks, leaning forward, elbows on his knees.

Sam is keeping a running commentary for Sierra. I can tell she is upset that I won't shift back to talk to them. My wolf is at least intimidating enough to keep them away. I don't want anyone trying to come close or embrace me. They don't get to be sorry for all the things they ignored in the past, because they feel bad now. My friend doesn't deserve this treatment and I would talk to her directly if I could, but I am holding out. I still have no reason to show them any kind of emotion and I can stay stoic in my wolf's form. She can choose to forgive me later or just keep the distance and let me go like everyone else.

"Can we jump back really quick to the part where she shifted at sixteen? That's incredible, Skylar!" My friend surprises me with her upbeat tone. "Your wolf must be really special for you to shift so young. I still haven't shifted yet." Sierra looks at me playfully. She doesn't strike me as someone who gets jealous over things out of her control. But, there is a little longing in her words. "I understand why the guys shifted early and at the same time too. You are all really close and have a tight knit group and to top it off you are all high ranking wolves training to be the next leaders. It makes sense that your wolves would come out and help you along with that. But, Skylar wasn't in line to be the next Beta or in a position for her wolf to be needed like that. So why did she come early? Why was it necessary, what happened?" She looks back at me, I'm pretty sure she set me up with that question. This is an answer that comes with a nightmare I don't want the guys or anyone to know. Something I have been avoiding telling her since the day we met. She knows it, too. She trying to force the confession out of me.

I close my eyes inside my wolf's head. I don't want to see their expressions through her very clear vision at my revelation. ***"She actually showed up after I received some of the scars on my back. Because of them."***

"She showed up because you were being attacked and, apparently tortured, didn't she?" Cameron whispers and my eyes fly open. He's the first to catch on, leaning forward, elbows on his knees, rubbing his mouth with his hands. He looks up slowly, waiting for my answer.

It's what I always thought, but my wolf and I never discussed it. I don't say that, though, My wolf nods her head in silent agreement.

"WHAT?!" My brother jumps up and shouts, his whole body vibrating. "It was so bad your wolf had to show up years early?! Dammit, Skylar, why didn't you say anything to anyone?" He's shaking so bad, and his eyes keep changing from gray to black, showing his wolf is fighting to come out. He's running his fingers in his hair and pulling at it so hard it's standing up in certain places.

My wolf lets out a warning growl, nothing offensive, just a warning to his wolf to get him in check. His fists are clenching and unclenching. We are ready for him to shift violently.

Oliver jumps up and places a hand on Mateo's shoulder to try and help calm him down. "Dude, she doesn't need this right now. She's got her reasons for not going to anyone and you getting all angry and huffy is not going to get you the answers that you want." Oliver's voice is deep and soothing, the grip on my brother's shoulder is anything but.

Mateo is breathing hard and struggling with his temper. I can feel the anger, worry and torment all rolling off of him in waves as he just stares at us.

"We need to help him or he's going to rage and tear this place apart, and the rest of your friends are going to get hurt trying to stop him. His

wolf is having a hard time controlling both of their emotions." My wolf is pleading for me to go to him. His wolf needs her, needs the comfort of his little sister. I'm still angry, but I get what she is saying. His anger is because of my situation and only I can calm him. Reluctantly I give in, his emotions are more important than mine right now.

"Fine, go to him." I take a deep breath and sigh.

Once again, their needs trump mine. We stand up slowly and walk over to him, rubbing up against his leg. I can feel his whole body shaking in anger. We just continue to circle him and nuzzle his legs. We come around to the front of him and look up into his face. He takes a few deep breaths and looks down at us, tears in his eyes. He's trying to hold in the sadness and anger he feels and slowly raises his hand to run it through our fur just behind my ear. My wolf purrs at the contact and she closes her eyes, letting the contact calm us both. I feel his weight shift and we open our eyes to see he has knelt in front of us, both hands on the sides of my wolf's face, looking us directly in the eyes.

"I'm so sorry, Sky. I know I can't take anything back or even begin to make it up to you, but I'm going to try. I thought if I just did what Dad asked and kept my distance, it would take his focus off of you. I guess that idea backfired. I never knew how bad it was, because I put blinders on and just hoped everything was okay since you never complained about anything. You never got sick or asked for anything. That wasn't because everything was fine though, was it?" My wolf just shakes her head. His tears are silently falling now. "I don't need details, if you don't want to share, but I need to know the worst, Sky. Why do you have scars across your back that never healed properly? It's been two years if you got them and your wolf at the same time. Why does it seem like you are a different person at school than on the training field or when you're just with us?"

"His intentions are true and real. Let them in a little. I understand why you don't want to give them names. You are right, they do not get to have revenge for what has been done to you. That is for you only. But, let them understand the result of their neglect so they can begin to

change their ways. They cannot grow without being taught. You are a teacher, teach them," my wolf advises.

I grumble in her head. This is exactly what I didn't want to do. I don't want to talk about the things in my nightmares. Just the thought hurts.

"They need something to work with. You can make it as simple or as detailed as you want. Maybe some graphic descriptions will be good for them, toughen them up a bit." Did she just make a joke out of my torture?

"Fine," I say to her. Then to the guys, *"I need some clothes, this will be easier to explain in human form. Sierra deserves to hear this from me directly."*

Before I finish my thought, large T-shirts are dangling in front of me. My wolf has to blink a couple times at the fast movement. She grabs one gently in her teeth. She inhales deeply, Dakota, the scent instantly calming me. We walk behind a tree and shift, then I pull on the over-sized shirt. I know these guys are significantly bigger than me, but jeez, the shirt sleeves reached past my elbows and the hem almost touched my knees. I have to try really hard to not think about the fact that Dakota is now shirtless, again, and the guys are all quick to literally give me the shirts off their backs.

I walk out and sit on the log across from my friends. I just stare into the fire. I'm not going to be able to look at them while I tell this story.

I don't want to throw blame their way, this isn't about that, but they also need to know they are a part of the problem. I take a deep breath, close my eyes, and steel myself to relive this story out loud for the first time.

Chapter 16

I take another deep breath in and let it out slowly, stalling as long as I can before beginning.

"It really started in middle school, nothing major, just getting pushed around for stopping other, younger, kids from getting pushed around or being verbally berated for no reason. I would tell them to stop." Deep breath. "Bullies don't like to be told what to do, so, naturally, more and more bullying happened.

As a Beta, my protective instinct kicked in and the damage to me wasn't that bad at first and I found out I healed pretty quickly from the physical stuff. Unfortunately, so did my bully. That's when my homework would go missing and I started having trouble with my grades. It wasn't from a lack of doing the work. It was literally being stolen or destroyed. Another thing my bully found out was the power they received from being known to beat up someone with Beta blood, and with Dad's very apparent and open dislike of me, it was like an invitation to try and harm me in some way. To see what injuries would last." I pause to take another breath. I've never put into words what being bullied is like. "The few times I was called into the principal's office for incidents, Dad was called in, he never listened to my side of the story and added to whatever beating I had taken before, right there in front of everyone." I cringe at the thought that I now know that wasn't normal. "This also gave the green light to my continued torture. The narrative that I was a bad kid that deserved punishment and should be used as an example was born and spread like wildfire."

Oliver opens his mouth to make a sound, I'm sure to ask the obvious question or give some helpful advice to 12-year-old me. I hold my hand up to stop him. I'm never going to get through this if they interrupt me.

"I did go to adults. Dad and the principal obviously didn't believe me and had no sympathy. Dad told me if I was too weak to handle my problems, then I was no daughter of his and not to make excuses. I went to the principal about the physical stuff happening to other kids. He decided I was exaggerating or making things up for attention. When I showed him my injuries, he told me something similar to Dad and I wasn't allowed to see the healer. We have had kids leave suddenly due to this bully after going to the proper adults to handle it or to try and help me by backing up my story. Teachers have also been removed from the school for trying to help me. I have since learned that school board members and elders are biased and only care for their own interests and not the interests of the students in the school. Those who don't like me have the whole board in their pocket. So I don't want to hear anything about telling someone, there is no one to tell. Anyone with power doesn't care or can't and I will not risk someone's livelihood because I got smacked around a few times." I can feel myself getting fired up at the injustice I always feel at the lack of action from the adults in my world.

"You could have come to us, we would have helped you." Cameron whispers, pointing to all of the guys who nod emphatically.

"Would you, really?" I cock an eyebrow looking at each one of them. They all nod again. "When? In the middle of your invite only circle of friends? While you were entertaining the entire school's population of girls learning the finer points of being men? At all the sporting events with those same people? Hanging out at the diner and wherever else you went? While you were all gone for the summer at training being groomed as the next leaders. None of you have ever been this accessible." I gesture wildly to them. I close my eyes and take another deep breath, I'm getting worked up and off track. They are not the enemy. They made plenty of mistakes, but that's not the focus.

"What about any of our interactions, before Sierra showed up, would suggest to me that you give two shits about me? When you were told openly and, many times, in my presence, that I am worthless and an unnecessary blight on the pack? Dad was never shy about his feelings for me and he never cared if I was in listening distance." I look at my brother, whose face has gone pale. Like any teenager, they probably tuned out and ignored my dad's rants. "Or when you were all spouting your 'survival of the fittest' mantra throughout the school. Telling everyone that they should handle their own issues, and you were all only going to deal with 'really major problems' whatever that means." I air quote, trying not to sound hateful but failing. The guys start shifting uncomfortably and Sierra is shooting daggers at them.

"You gave everyone free reign to openly put down people deemed less by teenage standards, not build them up. You praised people for beating others in training without a second thought to the person who tried their best and put in effort. There can only be one winner, sure, but that doesn't mean the person who lost is less than the person that won, specifically in training. Training is to get everyone better, to give pointers and tips to each person in a spar. To make the pack better, stronger, safer. You all promoted stepping on others to get ahead, and that all comes back to me." I'm now clenching and unclenching my fists as the words are just tumbling out. I'm blurting out all the things I have sworn never to say. Reveal feelings I thought I would never tell them. I stand up and pace. There's too much pent-up aggression flowing through me to sit still.

"Beat the Beta girl to prove you are better, her family supports the abuse." I point to my brother. "Beat her worse than the last person who beat her and you win the popular vote." I look at Sam. "Throw her into lockers, make her bleed at least once a week." Oliver gets my icy gaze next. "Steal her clothes and things from the locker room, throw them in the shower and pee on them." I look at Cam. "Chain and whip her in the locker room for asking too many questions in class and making you look stupid." I switch my gaze to Kota. "Blindfold and chain her up in an old storage shed and whip her to the point of throwing up and almost being unconscious, but don't let her pass out, oh no! She should feel the pain all because she did better than you at something and took the focus from the future leadership." My glare slides over all of them. "To make it more memorable, rub silver powder into the wounds making her flesh burn and scar so she'll never forget. Then drag her to the forest to bleed out and die a slow, painful death unless she is strong enough and worthy enough to survive. Because only those that are worthy survive." My tears are flowing now, my whole body shaking after my outburst. I sit slowly back on the log and manage to look up at them all after calming myself. Sierra has her hands over her mouth, tears shimmering in her eyes. They all look shocked and at a loss for words.

It only fuels my anger, but they asked for this, they wanted to know, and as much as I was trying to keep this hidden, I can't seem to stop the word vomit now that I have started. I can feel my confidence rising as I let each word go, like a weight is being lifted from my shoulders. I maintain eye contact with them now.

"The spot you found me tonight, do you want to know why it is my favorite spot, why it smells so much like me?" I whisper the question, none of them move, even the forest seems to be holding its breath waiting for me to speak. I feel a rush of morbid satisfaction at letting them in on my torture. "It's where I was dumped, where I survived, where I made the decision to live. I was left, bleeding out from the lashes I received for having the audacity to displease someone who thinks they have the right to behave this way. Because I talked to you, Mateo." I stare into my brother's soul. "And happened to be standing next to you." I tilt my head to the side and look between the twins. "The silver was added, because the previous whipping they gave me healed too quickly, the scarring wasn't gruesome enough. I go to that spot to remind myself that I am still here, I came out of that, without you or anyone else. My wolf stepped up when I had no one. She forced me to shift and caused me a little more pain in order to help me heal and live. I was there for two days." I pause, to let that sink in. I remember freezing at night and burning from the shift. "No one was looking for me. I wasn't important enough to miss, and I was only a mile or so from the packhouse backyard. So forgive me when I call bullshit on the thought of any of you helping me. You didn't notice when I was right there in front of you, and you didn't notice when I wasn't." Mouths drop. With all the things about these guys that are great, and I am coming to care for, this is their fatal flaw. They have been sheltered from the bad things that happen in a pack. They have never had to deal with real problems. No one is going to be terrible in front of people they want to impress. My brother was right, they have always had blinders on, they thought they would just magically have people fear and respect them and not cause problems out of that respect. They believe that they are untouchable, but at what cost? That respect doesn't apply to everyone, just them.

"You all have been a part of the problem since the beginning and don't think for a second you are going to show up at school threatening people on my behalf. Even being friends with you and being seen in public regularly with you hasn't stopped the bullying, it's just gotten more creative." I lift the side of Dakota's shirt to show the bruise on my ribs. "I do not need protectors, I have survived everything, so far, on my own. So don't even think about it, I am not weak and you will not treat me like I am or reinforce to people who believe I am. I know how strong I am, even if I don't act like it. I know that every hit I take is one that no one else has to receive. With all your training and status, none of you have ever actually had to fight *for* your pack members. Had Sierra not joined us this year and," I snark as an afterthought, "for some reason I still don't understand, chose to talk to me, none of you would be sitting here now, none of you would have looked twice in my direction. I was forced into your circle, she is the only reason any of you are paying attention to me now, listening to my story." I point at my still shocked friend. "But the problem is, have you even thought about any of the other kids going through what I am? I do my best, but I know kids are still getting hurt on purpose. You have pack members who are torturing other pack members without cause or consequence. So before you think about trying to save me or protect me, why don't you help someone else who actually needs it."

I get up and start walking towards the pathway that leads up to the packhouse yard. My eyes and head hurt from crying so much tonight. I need to sleep and then get back to my life, the way it was before the guys barged in and decided they all of a sudden needed to be a part of it.

"Sky, wait," Mateo calls, jogging after me.

"I'm done for tonight, please just let me go," I say weakly, continuing my way up the path, but slowing down. My wolf is still holding me back for some reason and I am too worn out to be stubborn against her.

"I'm not going to stop you, and I know it probably means nothing, but I am sorry. I had no idea, and I know that's on me, but for what it's worth, I love you." He wraps his big arms around me from behind and kisses the top of my head as he breathes in deep then sighs before letting me go.

I take a few more steps forward when I smell Oliver right before he wraps his arms around me, same as Mateo, but he kisses the side of my head before taking a deep breath of my scent. I can feel his whole body relax before he lets go of me. Sam repeats the hug, kissing the other side of my head, also taking a deep breath of my scent and noticeably relaxing. Sam releases me and I continue up the path. I'm too drained to wonder what is going on with all of them taking in my scent.

My tears start flowing again. I can feel their sincerity, their agony at being part of the reason for some of my suffering. No one else approaches me so I continue walking, trying to steady my breathing. Even though I told them I don't want apologies, it stings that the twins didn't follow suit with the other three and I don't expect anything from Sierra. She noticed within minutes that something was wrong with me when these guys have known me forever.

I make it to the packhouse backyard and feel like I have been walking for hours. The full out run and shifting like that took its toll, something I make note to work on. I can't have an energy drain just from shifting in a fight. As I turn towards my backyard, hands grab each of my upper arms to stop me. Kota and Cam's scent hits me at the same time and the warmth from their hands makes goosebumps rise up all over my body.

"Sky," they whisper in unison. I don't say anything, but I let them stop my movement. I'm still crying, but I can't open my mouth to speak. I've said all I need to tonight.

"Tell us what to do, Smalls," Dakota says.

"We need to fix this, start making things right," Cam follows up.

I breathe in shakily a few times. Anger and sadness both consume me. They need to figure this out on their own. I don't know what I need from them. "It's too late for me, I don't have much school left, then hopefully I can find my mate or go to Elite Warrior training and get away from the bullshit." I stare ahead of me, not really seeing anything. "Just don't let it happen to anyone else. See people, notice your pack members, all of them, not just the 'important' ones. Show them you are here for them, don't just say pretty words. *Show* them you are leaders, nobody actually cares about what you say, if your actions don't match."

"You want to leave?" Kota asks like he's been punched in the gut and out of breath.

After all that I said, he's focused on me not wanting to be in a place I'm not wanted. What the hell?

I can only whisper, "If you were me, would you want to stay?" I wait a couple breaths, they have no response. With that, I step out of their reach, continue walking home, and go straight to bed. I can't handle any more emotions today.

I stay in my room all day Sunday. Even Sierra gives me my space, but she makes sure I know she's giving me space today and only today via text, which did make me smile. How does she know me so well already? She knows what I need without having to ask, and she sees through my BS and calls me on it too. I'm sure she figured I was going to try and skip school tomorrow. There is just too much drama that I don't need and I have no idea what the guys are going to do with the information I gave them. I don't want to see that look in their eyes like I'm fragile. And after the mall display, Kaley will have something planned for me too.

I fall asleep quickly wearing Dakota's shirt. His scent makes me feel calm and relaxed. When I finally roll over and look at the clock it's after 2 p.m. I sit up quickly, I have never slept that long before without any nightmares waking me up. I actually feel really good, until I remember why I have Kota's shirt on in the first place, then the sadness takes over me again. I start to feel antsy after not training for two days so I move to go get in the shower. Once I am cleaned up, I change into training gear and head for the gym. Maybe lifting weights will burn off some of this energy. I take extra precautions leaving my house. I don't want to run into anyone. It's going to be exhausting avoiding all of them all of the time and they won't make it easy.

I make it to the gym and only a few people are here this afternoon. I put my headphones, phone, and water bottle down on a bench and begin setting up my weights for a warm-up. I can't help overhearing a couple of the guys talking about Elite Warrior training.

"Did you hear? There were so many applicants this year, they are holding trials in each pack before they will accept anyone," a tall guy I recognize from advanced training says.

"Yeah, someone told me the Alpha King himself is going to come to some of the trials," tall guy's friend responds. "And they are letting juniors and seniors join the trials. I guess even if they can't get chosen, they get seen by the recruiters and if you're good enough, they will remember you after you graduate."

I feel my heart flutter. Maybe I won't have as long as I thought. If I only have to make it through my last year at school, I can get out of here sooner than I thought. Elite Warrior training is year-round, and most attend while doing college courses. I just have to be good enough. My head and heart feel lighter, I have a renewed sense of purpose. Something finally just for me. I will have to talk to Luna Ava and her warriors at training this week.

Chapter 17

I blast through my workout, not going too heavy since I'm on my own, but I take all of my muscles to complete failure, the excitement of this new information fueling me. I have to start pushing myself...now. I need to be better, stronger, faster. I have a year to get ready.

I get home around 6:30 and head straight to the kitchen to grab some food. I didn't have more than my protein shake before my workout, which was a mistake. I am starving and my grumbling stomach is trying to eat itself from the inside out. If I don't eat, I'm going to be sore in the morning.

"Where have you been?! We eat dinner at six." A growl comes from the table making me jump and turn around gripping the edge of the counter.

"Oh, shit! I really wish people would stop that." My dad and brother's scent permeate the whole house, so I didn't expect them to be in here.

I look over to see my dad and Mateo sitting together at the kitchen table, plates half empty. They never eat in the kitchen. Mateo is looking at me, but his face is blank, he's trying to hide his emotions from me.

"You are never to be late for or miss a family dinner again. Do you understand?" My dad growls out.

I look at him confused, I can't even hide it. I have never been allowed to eat with them unless we had company. And as far as I can tell, there is or was no company. I take a look around the kitchen to make sure I didn't miss evidence of guests. "I don't understand, sir." I have nothing better to say.

"You will join us from now on, 6 p.m. every night, family dinner, that is an order." He's talking to his plate now. He can't even look at me when he's giving me his clipped directions. My blood starts to boil.

This has to be Mateo's doing after what I told him last night. I asked him not to try and fix things. I may want my dad to want me, but not by force. I can see in his eyes he's only doing this for Mateo's sake, not for me. To appease my brother, not because he suddenly feels affection for me. I take a deep breath to steady the anger that is now surging through me.

"Unfortunately, I have training every night during that time. I have had training during that time, seven days a week, for the last two years. You have never wanted me to sit with you before and I don't believe that you actually want me around now. So, no offense, *sir*, but I must decline your invitation. I will continue my regular schedule." I turn and walk out of the kitchen, my appetite long gone.

I hear the screech of chair legs and the unmistakable sound of my brother's footsteps. I don't slow for him this time, though. It is taking all I have to not turn around and rip him a new asshole. It's been less than twenty-four hours and he's already gone against what I asked of him and the guys.

"Shorty, wait." He tries for a playful tone with a small laugh and grabs my elbow when we reach the landing. I let him stop me, but I don't turn towards him. "He's trying, he even waited until 6:15 to start eating and sat at the kitchen table." The plea in his voice almost does me in, but I can't let it.

"No." I take a deep breath and blink back the tears forming. "You are trying, do not force something that isn't there. He will never love me the way I want him to and need him to. I have finally wrapped my head and my heart around that. I am the daily, living, reminder of the fact that he lost the most precious gift the moon goddess gives us. He and I are both counting the days to when I can leave and neither of us has to face each other ever again. I asked you not to try and fix anything." I take a deep shuddering breath and let a single tear fall before I walk to my door. "Goodnight, Mateo. I love you too," I say, not looking at him. I step through my door and head straight for the shower, my one and only source of emotional release.

I wake up feeling better than I thought after last night's train wreck ending. I make sure to get up extra early, eat really well, and head to the training grounds an hour before the guys usually meet up to drive there. I have decided it will take too much energy to actively avoid them all of the time, so I am just going to put as much distance as possible between us when I can. No more unnecessary rides to places five minutes away. No lingering after classes with any of them, including Sierra. They will just try and use our friendship against me, and it isn't fair to put her in the middle or make her choose.

I'm at the training grounds so early, not even Delta Kyle or any of the other training warriors are there yet. I start running laps at a nice leisurely pace to keep my mind from wandering.

"Seriously?! Now you're training earlier? Where are your extra-large shadows, still dragging themselves in?" Delta Kyle laughs at his own joke, and I just stare at him in disbelief.

"I actually wanted to ask you something before everyone else started showing up, I just guessed at what time you got in to start setting up. I'm usually busy warming up when you get here." I lie on the spot, I can't tell if he believes me or not. "I wanted to ask about the Elite Warrior training. Some rumors are flying around already and I am curious."

He crosses his giant arms over his chest and lifts an eyebrow at me. Definitely doesn't believe me, but now that I brought it up I really am curious. "Is it true they are holding trials because of the number of applications they are receiving?"

He stares at me and takes a deep breath before nodding his head once.

"And are they letting juniors and seniors join the trials for exposure? Will they choose any current students if they are good enough?"

Both eyebrows shot up at that. "Who did you get your information from, that was just a discussion we were having yesterday, nothing is set in stone about age restrictions."

My eyes go wide. I don't want to get the two warriors in trouble for gossiping about something that wasn't confirmed yet. "I was at the gym yesterday and heard a couple of guys in passing, that's all. I figured I would check the information with you. Is the Alpha King really going to attend some of the trials?" I cross my arms over my chest mirroring the Delta, trying to look calm and curious, but I am sure looking like a pouting child next to him, instead of a hulking warrior.

"Maybe. We do have some guest trainers today, so it will be interesting to see what they think about all of you."

Before I could ask anything else, people started filing into the large arena. We moved to the biggest space today because we were going to be fighting human to wolf. Not quite half the group could shift, but all the high schoolers were going to work in groups with a warrior. The warrior was going to be in wolf form, we were all staying human. Once we learn these basics and get comfortable, then they will start letting those of us who can to shift and reverse the training.

I didn't even have a chance to look around for a group to join when Sierra walks up behind me, linking my arm with hers and dragging me over to the guys who are in a back corner, looking disappointed.

"You didn't wait for us this morning." Sam tries the pouty lip, and I just look at the ground.

"Are you still mad at us? Cause I am running out of ways to apologize for the little stupid things and everything else is just going to take time. I don't think any of us can handle you avoiding us, Bite Size while we make up for literal years of stupidity." Oliver slides his arm across my shoulder to pull me into an involuntary side hug.

I just shake my head, keeping my eyes down. "I'm not mad, but it doesn't just go away." I sigh and rub my temples. "You have to remember I have been in basic isolation for most of my life, you guys are kind of a lot to handle all the time. Don't get your panties in a twist when I need to not be around you, and be okay if I don't tell you why." I shrug, it's as honest as I can be right now. I am avoiding them and will continue to separate myself from them, but it's going to have to be slow so they don't notice the change, I guess. I am leaving this pack when we graduate. The plan hasn't changed now that I have friends. I don't have a place here after school. My brother is the Beta, not me. And, yeah, I will admit to myself, the idea of returning as a warrior has crossed my mind recently, but I need to do something that is just mine, just for me. Having these guys too close is a problem I never considered. One or all of them might not let me leave if I let them get to attached. And don't want the guilt of leaving or the regret if I don't try.

"There you all are! I was wondering where the hottest and best fighters were hiding." The unmistakable peel of Kaley's voice rings out across the grounds. "I am so excited for training today, it should be so much fun! This is my favorite thing ever!" She doesn't even notice the weird looks she's getting from the crowd as they part like the sea to avoid her. She's here in a hot pink sports bra that's about two sizes too small, smashing her cleavage together and almost out the top with matching leggings. She looks like a highlighter. "I thought you boys could help me with some of my techniques. I really need help with submissions." She giggles and winks.

Everyone knows she doesn't train, so I'm not sure who she's trying to lie to right now. She really is stupid and completely self-absorbed. She is so focused on her own personal agenda that she has no idea that Delta Kyle stopped talking while she made her entrance and the whole crowd heard her stupid sexual innuendo, maybe that was her plan, to be the center of attention and make an entrance. I'm sure she doesn't even know or care what we are actually doing today. I just can't understand why no one reprimands her for it. The rest of us would be running until we vomit if we interrupted training.

Delta Kyle coughs to gain our attention back and resumes introducing the guest trainers, but I can't hear well over the conversation next to me. My wolf and I get more agitated the longer her screechy voice drones on.

"Training really is the best. I love getting all sweaty and the close combat moves can be used for so many different applications." She's giggling again. Who is she talking to? Everyone around her appears to be trying to ignore her like me.

"Who is she trying to fool? She barely attends training, let alone participates. Her acting skills are terrible," Sierra grumbles next to me.

"Our group is full, and we have different instructions from Delta Kyle, so you'll have to work with someone else today." Mateo steps towards her, blocking her path to the twins, pointing to another group on the other side of the arena.

"Awe, come on, Matty, I'm sure you have room for me. You know I won't be in the way." Sierra and I look at each other, mouthing 'Matty' in question. I have never once heard my brother go by that nickname. She runs a clawed finger down his arm then tries that hands-clasped swaying motion again. That little girl act must work for it to be her go-to movement.

"It's Mateo, and no, you can't fight at our level so you would be very much in the way, and you would probably get hurt. We are training with wolves today. Go find another group," He he says a bit more firmly at the end.

"You know you could be rough or gentle with me. And why are those two here, if you don't want girls in your group?" She pouts again, head tilting to one side quickly changing tactics. At least she's not yelling at me. She either is trying to use a sweet demeanor to get what she wants, even if she has to pretend to be nice to me and Sierra, or she found out quickly that threatening us is a very fast way to get on the guys' shit list.

"We didn't say we didn't want girls, Mateo said you don't fight at our level, I've actually never seen you fight at all. These two are warriors, train with us every day, and know how to keep up," Oliver supplies blandly while stepping next to my brother blocking the twins, clearly bored of having to explain this concept to her. "Go find another group so we can pay attention to Delta Kyle."

Kaley tries to look past them at the twins, clearly about to appeal to them to allow her to stay. Both Cameron and Dakota just point their fingers to the side without making eye contact. She huffs and glares at Sierra and I as she walks past our group and to one only feet from us, pushing another girl out of her way. How she thinks that behavior is going to gain loyalty from anyone is beyond me.

"It's her, isn't it?" Sierra whispers in my ear. I don't respond, I can't, she'll see through any lie I tell her, it's not the first time she's asked me and if I confirm it here, now, she's likely to rush over and rip Kaley's hair off. I keep looking straight ahead, trying desperately to hear the instructors over the blood pounding in my ears. "Fine, you ignoring me basically confirms it."

"Let it go, let's warm up," I say under my breath, making a point to look at the guys, hoping they aren't eavesdropping.

One of the guest trainers walks over to us first, I'm sure because the future Alphas are in our group. While Delta Kyle gets everyone else teamed up with pack warriors and starts their training, the guest trainer introduces himself to us.

"Hello, gentlemen, ladies. I'm Nickolas, one of the Elite Warrior trainers. I work closely with the Alpha King's personal warriors. I have heard great things about all of you." He looks at each of us in turn. "I wanted to watch each of you spar in human form before we started with the wolf versus human portion to get an idea of how all of you move as humans yourselves. Delta Kyle says you all train daily as a group. Are you all pretty comfortable being paired up at random?"

"Yes," we all say in unison, then laugh a bit. Warrior Nickolas just smiles.

"Alright then, let's see you and you together." He points to Sam and Mateo.

They are pretty evenly matched. Mateo has more muscle than Sam, but Sam's lean build is quicker. They both have advantages and disadvantages which they are quick to try and exploit from each other.

We play a pinning game several times a week. One of us is 'it' and has to fight off the rest for a certain amount of time. We change the length of time to keep us on our toes so we don't get complacent. The goal is to be the first to pin your opponent in a way that they can't release themselves, without causing them to lose consciousness. It's a great tactic for when you want to keep someone alive for questioning. It's fun because we get to work as a team against the person who is 'it' and that single person is fighting against six others at once. We have all agreed that it's not considered an official win for the person who is 'it' unless they have four or more submissions. And the group only gets a win if each person submits the person who is 'it' in the time period.

Mateo and Sam face off and waste no time fighting for dominance. Mateo leans down and tries to get Sam on the ground by taking out his legs, since Sam is weaker at grappling. Sam stands his ground, leans over my brother's back and grabs Mateo by the waist to steady himself and lands a few good punches to the kidneys, sending Mateo down to a knee. Mateo uses the downward motion to twist and pull Sam under him, essentially cushioning his fall. They go on for a few more minutes, until Warrior Nickolas calls them to a stop.

"I'm impressed, you both have a few things to work on, but your strength and speed is great. Who's next? How about you two?" He points to Kota and Sierra.

"Thank the goddess! I thought he was going to pair me with you since we are both girls. I don't know if I could handle you today." She laughs at me, and I roll my eyes, noticing Warrior Nickolas watching our exchange curiously.

"What am I? Chopped liver?" Kota tries and fails to look offended.

"You know what I mean, she's in rare form right now and super pissed at all of you. I don't want to be on the receiving end of anything she's dishing out today." The rest of the guys laugh. I just stare at all of them confused. Now they are making fun of the fact that I am mad at them? I don't get to dwell on it for very long though. Warrior Nickolas starts their fight pretty quickly.

He only let their fight go on for a few minutes as well. He really is just assessing our basic talents. It is fun watching him analyze. I wish I could hear the play-by-play going on in his head on all the corrections and what we are doing that really does impress him.

"Alright, you two." He points to Oliver and I.

"It was nice knowing you, man." Kota pats him on the shoulder.

"Shut up, you pansy."

We take our stance, and I wait for Oliver to make the first move. He's been getting faster with his reaction time since we all started training together. I try to take the time to read my opponent, study their stance and look for any initial weaknesses I can use early on. I'm not one for dragging out a fight if I can help it. I want a quick finish, which is something Oliver likes to push with me. He tries to wear me out, by keeping me moving and staying just out of reach for a full takedown with his long ass arms. I have to catch him off guard to get him to submit. We haven't trained together all weekend, and Oliver is the most adaptable of all the guys. He seems to read me the same way I read him. We almost move in sync, like the twins do.

We start circling each other. Neither wanting to make the first move. "You have to succumb to her wrath sometime, bro, might as well get it over with," Dakota shouts over at us.

"Yeah, she's been suppressing her anger at us all weekend, glad it's you and not me," Sam adds.

I'm not sure who they are trying to distract more, me or Oliver, but I have to tune them out and focus. Oliver's movements are more lithe today, like a panther stalking its prey. He's got something in mind and I can't spare an ounce of my attention on anyone else. Just as I have the thought, he strikes. Lunging forward, I thought he was going to grab my waist, but he drops down and grabs one of my legs trying to sweep it backward, knocking me to my front. I let the momentum take me and tuck my chin to roll forward, twisting slightly and planting my hands on the ground to throw a kick to his back before following through and jumping on his back, trying to get my arms around his thick neck. He's too fast for me though, spinning to a crouching position and grabbing at my legs again. This time knocking me to the ground, I keep one of my legs in between his and one around his waist to keep him from pinning my legs down. I bucked my hips trying to use the force from our fall, cause once we stop moving, he can use his large weight against me. He's thinking the same thing, trying to force me flat on my back grabbing one of my arms and trying to hold it down, so I do what any rational girl would do, I nailed him in the junk, well the very high inner thigh, I'm not that mean. Oliver grunts and slackens his grip on me. Using the distraction, I roll us over and get out from under him, but he recovers too quickly and gets up before I can grab him or throw a punch.

We both continue to move around each other throwing and taking hits pretty equally. He gets me in the ribs really well right over the bruise from yesterday and I can feel my lungs fighting for air. I land a good right hook to his cheek close to his ear, followed by a punch to the solar plexus. At least he's having as much trouble breathing as I am now. So many punches and kicks trying to gain a leg up in this fight, I'm losing track of what is working and what isn't. I feel like this fight is going on far longer than the rest of our friends' matches, but I'm not really sure, maybe it just feels longer since I can't breathe. Maybe Warrior Nickloas might actually want to see who will win.

After a few more minutes, Oliver is behind me with his bulky forearm around my neck. I struggle to find an opening in his arm to pull myself out, but his grip is solid. I manage to wriggle my hand up between my neck and his arm as I'm starting to see spots and pull back under his armpit, we are both so sweaty I slip out from his arm easily. Once I get loose, I bring his arm with me and effectively pin his arm behind his back. Before he can counter the movement. Warrior Nickolas stops us. "That was a really well-matched spar, but we have an odd man out. Skylar, are you up for a back-to-back match?"

"Sure, I guess." I'm panting and roll my shoulders and neck. At one point, Oliver had a lead on me and pulled me over his shoulder to body slam me pretty hard. I'm lucky he didn't dislocate anything.

"Do you need a minute to recover?" Warrior Nickolas looks at me with a strange look in his eye, and for some reason, it feels like a test.

"No. I mean, if we are going to be attacked, it's not like the opponents are going to come at us one at a time or give us snacks and water breaks." I shrug my shoulders and get set in front of Cam, who looks like he's going to enjoy this.

I notice there is less noise around us now, but I can't focus on that. Cam is great at spotting when you're distracted or have a weakness, like an injury. I actually like sparring with him, because he seems to become more difficult each time, like he learns and retains new information with each interaction. He's the opposite of Oliver, who improves his own skills.

Cam's not as fast as me, which is usually my saving grace, but he has had me pinned and submitted enough times to know how to break me quickly. But I have had him submitted too. His weakness is me, specifically. I'm not sure if it's because I'm a friend, Mateo's sister, or just my gender in general, but he tends to let me get too far in my fight, causing him injuries, before he puts in effort to take me down and it's a weakness I try to exploit. If I can wear him down a bit, he's easier for me to dominate.

"FIGHT!" Warrior Nickolas' voice booms from somewhere on my right. I move straight toward Cam, aiming to jump over his shoulder and onto his back like a monkey. We have been practicing multiple on one for a while now, so my stamina is pretty good, but damn is he strong. I got as far as moving around him and using his shoulder like a vault. I landed a great kidney punch across his back when he elbowed me in the side, in the same place Oliver hit me. Dirty fighter, well, two can play that game. I was knocked to the ground behind him with the rib hit. I roll out of the way, but I'm not fast enough, and he grabs one of my legs dragging me along the dirt back to him. I roll over and kick up wildly with my free leg, making contact, but I'm not sure what I hit. Then I hear a loud gasp from a lot of people, like a lot, a lot of people as I roll back over my shoulder to a crouching position.

I look up to see Cam holding his face and blood pouring out from his hands. I can't tell if it's from his nose or his mouth, but there is so much blood. He makes eye contact with me and several emotions cross his face at once. Surprise, pride, and then something more primal. I am in deep shit. He lunges for me, and I scramble back, knocking into a few people as I quickly stand and block a wide punch coming at me. He is throwing punch after punch, harder each time. I am able to block all of them for now, but they hurt and his speed is picking up and I won't be able to hold him off for long. I can see he thinks he has me trapped against the wall of people who have stopped to watch the spectacle. He lunges forward to try and grab me again and I use my shortness to my advantage and climb through his legs, turning to jump on his back and wrap my arm around his neck again. It's almost hard to lock my arms with the thickness of his neck and the blood flowing from his face making his skin slick, but I manage. And after what seems like another eternity, Warrior Nickolas calls us to a halt.

I let go and drop to the dirt behind Cam, and lay on my back, breathing heavily. Cam sits next to me, not even having to look to see where I am. His butt is even with my shoulders and his outstretched legs are almost as long as my whole body. If I wasn't so tired I would think it was funny.

"How dare you hit one of our future Alphas! You should be beaten and thrown out of the pack for your disrespect!" Oh, the dulcet tones of my favorite person. I just close my eyes and ignore her.

"What are you talking about, Kaley? They were sparring, like everyone else, bleeding and injuries happen. She makes us bleed all of the time actually." Sam cringes, and I really do giggle this time from my prone position on the ground. "That actually sounded way more pathetic out loud." He sits next to me. "Besides, did you see how many hits your future Alpha got in before she submitted him? I think it's safe to say they were pretty evenly matched."

"That was actually one of the best matches I've seen in a while." Warrior Nickolas walks over to us. His back to Kaley like she didn't even speak. "Now let's see what you all have against a wolf." His smile is one of a person who enjoys putting people through their paces with just a little bit of borderline torture to see where their breaking point is.

I am going to love this or hate it completely, but I guess this is like a snapshot of what Elite Warrior training will be like if I make it, so it won't matter if it sucks, I'd better get used to it. "Everyone back to your groups, your warrior will brief you on the basics of fighting against a wolf. You seven are with me." He points to us and starts to walk away to the farthest corner of the arena. Kota walks over and gives a hand to his brother to help him up, then reaches for me. We all turn to start walking slowly behind Warrior Nickolas.

"What about me, asshole?" Sam grumbles from the ground before helping himself up and following. None of us turn to him, but all of us are smiling and laughing low at his dramatics.

Chapter 18

"I would really like to train you separately from the others, you all are a distraction to them." He laughs to himself. "But I need to help the other trainers keep an eye on your pack members for this. The biggest thing you need to know is any attack will come as an ambush as much as possible. They will want to attack you in your human form since it is more vulnerable to injury. It has nothing to do with weakness, just the difference in the hide of the wolf versus the skin of the human. Any attacker will want to identify you and your mates, when you find them, because once they take out any of the leadership, the bond to the pack is weakened and you are all more vulnerable. Your Luna will be a major target, especially during the transition from one Alpha to the next. The Alpha or Alphas in this case will gain their full strength when they have marked and mated with their goddess given Luna on the full moon following the commitment ceremony. She will also gain full strength. That is why most packs have the commitment ceremony on the full moon, but that is not always possible for a variety of reasons. The time between mating and the full moon is the Alpha and Luna's weakest, which is why all the warriors and ranked members must be well trained. It is when packs are most often attacked. So, let's begin."

Nickolas proceeds to have the guys shift one at a time and tell us several weaknesses in the wolf's form that can be used to subdue the wolf long enough to get away. My wolf is grumbling around in my head the whole time, saying she isn't that weak and could never be taken out like that. She keeps a running commentary until Warrior Nickolas stops. "I can see in your eyes many of your wolves are fighting against my teaching. Understand these are not tactics to kill a wolf, they are right, it is very difficult as a human without weapons to kill a wolf. The whole point is to get away, or give yourself time to shift and have a more evenly matched fight. I'm not trying to bruise any egos, but you need to know what can be used against you, so your ego doesn't get you killed."

"Thank you for that. My wolf was starting to give me a migraine," Mateo says, and I smile. I was thinking the same thing.

"Okay, let's begin." Warrior Nickolas takes off his shirt and a I swear the heat goes up a bit. For being older he is a very nice-looking guy.

He talks us through what he wants to happen, then shifts and works with us each individually in slow motion.

"Damn, that man is packing!" Sierra mutters in my ear as Warrior Nickolas talks to Cam after their one-on-one. "I wonder if all the warriors are hung like that?"

"What?!" I try not to screech. I think I know what she's talking about, but I don't want to guess and be wrong. And I am sure as hell not asking here!

"I'm just saying he's built well in all the important places."

"Sierra!" I hiss. Now all I am trying to do is focus on his face. I can't unsee Warrior Nickolas' very naked body, and I did notice the same thing she did, but I would never say it out loud. Not here anyway. Now she put those thoughts in my head. And, I'm sure everyone heard it, and Sam doesn't seem to appreciate her observation.

When he gets to my turn, I am all sweaty and it isn't from the weather or the workout. I have read all kinds of books with plenty of descriptions, but I have never seen a naked man before. While I do think it is kind of a strange muscle...er...thing to appreciate. I do notice that all the lines on his abs seem to be pointing down, inviting me to look again. Ugh!

"Skylar?!" Warrior Nickolas says my name kind of like a question and for sure with some amusement. I think he has been giving me instructions, but I can't be sure. I am making a point to only look at his face, but I'm too distracted in my thoughts to listen.

Do I have my chin tilted too high for the occasion? Yes. Is my heart racing like I got caught with a dirty magazine? Also, yes. Am I going to change my focus before he shifts back into his wolf form? Absolutely not! I can already hear Sierra in my head now: 'Girl, we need to get you some experience.'

He shows me a maneuver I am supposed to perform on his wolf. He shifts and we walk through the movements, hand placements everything he can guide me through as his wolf, then he shifts back to give corrections. It would be helpful if he could just mindlink us, I can pretend nothing is awkward when he's covered in fur. It doesn't bother the guys since they shift together all of the time and Sierra clearly has no qualms with it, but I have just never seen one in real life and this is not the time to be curious. I have to shake my head a few times to keep my thoughts on track.

This part of the training is less grueling for us since we are all taking turns, watching, and analyzing each other, then taking time to ask questions and get answers.

When Delta Kyle finally comes over to check out our progress, I notice it's long after our usual ending time. The whole arena is already cleared out and the sun has passed completely over the arena showing late afternoon. How long have we been here? Time went so fast, but Omegas brought water and snacks continuously so we never really stopped to look at the time.

"You guys obviously missed meals and school today. You are all exempt from anything that was due or assigned today. Go clean up and you can all meet at the packhouse. the Alpha wants you all over for an early dinner and to talk about today's training."

The minute he mentioned dinner my stomach growls, loudly. My eyes go wide in embarrassment as I wrap my arms around my midsection.

"Let's get the gremlin fed before she devours us all." Dakota comes at me, and I start running. I can hear the rest of them following and the two adults just chuckling, watching our antics.

"You know I'll catch you eventually, right, Smalls?" Kota yells when I start zig zagging to stay out of his reach. "Or we can just herd you in."

I make the mistake of looking over my shoulder to see how far away he is, when I run smack into a hard chest, bounce off and start to fall towards the ground when strong hands grab my upper arms and steady me before I am whipped around and thrown over a shoulder. Of course they are all laughing. I am fighting a smile as I realize this is the only way they can catch me. They have to work together as a group, not one of them can do it on their own and that gives me some kind of weird pride. I realize from the scent of citrus that Cam has me and he is clearly not putting me down as we head out of the arena. I think this is the only way he has ever carried me, it's becoming his signature move.

"You are riding back with us, Tiny, don't argue." Cam's low growl makes my tummy flutter. "And you are not avoiding us anymore, so knock it off."

He stops walking suddenly and I feel myself being launched, only to land in another pair of large hands. Instinctually, I wrap my arms around a neck as hands grab under my knees and around my back.

"Umpf! You guys do realize I'm not actually a doll to throw around, right?!" I look up at Dakota who has this devilish grin on his face.

"But, it's too fun to resist." He gets dangerously close to my face before he opens the door with one hand and slides me between him and his brother.

We make the short trip back to the packhouse. As we all jump out of the truck, I am once again thrown over a shoulder.

"What now? I need to take a shower. I am covered in mud and sweat and Cam's blood. I wish I would have known your nose is a geyser before I kicked you." I look over at Cam as I figure out who has me now. "I would have chosen better." I laugh at my own joke, the only one who joins in is Sierra. Stupid boys, it's okay when it's me they make fun of, but not when the tables have been turned. I open my mouth to say so, when Oliver stops abruptly and jars my stomach into his shoulder. "What the..." He slides me down and places me gently on the ground before stepping in front of me, but not in my line of sight. His arm is stretched out across my waist, like he's ready to shove me behind him if needed.

"I'm here!" Really?! Is she singing now? She's like a cockroach, fucking everywhere. "I heard there was dinner with the Alpha and Luna, so I dressed up special." Kaley giggles, motioning to her very short black and purple bodycon dress with a deep v cut all the way to her belly button. I don't know how she thinks that's appropriate to wear to dinner with the Alpha and Luna. "You boys need to get cleaned up, why are you still all dirty from this morning's training? You're going to be late, and you can't make the Alpha and Luna wait. Cam, you can wear that nice black button down shirt and your pinstripe pants, and Dakota can wear his white button down with black slacks. I brought you both ties that will match my outfit perfectly." She giggles and claps like a toddler. I don't think she took a breath during all of that.

"I think you misheard, Kaley, we," Cam gestures to the group, "are having dinner with our parents and the Alpha King's warriors before they leave in the morning. It's not a formal event and we did not invite additional guests."

"What are you talking about? Daddy said that the Alpha was hosting the Elite Warriors, and I should be here to support you both since I will soon be leading this pack with you as Luna. It's the best time to learn all of my hosting duties as the next Luna, and what better way to learn than to be here with the current Luna while she entertains the Alpha King's warriors?"

Man, she is grasping at straws, and how many times can you use the word 'Luna' in a sentence?

"No, we've gone over this. We aren't twenty-one yet and have no idea who our Luna will be, stop trying to force this, it's not happening. We will only take our Goddess given mate and nothing else. You and your father need to figure this out." Dakota drops his fun personality. It's the first time I've heard something close to exasperation towards her.

"We are running late though, excuse us." Cameron, always the peacekeeper.

They both push past her, and Oliver shifts his arm, his large hand is on the small of my back and his large body is between her and I. Sam does the same for Sierra. I don't look her way, hoping she won't notice me, but that is wishful thinking.

"WHAT THE FUCK?! What is she doing here?!? You said no additional guests." Kaley has a pink claw pointed right at me. "If she is here, then I demand, as your girlfriend, to be here too." She stomps her heeled foot. "How does it look with you parading around with another girl all the time?"

Oliver moves me behind him so fast it takes me a second to blink and register it happened, Sam moves Sierra next to me and stands shoulder to shoulder with Oliver, blocking us both. The wall of male testosterone should piss me off and to some extent it does. But with Kaley, I will let them handle her as long as possible. I hope she doesn't take this as a threat or a 'na-na-nana-na' brag from me and take it out on some kid as retaliation. One day, I am going to have to face her and not let her win, but today isn't that day. I don't know what she will or won't do with the guys watching and I can't afford for any of the leaders, like my dad, see me get into a fight with her. That always ends badly for everyone but her.

"Well, it's about time you kids got here!" Luna Ava's beautiful voice rings over to us, I peek around Oliver's arm to take in the scene. Kaley's psycho face switches back to the sweet mask she wears to get adults to give her her own way.

"Luna! It's so great to see you! The guys were just telling me about dinner tonight. I hope you don't mind an addition to the table." Cue folded hands and the little girl twist. I have to admit, she put a good spin on the situation and a weaker person would have given in to her.

"Oh, I'm so sorry. I wish you would have called me, boys, but I only made enough for the usual group. Maybe another time...umm..."

"Kaley." She gives the Luna her name, her smile falters a bit. The Luna does not forget names.

"Right, Kaley. Maybe another time. Skylar, Sierra, come on, you can use my bathroom while the boys use the guest rooms. I want to hear all about training today. Lucas said it was amazing. Have a good evening, Kaley." Luna Ava waves her off and moves into the doorway, clearly the conversation is over and we are all happy to comply with the Luna's wishes.

Oliver turns around, keeping me directly in front of him, and pushes me toward the front door where Luna Ava is waiting; Sam and Sierra right behind.

Mateo and the twins bring up the rear. I can see in the reflection of the windows that none of them spare a backward glance at Kaley, and she looks murderous.

As soon as we're all inside, Luna Ava starts laughing. "You should have seen your faces when she tried to say you invited her for dinner." She grabs her stomach. "But her face when I said 'no' was even better. The Cunningham's have been trying since Kaley was born to find a way to force a chosen mate bond with the boys. It's getting absurd. Kevin showed up earlier today, I'm sure with the same intention of getting an invite to dinner. Anyway, you all really do smell, which I guess is to be expected when you train for almost ten hours. Girls, come on, I'll show you to my bathroom and we'll get you something to wear. I also want to know who made Cam bleed," she says sweetly, then turns to the guys. "Boys, move it!" They all hustle up the stairs to the second and third floors. Sierra and I giggle at how she can get these boys, who are easily twice her size and strength, to move like she electrocuted them.

The first floor houses the Alpha and Luna's offices to the left of the massive central staircase, the formal living room that is set up for pack meetings and other large events to the right of the staircase and the massive kitchen at the back. The second floor of the packhouse is for guests. There are six large rooms, three to each side of the staircase. The main staircase stops at a beautiful walkway on the second floor where you have a great vantage point of the front door and living room. I'm sure many speeches and grand entrances have been made on this set of stairs. Alpha Lucas does as few unnecessary speeches as possible.

From what I have heard, each guest room was individually decorated to perfection by the Luna herself. They are large enough to make any neighboring Alpha feel welcome and comfortable with their own ensuite bathroom and minibar, but not obnoxiously overdone.

The third floor is for the twins. I believe there are actually four bedrooms on their floor, for the four kids their ancestor had when he built it originally. I think I heard Mateo say that one room has been turned into a study of sorts and another into a game room, then each twin has their own room.

The fourth floor is the Alpha and Luna's floor. No one but the Alpha, Luna, and their kids go up there. It's the one place they can just be. Away from all the pack business and responsibilities. Luna Ava leads us to an elevator housed behind the staircase that goes up the center of the house to her floor. It's hidden in plain sight and can be locked down like the staircase that takes you from the second floor to the twins' floor. It helps keep people from snooping around during parties.

I am actually nervous going up to the top floor. It's like being invited to the inner circle. We arrive at the top floor and the elevator opens to a small sitting room. We step out and directly across from us is a gorgeous fireplace that is surrounded by floor to ceiling bookshelves. Two oversized armchairs sit facing the fireplace. It is so inviting, I want to just plop down and get lost in a book. The room is bright white with dark wood beams across the ceiling and a dark wood floor covered in a very comfy looking area rug. It's such a contrast to the lower floors, which are more soft and neutral. The walls and furniture are pure white, the floor is darkwood to match the beams. Little accents of forest greens and navy blue are around the room, but subtly done. I am totally blown away with just the entry, I have completely forgotten why we are here.

"I thought you might like the sitting room." Luna Ava gives a small laugh as she places her hand on my shoulder. "If you ever need an escape, my library downstairs is the same, you can always come over." She gives my shoulder a squeeze before letting go and walking ahead of us. I smile, never intending on taking her up on that invitation. The little spot in her garden outside is enough for me.

The sitting room is separated from a small living room and kitchen to the left of it by a short white cabinet that houses books on the sitting room side and closed storage on the other. A large white L shaped couch faces another fireplace that has a large framed abstract picture over the mantle. Just beyond that a small kitchen filled the end of the long rectangular room. The clean white theme extends here too. White cabinets with a light gray countertop, with an island in the center matching the rest of the kitchen.

"The bathroom is just through there." She points to the right, where you can see a massive king-sized bed with a fluffy white comforter that makes it look like a cloud that I would really like to lie on. Just beyond that double doors open to the bathroom. "I will grab you both some clothes and put some snacks out. I'm sure you could use an energy boost after putting those boys in their places." She laughs as she points us through the open concept area.

"Oh shit! I think this bathroom is as big as my whole room at home!" Sierra laughs as we walk in and just starts stripping in front of me.

"What are you doing?!" I all but shout at her while turning around.

"What? We have the same parts, and the Luna and I have both seen your scars. Stop being shy, this will go faster and there are four shower heads in this shower fit for twenty. We can both shower on either side and get done more quickly. I am hungry and I want to hang out by that fireplace. When are we ever going to be in the Alpha suite again?" She lifts an eyebrow at me as she steps to the far side of the shower.

"Fine. This is really weird, though."

"What's weird? It's no different than a communal shower in the locker room."

"You forget I use the stalls for obvious reasons. This communal thing is weird." I repeat, stepping to the other side, keeping my back to her and showering faster than I ever have before. This is really uncomfortable, even with Sierra.

"You won't think it's weird when it's you and your mates." She giggles.

"What?! I have barely seen a guy naked, being around Warrior Nickolas today was awkward enough. I am not even thinking about any of that right now. And what do you mean 'mates'?"

She just steps around me and heads out of the bathroom, towel tied around her body, pretending like I didn't say a thing.

I wrap up in a fluffy white towel and walk out to see two sets of clothes on the bed. It looks like the boys' clothes, though. I figured she would have given us something of hers that would fit us better and frankly, look nicer for guests. Interesting. Sierra walks straight toward the set that smells like Sam's and starts getting dressed right away. I pull on the other set of clothes. The shorts were Olivers, the tank top (that fits me like a dress) is Dakota's, sweatpants are my brother's, and the sweatshirt is Cam's. I'm not sure why she gave me a piece from each of them. That is a question for later. At least I have layers, considering I have no underwear or a bra on now.

We both sit at her island eating off the snack tray she left us. I am more than happy to sit here and continue avoiding the guys for as long as everyone will let me. Cam called me out on my avoidance, but I can't think of anything else. I need to stay away from them. Kaley is still hurting kids and after being ignored and blatantly left out today at training and now for dinner, this week is going to suck for anyone unlucky enough to be in her path.

"Alright girls, the boys are all done and setting up the back yard, the Alpha and Beta are on grill duty as usual. Let's go relax by the pool." Luna Ava comes strutting in just as we finished eating.

"I don't know if I can eat anymore." Sierra rubs her belly. "Your snacks are too good, I couldn't stop." She giggles.

"You train as hard as these boys, you can put down plenty. Let's go." She grabs me gently by the shoulder, basically telling me she is aware of my avoidance too and will not allow it any more than Cam will.

The patio surrounding the pool looks similar to my birthday, two days ago. They must do this a lot, because it took no effort for them to get everything set up. It makes me smile to know that I can be a part of this for now, even if it's temporary, it feels good to be included and to let myself be included.

The long table is filled with people. All the warriors that helped out with training are here, warrior Nickolas and another of the Alpha King's warriors are in conversation with Delta Kyle. Gamma Brett and Gwen are talking with the guys animatedly. Whatever the story is, it's hilarious to everyone but Gamma Brett.

"We're all here now," Luna Ava announces our presence as we walk over to the table. There aren't any available seats for Sierra or I. My friend walks up to stand by Sam, and I move between my brother and Cam. "We just want to thank you all for coming to our special training today. We wish you could stay longer, these kids looked amazing, and came home tired and completely disgusting. I know that they enjoyed it immensely." She stands at the head of the table addressing everyone but not making it awkward. "Now let's enjoy some food!" She claps and everyone starts moving to the kitchen to get food and drinks before coming back to the table.

Sierra plants herself on Sam's lap. I know they both claim it's 'nothing' but the way they move together is not 'nothing.' Even I can see that. Maybe they are both just having fun before finding their mates in a couple years. They seem to get along really well and there isn't any of the drama that I see with other couples at school. Some girls are offended by everything their boyfriends do. It's like they live to be mad at someone, I don't know how they go through life like that. Sierra and Sam make it look easy, more than friends, but nothing crazy or over dramatic. I wonder what it would be like to find someone like that?

"Whatcha thinking about so hard, Smalls?" Dakota says right next to my ear. "I can almost see the steam coming out of your ears." I had stopped walking in my assessment of the seating. I didn't realize I stopped in anyone's path, lost in my thoughts.

I jumped a bit at his closeness. "Uh, nothing. Just thinking about where to sit." I lie quickly. "All the chairs seem to be taken."

"Come with me." He takes my plate so I can't argue and heads toward the table where Cam has pulled up a bench. They both sit down on it, effectively taking up the whole thing and I am super confused until Kota pulls me around in the small space in front of him and Cam, then pulls me down so I am straddling one of each of their legs, officially making me look like a toddler on their knees.

They each wrap an arm loosely across my legs and I can feel my cheeks burn at being so close to both of them like this. It's one thing for them all to throw me around when we are at training or messing around. That feels like brotherly affection, but like this, it's different. I can't even touch the ground sitting on their laps like this. It's the first time being small has made me flustered. I try to wiggle forward and put my feet on the ground so I can take a little weight off their legs, but someone grabs my knee.

"Let's not do that, Tiny. Otherwise we will have a problem you won't want to fix," Cam whispers low so only Kota and I hear. I freeze, Kota lets out a small huff of amusement. I'm not even sure if I can move at all now. Logically, I know he's just teasing me, but this is so uncomfortable. This is not a situation I have ever had to deal with before. My heart is racing and feels like it is going to pound out of my chest. I don't even feel like this on a hard workout day. And I am sure they can hear my erratic heart, making me blush harder.

"Breathe, Smalls. And relax," Kota whispers.

I do my best to sit and join in the small conversations going around the table. There are so many people here, it's almost overwhelming. I don't have to speak much, which helps a little. As everyone eats and talks, Cam moves his left arm behind my back, but Kota adjusts so he can eat with his right hand. As soon as he takes a bite though, he puts down his fork and drapes his massive arm across my lap so I essentially have a twin seat belt. I have no idea what to do, I'm afraid to move. I've never been close to a boy like this, ever.

"You feeling okay, Bite Size? You've barely touched your food," Oliver asks from next to Kota.

Why do these guys notice stupid things like my eating habits, but can't wrap their heads around shit going down at or around school?

Before I can answer, Warrior Nickolas looks over at us. "How long have you all been training together? You move like a unit. Even when you were paired up, the rest adjusted around the pair like a protection detail. It takes years for most teams to gain that."

"We have all been training since we were about five. All the guys have been doing the extra summer training at the Alpha King's training compound since the eighth grade. Sierra and Smalls joined us back in November," Kota says shrugging after swallowing a mouthful of food.

"Really?! I never would have known they joined your training recently," Nickolas replies.

Sierra snorted. "We didn't just start training. We both have been training independently as long as the guys have. We just allowed them to join the extra training that we do," Sierra chimes in and I'm glad she did, I'm not quite sure how to take his comment. It could have been either a compliment or an insult. Warrior Nickolas eases my mind with his reply.

"I wasn't implying that you were untrained. Anyone who watched knows the both of you are top tier warriors. I only meant to get that level of nonverbal understanding and have a natural trust and a connection to move the way you all do, usually takes years and a lot of real-world experience. It's impressive. More impressive knowing you all became a full group roughly six months ago." He thinks for a minute and comes back with: "What do you mean you allowed *them* to join you?" He gestures to the guys when he says 'them.'

"Well, the crazy small girl here trains like she's preparing for the next apocalypse. You saw her today. She's the only one that went two rounds, and she did it back-to-back against the future Gamma and a future Alpha and she handed both of them their asses, barely breaking a sweat. Then to wrap it all up nicely, she completed the human versus wolf training and the only one you yourself couldn't submit. And we were with you for over six hours *after* the rest of the training group left. She got there before all of us, meaning she probably did an hour of cardio before anyone else showed up. Today was a 'regular' day for her." She air quotes. "She's also the top student and helps Delta Kyle train all the juniors and pups. Yeah... we all train with her." Sierra giggles and the rest of the table follows suit. My eyes are wide, and I can feel my cheeks flush at her words. I can't look anyone in the eye, I hate having this much attention on me. Now they all know I am a freak.

Chapter 19

I just want to crawl in a hole. I know my cheeks are flaming and I focus very hard on the uneaten food on my plate. I can't make eye contact with anyone. I feel like such a freak. No teenager acts the way I do. I didn't realize I brought that much attention to myself today. Sierra isn't one to exaggerate or embellish. If she noticed all of that, who else did? I really don't like everyone staring at me either, and I can feel the pressure of their eyes on me. I have to figure out a way to change the subject.

I clear my throat abruptly. "So I heard that you are doing trials for Elite Warrior training because there are so many applicants and you're going to let high schoolers participate. Is that true?" I blurt in one breath. "Are you going to start training high schoolers to be Elite Warriors?" I'm hoping to get someone else talking and take the conversation in a different direction.

"Uh, yeah." Nickolas coughs and looks a little taken aback. "Many packs want their warriors trained well and going through the two-year program allows us to fully train Elite Warriors and get them real life experience in peacekeeping, rescue and recovery, and battle strategy. We don't just train for war and not all packs understand that, so they have been sending more and more warriors for the Elite program trying to get enforcers and shirk their obligations to train their own members, but we fail most of them out within the first two days. We now have a trial that lets us evaluate if someone is right to train in the elite program. It has become invite only."

"You fail them in two days?" Mateo asks. "Damn, isn't that harsh? It's hard to get to know someone in just two days."

"That's the point, though. To not know them, only to see them for the potential that they do or don't have to be an Elite Warrior. There are qualities we have to see that cannot necessarily be taught. It can't be personal, we all have to detach, that's the job. It's an intense line of work and we train as such. There isn't anything wrong with pack warriors, they are actually crucial to the safety and well-being of each pack, and we have trainers for them as well, but the Elite Warriors are utilized differently so they are trained differently." He finishes off vaguely, looking at all the warriors surrounding him. He has clearly had this debate before and wants to avoid a conflict.

"Do you implement the same training tactics for the summer ranked training for us that you do in the Elite training?" Oliver, of course, wants to know if he's missing out on something.

"Some things, yes. You have to remember ranked members, like you guys, have a pack to run. So while you need to know how to fight and protect your pack, the goal is to teach you how to lessen the need for that. To teach you to always be ready for anything, but conflict resolution, pack growth and camaraderie are more important here on the home front. You have and train warriors for a reason, to protect and fight on the front lines when necessary. The Elite Warriors are sent on some of the most dangerous missions. We would never send a future Gamma on a mission, for example, where the possibility of not coming home is high and that is almost the whole scope of an Elite Warrior's job description. They are required to go undercover and sometimes go dark for months or years. A certain personality is needed to do that."

"Damn, that sounds nuts and yet I have FOMO all at the same time." Sam shakes his head and everyone laughs, breaking the tension.

I almost hate to admit it, but I agree with Sam. It sounds nuts and yet it's exactly what I need. To get out of this pack and away from Kaley and all of her bullshit. We all finish eating and the adults start conversing in their own little small groups. Luna Ava makes sure everyone has plenty to eat and drink, and

I'm able to finally scarf down my food when the guys get up and leave to start their usual clean up routine. With so many people it took a few trips, so I didn't feel super weird since several other people were still picking at their plates too.

"Warrior Nickolas, how will the trials work? Obviously you are looking for recruits now, but are you also scouting for the future? Will you be doing the same two-day elimination you have at your compound?" I can't help but wonder if I could do it and get out of here sooner than I thought.

"Why are you so caught up in this warrior training? It is serious business and has nothing to do with you. As soon as you graduate, you'll find your mate, settle down, and give him pups right away. You have no need for the training you do as it is," my father chimes in. I have successfully avoided him all night. He's not looking at me, but there is no doubt to anyone who knows our relationship, who he is talking to. If any of the Elite Warriors thought his comment was out of place, they didn't show it.

I keep my face as neutral as possible. "I am just curious, that's all. Hearing how other packs do things is always fascinating. It helps to have knowledge of other pack's customs and traditions, training is no different. It will be especially important if my mate happens to be in another pack."

CRASH! An explosion of glass and metal has us all jumping.

We all turn to look at the kitchen where Oliver and Mateo are scrambling to pick up broken pieces of what I think was several plates.

"Bite Size, you really have to stop talking about leaving." Oliver huff's loud enough for everyone to hear and giving me the side eye. The rest of the guys give me a similar look.

How did he even hear me? They are like forty feet away, with water running, banging dishes around, and many conversations going on. I mean, the glass door panels that make up the patio wall of the kitchen are open completely today, since it's nice out. There is no barrier between the massive table by the pool and the kitchen, but still there are like 20 people between me and them and not everyone is listening to the conversation Nickolas and I are having. Several are talking amongst themselves adding to the noise.

"What's wrong with them?" Gamma Brett asks, turning his attention back to me. "They look ready to kill someone."

"They are not dealing with the idea that Sky is a very strong Beta and therefore probably going to be mated to a high-ranking wolf, who is possibly NOT IN THIS PACK!" she shouts over her shoulder in the direction of the kitchen. Which is followed by more banging. "They are not liking the idea or taking the news well." She shrugs.

The adults around us all laugh a bit, but I don't miss the look that passes amongst the Luna, Alpha, Gamma, and Delta. Our parents are keeping something from us, or have information we don't about mates and clearly not in the mood to share. I take a breath in and fight an eye roll.

Warrior Nickolas shakes his head and looks back at me. "To answer your question, Skylar, we will be allowing potential candidates to do some portions of the trials. We can't give you everything because some aspects need to be done in the moment. We also adapt the training regularly so things may change or evolve. We don't usually take anyone under 20, but again we don't work in absolutes. We also prefer mateless warriors. Having a mate complicates missions and puts a target on the mate, should someone want to use them as leverage or take them as a hostage."

No mate while a warrior, good to know.

"We have to head home this week, but we'll be back the following week to begin the trials here at Blue Crescent. We are bringing in potentials from the four surrounding packs as well. You should join us. It will be interesting to see you up against people you don't train with every day. In fact I insist that you join us, I think you would give a few of my team members a run for their money." He laughs and so does his partner.

I can't help but smile, I know he's just stroking my ego. There is no way I would give any of those guys a run for their money, but I like that he's trying to make me feel better after my father basically said I'm not good for anything but being a baby making machine.

"Well, all of this training talk is fascinating, but we need our friends for some well-deserved down time." Sam slides my chair back and throws me over his shoulder before I can even register what is happening.

"You guys do realize that my legs work, right? I mean, the amount of takedowns today should be proof enough." I laugh lifting my head up just as a crack sounds and my buttcheek is on fire. "Ow! What the hell?"

"No sass from you, Smalls. You would never leave a conversation about fighting willingly," Kota says low, but I know everyone heard. I laugh again as I hear Sierra squeal too, meaning someone pulled a caveman on her. At least I'm not the only one this time. I can see her brown hair bouncing to my right as I look around Sam's back, Mateo has her and the rest of the adults are laughing at us.

They walk us inside, up the stairs, and down the hallway to the hidden staircase that leads up to the third floor. Cam reaches a keypad, types in a code, then presses his thumb down. I never realized how much security they had for their private areas. I don't remember the Luna doing anything like this to get on the elevator to the fourth floor.

"What's with the James Bond security?" Sierra asks. I love that she says what I'm thinking.

"We've had a few incidents with people invading our space and the security that seems to work for our parents, doesn't stop people from trying to get to us, so we improved it." Cam looks over his shoulder towards me as I am propping my upper body on Sam's shoulders to try and look around his big head.

"Translation. They have had stalker girls trying to get up to their rooms, because one romp in the sheets wasn't enough." Sierra laughs still hanging over Mateo's shoulder, but she has her hands on his butt, pushing herself up to look around to me.

"Ding, ding, ding!" Kota says, touching his nose and opening the door to the staircase. We all head up, Sierra and I still hanging from shoulders.

"Gross, I was kind of kidding. I don't want to go anywhere near where you guys bang your little tramps." I can't see her anymore now that we are traveling single file up the steps, but I can imagine the difficulty she is giving my brother.

"First, we don't bring girls up here. Second, our rooms are cleaned regularly even if we did. Third, we are going to the media room anyway, so relax," Cam says somewhere in front of us as we hit their landing.

Sam finally sets me down and I am in a big open entryway. There is a sitting area and fireplace here, just like on the Alpha and Luna's floor. The difference here is everything is earthy colors. Dark browns, greens, and beiges. It feels more like a log cabin here. The dark brown leather couch in front of the fireplace looks completely inviting, but I ignore it and keep looking around. There is a dimly lit hallway headed off either side of the fireplace wall. I assume that's where the four bedrooms are. Opposite the fireplace is a wall of glass and a small balcony. The balcony looks out at the forest behind the house. The view is incredible. The sun has begun to set, and the trees look like they are on fire.

"Come on, Shorty, you have plenty of time to enjoy the view later. It's movie night." Mateo wraps his arm around my neck, pulling me into a head-lock and dragging me down the hallway. He pulls me into a room that's probably bigger than my bedroom at home, but barely furnished. There's a large dark gray U-shaped couch in the center facing a long flat wall. The walls are a shade of navy blue. The carpet is a marbled pattern of grays and whites. The black curtains hang at four-foot intervals along the wall. Clearly, this is designed for the best movie watching experience. Along the back wall there is a narrow bar top with four stools, behind are shelves fully stocked to entertain. Mateo marches me over to the couch and sweeps my legs out from under me, throwing me over the back of the couch right in the center.

"Umpf! Seriously, did you need to throw me?"

"If I would have left you out there any longer you would have noticed the bookshelves and started drooling, we never would have gotten you in here after that." Mateo laughs at me.

"Whatever, I probably wouldn't have turned around, the view was awesome. You would have lost me to the balcony and the sunset. Will you get me a water while you're up?" I smile as sweetly as I can at him.

"Here you go, Little Bit." Sam hands me a water bottle before jumping over the back of the couch.

I giggle as he cuddles up to my side on the enormous couch. The couch is deep enough to be considered a bed for someone my size but also almost the full width of the room. There is just enough space to walk around on either side, but clearly none of these guys walk the long way, they just jump over the back.

Mateo lands on my other side and I lean into him. Sierra moves to sit in between Sam and I which makes me laugh even more as she wiggles in.

"Hey! No hogging the girls!" Kota whines.

"You snooze, you lose, sorry brother." Sam chuckles up at him. Kota responds by smacking him in the back of the head as he jumps over the back of the couch.

This starts an all-out wrestling match on and over the couches. Sierra and I move to the corners to avoid being trampled, but laughing hysterically. Are they really fighting over who sits next to us? How old are they? Five?

Cam, Kota, and Oliver all jump over the couch tackling Sam together and all four fall to the floor. Mateo scoots back towards me laughing, but they don't leave him out for long. Someone grabs for his foot and drags him to the floor, making me squeal again, avoiding his flailing arms. I have no idea what they are even trying to accomplish with this type of wrestling. Clearly there won't be a winner, but they seem to be enjoying themselves. Arms and legs are flying everywhere and all you can hear is our laughter. It is so great to feel like this, they make me feel so good just being here in their little inner circle, the one they don't show to the rest of the world.

It hits me that I don't know if I ever would have been able to keep my distance from them for very long. They brighten my day and don't even realize it. Just as I let that thought warm me up, a prickle of ice crackles at the base of my skull. I am still going to leave. Leave this, them, and for the first time ever I find myself wondering 'what would happen if I stay?' But I shake it off. Nothing would get better for me. I need to get better. I need to be able to stand up to Kaley and to do that I need to leave. But, what if they don't want me when I get back? The prickle of ice trickles down my arms and through my chest making it hard to breathe.

I shake my head of the thoughts before they go too far as the guys slow down, all panting harder than they do at training. Cam is lying on his side holding Mateo's legs, who is lying face down across Sam's chest. Sam has a hold of Oliver's legs, who has Kota in a headlock. This is the most ridiculous thing I have ever seen. My mood is instantly lifted, they just have that effect.

"You're at a standstill, what are you all going to do?" I ask, truly wondering if they are going to just let go and call it a draw. Knowing them, there will need to be a winner.

"Who do you want to sit by, Bite Size?" Oliver asks. I knew it! He's gripping Kota a little tighter, making him laugh or cough, I'm not really sure.

Oh, no! I feel my eyes widen. I am not the deciding factor here. "I'm going to sit by Sierra, I cuddle up to her. Where are the rest of you going to be?" That is about as neutral as I can be.

Sierra laughs loudly. "See, I am better than all of you combined!"

"Nope, she's mine." Sam lets go of Oliver, wriggles out from under Mateo, and jumps up to grab Sierra around the waist, pulling her into one of the corners of the couch.

The rest of the guys figure out quickly that they need to move, and I am tackled and pulled around again. We finally settled with me in the center of the couch, sitting with my legs folded in front of me, Cam to my right with Sierra and Sam to his right, then Oliver to my left and Mateo on his other side. Kota sits on a cushion on the floor with his head tilted back on my knee. I wish I could tell you what the movie is even about, but I don't think I made it through the opening credits. I am so comfortable surrounded by the guys. The warmth radiating off all of them is enough to put me into a comfy coma. Add to that the restless night of non-sleep and the amount of effort we exerted today, my body and mind are toast.

At one point, I wake up and completely forget where I am and almost freak out when I can't move my legs. The familiar scents of the guys is what calms me down. I look around in the dim light coming from a little night light behind the bar, I'm lying in Cam's lap, and Oliver is using my butt as a pillow, his arms having my lower legs locked together. There is no way I am getting out of this hold, so I adjust my head and arms. I brush hair in front of me and notice Kota still sitting in front of me on the floor, his head tilted back in the little spoon space next to my legs. I run my hands through his hair. The silky feel sends a shiver up my arm causing me to take a deep breath in, and I swear I hear him purr and feel the rumble go through his whole body. The last thing I remember is a huge smile on my face, that I have no control over as my eyes flutter shut.

Chapter 20

When I wake up next, I am in a bed and the room is still dark with just the light from the moon shining through the sheer curtains. I stretch and take a deep breath in. This smell is all Kota. I am so comfortable, I don't want to leave, but curiosity gets the better of me. I slowly sit up and look around, interested in how he lives when no one is looking. I am lying in the middle of a king-sized bed with the softest light blue comforter I have ever felt. The room itself has minimal furnishings. He either doesn't spend a lot of time here or just doesn't like excess stuff. I find that interesting for the more happy-go-lucky twin. The walls are a dark gray. There are double doors on either side of the bed probably leading to a closet and bathroom. The wall to the right of the bed is almost all windows. The cream curtains are sheer to let in light but keep privacy. It looks out over the front drive of the house. The wall opposite of the bed has a long deep cabinet with a marble top and three floating glass shelves above it. The wall to the left of the bed has a few framed photos of the twins together and them with the rest of the guys.

I slowly climb out of the bed wanting to get a closer look at what he thinks of as things important enough to remember and display. There are no pictures smaller than an 8x10. The largest in the center is a copy of the same family picture that's down in the main hallway. One of him and Cam in sharp black suits posing together in an unfamiliar garden. Probably the second biggest is a picture of the five boys together, maybe a few years ago, all shirtless in swim trunks sitting on a log in front of a lake. They look sun-kissed, soaked, and happy, like they are having the time of their lives. I wonder if this was their first summer away. The rest are other pictures of him and the guys. As I turn to walk towards the door to see where everyone else is at, I notice a picture on the bedside table and my heart rate speeds up. It's like my body has a mind of its own and moves me towards the photo. I pick it up and just stare. I don't remember anyone taking pictures the night of my party, but it is one of all five boys, Sierra and I laughing at the table by the pool. We all had cake so it was after my embarrassing crying episode, but it doesn't look like I cried at all from this photo. There is a light in my eyes, and I truly look relaxed with them, like sitting there and having fun is something we do all the time.

I set the photo down before I can dwell on why this one is by his bed and how fast he printed and framed it. I head toward the door and, stepping out into the hallway, realize have no idea what time it is. With all the minimal stuff in Kota's room there was no clock either. I'm sure he just uses his phone. The doors to Cam's room and the office are closed. So I head to the media room to find Mateo and Oliver sprawled on the couch. Sam and Sierra must be on the guest bed, but where did Kota sleep?

I walk over to the ottoman where my phone is laying and see that it's 4 a.m. My body is just hardwired for this time of the morning I guess. I'm actually a little sore from the very long training yesterday, but I can't skip today, nor can I skip school. I'm sure my dad was pissed yesterday, but with the company we have, he won't say anything about it. I have a suspicion that's why I am here at the packhouse rather than at home, but that won't fly today.

At least Luna Ava gave me leggings and a sports bra. I can get my morning training in without going home. I can wait to go home and change when Mateo does. Being with him may lessen the fallout of skipping school and not going home at all last night.

I learned my lesson though, these boys will come find me and they will be pissed if they have to search again. So I find a piece of paper in Kota's room, write a simple note telling them I have to run and will meet them at the training grounds. I leave it on my brother's phone.

"Let's hope this will be enough 'notice' for them," I say to my wolf.

She just laughs. *"You do realize how protective of you they are, right?"*

"Yes, but is that normal? I mean, they have known me forever and have never been this 'in my personal space' before."

"They are all 19 now, maybe they are developing mate senses early."

"All of them? There is no way I am a mate to all of them, even Mateo is different and the thought of that is just weird."

"Okay, so maybe it's too early for mate talk, but I agree they are acting differently. There's something special about you, that much I can tell."

"What does that even mean? Aren't you supposed to be like old and wise? Do you know more and just can't say because the Goddess will punish you?"

"This isn't a spy novel." She laughs at me. *"There are things I know from my past humans, but no, I don't have any hidden knowledge or agenda. I am going through this right along with you and your friends."*

"They are still weird. Let's go run before training, I need to clear my head. Especially if the warriors are training us again. It's been a long time since I was this sore, so I need a slow warm-up today."

Cam and Kota are annoyed at me for not waking anyone, but in the end decided that since I left a note and told them where I was going to be...and that's where they found me... I should be forgiven. I just roll my eyes. Boys are stupid sometimes.

We get to train with the warriors this morning, but instead of leading, they join in our regular sessions. I'm selected to work with Warrior Nickolas and

Warrior Thomas much to the guys' annoyance. They probably think I am hogging the trainer's attention. After a while though, the trainers begin to work with everyone pretty equally. I'm not sure if it's on purpose, but they wander towards our group more often to give tips and correct movements. They do give Sierra and I more attention than the guys and their complaints become more vocal. Training is not as intense today, everyone is sore and slow after going against wolves yesterday, so we stick to the standard two-hour time with very little excitement.

Sweaty and laughing, Sierra and I beat the guys out to the truck. "What is taking you so long? I have a test today and I'm not a future Alpha who can get away with walking into class whenever I feel like it," I whine at the top of my lungs.

"We're coming, keep your shorts on!" Kota yells across the parking lot.

"Or don't. I'd be okay with that too!" Sam laughs right before my brother knocks him in the back of the head.

"Knock it off, asshole."

"What? This is not a new sentiment. They are both hot and you, my friend, are going to have to get over the fact that all these guys," he twirls his hand over his head, "fantasize about your beautiful sister and her equally beautiful friend. And after the ass whooping they both gave us, I'm sure the wet dreams are going to be more intense." Sam laughs as my brother chases him around the truck, muttering unintelligible curses.

Once Oliver and Cam round up my brother and Sam from the ground where they ended up wrestling, we get in the truck and drive toward the packhouse. Sam is laughing and continuing to egg on my brother. My brother is getting progressively more irritated with his friend. We pull into the packhouse parking lot, I jump out and turn to walk toward the Beta house when Cam stops me.

"Where are you going?" he asks, holding onto my elbow.

"Home, to change for school." I raise an eyebrow at him and then look pointedly at his hand on my arm. "I really can't be late, and I need clothes that are actually mine for school."

"All your stuff is here. We had it brought over this morning."

My face falls, "Wait, what?! Why is my stuff here? And why is this the first I am hearing about being moved into the packhouse? Mateo!" I shout.

"Yeah, we were supposed to talk to you about it last night, I guess we were just having such a good time, it slipped my mind." My brother looks at me, shrugging his shoulders, not looking apologetic at all.

"It slipped your mind that I was going to be moved out of my home? Do the Luna and Alpha know? Does Dad know?!" I run my fingers through my hair. "Oh, Goddess, he is going to be so pissed. Or maybe not. Did he kick me out? Is that what happened?" I look from my brother to each of my confused friends. "He hates me so much that he doesn't even want me in his house now either?" I'm starting to spiral and can feel the tears start to sting behind my eyes as I pace next to the truck. I rub my temples with both of my hands and I blink them back as best I can, I cannot lose control here. Deep breath. I just want to run to my room and cry at the thought of not having a home anymore, but, I freeze, I don't even know where I would run to now.

"Hey, hey, breathe. It's not like that." Mateo pulls me into a hug. "I wanted you out of his house, that's all. I'm tired of the way he acts towards you. You are better off here, with Luna Ava. I didn't think it would be that big of a deal." Mateo is rocking me and stroking my hair while I struggle to breathe normally.

I should be thankful that he finally sees me, sees what being around my father does to me, but I am pissed. It's just another decision that was made for me, about me, but without me. I take a deep breath, and I push him away firmly.

"You didn't think it would be a big deal to pack up my things and rip me from the only place I have ever known because *now* you don't like the way he treats me? Newsflash, asshole, that man has never loved me, never wanted me, and never will." I gesture towards my former home. "He has tolerated my existence for eighteen years and I have tolerated the neglect. Stop trying to think for me. I come and go as I please, thanks to that neglect. I eat where and when I want, thanks to that neglect. I have been on my own my entire life, you do not get to come in now and try to be the fucking hero." I stop and close my eyes, take a deep breath, then look at my brother and the rest of the guys and Sierra. "I know you all want to help, and that you mean well, but don't presume there is an easy fix to what is going on. Thank you for bringing me closer to Luna Ava, but talk to me before you do anything else that drastically changes anything for me, make sure it's what I actually want and not what makes you feel better. Now show me my room. I need to get ready for school." I turn around and walk toward the packhouse front door where I see Luna Ava standing waiting for us. Why is she smiling like that?

"Well said, my dear, teach those boys to think first instead of throwing stuff at the wall and seeing what sticks." She laughs, and Sierra comes up behind me linking her arm with mine. "But, seeing as they have already had all of your stuff moved and I anticipated you being angry with them, I will show you to your new room while you ignore them." She walks us up the stairs to the second floor and to the right around the wall that houses the elevator. She punches in a code to the third-floor staircase and leads me up.

"You put me on the third floor? With the twins?" I ask her back as we ascend.

"After some thought and your very colorful interaction with that girl yesterday, I thought it would be a good idea to not have you on a floor that literally everybody has access to. So I have your things in the boys' study."

"I don't want to take over one of their spaces." I almost fall backwards down the stairs.

"Nonsense, they both have desks in their rooms where they do homework and if they are working on anything for pack business, they do it in the Alpha's office on the main level. They never actually use this room, it gets more use when all the boys stay."

"I don't want to be in the way of that either. This is messing with more than just me, I don't want to inconvenience anyone."

"Trust me, you are not an inconvenience, and besides, this way you and Sierra have a bed here when you stay now, and the boys just sleep wherever they are anyway, they don't actually need a bed as I'm sure you figured out last night.

Besides, your room is done now, and I won't be returning anything." She stops at the door next to the media room, turns the handle, and pushes it open.

It's incredible. The layout is the same as Kota's room. From the door to the right is an enormous white four poster king sized bed. The comforter is the same pale blue fluffy cloud that Kota has. There are double doors on either side of the bed, I can see the bathroom light on beyond one of the open doors. To the left of the bedroom door is the most eye-catching fireplace surrounded by stones of all shapes and sizes in varying shades of gray and blue. A sleek TV hangs above it, but the best part is the floor to ceiling bookshelves that flank the fireplace and are completely filled. Two very familiar oversized armchairs sit in front of the fireplace. A desk sits between the door and one of the bookshelves, complete with a comfy chair holding my backpack and the rest of my things from my desk at home. Everything is white and clean, even the floor is a whitewashed wood with area rugs to tie in the different spaces of the room. Two windows let in a decent amount of light with soft white sheer curtains.

"I hope you like it, my dear. The boys really did mean well, and they know now that your relationship with your father is not as amicable as they thought. They want to see you happy and are hoping this may help that along, although they will never be able to put all of that into words." All three of us laugh. "Now get ready for school, all of your things are in the closet and Sierra, I had a few things in your size put in there as well, you know, for times like these." She winks at us. "Then we have breakfast waiting."

We both shower and dress in record time. Sierra let me try out my shower by myself, but still laughed through the door at my prude-ishness. I organize my bag, and we head downstairs to the rumble of noise I have become familiar with on Saturday mornings. I slip my bag off my shoulder and take a seat at the large island next to Sierra not making eye contact with the guys even though they have stopped talking and are all burning holes in the sides of our heads. I have forgiven them and actually love my room, but Sierra and I decided they need to fester just a little bit longer. The Luna seems to approve as she comes up and gives us plates filled with food while leaving them to fend for themselves. She starts asking how I like my new room and anything else I may need and then moves onto other mundane topics, waiting to see who will crack first. It was not who I expected.

"Are you really still mad at us, Bite Size, or just proving a point?" Oliver asks from across the room. "Cause the silent treatment sucks."

I look right at him and try not to growl. "I am mad that a major decision was made about me, without even a thought to consult me. I may let you all toss me around like a shared toy, but this is a big deal and as much as I am glad that I have some separation now from a bad situation, you didn't even think to find out if I would have any reason to not go along with the idea." They all nodded their heads. "You don't know what goes on in here," I point to my head, "it's weird for me to be wanted, for people to want me to be around, wrap your heads around that. You need to give me time, and be okay if it takes me time, to make decisions and process things. Now let's get to school, we're going to be late." I jump up and grab my bag before the conversation gets any deeper.

Chapter 21

Once we get to school, the energy in the air is palpable. Something is different today. All the kids are buzzing. What could have happened in the last hour since training ended?

Kaley runs up to the twins who are leading our group up the wide path to school, and grabs both by an arm.

"Oh. My. Goddess! Did you hear?" She punctuates every word. "The trials for Elite Warrior training are going to be at the end of this week. Isn't that so exciting? I heard the Alpha King himself is going to come down, since he heard so many great things about all of us from training yesterday."

"What does she mean by 'us?' She didn't actually do much of anything but parade around in her pink outfit," Sierra whispers to me, and we exchange an eye roll, but say nothing else.

"You guys have done such a great job training everyone and leading. I bet that's why he's really coming. He wants to see all the high ranking wolves in action. I can't wait to sit next to you while our best warriors show off their skills." She jumps up and kisses Cam on the cheek unexpectedly and turns toward Kota who steps back to avoid the assault. Cam looks like someone slapped him and he's pissed. He is rarely pissed enough to let it show on his face. Kaley doesn't seem to notice looking at all the guys and bouncing on her toes.

"We'll see. Our parents usually have plans when we have guests. Not sure what they will expect of us if the Alpha King is truly coming. This is the first we are hearing these rumors." Cam breathes out, always the diplomat.

"I'm sure they will expect the future Alphas and their Luna as well as the rest of our future leaders to be present for all of it." She looks around at the guys and giggles as she playfully slaps him in the arm.

Oliver clears his throat. "We don't know who our future Luna is, and I'm sure if the Alpha King wants people present, he will let us know who will be allowed in his presence, there are protocols for that. We're going to be late, let's go." He doesn't wait, just steps around Kaley and the rest of us follow without looking back.

Tuesday and Wednesday are a blur of activity. Training remains the same and the Elite Warriors end up sticking around because they are, in fact, running trials on Thursday and Friday. No one mentions why the timeline got moved up a week, and I am too afraid to mention it. I do want to participate if they will let me.

The school board decides to cancel regular classes after training Wednesday morning so our higher level students can spend time focusing on getting ready and the younger kids are just too wound up with excitement over the whole thing to focus. I train like normal, and the guys and Sierra grudgingly come along.

No one has confirmed whether or not the Alpha King is going to actually attend, but the high school rumor mill spread that information like wildfire. The dance is also next Saturday night so there will be several things to celebrate. Which is our current topic of discussion. We are all sitting in our usual booth at the diner devouring our usual meals. Martha always throws extra fries on my plate or brings me a milkshake, even when I don't order one. Sam is still trying to get her to give him extras.

"We have to go as a group, it's the only logical thing. No one takes a date to the spring dance because of the mating celebration, but I still want a reason to tell Marnie I can't go with her." We all laugh at Mateo. "She has told me twice a day, every day, for two weeks what time to pick her up and what color shirt to wear so we match. This bitch is crazy!"

"She's going to have a rude awakening when she's waiting and no one shows." Sam laughs.

"Jeanie tried the same thing, but I shut her down and I blocked her, so if she's tried since I have no idea." Oliver shrugs his shoulders and lets out a huff that I think might have been a rare laugh.

"What about Kaley? Has she tried to rope the two of you into taking her?" Sierra asks the twins.

"She did, I told her we were taking Skylar." Kota shrugs his shoulders. My eyes went wide, fork clattering to my plate as I choke on my food.

When I get control of myself, I shout, "You what!?!" Now she really is going to try and kill me.

"Relax, it wasn't a lie since we are all going together."

"You know you need to put a protective detail on Sky now, right?" Sierra looks between the two of them who appear to have been hit with a stupid stick. "I'm kind of joking, but kind of not. Kaley is willing to do anything to get close to the two of you including harming people. We've seen it."

"Sky will be fine. She's taken down pretty much everyone in the pack who can actually fight. I'm not worried about fucking Kaley," Kota finishes. He has no idea, it's never Kaley who gets her hands dirty and they never come at me one at a time. I completely lose my appetite and push my plate away. Sierra gives me a sympathetic look.

At least we don't have school, that will help me avoid her. Although she has actually been coming to training every morning dressed in workout gear. She doesn't appear to do much, but she's good at looking busy. We all leave looking like something the cat dragged in while she looks exactly as she showed up.

"She won't fool people for long. She's trying to impress the Elite Warriors by pretending to be involved. We just need to keep our head down and make a good impression so they will take us next year. Then we can get away from her for a bit." My wolf calms me.

"I know, I just hope that she doesn't start bullying other kids while we are gone. She's starting to get worse with her bow-to-me Luna tirades."

"Hey, Shorty, where'd you go?" Mateo looks at me, concern clouding his eyes. "You know we won't let anything happen to you, right?" This comment, of course, gets the attention of the others.

"It's not me who needs protection." I move to get up, annoyed that they are so short sighted still, even after what I told them about the bullying in school. I take the bullying so no one else has to. And I have told all the kids not to fight on school grounds since they are the ones most likely to get into trouble for it. They just come to me.

I walk toward the door and start a slow jog back over to the training field. I need to hit the gym and punch something that won't actually get hurt if I put my full rage into it. I know they are following me, but at a distance. They have at least picked up on when I need some time to myself. It doesn't mean that they actually leave me alone or understand, they just don't try to engage, and I have stopped trying to run and hide from them when I am upset. I just kind of shut down verbally. It's only been about six months since we have been hanging out and I still find myself overwhelmed at all of them being around all of the time. There are moments when I do miss the quiet and peace of being by myself.

I make the effort not to rip the door open as I reach the entrance to the gym that's attached to the main training grounds. I'm not here much since I prefer to train outdoors no matter the weather. But the weights and the punching bags are a great way to release pent up frustrations quickly. Also the guys can all be here with me without being in my way or in my space. It's the best compromise I can give them. I walk over to the stereo, hook up my phone and blast the loudest, most aggressive rock playlist I have. The guitar and drums fuel my irritation and help me channel the rage that has been slowly building up as the year has gone on.

I walk to the wall and grab a spare set of wraps for my hands and begin the irritatingly long process of wrapping my knuckles. I prefer the MMA wraps to boxing gloves, it's closer to the real thing and I tend to not overdo it since the pain comes more quickly. I get one done and struggle with the other since it's my off hand. Without a word, large hands grab the wrap and my hand and begin the process of securing my knuckles. I don't look up, I don't have to, each of these guys brings me comfort in their own ways. Oliver is the one who originally showed me how to wrap properly so I did less damage to my hands. He always makes sure I'm safe, but never tries to stop me from letting out my anger in a constructive way. That's the part of me he seems to understand and can sympathize with. When he's finished, he just turns silently and walks away, leaving me to my thoughts.

I begin a slow warm up keeping my back to them, I don't need to see worried gazes. For some reason, my silence garners more attention than when I yell at them. I circle my arms and stretch, then shadow box before fully turning to the bag. My body is still pretty loose from the workout we finished only a couple hours ago. I go through a series of punches that Oliver taught me, then move on to kicks. I have no idea how long I have been at it, but I feel a tap on my shoulder, and I turn, seeing Dakota with a set of handbags. He also says nothing, just holds up his covered hands. He's trying to bring me back to the group, one person at a time. I follow his cues with the bags, punching and kicking as fast and hard as possible. I then feel another tap and see Cameron behind me with another set of handbags. I don't think, I just go with it. I'm learning to trust them more and more. I still don't tell them everything, I don't think they will ever learn about all of the bullying, it's been too much for too long. But, I'm not actively trying to shut them all out anymore. Eventually Sierra, Sam, Oliver, and my brother all join so I'm surrounded, taking cues from each direction. They know that I need to burn out whatever emotions are coursing through me, even if they have no idea what or why.

Finally, when I am a panting, sweaty mess, I drop my arms and just look around at my friends. My playlist ran out long ago, so it is just silent other than the sound of our heavy breathing. I walk to my brother and put my forehead on his massive chest. He wraps me up in a tight hug and kisses the top of my head then lets me go.

Sierra walks up to me and throws her arm around my shoulder. "Let's go, we all need to shower, and I need a serious meal after the last three hours. You sure know how to make me earn my food, girl."

"Oh Goddess! I didn't realize how long I kept you here. You didn't have to stay with me." I groan as I take off the, now soaked, hand wraps and throw them in the laundry bin. "I know you all have other things you could be doing. You don't have to babysit me, it's not like I go far." I giggle at my own joke, but I seem to be the only one who thinks it's funny.

"Little Bit, we aren't babysitting you. We upset you. And I'm leaning more towards pissed you off based on the way my hands feel after that beating. You really hold back during training, don't you?" I chuckle as Sam dramatically shakes his hands. I didn't hit them that hard. "I'm sure everyone feels the same, but I worry about you when you go all silent treatment. You're actually really scary."

I just roll my eyes. "Kaley hates any girl in your vicinity, she wants to be Luna and she thinks I am a problem. She is actively trying to remove any problems to her goal. You implying that I am your date," I look at the twins, "is a problem." I shrug and leave it at that. They have been better about paying attention to the pack members and have shut down a lot of the unnecessary bullying that has been happening, but they have still never seen Kaley in action.

"She still won't do anything to you, she's not that stupid. She knows that we care about you, she wouldn't risk getting on our bad side by hurting you," Kota chimes in as we make our way to the truck. I share a look with Sierra, she's guessed and tried to get me to admit that Kaley is behind the worst of my torture, but I still won't confirm or deny it.

Climbing into our usual places, Sierra mutters, "You'd be surprised what some people will do for a position of power." Either the guys don't hear, or they don't know how to respond, they stay silent. Just as we all get settled all of our phones go off.

> **Luna Ava: Tell Skylar to stop training you all to death and all of you get to the packhouse. Be**

showered and dressed nicely in 30 minutes. I have clothes for the girls, they can get ready with me.

Oliver: Yes, ma'am.

Sam: Do you love the girls more than me now?

Kota: *thumbs up* emoji

Cam: We'll see you soon.

Mateo: On our way.

"We are all together, why do you all respond?" Sierra asks, looking up from her phone. I was thinking the same thing.

All the guys let out a little laugh. "What?" I ask as our phones ping again.

Luna Ava: Girls?

"She wants confirmation from all of us. She found out the hard way that some of us pretend like we don't get the message and claim plausible deniability." Cam laughs.

"It was one time! And she won't let it go," Sam exclaims.

"And now we all suffer, if we don't all respond. It's her proof, so none of us can get out of anything with her." Oliver rolls his eyes next to me.

Another ping.

Luna Ava: GIRLS!

Me: With the guys, on our way now.

Sierra: See you!

We are all laughing as we pull into the garage not a minute after sending our responses. Sierra and I rush upstairs to the Luna's floor and she is waiting for us outside the elevator.

"Quickly, into the shower please. We have no time to lose." She claps her hands, pushing both of us towards the bathroom. "And give me those things, you have been training most of the day, they are disgusting." We both laugh at her. "You two are as bad as the boys."

"Don't blame me, Luna Ava, blame the little tyrant over here. She's trying to get noticed by the warriors so she can get recruited and get out of here." Sierra blurts out as we both undress and drop our clothes in a pile, stepping into the already warm running shower. I have definitely lost my shyness with these two. I still make sure my scars are covered at all times, but the guys have seen them now, so I'm not as afraid if my shirt rides up. But, the looks they get when I catch them staring at my injuries, that guilt is something I don't enjoy.

"What? Sky, you really want to leave?" I can hear her move into the bathroom. "What about your mate and graduating school?" She leans against the sink, crossing her arms like she's stealing herself for bad news.

"They don't start taking trainees until twenty, so I won't even qualify for two years at the earliest. I just want to get on their radar, Warrior Nickolas said that anyone in high school could be invited to do the trials. That it will give a baseline for what the warriors might be looking for in the future.

"But that training is two years, what would the boys do without you?"

"They didn't even notice me until this year, and I have literally been under their noses my whole life. Truthfully, they will probably score more dates if they aren't hanging out with me. I've been thinking about doing the warrior training for a long time. There really isn't much available to me here as the Beta's second child and daughter. I am going to finish high school early anyway and even do college courses while at Elite so I won't be delaying anything or holding myself back. There are a lot of reasons for me to go and do this."

"Is your father one of those reasons?" I hear the clip in her words.

"He's not *NOT* a reason. I want to go and do something with myself, use my skills to make other people better. And if I go now, then I will be back just after I turn twenty-two and am ready and able to find my mate." I try to sound cheerful at the prospect. I turn off the water and we step out to her holding towels, looking lost in thought. I wrap the towel around myself and grab her hands making her look at me. "I promise, I'm not trying to run away, but I have to try this, I need to do something that makes me feel accomplished and right now I don't have that. I promise that I will come back." I look her straight in the eyes for a moment before she pulls me in for a tight hug.

Chapter 22

She shakes her head as she releases me. "Okay, we have to get you both dolled up a bit, this is not our usual casual dinner. Let's get started on your hair and make-up." She claps, changing the subject abruptly. I wonder who's coming to dinner. We spend the next twenty minutes getting ready to the Luna's specifications. She dresses us in light sleeveless maxi dresses: mine navy blue with a deep V-neck and wide straps, cinched at the empire waist to highlight my curves; Sierra's a muted red, accentuating her hair and eyes, with delicate spaghetti straps that look fragile. We finish with matching comfortable wedges.

As we are doing a final look in the mirror, Luna Ava walks out of her closet in a pristine white cocktail dress complete with dainty chandelier earrings and grecian sandals with straps wrapped around her ankles.

"Wow! You look amazing," Sierra beams at her.

"What? This old thing." She laughs at us. "Actually, this is my favorite dress, I have it in every color. It's so comfy and I can dress it up or down."

"Speaking of, why are we dressing up? Your backyard barbecues have never been fancy before?" I look at her in the mirror.

"We have some special guests tonight, and we are right on time to annoy all of the men!" She giggles like a teenager and we join in. She is as much trouble as Sam sometimes. She leads us through the sitting room to the elevator. It dings and we all step in.

"How are we annoying the guys?" Sierra asks, looking just as amused.

"I told them to be ready in thirty minutes. It's been an hour and a half. And they had all better be waiting with bated breath for our arrival." We laugh at her dramatics. "If I told them how long they really had, they would have taken their time to get you two back to me and I couldn't have that."

The elevator chimes and comes to a stop. The doors open to the hallway just off the kitchen and we can hear lots of chatter.

"Luna Ava, what's going on? Who's here?" I ask, a little worried that I shouldn't be here.

"With the trials tomorrow we have a few guests, so I am hosting a little get together to introduce everyone." She is super vague. She's never been purposefully vague with us before. What is going on?

My pride won't let me run and hide, no matter how much my brain thinks that is the better option. We follow the sounds of the voices into the kitchen, and it is a sight full of massive guys and a handful of women. The Alpha is in a navy blue suit with a white button-down shirt, no tie, and the top button undone. Looking business casual. The rest of the pack leaders are dressed similarly, all dark suits and white shirts. They look like they just got done with a business meeting. Delta Gwen has a beautiful dark purple cocktail dress on. I don't know if I have ever seen her dressed up with heels on before. I always thought she was pretty, but she is gorgeous in this halter dress that shows off all her strong, defined muscles. She doesn't look unfeminine, she looks like a badass. And don't get me started on her black lace up heels. The sheer patterned material looks soft and goes up tall past her ankle with thick purple satin ribbon lacing the front.

Once I stop drooling over Delta Gwen's shoes, I notice all my guys are in dress slacks and button-down shirts like their fathers. The twins, who don't usually dress alike, are in matching silver-gray shirts that have a shine to them with black pants. The silver of the shirt highlights their very different eye colors, but makes them brighter somehow. Their hair is combed back off their faces and gelled to perfection. Oliver is in all black as usual, his sleeves rolled up showing off the corded muscles of his forearms and the tattoos that are slowly beginning to crawl down his arms. He updated the severe fade and hard part of his hair giving him a mafia intensity. Sam is in a soft pink shirt, showing off his flamboyant nature without being overwhelming, golden waves tamed for once. My brother is in a navy-blue shirt that oddly seems to match my dress and slate gray pants, his straight blonde hair styled into sharp points looking stylishly messy. Everything fits these guys to perfection showing off their hard earned physiques. Man, it just got hot in here. Sierra's elbow to my ribs means she agrees.

These boys are out of their usual attire so this must be really important. As I finish my assessment of the people I know, I find three that are unfamiliar to me, standing at the far end of the kitchen talking with Warrior Nickloas and Warrior Thomas. They are all giving off an almost overwhelming aura of dominance and power. Before I can question the Luna, we are noticed by Alpha Lucas.

"Ladies! Now I understand the wait, you all look beautiful." The Alpha comes over to us and wraps his arm around Luna Ava, pulling her close, and whispering something in her ear that makes her blush. Sierra and I giggle. "Let me introduce you to our guests for the next few days. Alpha King Reginald and Luna Queen Anne and their eldest son Prince Alexander." He motions to each as they are introduced.

I can feel my pulse quicken and I'm sure everyone can hear it. The Alpha King is here? And we are meeting him. What in the hell am I supposed to do? I have no idea how to behave with royalty, this is not what I train for. All this high and mighty, classy stuff is not where I belong. I feel like it's a set up and this is why the Luna said nothing about who we were meeting.

I feel a hand wrap around my back and upper arm. "Breathe, child, it's okay," Luna Ava whispers in my ear giving me a squeeze. "They are here for the trials and since you all live here anyway, we wanted to make introductions in a less public way." She finishes out to the group at large before steering us over to the Luna Queen and the prince. "Queen Anne, I want to introduce you to Sierra and Skylar. They are some of our best fighters and brightest students."

"Oh my! Are these the two who gave you a run for your money, Nickolas?" Her sweet voice carries over the room and everyone goes quiet at her question, making me more nervous like maybe I did something wrong.

"Yes, ma'am. I've never had students with such natural talent and quick to pick up new skills. That little firecracker even left me with a couple bruises to help me remember her by." He and Warrior Thomas laugh.

My eyes go wide. I didn't know I left bruises on him, he never said I was training too rough. My face is heating more than ever. If I get any more embarrassed, I'm going to look like a tomato.

"Don't look so shocked, dear. It is an accomplishment that you were able to fight him off, let alone leave proof. He has been without a real opponent for a while now. I can't wait to see what you'll do when you are fully trained." The Alpha King chuckles at me.

I give him a small smile, I have no other reply. How do you respond to a statement like that? I think it was a complement at least.

"And Sierra, my dear, how have you been? I know spending the year here was not the most ideal situation, but you seem to have made yourself right at home."

"I have, sir, thank you." She just smiles back at him and leans into me slightly. I forgot that she actually lives in his pack and her parents work closely with him. That is why she isn't nervous, this is nothing new for her. She probably talks to him all the time.

"Wait, you took on Nickolas? And beat him?" The the prince finally speaks up. He has a deeper voice, commanding and clear, but unsure. Like he is still growing into it. He can't be much older than us by the look of his face, but he is already massive. Bigger than all the guys. That has to be the Alpha King genes at work.

I thought the twins were big guys, but he has to be pushing six and a half feet if not more and at least three of me wide. He has dark blonde hair with some natural highlights indicating he spends a good amount of time outside. His brown eyes are kind and searching, like he is looking into your soul. He has a toned face and sharp jawline. I can see the muscle he has packed on, even through his three-piece forest green suit. He is very handsome. I'm sure like our guys, he has girls fawning all over him. I fight an eye roll at all of them and their good looks. I did not 'beat' Warrior Nickolas, he just couldn't submit me. I can't seem to form those words, so I nod my head at his question like an idiot. I can feel his body heat radiating off of him and it is comforting and intimidating all at the same time and my brain feels fuzzy.

"My friend is just modest, she is the best warrior in the pack. She's even better than our Delta and his current trainers." Sierra looks at Delta Kyle and winks.

"You're not wrong," he confirms, walking over to us. "This girl puts me to shame as far as her training time each day goes, and she does it all while maintaining her extremely high grades and helping me train our pups."

"Really?" Prince Alexander asks.

"I just like to train, that's all." I whisper and shrug my shoulders. "It's really not that big a deal. I don't like a lot of down time." I am painfully aware of my awkwardness. I don't know where to look. Am I allowed to make eye contact with them? My arms are hanging by my side all weird, so I try clasping them behind my back and that just seems more strange. I have no idea what I am doing and fidgeting is not helping my anxiety.

"Time to eat." I am saved by Luna Ava calling us to the formal dining room, we all head that way slowly. Some separate conversations have started and I feel less exposed. I fall to the back, unsure where I should be in this group.

The long rectangular table is set beautifully with a white linen tablecloth and a gold runner down the middle. Low candle and flower arrangements are dispersed along the runner, low enough that conversation can be had across the table. The food smells delicious as always, set in silver warmers on a buffet along a back wall with omegas waiting to serve us. I have never seen anything so fancy in my whole life.

I grab Sierra's hand, silently pleading for her to stay close to me. She gives my hand a little squeeze and then smiles at me. As we make our way around the table, a soft hand touches the small of my back startling me. My body reacts with a quick inhale of breath as I turn to see who's touching me.

"Would you mind sitting next to me? I would love to hear more about what you and your pack do with training your young pups." Alexander is really close to my ear.

I hear a huff, but when I look around, I'm not sure who it came from. I nod my head, still too stupid to form real words. I blink and clear my throat. He wants to talk pups and workouts, I can do that. "Sure, I would love to hear more about the Elite Warrior training and some of the battle strategies you use." He does not remove his hand from my back, instead guiding me to one end of the table where the Alpha King and Luna Queen are standing.

"Does everyone have a seat? Perfect! Let's eat." Luna Ava moves around her chair as Alpha Lucas holds it for her. The Alpha King does the same for his queen. Delta Kyle helps Gwen, Alexander holds my chair for me, and Sam has Sierra's next to me. The rest of the guys wait until all the ladies are seated before they take their own. It's so strange to watch them in such a formal setting and to perform the protocols like it's second nature.

Our first course is soup, and I am so hungry I don't really pay attention to anything around me, catching bits of different conversations here and there, but my focus is on slowly eating, so I don't look like a barbarian, until I have finished my whole bowl.

When I look up, I notice the rest of my friends have finished theirs as well. We are all famished after the extra 'angry' training I made them do. I kind of feel bad now.

"So how do you get your pups to train? Nickolas says you start with them at five years old. That's really young." Alexander looks at me from my left.

I can see Nickolas and Thomas across from me waiting for my answer too. "We turn everything into games mostly. They love the idea of challenges so we time everything or give them a number to hit and they have goals each week. We have also adapted a lot of normal games to fit with what we want for training like Tag, Capture the Flag, Hide and Seek, things like that. It seems to work for us." I shrug again like, it's nothing.

"Let's be clear, she adapts the games to fit what I want them to learn each week. They also seem to like that she is closer to them in age. She's thirteen years older than our youngest pup but pretty close to their size." He and all my friends laugh at me. I roll my eyes. The short jokes will never go away. "They respond better to her than adult trainers most of the time," Delta Kyle adds to the conversation from next to Warrior Thomas. "We all have our strengths and weaknesses as trainers, hers is keeping the young ones engaged and wanting to return."

"I would love to see that sometime." Alexander smiles at me.

"Sure, the training is open for anyone to come watch." I smile back and I swear I hear a low rumble. Alexander's eyes lift from mine to look over my shoulder at someone, but when I follow his line of sight, no one is looking our way.

Dinner continues with a salad course, then the main course with steak, asparagus, mashed potatoes, and the most melt-in-your-mouth dinner rolls I have ever had. The conversation flows easily, and I really like the Alpha King and Luna Queen, they seem so much more down to earth than I thought they would be. I hear a little more about Elite Warrior training and about the ranked training the boys go through. It's fun to hear stories from the Alpha King about all my guys and Prince Alexander from their time together. A strange feeling comes over me when I notice for the first time how far away all my guys are seated, though. It didn't hit me right away since I was so interested in hearing from the prince and Warriors Nickolas and Thomas about training. But, now the distance is becoming uncomfortable.

The Alpha King sits at the head of the table on our end, the Luna Queen to his left, and Prince Alexander to his right. Warriors Nickolas and Thomas sit next to the Luna Queen, Deltas Kyle and Gwen next to them. Oliver, Kota, and Luna Ava finish out their side of the table. I am next to Prince Alexander, Sierra to my right, followed by Sam, Gamma Brett, Mateo, our father, and Cam. At the other head of the table is Alpha Lucas. I have to wonder if we were purposely spread out.

As we are being served dessert, a luscious chocolate cake with chocolate drizzle and vanilla ice cream on the side, Sierra addresses the prince next to me.

"So, Prince Alexander, are you done with school now? What are your next big plans since you don't seem to be jumping at the throne right away?" I look at her wide-eyed. That was kind of a bold question to ask the prince.

He just laughs. "No, I don't plan to overthrow my father anytime soon, he's doing just fine. And it's Xander to my friends." He looks at her then at me before continuing. "I did graduate college this year, so my next big task is to find my mate and the next Luna Queen." He looks at me again for a little too long. I look away then around the room and Oliver and Kota do not look happy, but are trying to hide it. Xander clears his throat, but I don't look back at him when he continues. "I plan to travel a bit, get to know the packs in our kingdom and continue training with my father."

"That's the task of all leaders, isn't it? Find the mate the Goddess designed for you, to make you the strongest and best you can be," The the Alpha King says, breaking the little tension that has developed in the room, slapping his son on the shoulder. Sierra keeps the conversation surface level after that. Something happened, but I have no idea what. Just another thing to ask her about.

"Why don't we have drinks on the patio?" Luna Ava asks the group at large once we are all done with dessert.

"I would, Luna, but I have a series of trials to set up in the morning. I think we are going to call it a night." Delta Kyle stands and helps his mate up. "Sam, are you staying tonight?"

"Probably. We will head over to the trials together in the morning, and no, Little Bit, none of us are training in the morning, including you. We have done so much extra training with you, my clothes don't fit." He holds up his arms and flexes in his dress shirt, which is threatening to shred any second. The rest of the guys, Sierra, and I laugh. He's not wrong though. For being the leanest he has probably added 20 more pounds of muscle since they have started keeping up with my training schedule. The rest of the guys have gained too, but it's just more noticeable on Sam.

We all start to get up and head toward the back patio still laughing at him. "You made them all look like that?" Xander asks, surprised.

"No, they made themselves look like that, by keeping a training schedule that just happens to match mine."

"Don't be modest, Bite Size. You kick our asses now and we have all improved. We had to get better if we didn't want to be shown up by you at every turn. It was getting embarrassing." Oliver walks next to me and throws a possessive arm over my shoulder, pulling me close. "This is definitely your fault." He flexes the arm around my neck, and gives me a rare half smile. This one is less sweet and more like he's up to something, though.

"You all seem to call her something different. How...*endearing*." I hear the sarcasm. "Does that bother you at all?" Xander looks at me from my other side, Oliver's arm still firmly planted on my shoulder as we make our way to the covered patio seating. Xander sounds a little like he's trying to gaslight the guys.

Chapter 23

"Not really. It started as a joke and then just stuck. They aren't making fun of me, just stating the obvious size difference and now that all of them have put on more muscle it's even worse and I don't think any of them are done growing, but I'm pretty sure I am." I roll my eyes at Sierra who laughs. Once we catch up to everyone else, Kota grabs me around the waist and pulls me onto his lap. Cam is on one side of him, Mateo takes the other. Sam sits next to Cam, pulling Sierra into his lap and I can feel Oliver come up behind Kota and I. There is no room for Xander to sit anywhere near me now. I can't decide if the gesture is cute or frustrating.

"What is going on?" I link all five of them.

"He's just getting too close for comfort," Kota responds.

I chance a look at Sierra and see she is fighting a smile. This whole situation is totally funny to her, so it can't be all bad, right?

"Yours... or mine?" I'm feeling a little feisty right now and go with it based on her reaction.

"Both." I don't love Oliver's clipped reply. I roll my eyes.

"He just got too comfortable too fast. And like he said, he's looking for his mate, he's going to snuggle up to any single female right now." If Cam is trying to placate me with logic, he just lost.

"So, you are saying he's doing the same thing as all of you? And what guy says 'snuggle'?" No response.

I get up from Kota's lap. "Where are you going?" He jumps forward to try and grab my hand, but I pull out of his reach before he can.

"The bathroom. Is that okay with you? Or is my leash not that long?" I say keeping my voice low and calm while raising my eyebrow at them, looking each of the six guys in the eye, challenging what they are doing openly. No one replies. I look at Sierra, silently asking for her to join me.

She gets up smiling the biggest smile ever. Oliver goes to get up too. "Nope, you sit right back down. And if any of you try to follow me, I will throat punch you into the pool." As I start to turn, Xander makes a move to get up. "You too. Sit down. You all can finish your pissing match while we're gone." I roll my eyes, and Sierra openly laughs now, and I think I heard laughter come from the adults sitting on the other side of the patio.

Sierra and I walk into the house and straight toward the stairs. I know there are bathrooms on the main floor, but I have to figure out what is going on and I can't do that where everyone can hear me. And I just need a break from all their posturing. We head straight up to my room.

"What the hell was all of that?" I ask her as soon as my door is closed, and locked, for good measure. I fling my hands in the air.

"Your boys are jealous. You have never talked to a guy outside of our group before."

"What do you mean? I talk to guys at training all the time." I rub my forehead.

"Not like this. This time it was a guy they have no control over, openly flirting with you and they got a rude awakening. They like you in this little bubble and you keep talking about wanting to leave, this is the first time they saw that idea as something real and they went into possessive mode. But they also have to follow protocols with the Alpha King here. They couldn't argue about where you sat since Xander claimed your attention. You will have a shadow the rest of the time they are visiting. I don't think any of the guys have ever been jealous and helpless to do anything about it before. It's an amusing look on them." She giggles.

"I don't understand, we are all just friends. No guy has ever looked at me before because I am nothing to look at, this is so weird. I have no idea what I am doing, Sierra. He was flirting?!" My voice goes up an octave asking the question and pacing around my room.

"Oh, my poor sheltered girl. I don't understand how you don't see it. The guys are not the only ones who have changed. You just don't look in the mirror much. You are gorgeous and strong and smart and independent. You are probably the only girl who hasn't thrown yourself at any of them, the prince included. You treat them like normal people, not fawning over them like celebrities. You aren't afraid to publicly humiliate them, it's refreshing for them. I'm sure, just now, was the first time someone, who isn't his mother, has put the prince in his place in front of other people. Same for the guys. No one tells them 'no' or to stay put. You are on fire tonight." She starts laughing again.

"Okay, but what do I do about it? And stop laughing at me. This is so weird. I don't want to offend anyone or hurt feelings." I flop back on my bed, my long hair fanning out around me. "I have no experience with boys like this, give me training and beating the crap out of them any day."

"Well, you can go down, sit back on Kota's lap, or whoever caveman's you first and keep having awkward conversations or we can go talk to the adults and make the boys sweat and get their acts together. Either way, I'm going to enjoy myself." She giggles and claps her hands.

"Ugh! Let's go." I have no idea what I am going to do with her suggestion. Once we get back outside, though, my decision is made for me.

"Skylar! Come here, kiddo, I have a question." We turn and walk towards the adults, leaving the boys watching out retreating backs. "What do you know about border security?" Warrior Nickolas asks when we are close enough.

"A little, I run our border every day and see patrols. I know some areas are more heavily monitored than others. I guess it all depends on the terrain, if the territory on the outside of the borders is open or belongs to a neighboring pack, things like that. Why?" I sit in a chair next to him at their table, Sierra next to me. It's almost strange to not be in someone's lap out here.

"Let me put a hypothetical scenario out there and see what you think."

He spends about ten minutes moving things from the table around giving me general topography. Furthest from me is a crescent shaped mountain range with a lake at the base, what he called the packhouse is to the left of the lake, butting up to the curved end of the range. He hesitates when he says 'packhouse' so this is code for something important. From the packhouse he describes different structures that fan out towards a forest line, like a sun burst. Just beyond the forest line are small clearings, miles apart, each with a different function, but he doesn't elaborate on that.

"So the dilemma is rogue attacks are coming at different times and from different locations. How would you set up patrols to guard an area like this? With the obvious goal of keeping them away from the packhouse, but also keeping innocent people in these other areas safe."

"That's it? That's all the info and you want a full patrol schedule?" He just nods his head with a little smirk on his face. Alpha Lucas and the Alpha King are both watching intently giving nothing away. "Okay, I'll bite, it's like a pop quiz in battle strategy class." I shrug, studying the table.

"You're in a battle strategy class?" my father asks.

"Yeah. I needed to fill my day since most of my graduating requirements are already done. I'm in several senior specialized classes." I shrug, not taking my focus off of the table. "How many are on patrol at any given time?" I look up at Nickolas, giving my dad the brush off.

"You can have as many as you think you would need to run rotations."

Again, vague. Apparently, I am being tested. Alright, let's see.

"Well, there are a lot of variables that I don't have that would help in this situation." I side eye him. He gives me nothing. "For instance, what is the mountain range like? Is it all forest and trees? Easy to climb? If that is the case, then I would put up watch structures with motion sensors sporadically a minimum of a mile radius out and go up to five miles if the terrain is easy considering how close the packhouse is to the base of the mountain. If it's all rock and pretty open, less patrol would need to be done from the mountain itself since it could be monitored from the ground and extra resources could be used elsewhere, but motion sensors in both cases would be helpful." I look at the example he set up again. "I would also run patrols around the lake and have more or less depending on visibility, but it being at the base of the mountain would make it easy for an enemy to sit in the caves and crevices of the mountain, here," I indicate, "and observe across the lake, without being seen and the water would dim or mask the scent."

I grab a drink of water as I analyze the 'forest' portion of his example. I am really getting into my territory dissection, this is way more my speed than all the flirting talk from earlier.

I stand up to get a better viewpoint. "The clearings are obviously serving some sort of purpose, meaning pack members are probably here, but there is so much space that a trained person would be able to get past undetected. I would run patrol patterns in an arc here," I point from the East to the West side of the map, "As as well as patrols running North and South in groups of two or four. Having their paths staggered in waves ensures that way no one area is unprotected for long, and the full entire grid is covered. If you are having rogue attacks regularly, I would have patrol check in every hour, but from a different point in their path to keep communication open and minds sharp, especially at night. If there are specific paths in or out of the territory, I would have those monitored too. It's easy for hostile wolves to keep their bearings if there is a road or river to follow. And even if they know you have hidden warriors, they will focus on the ones that can be seen first. I would also use motion sensor cameras that can be monitored at the packhouse or other central location. More than one set of eyes is always better. Your warriors can use them if for some reason they can't mindlink, giving a better early warning."

I look up to see Alpha Lucas smiling his gentle smile, the one he wears when he is in 'dad mode,' Luna Ava and Luna Queen Anne look impressed, but not surprised.

"Is that right? I know I am being tested right now, and you are all staring and making me anxious." I am wringing my hands and have to bite down on my lips to keep from trying to fill the silence with nervous chatter.

The Alpha King responds first, "Very impressive, my dear. And you have no training in border security or patrols?"

"No, sir. Only the little we have started studying in battle classes."

"Bah! None of this 'sir' stuff." I jump at his exclamation. "Alpha Reggie to you. And you seem to have a natural eye and realistic notion for what is needed. Let me ask you this, what would you do if you were protecting the Luna in an attack on this territory?"

"Where is the attack coming from, sir?" He looks at me, eyebrows pressed together. My eyes go wide, unsure of what I did to earn that look for a moment, then it dawns on me. "Sorry, Alpha Reggie."

"Let's say multidirectional attack. One from the mountains, one from the east entrance, and one from the west just beyond the lake."

"Does the packhouse have a safe room?" I ask without looking up from the 'map' made of glasses, bottles, napkins, and phones on the table, making a mental picture for myself.

"Let's say no safe room."

"I would have the Luna suppress her Aura and shift, we would run up the middle, trying to avoid the attacks from the East and West. Most Lunas would want to stay and fight or care for their pack, but keeping her safe keeps the pack fighting. She can keep morale boosted via the mind link as long as she is in range on the territory. If her Aura is suppressed then it will take longer for the rogues to find her, giving warriors time to fend off the attack. More than likely, if the Luna is the target, the attackers will check the packhouse first and look for a safe room for her to be holed up in, that will also buy time if there is a rumor of a safe room planted.

"What if there is an actual safe room?"

"I would hope that it has two exits, like a rabbit hole, otherwise they can just sit on it, keeping her hostage and wait for her to need food and water. I would also hope it's built into the mountain, giving you options for exits. If your architect was skilled, it could be a tunnel system that needs to be navigated like a maze to find." I'm just letting my imagination run wild now. "You could also have more than one option for an exit with the maze system. It could double to protect non-warriors of the pack in any type of emergency if food is stored and you can locate a source of clean water. It could be a place to keep your pack safe or as an evacuation point." I look up smiling at all of the possibilities.

"Well now, I'm going to have to see how creative my architect can be." Alpha Reggie chuckles at me.

"Wait, what? The Royal Pack?!"

"This is the basic makeup of the Royal territory and you, my dear, have picked apart our entire protective strategy. Your fan club back there has spent the last two summers here at the training grounds." He points to a clearing close to the lake and I think of the picture in Kota's room. I take a slow breath, my eyes go wide, and I can't utter words. I sit slowly as I process what he just told me. Did I offend him? Did I just embarrass myself?

"Don't look like that. You didn't say anything wrong, but as you said— having a fresh set of eyes always brings new light. Sometimes we get so familiar with things we don't actually see them. Like you mentioning only one exit in the safe room. It seems common sense to have multiple exit points the way you explained it, but no one else thought of it. We have always put focus on the outer border, and that has worked just fine. The mountain has never been thought of for its extended use either. I'm not so full of myself as to think I have all the answers all of the time. So thank you for your insight, my dear." He smiles at me, and I can't help but smile back. "Well, this has been a very enlightening evening, but we are off to bed. My patrols have joined yours, so just let someone know if you plan on coming or going in the wee hours of the night." He looks right at me and winks. My eyes go wide. He just called me out!

"Nope." I jump at the voice behind me. "Tiny has no plans in the morning. Goodnight, sir," Cam says, then reaches for my hand, something none of them have ever done. I take it and stand, saying a quick goodnight to everyone while letting Cam lead me and the rest of our group inside. Just before we cross into the kitchen, I hear Alpha Reggie ask, "Do they always flank her like that?"

"Uh huh, and I don't even think they realize that they are doing it…" I don't hear the rest of Alpha Lucas' comment as we make our way through the kitchen. We head up the main staircase, Cam is not letting go of my hand under any circumstances.

"Hey, Skylar." We stop just before the door to the third floor and turn around to see Prince Xander right behind our group. "Can I walk you to your room?"

"She stays on the third floor," Kota responds a little curtly. Xander's eyes snap to him.

"Oh, okay. Um, who are you sitting with during the trials tomorrow?"

I can feel the testosterone flex in the air around me. "Don't," I whisper to the guys as Cam's hand tightens around mine. To Prince Xander. "I'm not sitting with anyone tomorrow." He looks confused, so I elaborate. "I'm joining the trials, so I will be on the ground with the warriors. I'm not really the sit-in-the-stands-and-watch type." I keep the conversation going as if we aren't being eavesdropped on by all of my friends. "We'll see you tomorrow for breakfast." I smile at him and place my freehand on his forearm for a brief second. I do like him and had fun talking to someone other than my usual guys. He really is very handsome, but I just don't have that same pull I have with the guys. It would be nice to be on friendly terms with the Alpha Prince, though. "Goodnight, Prince Xander." I smile one more time and turn back to the door before anything else embarrassing happens tonight.

Kota lets us into the stairwell, and we all file up. "Man, I am beat. What time do we have to have Little Bit down to the training grounds?" Sam asks from somewhere behind me, breaking the silence.

"Warriors arrive at 10 and the trials start at noon," Cam calls back. "Oh, and Tiny, Delta Kyle wanted me to tell you, that you are not allowed anywhere near the training grounds before 9:30, so you are hereby forced to sleep in and lay around, no matter what time you get up." A soft chuckle runs through him.

"So, what do I do when my body decides 4 a.m. is the time I need to be up? I will go nuts, just sitting around waiting for the rest of you to come out of your comas," I ask a little flippantly.

"Come find one of us and we will *snuggle* you back to sleep," Oliver whispers in my ear and it gives me goosebumps, but I'm not sure if it's a good or a bad thing.

"Alright, Tiny has her room officially now, someone can crash in Kota's room, two of you on the couch and Sierra, you can decide who you're spooning with tonight." Cam laughs again.

"Where is Kota going to sleep?" I ask after doing the math in my head.

"We usually share," the twins say in unison.

"We don't spend many nights apart, never have," Kota explains when he sees my questioning look. Now I know why I was able to sleep in his room the other night.

"Okay, goodnight, boys, Sierra," I say before turning towards my room. It's so crazy to think I have a room in the packhouse. But I don't dwell on it. I need to get away from all the masculine energy.

Chapter 24

"Wait up there, Shorty." Mateo pulls me into a hug from the back and kisses the crown of my head like he did the other night. Sam and Oliver hug and kiss me on either temple too. Sierra walks by me, laughing.

"They can't even let you go long enough to get some sleep. I need to get out of this dress and into some pj's, I'll see you when they are done with you." She squeezes my arm gently before going into my room.

Mateo, Sam, and Oliver all walk away to wherever they are crashing for the night. I turn and see it's just the twins and I left in the hallway. They both have their shirts untucked and hands in their pockets, standing side by side looking almost shy in their slightly messy hotness. I take a breath and wait just a moment to see what they will do. When they make no indication of moving, I decide to tease them a little.

"What? No goodnight kiss from my future Alphas? I'm a little disappointed."

Neither move, but they do look at each other before bringing their focus back to me. Then they both stalk the measly four steps towards me, Cam stands in front of me, Kota at my back. They are pressed so close to me, I could probably pick my legs up off the ground and I wouldn't fall. Ever so slowly, they both bend down and touch an ear with their lips. My breath catches in my throat.

"When we kiss you…"

"It won't be on the forehead…"

"In the middle of the hallway…"

They both run their noses from my ear, down my neck to my shoulder and back up, perfectly in sync. Then they both slowly stand to their full height, but don't move away from me.

"Breathe, Skylar," one says, I have no idea, I'm so disoriented. I take a deep breath in and realize I have been going without oxygen for a bit as my chest starts to heave like I have been jogging. "You also have to let go, if you want us to leave." A husky low sound sends chills down my body again.

I focus my eyes and see at some point during that interaction I grabbed a wrist in each hand, one in front of me and one behind. When did that happen? I don't even remember moving. I slowly let go of my vice grip, clearly trying to keep myself upright. Once free, they both slowly move away from me towards Cam's room, hands still in their pockets. They never once touched me.

"If you have trouble sleeping, you know where to find us," Kota says and winks over his shoulder.

I shake my head a little and turn back toward my room, where Sierra is staring at me through a crack in my door with the biggest smile on her face. When I get close enough, she grabs my arm, drags me inside, and slams the door.

"That was *THE* hottest thing I have ever seen!" She she squeals. "And they didn't even lay a hand on you. What did they say?"

"Umm, that when they kiss me, it won't be on my forehead in the middle of the hallway," I whisper like a question, still a little dazed.

"Oh Goddess, do they have it bad for you. No wonder they went possessive on you tonight. The Alphas found out they have competition and are staking their claim."

"What? No! Why would they do that? We are friends, it would just be weird, if something happened."

"But don't act like that little interaction didn't excite you. You are still in a haze. I'm not sure if I have seen them flirt like that with anyone."

"What do you mean like that? They are surrounded by girls all of the time." I'm trying to shake myself out of this brain fog they put me in. I head to the closet to find something to sleep in. As I'm digging through the drawer for a pair of shorts, she responds.

"Two on one." Did she just purr? "They don't flirt or target a girl together like that, and I spend more time with them around other people than you do."

"Oh." I can't think of anything else to say. "Are you going to stay here with me or do you want to go stay with Sam?"

"Maybe a bit of both. We need to unpack this new development with the twins, then I for sure cannot sleep without Sam, but he's patient, he'll wait up all night if I want him to." She shrugs and we both laugh.

We crawl in my bed and under the comforter and she talks me through the finer points of understanding boy behavior. I don't really care. No, that's a lie, I do care but I'm not ready to say that out loud and I don't really understand, but it is fun to talk about something that isn't training or homework for a change so I just listen. It's the first time I've ever just sat here and been a teenager. It's a mind-blowing concept for me. It's not long before I am dozing off in my cloud of a bed. She kisses me on the forehead and says good night as I drift off to sleep.

I roll over and stretch, I have no idea what time it is, but there is no light coming through my window. I can only assume it's my usual early wake-up. I get up, use the bathroom, and then wander around my room. My room. Just the phrase makes me feel light and happy. I can't believe Mateo brought me here to get me away from our father, to give me some level of peace and acceptance. I try to read in my new lounge chair, but I am too antsy. I need to get up and move, but I believe Sam's threat and I don't dare try to leave to go for a run. I could go see the twins, they said I 'know where to find them' if I can't sleep. Sierra confirmed they were definitely flirting with me, which means so was Oliver, and Sam always flirts and that makes butterflies erupt in my stomach.

I have never thought of any of the guys like that before. Sure, they are all drop-dead gorgeous and they all have the egos to back up their looks, but I never considered anything more than friendship with any of them. Until last night...when the twins invaded my personal space in a way that left my brain fuzzy and my legs weak and neither of them even touched me. Come to think of it, of all the guys the twins touch me the least. Mateo, Sam, and Oliver will put an arm around my shoulder or hold my hand when we walk. In fact, someone seems to always have physical contact with me. The twins are just there in proximity unless I am on one of their laps with a lazy arm around my back. Huh.

I move to my door hesitating for only a second so I can't talk myself out of this. I tiptoe towards Cam's room, not wanting to be caught sneaking to them. I don't know why it bothers me, we all cuddle together and basically sleep wherever, but now it feels different. I get to his door and hesitate. Do I knock? Just walk in? I have no idea what I am doing or how any of this works. I shake my hands out, take a deep breath and turn the handle. Don't overthink this. The door slowly opens, and I peek around it. In the dim light from the hallway, I see the setup is exactly the same as Kota's, same color, layout, everything, even the pictures on the walls. This twin thing is interesting. I look over at the massive bed in the middle of the room and see two of the most beautiful men ever. With their eyes closed, they are identical in almost every way. If you don't really know them, there's no way to tell them apart like this. Kota is in dark shorts, lying on his stomach, his right arm up over his head, left down by his side. His playful smirk is long gone, and he just looks sweet. The muscles in his back and shoulders are defined and show off his strength even in this relaxed state. Cam is in dark shorts as well, but laying on his back. One arm over his eyes, the other across his stomach, thumb tucked into his waistband. His usual serious look is relaxed. And those abs, oh Goddess help me.

The small space between them seems to be calling to me. I pad toward the foot of the bed and slowly crawl over the comforter that's piled between the two of them. I can feel their body heat from here and their combined scents of citrus and cinnamon is heavenly. My pulse instantly slows, like my body knows I'm safe. I move all the way up to the pillows and lie down on my side, facing Cam. I take another deep breath in and my eyelids droop. I melt into the bed, both Cam and Kota shift. Kota, against my back, and he wraps his arm over my stomach and buries his nose in my hair. Cam turns to face me, glides his hand down my side and rests his large hand on my hip with his fingers extending toward my butt. His head leans towards me, lips grazing my forehead. That's the last thing I remember before I am dead to the world.

"WHERE IS SHE?! IF SHE LEFT WITHOUT US, I AM REALLY GO-ING TO KILL HER!" The door to the room bangs off the wall as my eyes fly open and my breath hitches, but I can't move anything.

What? Where am I? I take another deep breath and try to look around. Then the familiar scent settles in and I remember, I crawled in bed with the twins when I couldn't sleep last night. Oh jeez, I crawled in bed with the twins! What was I thinking? Before I can move or say anything, a gravelly voice speaks up.

"Are you sure you looked everywhere for her?" Cam asks from in front of me. His breath fans over the top of my head that moves the baby hairs slightly.

I can hear footsteps pacing the room. "Yes. Her room is empty, she's not downstairs in the kitchen or in the Luna's office. We told her not to go without us, it's 8, where else would she be if she didn't leave?" I flinch hearing the time, I never sleep this late. How did I manage that? My brain is running a mile a minute as I start to get uncomfortable at how close and intimate this feels. Hands flex on my hip and on my stomach. I stop moving.

"I'm sure if you take a deep breath and calm down, you will be able to find her," Kota says behind me. I can feel him huff into my hair behind me and I know he is smiling. They are clearly enjoying my brother's torment, and I have to admit, it is kind of funny. He hasn't noticed I'm sandwiched between the two people he's freaking out to.

"Fine." I could hear him taking a deep breath. "Wait!... What the fuck is going on?!"

Both twins are laughing now, but they haven't moved from our pretzel position. "Okay, you've had your fun with him, but I need to pee, so let me go," I tell them, pushing up from Cam's well-defined chest, covering up my awkwardness with my own laugh.

I climb down between them, step off the bed softly, and walk past my brother not looking at anyone. I keep my gaze down as I walk past the rest of our friends hovering in the hallway. I can imagine what Sierra's knowing grin looks like, Oliver's confusion and Sam still waking up. I don't want to know, I just move past all of them, into my room and straight to the bathroom to do what I need to do to get ready for trials.

I'm ready in 20 minutes, I couldn't stall any longer than that. I pull on black leggings, a black sports bra, and black tank top that has a high neck. I don't know what the trials are going to consist of, but I'm sure the more of my skin that is protected the better. I pull my long blonde hair up into a high ponytail and throw on my new tennis shoes. Somehow, the Luna knew I busted through my last pair. I walk out of my room to see all my friends waiting for me on the couches in the sitting area ready to go. No one says anything about where they found me this morning. We just walk to the stairwell and head down to the kitchen for breakfast.

"You seven really do travel as a pack, don't you?"

"Good morning, Alpha Reggie!" I say, walking to the island covered in food. "Good morning, Luna Anne, Prince Xander." I acknowledge them as I get closer. The rest of my friends form a line behind me to get food, and I follow Cam and Kota to the large kitchen table set near the patio windows. We all slide into our own chairs and dig in.

"Are you really going to go through the trials today?" Prince Xander asks. "They are brutal."

"Yep. I'm too young to join, but the more experience the better for when I am able to fully participate."

"I don't know if I'm going to be able to watch that." He looks like he might be sick. He barely knows me, why would he be this emotional about it?

"Now, son, don't go giving anything away. No advantages to our young friend here. We can't be showing any favoritism." Alpha Reggie winks at me and I smile, but start to feel an unease set in.

I have to force food down after that little interaction. Who knows how long the trials will be and if we will get food or water during it, but I am not hungry at all. That's new. I'm actually nervous for something. I don't know how to feel about that. At 9:30, I stand up from my chair and I look at everyone.

"Okay, I have held off as long as possible, I need to go or I am going to go crazy. Delta Kyle can deal with me being 30 minutes early." Everyone smiles and I turn towards the door before they can laugh at me. I am already nervous, I can't handle the playful teasing this morning. I just need to get there and get my head in the zone. Just when I think they are all going to let me have my space, I'm scooped up and thrown over a shoulder. The thick honey scent tells me it's Oliver.

"You didn't think we were going to let you head to the trials alone, did you? You are about to do something massive without us. We are going to go with you as far as we can."

"Can I at least be cavemaned in an upright position?" I giggle at him.

"Fine, you can climb on my back, but you are staying with me. The twins got you all night." Is that jealousy?

Without putting me on the ground, I scramble to his back. My legs are too short to lock around his waist, so he links his hands together under my butt for me to sit on. I wrap my arms around his neck and rest my chin on his shoulder.

"Are you jealous?" I tilt my face to his to see his reaction.

Nothing on his face changes, but his skin ripples with goosebumps as he turns just enough to look me in the eye. "Maybe."

His pace doesn't slow, we are clearly not taking the truck. I take a moment to notice where everyone else is. They are all loosely walking behind us, but seem to be giving Oliver and I space.

"Look, I don't know what is going on, but we are all drawn to you for some reason. We all feel it. I just know that I like being near you, I like having physical contact with you. It's hard to explain. It is definitely more intense than brotherly affection, but I don't know if it's the same as the way Cam and Kota feel. You keep me calm, keep my head on straight. When we thought you left this morning, I thought I was going to have a panic attack, then we found you and the first thought in my head was, 'I wish they found you with me.'" He clears his throat. "I don't know what to do with that information, but I want you to know, we all need you. You have your reasons for wanting to leave and I hope someday you'll trust us enough to tell us the whole truth, but the idea of you leaving is making us all a little crazy, so you are going to have to deal with us being clingy and possessive, and yes, even a little jealous."

He turns his head forward and keeps walking. Holy shit! First, that is the most words at one time he has ever said to me, but it is also the most truth I have gotten from any of them. At least it explains their weird behavior recently and why they went all Alpha male last night. I do the only thing I can think of in the moment and hug his neck tighter, burying my nose in the crook between his shoulder and neck taking in his honey scent, calming my nerves as we get closer to the training grounds they are holding the trials at for the next two days.

"Thank you for explaining," I whisper into his neck and goosebumps ripple down his arms again, but he has no other reaction.

Chapter 25

"Okay, my little love doves, we have to go and join the rest of the crowd and cheer on our favorite girl." Sam comes bounding up to Oliver and I.

I jump down from Oliver's back and wrap my arms around Sam's waist, and he kisses the top of my head. "Mateo steps up and I do the same thing. I turn to Oliver and wrap my arms around his neck, he stands, lifting me off my feet and squeezes me tight for just a second before letting me go. Sierra wraps her arms round my neck and pulls me close.

"I want to know what that is all about, but later. Now focus and kick everyone's ass like always." She pulls back and we both laugh.

I step up to the twins and they do their usual sandwich, Cam in front and Kota behind. They both have their hands in their pockets again, like they are actively trying not to touch me. Cam leans down to my ear. "Do yourself proud, Tiny, we will be cheering you on." He brushes his cheek next to mine, his nose running along my ear. Then he pulls back, and I turn to Kota.

"Kick some ass, Smalls. I can't wait to watch you put someone else through the wringer." I can feel him smile as he rubs his cheek on mine the same as Cam. It's like they are both trying to leave their scent on me before I go.

They leave me at the gate of the arena where the Royal guards are waiting for the crowd of candidates to begin lining up. I am getting my head in the game and focused on unknown physical and mental tests they will put us through. When the only thing that could possibly break my concentration did.

"HEY, BOYS!! I'm so glad you waited for me, thank you so much, it's so sweet of you." The grating high pitched, nails on a chalkboard sound breaks every ounce of calm demeanor the guys left me with.

"Kaley, not now. Run along and find your little minions. We have no plans to put up with you or your antics today, it's too important. You have not been invited to the Alpha's box, and we wouldn't have room for you if you were," Sierra states matter of factly. I chance a look over my shoulder to see my friends didn't go far from me, and Sierra made her claims loud enough for all the patrol guards to hear; she knows exactly what she's doing, putting them on alert. My best friend is her own force to be reckoned with.

"How dare you speak to your future Luna like that, you lowly little bitch. Cameron, Dakota, tell her I am sitting with you, as your future mate we should be seen at functions like these as a united front." She flips her hair over her shoulder dramatically.

"Just so we are clear," Sierra's voice gets dangerously low, but still loud enough to be heard by the growing crowd of spectators that have started to show up early to get good seats. She closes the distance between her and Kaley. "I outrank you on so many levels and you only want to be seen, you couldn't care less who you are with so long as you feel special in the Alpha's box. You bring no value to any of us, walk away before I have the guards remove you." She spares me a quick look and wink over Kaley's shoulder, and I just smile back. She's not going to let that waste of space anywhere near my guys or let her ruin my day. It instantly puts me at ease.

Huh. I wonder when I actively started to think of them as 'my guys'? But they are, aren't they? The twins said as much last night, Oliver said so on the way here. Ugh! Boys are so complicated.

But before I can get lost in my thoughts, Delta Kyle comes out of the gates that have been strategically covered so you can't see into the arena.

"I'm impressed. I didn't think you would be able to hold off. I was ready to fight with you at 5 a.m." He laughs at me.

I roll my eyes. "Ha ha, very funny. I wasn't given a choice really. I was threatened by the guys, and they made sure the Alpha King's patrol knew I wasn't supposed to leave early, so here I am, almost not early."

"Well, let's get your name on the register and wait for the rest of the slackers to show up." He hands me a clipboard that asks for basic information, like my name, contact info, and pack affiliation.

At 10 the last of the competitors show up. I have no idea what the actual number is, but it feels like about a hundred people of all ages are here. Once everyone is signed in, they divide us into groups. The high schoolers who are just here for exhibition purposes, those 20-40, and then anyone over 40. Since we age more slowly than humans do, our fighters continue until well into their seventies without issue. They don't divide male and female though, which I appreciate. There are a fair number of females here, but we are far outnumbered by the men.

"Now that you are all in your groups," Warrior Nickolas calls out, "we will send you to your designated area. Once there, we will pair you at random to spar one on one, two on one and wolf to human. Listen for instructions, the pace will go quickly. You will be scored on many different aspects, but most of all your ability to not get submitted by your opponent. From there we will combine the groups, put you in order of score totals and spar again. Once that round is complete, we will make our first round of cuts, then the gauntlet. Alright, let's go."

A hand shoots up from the crowd over in the 20–40 year-old group. "When will we break for meals during all of this?" A high male voice asks, and I have to fight an eye roll.

"You won't..." Warrior Nickolas deadpans. "this is not a leisure training, you are about to fight for your life. If you are not prepared to do that, the gate to the spectators is that way." Warrior Nickolas points then turns and walks away without another word or to see if Wimpy sticks around or not.

A low murmur comes over all the contestants. I figured as much, you don't get breaks and days off as an Elite Warrior in a real battle. This is what he meant by packs sending whoever and them not even being ready to train.

A whistle blows and we all file to our respective designated areas. The volume of the crowd cranks to deafening, someone has clearly fired them up. I chance a look at the Alpha's box which has low walls blocking them from the rest of the crowd. The Alpha, Luna, Alpha King, and Luna Queen are sitting in the top row, with two soldiers sitting behind the Alpha King. The rest of our pack's ranked members are sitting in the row in front of them along with, I assume, more warriors or ranked members of the Alpha King. In the very front row is my crew all clapping and cheering me on, and in Sam's case, obnoxiously loudly, accompanied by a dance. I also notice Kaley found a way to sit right in front of where the twins are to make it appear that she is close to them, the only thing separating them is the three foot wall behind her. I just roll my eyes and tune everything out. She isn't my problem today.

Each group has two Elite Warriors giving out instructions and pairing us off. My first opponent is a guy I have never seen before, but about Oliver's size. He smiles, says 'hi,' and tries to tell me his name. I just nod in response and move to my side of our fighting circle. I'm not here to make friends, just to see what I am actually capable of.

A horn blares, and everything turns into a blur. Arms are flying, legs kicking, bodies being thrown in every direction. No one is screaming or shouting in pain, no true warrior would do that, but there are lots of grunts and groans and muffled sounds of discomfort. I have no idea how long I fight with my first opponent, who is big and very strong, but not fast enough to get any real hits on me, when two warriors walk up, tap us on the shoulder and point us each in another direction. I have a new target and don't hesitate. This goes on for so long—; fight, tap, change opponent—; I have lost track of how many opponents I have come up against. I do notice the field is becoming more and more open, like we are gaining space. I shove that thought to the back of my mind for now and will ask the guys later.

When I feel like I am going to pass out from exhaustion, dehydration, hunger, or maybe all three at the same time, someone runs by me and tosses a bag and then disappears in the crowd before I even catch it. The two people I was fighting have disappeared too. I look around to make sure another person hasn't been sent to attack me before I look down at the bag. It contains a bright yellow shirt, food rations, a bottle of water and a first aid kit. Most of it makes sense, the shirt I'm not sure about, though.

"Find your respective colors' corner and follow the instructions while you refuel," Warrior Nickolas' voice booms over a bull horn.

I head to the corner of the arena that has a yellow flag. Three other people join me. My first sparring partner who seems to have done well for himself, he doesn't look like he sustained many injuries anyway. A poor guy who looks like he has been a human punching bag stumbles over. He has a cut across his right eyebrow that is bleeding into his eye, his nose is for sure broken, and his lip is split and bleeding. His whole face is going to be bruised soon, I hope his eyes don't swell shut while we are trying to complete this course. It's clearly a teamwork drill. The girl is one of the last opponents I had, and she was giving me a run for my money and a good nose bleed Cam would be proud of. None of them look to be current students so maybe in the 20-30 group.

I start to wonder why I was put with a group of people actually competing for a training spot when Warrior Nickolas announces, "You have five minutes to strategize and tend to wounds, then the horn will blow. From then, you will have 30 minutes to complete your task."

"What task?" The the girl asks as we all do the obvious and put on our team shirts.

I dump my bag and so does my first fighter. Where I have a first aid kit he has rope.

"Check your bags, we all have different things... and come here," I gesture to the injured guy. "Let me reset your nose so it can at least start to heal."

The girl dumps her bag and a card falls out. The only thing on it is 'Capture The Flag.' My eyes light up, yes!

"What's got you looking so happy?" First first guy asks.

"It's my favorite game. Looks like this is a team effort. You are the tallest, can you see where they may have hung the yellow flag?" I ask while I am still tending to injured guy. "My name is Sky."

Injured guy looks at me. "I'm Jeff, how'd you learn to do this?"

"You can flirt with her later. I see it. I'm Lillian. Can he move yet?" The girl rapidly fires at me.

"Everyone eat and sip water so you don't get a cramp or throw up, it will slow us down." I turn to see where Lillian is pointing. "I see it too, he should be good to go. Let's assume that we have to get it and return it as a team. Who's the best scout?" I look at Lillian and First Guy. I don't even bother with Jeff for now, once I see him move, I'll decide if I trust him to help.

"I'm a good scout, once we get over there, I can keep anyone away who may try to intercept you, guys." First guy shrugs. "Name's Wyatt."

"Okay, you're pretty fast so we should work together to get to our flag." I look at Lillian and she nods. "Jeff, can you be on the lookout for other team flags as we move?"

"Sure can, then I can help Wyatt with scouting."

"Alright, Lillian, lead us out, I'll cover your back. Jeff, follow me, and Wyatt can bring up the rear. Our flag is on top of the rope climb, but it looks like they took the ropes off completely, so we are going to have to scale the obstacle course." I point out to Lillian, "The best spot is there to the right. The cargo net bracing is the most direct route, and we should be able to jump from there, as long as we aren't intercepted. I do have a couple back up ideas, but let's hope we don't have to use them." I smile at her, and surprisingly she smiles back with a mischievous grin. Perfect, someone else just as crazy as me.

We line up and the horn blows. The four of us take off behind Lillian, and she follows the path I gave her perfectly. There is so much debris on this portion of the arena, it looks like a paintball field. I can hear others shouting directions to each other, but we stay as quiet as possible. I figure we can rest up a bit if we don't have to fight our way to the flag. She follows a path that takes us around the outer edge, Poor Wyatt is so big he barely fits, but he squeezes through, and we come around to one side of the cargo net.

"Alright, this is where we let go of our cover, Wyatt, Jeff? You guys ready?" I whisper over my shoulder.

"Yes." They they replied together.

"Keep track of the other teams, we don't know how big they are, assume we are outnumbered and fight like we are. Also be on the lookout for Warriors they might try to mess with us. Let's go."

Lillian and I do a running crouch to the other edge of the cargo net. It would be stupid to scale it and then have to climb across. I head up first and can hear Lillian right behind me, she struggles a bit as the net swings and shakes below me, but she keeps up. Once we are halfway up, six people run out from various places along the ground. Wyatt is able to stop two with swift hits to the head, they go down hard. I cringe, I was on the other side of those a while ago and don't envy his opponents. Jeff is fighting with one, and I have to say is putting up a good fight even with his injuries.

"Let's go!" I shout to Lillian and hear a string of curse words with every movement. It actually makes me smile. Once we get to the top, I help Lillian onto the beam. "It's a ten-foot jump, you have to take a running start."

"You act like you've done something this stupid before."

"Yep." Is is all I say before I take off across the support beam and launch myself onto the rope climb support.

"That's all you girl, I'll catch you when you come back." She laughs.

I grab the flag and go to put it in my bag, but as I am, I have a thought and move it to my sports bra then make a show of closing and securing the bag on my back before running and jumping back.

"You were right— we are surrounded, how are we going to get out of here with the guys? Wyatt isn't fast enough to get up here, and Jeff can only handle one person at a time."

"I can handle several at a time, here, you take the bag and wait until we clear a path, then we can all run together." Let's see who takes the bait.

We move down and Lillian stays out of reach with both my backpack and hers on her. I jump in and start helping Wyatt clear out a path, there are only about ten people left and he's knocked a few of them out. Once we get a couple more subdued, I call up to Lillian.

"Get ready! Jeff, flank her right, I will take her left then Wyatt can watch our backs. 3. 2. 1. Go!"

Lillian drops down and starts to run, Jeff runs to position on her right side, I follow up on her left. Wyatt grunts like he got hit and I risk a look back and see someone barreling at Lillian's back. I move to intercept him, but his momentum is too much and all three of us go toppling head over feet. The guy grabs both backpacks and takes off hooting and hollering to his friends. Lillian moves to get up and chase him, so does Wyatt.

"Let it go, let's just get back to our side before time runs out, we only have 2 minutes."

"But, it doesn't matter if we don't have our flag," She she whines as she stops moving.

I open my eyes wide and say again, "We should get back to our side before time runs out."

"Ah!" Jeff says and jumps up to wrap a sympathetic arm around her gently guiding us to our corner, but she starts to dig her heels in. Then Jeff looks over his shoulder. "Would you please?"

The next thing I know, Wyatt has Lillian in a fireman's carry and we are slowly jogging back to our side while the other team is still having a party in the center. I don't even think they checked the bags yet. We all step over our line, just as the buzzer goes off. There are cheers and boos from the crowd.

Warrior Nickolas walks to the group holding our bags, while medical staff goes to tend to the injured people. He holds out his hand to the leader of the group. The leader smuggly opens one of the bags and rummages around. There wasn't enough stuff in them for the amount of time he's taking. Panicking, he flips it over and dumps it out, no flag. He moves to the second bag, and the looks on the faces of his teammates change to worry. He wastes no time dumping the bag and finding no flag. Warrior Nickolas looks over at us and Jeff looks right at me smiling, as does Wyatt who caught on. Lilian looks around confused, then I pull the flag out of my sports bra and wave it around. My team and the crowd goes nuts. I have never heard it this loud in the arena before. The vibrations of all of the voices are rumbling the ground we are standing on. My team all hugs and we are laughing, Lilian is pissed I didn't tell her, but I had no way to and not give it away. I should tell her to pay better attention. The guys caught on quickly enough. But, I'm too happy to give her a hard time.

I try to look in the stand for my friends, but there are so many people surrounding our group, I can only see what's right in front of me.

"You are sneaky. I'm going to have to keep my eye on you." Lillian jokes in my ear, giving me another hug.

Chapter 26

The medical team comes to check on all of us, bringing more water and food. We are each subjected to a full exam by a pair of healers, one werewolf and one witch. I know about witches, but I've never met one, we don't have any in or near our pack. I wasn't sure what to expect. The werewolf did a physical examination notating any injuries, including the smallest cut on my cheek. Then the witch stepped up and held her open hands about six inches from my body. I can feel the hum of power like a soft brush grazing over my skin.

"Can I ask what you are checking for?" I question softly.

Her emerald green eyes stay unfocused and staring at my forehead. She's in full concentration. Maybe she can't hear me. "She's checking for anything internal." The werewolf healer says softly. "With this many warriors, it's faster to do a scan like this to ascertain the worst injuries so we can prioritize."

"That is so amazing! She can really tell if I have, say, a damaged organ or something?"

"Yes. Now will you stop moving? I don't think I have ever had anyone excited about an examination before. You must be new to this." I immediately hold still. I'm curious what she will find. I also wonder if she can feel old injuries. I try not to let that worry show on my face. The witch doesn't say anything else to me or her partner, but they are communicating somehow, cause the werewolf is taking notes and scribbling quickly. A glance around shows the others taking lots of notes too, so I try not to worry about it.

Once everyone has been cleared, we are all brought back to the sparring side of the arena and told to sit while we wait for instructions for tomorrow. I sit with my team and lose track of how many protein bars I smash as Nickolas talks. It's been a long time since I was this hungry. We are told we have to be back again at 10 a.m. That is the only real information we get, that and 'everyone here did well today.' Whatever the hell that is supposed to mean. Based on the way everyone looks, if this is 'well,' tomorrow is going to suck. I grunt as I move to get up to go find the guys and get real food.

"I thought they were going to do cuts today," Jeff mutters out, following me.

"Me too," Wyatt says, looking around.

"Maybe they will still announce that later or individually." Lilian shrugs.

"Or maybe anyone who didn't make it to the capture the flag round is out," I say more a question. "There weren't many teams in the game, but I'm not sure if that was an injury thing or a cut thing. We'll find out tomorrow I guess. I need to go get food, before I pass out from starvation. I'll see you guys tomorrow." I wave to them as I turn and see my guys walking up to me, grinning from ear to ear.

My face breaks out into a smile I can't control as I run straight at my brother and jump into his arms. He spins me around. "You were incredible, Shorty, I can't believe you just did all that." He puts me down and I go to hug Sam who is giggling like a hyena and sways me side to side.

"Of course you got Capture the Flag as a test. That jump was epic!"

"The flag in the bra thing, seems to be your go-to. You're going to have to change it up now or people are going to figure you out and start digging in your clothes," Oliver teases me as I turn and hug him around the neck again. "...and we won't be having any of that, you hear?" he whispers in my ear, and I'm sure I am blushing again as I let go.

I step in between the twins and smile up at them. "I need to eat and then I need to sleep. It took me too long to figure out what makes me comfortable enough to sleep in my new home."

"Whatever you want, Tiny," Cam says, smiling at me.

"Mom is waiting for us." Kota holds out his hand to me, I take it without hesitation.

"She thought five hours was enough and will probably try to fuss over you for a little while," Cam says, sliding his hand onto my lower back. "It's probably best to give in." He huffs a laugh under his breath and I smile.

"Let me know if you need another piggyback ride, Bite Size, you took a few good hits today," Oliver says directly behind me.

"I'm good. I'm not fragile, guys, just tired. The walk will help my muscles cool down anyway. I have a feeling tomorrow is going to suck just as much." They all laugh with me, but no one argues.

We all walk into the pack house and as promised, Luna Ava greets us at the door and moves straight to me, cupping my face in both hands. "That was harder to watch than I thought it would be. I've seen you fight and I know that you can take care of yourself, but it is different knowing you are with the boys and they don't mean you any real harm. And you are going to do this and more again tomorrow." She blows a breath out of her puffed cheeks and I do the only thing I think I can in this moment. I wrap my arms around her and let her pull me into a hug. The kind of hug that a parent gives a child to lend them strength and tell them it will be okay without using words. As much as she doesn't want to see me do this, she won't stop me either. Nor will she stay away because it's difficult to watch. She will be there to support me, because this is something that I want for myself and she knows how badly I want it. She will cheer me on in a way she's never been able to publicly before. My heart clenches then explodes at the thought of an adult rooting for me to succeed.

"I need to shower, I am so gross," I say, muffled into her shoulder.

"Okay, hun. Do you want dinner down here, or do you want to eat upstairs?" The watery sound of of her voice tells me she is close to tears, but fighting it. Neither of us wants to get emotional here.

"Would it be okay if I eat upstairs? I don't want to be rude, with the Alpha King here as your guest." I pull back and look up at her cringing a little bit. I'm worried about appearances, it's part of my upbringing, my DNA. I don't want to offend the royalty that they are hosting, just because I am too tired to socialize.

"Of course you can. He will not be offended at all. He saw first hand what you did today and will completely understand. Would you mind if I send Xander up? I think he is bored hanging with all of the adults and would probably like some time with kids closer to his age."

"Yes! Of course." I almost shout and I feel more than hear a low rumble behind me. I look over my shoulder with a scowl, I don't know who it was, but this pissing match is stupid. "That would be great, we can set up in the media room." I smile at her and start for the stairs.

"I'll send Xander up when I send food up. That should give *you* plenty of time to shower and change. That will give the *boys* time to put their protective cavemen away as well."

"Mom!"

"What, Dakota?" Damn! The snap in her voice could break glass and she used his whole name. "You five have been acting crazy, she is not a tree for you to pee on every time another male your age comes around. Save that for your mate, Goddess help her." And with that, she walks around the stairs, presumably to the kitchen to get food ready, leaving the boys staring with their jaws on the floor.

I laugh and run up the stairs, not waiting for the guys to come out of their dumbstruck state at what she said. Sierra follows me, and we laugh all the way to my room.

"You really did kick ass today, girl. You should have seen how fast some of the other contenders went down. I get what Warrior Nickolas was talking about, though. People want the best or want to be the best, but most of them haven't put in the work and they aren't ready for all of that, and it's a joke." Sierra's rattling off as I come out of the bathroom, having showered quickly. I thought I might fall asleep if I stayed under the warm stream too long.

"You'll have to tell me more from the stands, it was so crazy on the field, I didn't always know what was going on, and they just tapped us to point out our new target during the sparring part. There wasn't time to think at all." I tell her my version of the whole contest, and she fills in the gaps from her vantage point in the stands as I get dressed in comfy sweats and a T-shirt. We settle in my bed excitedly analyzing everything.

"I can't believe it went on for five hours. I didn't feel that long while I was doing it, but now it feels like longer." I smile. "I've trained that long before, but this was different. I had to rely on others I've never met before and just had to trust that we were all on the same page, without any kind of introduction or anything. I barely got their names before we had to start. This was all business, and I think I really like it. I liked the rush of adrenaline I got when the horn blew and all hell broke loose. There was no time to overthink, you had to just use instinct. Does that even make sense?" Sierra laughs at me when I confess my feelings.

"Of course, you enjoyed that. You finally got to be completely you, no holding back."

Knock. Knock. Knock.

"You ladies decent? I'm coming in either way, the warning is a courtesy." He sing-songs as my door flies open and Sam walks in, flops on my bed, then rolls to his side propping his head in one of his hands. "So, what are we gossiping about? It's me, right? Tell me it's me, even if it's not." We both burst out laughing. "All jokes aside, your fan club is here and we need a mediator. I don't know what you did, but territorial doesn't even begin to describe the vibe." I laugh again, letting him pull me to my feet and lead us to the media room.

The 'U' shaped modular couch has been moved and adjusted to line the two side walls with a large table set in the middle covered with a spread made for the King.

"It is official, you are her favorite." Mateo laughs at me." I don't think we exist anymore."

"Stop, this is not all for me, this is for all of us." I plop into the middle of the far couch and start digging in. I am too hungry to wait for anyone.

"Umm, no. Had we done double what you did today, she would have sent a plate of sandwiches and water and called it a night if we couldn't be bothered to come down to the kitchen and eat with everyone." Dakota laughs from the bar where he is standing with Xander, who's looking awkward.

"Xander, come sit by me, you have to tell me what you thought of the trials today and give me any inside tips for tomorrow." I looked over at him and caught Sierra's eye, she winks at me knowing what I'm doing.

Chapter 27

Sierra moves to sit on my right side, and Xander slowly moves to my left while the rest of the guys look dumbfounded at my request. They don't get to be rude and treat me like a toy they don't want to share, so they can learn to act like decent people or suffer.

Xander flops next to me, but wisely keeps a visible distance between us. We eat and talk, Sierra joining in the conversation. Eventually, the guys resign themselves to the fact that I am going to include Xander and join us. Once we all started talking and relaxing it was actually fun. Xander is a mix of Dakota and Sam, but has Cam's responsible oldest child vibe. I really need to ask about his younger siblings.

Once the food was done, the guys cleared the tables and put everything into the hallway for the house staff to get and we all moved the couch back to its 'U' position. This time Kota was not missing out, he grabbed me by the waist and pulled me to the center of the couch, my brother flops next to me and the rest of our group, including Xander, settles in for a movie.

The opening credits weren't even done before my eyes started drooping and I lean my head to nestle on Dakota's shoulder. He drapes a warm, lazy arm over my knees tucked into his side and I don't remember anything else.

I wake up earlier than expected considering how tired I was from yesterday. I can smell Luna Ava approach, then she makes herself known with a soft knock on my door, before bringing in a full tray of steaming breakfast foods. She knew

I would still want to be up first and sit in the peace and quiet for a bit before the guys barrel in.

"This looks amazing. Thank you!" I beam at her. I startle as Sierra stirs next to me, pulling my attention. It was then that I realized I was in my room, in my own bed. I think this might be the first time I have actually slept in here overnight. I wonder if she came in on her own, was assigned to me, or had to fight for her spot?

"It's nothing, sweet girl. Now eat, both of you, before the boys smell food and come running. I don't usually bring food up here for them."

"They may have mentioned that once or twice last night when they saw what you sent up for dinner." Sierra yawns by me. "They did call Sky your favorite and pouted about it."

Luna Ava just laughed before turning around and walking towards my door. "You have about an hour before you need to get ready, I know you like to get to the training grounds early. It's almost 8 a.m."

It's strange to be so comfortable in this house that I sleep in so late, no matter where I end up actually sleeping. "How did we get in here? The last thing I remember was starting a movie and leaning on Dakota's shoulder." I look over at Sierra as I crawl to the end of the bed and start digging into the plate with pancakes.

She giggles and follows me to the food. "Well, you made it all of five minutes before you were snuggled into Dakota and snoring."

"I do not snore!" I gasp and freeze mid-grab, staring at her. I can't snore, how embarrassing would that be? I'm looking at her with a forkful of pancake halfway to my mouth, waiting for her answer.

"You do, but it's cute. What was more cute was how much gloating Kota did while you were holding on tight to his arm. You were using him like a body pillow." She laughs, "There was even a little scuffle about who was going to carry you to bed and then, where you were going to sleep. Your brother eventually won and put you here, then asked me to stay with you to keep the rest of them out so you could get enough sleep for today."

She shoves her mouth full of whipped cream covered pancakes and smiles at me.

I swallow hard. "That's the dumbest thing I have ever heard. There's no way they fought over carrying me." I roll my eyes and stuffed my own face with another bite of food. She just shrugs her shoulders at me.

I don't understand them sometimes. Their attention can be a lot to handle, and I don't get why so much of it's directed at me. I mean we're friends now, but no one except Sam does that with Sierra and we all started hanging out at the same time. Just thinking about them makes me tired.

Speaking of them, it wasn't long until we were joined by all the guys, including Xander, and they polished off everything that we didn't eat. And even though she said it was for us, Luna Ava made plenty for the boys too. She knew that they would end up here.

It took some convincing, and threatening on Sierra's part, to get them to leave so I could change. I decided on more grubby clothes today, knowing we were going to be in wolf form. I wasn't sure if we would have to shift unexpectedly and tear through clothes, and I can't risk tearing through my favorite stuff. Again.

Just like yesterday, I got a piggyback ride from Oliver. He and Sam played rock, paper, scissors for it. My brother and the twins just shake their heads and smile at the antics, but they didn't argue. More confusing things about these boys to pack away and discuss with Sierra later. Xander, however, looked confused as he watched the scene play out, but said nothing and joined us on the short walk over to the training grounds. I am the first to arrive again, but not by much. Wyatt, Jeff, and Lillian all walk over to say hello and I introduce the groups. There were a lot of titles to throw around. I now know I take for granted the fact that I get to call all of these friends by only their first names. The 'future this' and 'future that' part of the title got old by the third time I had to say it.

The guys and Sierra leave me to go and sit in the Alpha's box to watch. As soon as they walked away, I could feel my anticipation start to rise again. We are going to be in wolf form today. Only a handful of people even know I have a wolf let alone have seen her. I find myself wondering if my dad is going to be angry that I didn't say anything about it to him, or if he will be pleased that I was strong enough to shift so early.

I didn't get a chance to fall too deep into those thoughts though as Delta Kyle walks up and gets our attention.

"Alright, today we will begin similar to yesterday. You will all be broken down to fight one on one in your wolf forms. Our instructors will give you your opponents as you go, similar to yesterday. We will divide you into males and females at first, then mix you up according to your fighting skills and styles. There are changing tents lined up along the edges of the arena. This will give you the chance to change and our instructors a chance to get to know your wolf form without having to strip awkwardly in front of hundreds of people." He smiles warmly.

Our whole crowd lets out a little chuckle, but you can feel the collective sigh of relief too. I know I will breathe easier without having to get naked in front of everyone. That was my biggest fear this morning. I don't want to have to explain my scars to anyone, especially not right now. I came prepared to just shift and tear through my clothes, though. Sierra has a backpack with backups for me.

Delta Kyle gives a few more instructions then leads us in and shows us our respective tents. While we are walking, I can see Lillian looking at me every couple seconds from the corner of my eye. She follows me back toward the furthest corner from the tent opening.

"Why do you keep looking at me like that?" I question her as I sit down on a bench and slowly work my shoes off.

"How are you even going to do this? You're only like fifteen/sixteen, right? You can't go human against wolf. Especially those Elite wolves."

"Umm, I actually got my wolf a while ago." I shrug, trying to make it seem like it's not a big deal. "That's why Delta Kyle was given permission to let me join trials. And, we train human versus wolf, so that's not really new either." I skipped over confirming how old I was, hoping she doesn't notice or doesn't bring it up again.

Her eyes go wide, and I thought I was going to have to help her pick her jaw up off the floor.

"You have had your wolf for a while?! Holy shit! But, for real, how long is a while?"

"I'm a Beta and my brother and his friends got their wolves around the same time. I just figured that was normal." I shrug again, hoping she believes the flimsy lie. I figure if I play innocent, she'll drop it. I was rewarded with one more quizzical look. Then she began to focus on her own changing.

There were only about 50 or so people left in the trial, and of those about 20 women. It was nice to know that female warriors are appreciated and not as few and far between as I had thought.

The female warriors assisting us have girls change and shift a few at a time and make note of the wolf's color, scent, and other markings. I hang at the back, not really having to act nervous. I tell Lillian to go before me, that I need a minute before I head out. Once everyone is out of the entrance, I head forward, still clothed, toward the warriors taking notes.

"Can you not shift yet, sweetheart? I thought you looked a little young," the taller of the two said.

"No, it's not that. Can I ask a favor? Can you only make note of the markings on my wolf?" I asked quickly, not wanting to miss anything.

"I'm not sure what you mean, honey, but we can do that, I guess." She's still looking at me funny.

With that I nodded and began to undress, trying to keep my back away from them as much as possible, but I won't have much control when my wolf starts to take over to shift. My shift was quick, but I didn't miss the intake of breath before it was complete. I know they saw my back and the ugly scars I get to carry around. I just hope they don't ask about them later or mention them to anyone. The last thing I need is for them to start asking questions.

"You are beautiful!" The the shorter warrior exclaims. "I don't think I have ever seen a pure black wolf before. It's so rare to not have any other markings."

"I told you we are special," My wolf gloats to me.

"Whatever, let's go before they send a search party in here for us."

We trot out and blend right into the group, then take the position given to us by the warriors who are helping with the trials. We square up to a beautiful brown wolf with red tinting the ends of the fur. She isn't from our pack, that's all I can tell. As soon as the whistle is blown, we are in full focus. If I thought yesterday's battles were tough, today's have blown the whole thought out of the water. The second the whistle blows, all that can be seen is fur, teeth, and claws. Because the fighting was so fierce and fast, the warriors had to jump into the fray to get our attention in order to direct us to another opponent.

Sparring in wolf form was exhilarating. I have never had this much fun or felt this powerful in my life. My wolf and I are giddy. I wonder if she can smile? I lose track of how many opponents they put me against. They never let anyone get to the point of being pinned. I'm not sure if that was because all of the fighters were just that good and we were all having trouble submitting each other or if they wanted to preserve energy to see us against a bunch of different opponents.

After the individual rounds we were told to simply 'get past the line of warriors.' I wasn't sure what kind of task that was until I saw all of the Elite Warriors saunter out in their wolf forms looking intimidating and ready for battle. They take up a defensive stance in a semicircle around the obstacle course. Similar to yesterday, there were barriers and other things added to give us cover, but I have a feeling we were all royally screwed.

Delta Kyle blew a whistle, and we all run toward the hostile wolves, ready to prove we are not worthy to join their ranks. I focused on the line. They all seemed to be hyper aware of their surroundings, all taking on more than one wolf at a time and at lightning speed. I had to remind myself I was a part of this whole show, and I couldn't sit here and watch in awe at the graceful and deadly movements of these highly trained machines. I couldn't ignore it either. It was almost magical.

Some wolves just ran forward head on into the line trying the most obvious way to get your ass beat. Others tried to dart between the things piled up, but not really looking at their surroundings for the best ways to move and getting caught up by an Elite Warrior before getting too far. I belly crawled from one hiding spot to another, keeping myself as small as possible. There are benefits to being my size. I made it to a low woodpile about 20 feet from the ropes course side of the obstacle.

The Elite Warriors were pinning wolves left and right like it didn't cost them any energy or effort at all. My plan was to find a gap when two were focused elsewhere, but they never strayed from their general positions. If one wolf moved, the whole unit shifted. I have no idea how long I stood there and just observed their movements, it was like a dance, so mesmerizing. A loud snarl broke me from my trance, and I saw a huge gray wolf with black markings barreling towards me. My wolf scrambled back and tried to get around the other side of the woodpile only to be met with three other wolves, I had been corralled. How did that happen? They were all just engaged with other people not a minute ago. Damn, they work fast. Now the question is, do I fight and try to keep going or surrender? Before I can answer my own question with some form of action, a whistle is blown.

"You all did a great job today. The warriors have a lot to discuss. Please go and change and meet at the pack house to celebrate a successful trial session. You all deserve it."

All of the wolves dispersed back to the changing tents, and I vaguely heard the crowd cheering. I completely forgot we were being observed. I was so engrossed in the fighting, it felt like a normal training day, just with really well-trained adversaries.

We walked back towards the tent and were stopped by Delta Kyle. "Good job today, kid. I'm not gonna lie, I was a little worried about today. I know you have been training in your wolf form, but clearly more than I even knew."

My wolf nods her head accepting the compliment for me. *"Thank you. I appreciate all your help. I just hope it was enough to get me on their radar for when I can actually be accepted into the program."*

"I don't think that is anything you will ever have to worry about. I don't think I am supposed to tell you this, but, you went up against the most opponents yesterday and today and got the closest to the target as a wolf today."

"There's no way! I was watching some of these guys fight. It was crazy. And there has to be people that got just as close today, I was so far from the target, and I didn't even engage until the very end when they cornered me."

He just shook his head. "Nope, but I think your tent is clear and you have some friends who want to celebrate your success with you. Go change. I'll see you at the pack house." He winked at me before walking away.

I turned around to see that almost everyone had cleared out of the arena, and I had an even bigger appreciation for Delta Kyle. He knows I keep my scars to myself and gave me the excuse to not have to change in the excited tent with others, where I would more than likely be cornered and asked a ton of questions. He does it all without pushing for more information, even though I know it bothers him to not know what is really going on.

I change quickly and head out the gates of the arena and get immediately thrown into the air. I have no idea what is going on, but I am weightless with my hair wrapped around my face so I can't see up from down. Then a pair of warm, calloused hands grab me and a familiar salty ocean scent wraps around me. Sam.

Chapter 28

"Holy shit, Little Bit! I thought yesterday was amazing, but I don't think I have ever seen you move that fast. You've been holding out on us." He pouts a little at me.

"Alright, put her down so we can share her." Sierra giggles.

Sam places me on my feet and she wraps me in a tight hug. "There were a couple times there I was actually afraid for your safety. That was harder to watch than yesterday. I don't like being on the sidelines at all." She lets out an amused huff, but there is something else there I can't quite place.

I don't have time to dwell on her meaning as my brother grabs me up in a hug. "You should have heard Dad's reaction when I explained which wolf was you. I don't know if I have heard him cuss that much in my life and most of it was at me and Delta Kyle. I don't think he believed that you could shift until then."

He places me down in front of Oliver, who says nothing, but hugs me tightly and buries his nose in my neck, inhaling deeply. He steps back and the twins do the same. Again, actions I don't totally understand, but I don't get the chance to think about them when Xander walks up.

"That was amazing!" He grabs each of my shoulders in his massive hands and stares down at me. He looks a little disheveled, like he was nervous for me too and ran his hands through his hair a bunch. His suit is rumpled, and his tie is crooked, but the look on his face is elated. "I have never seen our top warriors have real competition outside their own circle. You were incredible!" He pulls me in for a quick hug, then pushes me out to a safe arm's length distance when a low growl sounds behind me. "You went against each warrior that travels with my dad and mom personally! They heard about you yesterday and asked to join in."

That was news none of us expected to hear. It was all such a blur though, I couldn't pick the wolves I fought out of a line up if I tried. Still in Xander's hands, I turned to look at the guys, "Can we go eat please? I am starving!"

"Of course, Smalls, but this time you're mine!" Kota swings me on his back and starts running. The rest of the guys are laughing and running to catch up.

It took us no time to run to the packhouse which is completely overflowing with people. The front doors are thrown wide open and groups of people are milling around the front lawn and porch all talking and enjoying themselves. I can hear the music coming from the back yard and can smell the delicious scent of barbeque billowing from the Alpha's pride and joy grill.

"Kota, can you run me upstairs for a quick shower and change of clothes?" I pat his chest, making sure he's listening over the sounds emanating around us.

"Sure, Smalls, I would love to get you all cleaned up," He he says in a tone I've never heard from him before. The low rumble vibrates through my whole body. Then he looks over his shoulder and winks at me, then I catch on to what he's implying.

"Ugh! NO! Get your head out of the gutter. Just take me to our floor." I roll my eyes back at him.

"You said it not me, Smalls. I can keep it quick though, so no one suspects." He chuckles again.

"Will you stop! I'll just go myself, you are being weird." I tried to jump off his back as he reached the porch, but he has a death grip on my thighs. I was not going anywhere without a scene, and we both know I won't cause a scene at Luna Ava's party. Stupid boys. "Fine, just move it, I don't want to keep your mom waiting. She's probably expecting you and the guys to play your parts as hosts and is not happy it took us this long to get back."

"Mom knows where we are, it's fine. Besides, she wants you, not the rest of us. You are the jewel of the pack right now, from what I overheard in the stands." He nonchalantly throws that out as we make it to the door to their floor and starts punching in the code.

"You are full of shit." I scoff. "I can't even compete for a real spot yet, no one was even looking at me with so many actual candidates."

He turns to respond, but is interrupted by my favorite sound on the planet.

"Oh, my goddess! Babe, there you are, I've been waiting forever. You totally need to get downstairs. The Alpha King is waiting to talk to you and your brother, you really can't keep him waiting any longer. He probably wants to hear about all the great plans we have to make this pack even better when we are Alphas and Luna. Where is your brother?" She's looking around like Kota is somehow hiding his massive doppelgänger.

Kota puts his hand up to stop her rambling. She either hasn't noticed me on his back or is choosing to pretend that I'm not here. My guess is the latter. "Kaley, who am I?"

"What?" She opens her eyes wide and tries to look innocent.

"Who. Am. I? It's not a hard question. Or at least it shouldn't be." Kota shrugs, bouncing me with his boulder sized shoulders.

"You are a future Alpha, silly. That's such a weird question." She giggles and air swats him.

"My name. Say my name. Which future Alpha am I?" It hit me then. She can't tell them apart. I never thought of it until now, but she never calls them by their names initially. It's not funny but at the same time, it is to me. I bury my face in the back of Kota's neck to stifle a giggle of my own. Can't she just tell by their scents who they are? She can't be that stupid. Kota lets out a purr-like sound from his chest, and I pop back up looking at him with my eyebrows furrowed.

"Smalls, you probably shouldn't do that, unless you want our previous conversation to become a reality."

My eyes go wide again. Kaley raises her eyes to me, "I'm sure you're capable of walking on your own, stop playing the victim and making him slave over you. It isn't appropriate for a future Alpha to be schlepping the help around." She places a manicured hand on her hip.

"Kaley, you never answered my question. Who am I?" Kota gains her attention again, and for once, she looks nervous.

"Uh, well…" Kaley starts to stutter out and takes time to smooth and adjust her livid pink dress, probably hoping to stall long enough for our hurricane of friends to come blasting up the stairs and save her from answering the question.

"Would you quit hogging my little sister?" My brother comes up and she uses the distraction to step back a little. "Where are you guys going anyway? The party's downstairs." Mateo looks at Kota and I suspiciously, folding his arms.

"I was trying to go upstairs and clean up a bit before I went down. I am disgusting from the trials today, but all of you think I am not capable of walking," I swing my arms and legs helplessly to make my point, "so I'm stuck here while Kota finishes up his conversation." I realize what I did the second his name left my lips. I gasp and whisper, "Sorry," into the shell of his ear and he shivers.

"See, Dakota, even she thinks you need to put her down and come with me to talk to the Alpha King." Kaley jumps into the conversation again and twists my words to her advantage.

"We'll be down in a bit, you should go and rejoin the party," Kota says turning, still holding my thigh tight with one hand while he punches in the code to the door with the other. I didn't miss the way he turned to block Kaley's view of the keypad. If she noticed too, she wisely didn't say anything.

"Well, I guess I could walk down with her," She points to Sierra, "and we could wait for you guys together." She's grasping at straws now.

Kota has the door open, and we all turn to look at her, the guys just as confused as me.

"Sky needs to go to her room and change first, and Sierra needs to check her for injuries that might need to be dealt with. She took a couple of hard hits today. We'll see you in a little bit, Kaley." My brother's words were polite and about as final as you can get and Kota took the out, turning back towards the doorway and the stairs leading to our floor.

We started the walk up and I can feel the rest of my friends behind us, moving in a bit of a rush. I heard Oliver at the back, "No, you are not allowed on the third floor." A growl rumbles from him that sets my stomach buzzing, but not in a bad way. "Move. Your. Fingers," he says clipped and then takes an audible breath through his nose. "...so they don't get crushed. Mateo said we'll see you later." Then the distinct click of the door and lock engaging.

"She's getting more and more desperate and bold, you two are going to have to watch yourselves," Sam says somewhere behind me.

"Yeah, but she still has no idea which one of us is which, and doesn't give a shit. Even if we wanted to take a chosen mate, why would we choose someone who can't and doesn't even try to tell us apart?" Kota says over his shoulder. "She just likes the idea of status and thinks being Luna is just throwing parties, spending money she hasn't earned, and parading around in front of people. She has no idea how much work our mom does on her own on top of everything she does with Dad."

"Wait! She really can't tell you two apart? Like, at all?" I ask from my perch. I thought she might be trying to play cute or something.

"No, most people can't. They tend to just see us as one collective unit." Cam sighs behind me.

"Even we have a hard time when they dress the same," Mateo says.

"How is that possible?" I scoff. We make it to our floor and Kota finally put me down. I wiggle my legs a little to wake them up from having to straddle Kota's wide back for so long. "There are so many things about you both that are different."

"Like what?" Cam asks, crossing his arms, almost in a challenge.

"Well for one, you both have different colored eyes. That's a dead giveaway, if anyone pays attention." I rolled my own eyes as if it was obvious.

"To anyone who looks at us our eyes are teal, the exact same shade," Kota says with his eyebrow raised.

"What? No, they aren't!" They have to be trying to mess with me now. "Cam's eyes are green. It's a really pretty bright emerald shade and Kota's are blue, like the Caribbean Ocean. I could see how, if you mixed the colors, that it would look teal, though." I said the last part more to myself than anyone else. "And your scents are different, just to name a few. How could anyone mix you guys up?" I shrug my shoulders and turn towards my room to go get cleaned up and changed.

"Wait, wait, wait! They smell different to you?!" Sam almost shouts. "How is that even possible, when they smell the exact same to the rest of us?"

"Huh?" I turn back around. "What do you mean they smell exactly the same to all of you? Cam smells like a mix of oranges and lemons. It's a really clean citrus smell, and Kota smells like sweet cinnamon. When they stand together, they smell like fall." I can't help myself, I close my eyes and take a deep breath. Their scents are actually really calming.

When I open my eyes, everyone is staring at me like I have lost my mind and I'm starting to feel self-conscious.

"So you're telling me, you would know who was standing next to you based on our scent and eye color alone? Even if we were dressed exactly the same?" Kota asks.

"Yeah, probably." I shrug.

"Our parents can't even do that," Cam says. His tone is strange, like disbelief laced with curiosity.

"Okay, you guys are being weird. I'm going to jump in the shower quick and change. Give me five minutes." I turn around again and head to my room. I can hear them muttering, but I tune it out. They are being so weird about this whole telling them apart thing. It's not that big of a deal. Of course they smell different, they are two separate people. They have different features like eye color and their builds are a bit different, even if it is subtle. Their hair isn't even cut or styled the same. If people are too dense to notice those kinds of differences and see them as individuals, they don't deserve to be considered friends.

I get in and out of the shower in record time and notice an outfit placed on my bed. I'm sure Sierra is responsible. Making sure I dress the part of a non-awkward pack member instead of the recluse I am. I had to let out a laugh when I noticed two full outfits as I walked closer to my bed to examine what she decided is acceptable. One is a subtle but statement-making yellow halter dress that is far too short for my comfort level. The other is a pair of dark washed skinny jeans and an oversized white sweater with an off the shoulder cut neckline. It looks amazingly soft and feminine. She at least left a cute bralette with a full back intricate lace pattern. And tan ankle boots were left on the floor. Apparently, she thought they went with either outfit. I obviously chose the jeans. She lost her mind thinking I was going to voluntarily wear a dress to a backyard party. But, I'm sure she knew that and laid the dress out to keep me from complaining about the dressy sweater and heels. It's sad she knows me so well.

"You ready yet?" The devil herself calls from the door.

"Almost, just need to get dressed and throw my hair up." I don't need to do anything fancy, it's a bunch of warriors, not diplomats from other packs.

"Absolutely not!" She scoffs. "Get dressed, I'm doing your hair. "

"We can't take forever, the guys will come barging in here and carry us down the stairs. I would like to walk back down on my own two feet, thank you very much."

"It will only take a second. You don't even need make-up, you're already so tan from training, but I want you to get a little of your hair out of your face." She gives me a deep side part, then finger combs my hair. Instead of tucking my hair behind my ear on the part side, she whips two jeweled clips out of nowhere and pins the loose strands back. It's super simple, but looks like I put effort in, even with still damp hair. I can't help smiling at my reflection. She always knows how to dress me up, but keep me comfortable.

"They are literally about to bang on the door, let's go." I push back from the vanity.

"What? How do you know that?" She looks at me funny again.

"I can smell them from here." The vanity is just outside my bathroom, on the other side of the room from my door. "Kota and Oliver are right behind my door, Cam is further away behind Kota, and Mateo and Sam are behind all of them." I shrug, heading to the door and throwing it open.

Kota had his hand raised to knock, but they all had varying looks of surprise.

"Holy shit! How did you do that?" Sierra breathes out behind me. "I couldn't smell them till we were halfway across the room. And you got the order correct. Or at least I think you did. Did you guys change?" She asks the twins.

They both nod. "Call it a social experiment." Cam says, looking straight at me.

"What are you trying to prove, Cam?" I ask, really intrigued.

"That, so far, you are the only person who has been able to say who is who while we are dressed the same, without hints."

"I told you, you both have different scents and eye color. That alone should be enough if people pay attention. Your hair is usually done differently, and your builds are slightly different. There are so many things that make you each unique, I don't understand."

"And I really want to unpack the fact that you are the only one who sees those differences, but Mom is starting to get impatient, we have to go." Cam smiles at me and reaches for my hand.

I take it and let him lead me down the stairs, but let go when we get to the second floor landing as we are accosted by people. There are so many more people now than when we went up not even fifteen minutes ago and everyone wants to talk to the guys and Sierra, and surprisingly, me. We all kind of spread out mingling with the crowd, but I can still see all of them. Thank the goddess all my friends are tall. A guy I know I have seen around gets close to me and starts going on and on about something in the trials. I'm not really sure what he's talking about though, he's talking too fast to keep up and most of it is mumbled. I don't really notice how close he is until I feel something brush my hand, I look down and see him stroking the outside of my hand and wrist with one finger. When I look up, he's only a couple of inches from me and I freeze.

"Why don't we go take a walk?" Rando says in a low voice, that, I'm sure, was meant to be inviting, but I am just stuck having never been flirted with by anyone other than the guys, who I don't take seriously at all. He slowly starts to trail his hand up my statue-like arm and gently wraps his hand around my bicep. I want to move, but my body is not listening to my brain. "You seem like the type who likes a good rough time." My eyebrows shoot up into my hairline and I try to step back, but his grip tightens.

"No thanks, I'm good." Is all I could sputter out.

"I was promised a really good time with you, and I don't intend on missing out on all the fun everyone else has been having. Watching you fight today makes me even more excited. I wonder how much you could handle before you break."

"What are you talking about?" Of course the insult brings me out of my scared state. "Let go of me," I say strong and stern, trying to keep my composure. I won't start a fight in the packhouse while the Luna is hosting, but this guy is giving me the creeps and has clearly been misinformed about me.

"Not a chance, I want what I was promised." He growls low and goes to pull my arm again. He clearly thinks he can overpower me. He must not have really been paying attention to my fighting the last two days. I pull my arm back, but he doesn't release his hold, just lets me pull him in closer. "See, I knew you couldn't resist me," he says close to my ear, then a deep menacing growl rumbles directly behind me. I can feel Oliver's body heat warming my back.

"I suggest you keep your hands to yourself, Micah, if you value the use of them." Oliver's arm wraps around my waist and pulls my back completely against him. "She said no, hear the rejection, get over yourself and move on." He's still looking directly at Micah, but talking to me, "Come on Skylar, the Luna will be looking for her favorite girl." A threat was clearly implied here. I could feel the menacing aura coming off of Oliver. Micah steps back, looking pissed.

Oliver moves to my side, but doesn't take his arm off of me as we move down the big staircase to the first floor and on through the kitchen to the back patio. He doesn't release me until we get next to the Luna and Alpha and the rest of the guys. He more or less places me between Luna Ava and Sierra and then steps back by Mateo. Based on the dark look that crosses my brother's face, he was told of what just happened with Micah over their mindlink. A low rumble comes from Cam and Kota on the other side of the Alpha. Oh, goody, they are having a conversation about me and my completely lame situation upstairs. it's not as if my frozen reaction to being flirted with? accosted? propositioned? Wasn't embarrassing enough, now they all know how lame I am.

"Whatever you guys are talking about, knock it off. People are star-ing." I hope that is the end of it, but that would be wishful thinking.

"Someone put their hands on you, Sky, without your permission. And after you told them to back off," Cam says plainly, no judgement or accusation. I didn't miss the use of my name either.

"We've been through this, it's not the first time, and Oliver did step in before there was a problem that would have caused a scene. Now stop, your mom and dad look like they want to speak."

"I had better get a full explanation of what that was," Sierra says in my ear.

I roll my eyes slightly. "Was it that obvious? Just the boys being overprotec-tive."

"Well, you did kind of challenge them to pay attention, now you have five bodyguards. And that was more than just being protective, their auras are in full force right now. If they were full leaders everyone would be in submission right now." She huffs out in a whisper, and I have to fight a smile, it's not that bad.

Luna Ava clears her throat as she and Alpha Lucas stand, stopping all con-versations.

Chapter 29

"We first want to thank Alpha King Reginald and Luna Queen Anne and their son Prince Alexander for joining us this week for Elite Warrior trials. It truly is an honor to be a host pack, and I know all of our young trainees have had an amazing time with your warriors. I know they are all excited to put their new knowledge to use. It was also nice to have some friendly neighboring pack training, everyone involved learned a great deal and I wish you all luck in your placements with the Elite Warriors." A polite amount of clapping follows.

Alpha Reggie follows up with congratulations to all who participated in the trials, stating his trainers have been left with some tough decisions to make. "We are also excited to see the young leaders at the training grounds here in a few weeks. Now that I have seen how much they have grown and what they are capable of here on their home turf, I can't wait to see them challenged again this summer. I may have to rethink some of our strategies seeing your young warriors train." He chuckles and everyone else follows suit before Alpha Lucas finishes.

"We are here to not only celebrate the end of the trials and their success, we are celebrating the end of the year, with many of our graduating pack members moving onto great and successful careers, and our own future leaders heading into the next phase of their training. With their departure, following the mating ball next weekend, we want to wish them well and good luck on their journey this summer. And from the sounds of it, they will need all the luck they can get."

More laughter follows. "Please eat and enjoy yourselves, our pack has much to be thankful for."

With that, both Alphas sit down and look, relieved maybe, that the formalities are all over. I look around at the crowd milling about. This is what I imagine parties for the guys to be like, people crawling everywhere, standing room only and a constant hum of conversation. The buzz is almost palpable. It's a weird sensation and I find myself smiling again for no reason other than I'm included this time.

"Sky, come sit with us," Luna Ava calls me over. "We are all dying to hear about the trials. I was so excited to see your wolf out, she is so beautiful and she has definitely gotten stronger since the last time I saw her."

I moved into the chair she offered me and just smiled at the compliment. I didn't know what else to say. My wolf is just purring in my head at being called beautiful and strong. "She has grown since I've gotten her. I wasn't sure if that was normal, or if she still needs to grow since I got her so early. I have meant to ask Doc T in anatomy or maybe Mr. Lyons in history what they think."

"I don't know if I have ever heard of a wolf growing after they show up, but maybe you're right, you got her very young. You are going to be a force when you are fully trained, based on what I have seen over the last two days," Alpha Reggie says.

I just smile again. I don't really know what to do with all of these compliments. Before I have to really come up with anything though, a plate is placed in front of me and Kota kisses the side of my head before sitting down next to me. Another plate is placed next to that and Cam kisses the other side of my head then moves to sit across from me.

I look to my left. "Dakota, what is all of this?" I figure I would make a point of naming them while they are on this social experiment thing.

"We didn't think you would ever get a chance to eat, so we brought a little of all of your favorites." Then he looks at his brother. "She's still the only one." Cam says across from me.

"Only one, what?" Luna Ava asks with an eyebrow raised. What are the two of you up to?

"She's the only person who can tell us apart when we look exactly the same, don't speak and give no hints," Kota says.

"She's the first person to call us by name since we came downstairs dressed the same. It's actually kind of funny." Cam adds.

"You can tell them apart like this?" Luna Ava looks impressed, gesturing to the twins. "Even I have trouble sometimes. Especially when they are purposely trying to be difficult." She lifts an eyebrow at them, and I smile

"Yes. I can't believe you two are still on this topic, but to be fair there are a bunch of things that set them apart, if people pay attention. I keep telling them that. And thank you for the food, I am starving," I say, becoming a little annoyed that they don't believe me.

"You seem to be the only person aware of those differences, though. For example, Mom, what color are our eyes?" Kota looks pointedly at Luna Ava.

"You both have that beautiful teal color, why?"

"Sky, tell her what you see." He looks at me.

Now I'm nervous about being put on the spot. I take my time swallowing the large mouthful of food I just shoved, unladylike, in my face. "To me, Cam's eyes are emerald green and Kota's are ocean blue. They aren't the same shade, but I can see how blended they would be a teal color."

"Now, Mom, what is our scent?" Cam asks, in full investigation mode now. It makes us both smile.

She gives me a wink and I know that she is just placating them. "You both smell like the holidays, like citrus and spice. It is actually one of my favorite smells." She giggles a little, and I think they both blush. Interesting.

"Skylar?" He doesn't even finish the question.

"Cameron is the one who smells like citrus, and Dakota smells like cinnamon." I roll my eyes as I smile at them, using their full names, like they are using mine. "Just to finish my observations, so I can eat, Cam is slightly taller while Dakota is set wider in the shoulders. Their hair is different, even now when they have tried to comb it the same, Dakota's has more waves and Cam's is a shade darker. There are a few more subtle differences, but you get the idea, they find novelty in the fact that I can tell them apart."

I look away from the twins at the Alphas and Lunas who all look surprised. "Now I'm curious if you could tell them apart in a black and white photo. We'll have to test that sometime," Alpha Lucas says. "But, right now, leave the poor girl alone and let her eat. She took out like 20 wolves today." He winks at me, and I give him an appreciative smile.

"Speaking of kicking ass and taking names, I've got my eye on you, little one. You gave some of my best personal warriors a run for their money and even put Xander in his place."

I choke on my drink, "WHAT!? He never said he went up against me!" I look around for Xander, but he's nowhere to be found. "Did you guys know?" I look at the twins, who at least look sheepish. "Seriously?! Why didn't you guys say anything? Which one was he?"

"That, we are not telling you, Tiny. If he feels like telling you which royally beaten wolf was his, he can do that. If I was him, I would take that info to the grave." Cam laughs and so does everyone else.

We all break into smaller conversations after that, and I just enjoy listening and watching all that is happening around me while I gladly eat all of the food that Cam and Kota brought me. I was having such a good time, I didn't even notice that the sun had set, the patio lights were on and the soft music was slowly turning to more upbeat dance music.

All of a sudden my chair spins around and I am being dragged to my feet. "Come on, Little Bit, this is my jam." Sam pulls me onto the glass cover over the pool that has been made into a makeshift dance floor to an old hip hop song where the only required dance move is jumping around. I couldn't help but laugh and join in, this I could do, normal dancing was not my thing. Every song after that was probably from the late 90's or early 2000's intermixed with every possible song that could tempt the girls present to act like strippers thrown in. I tried to leave the floor everytime one of those songs came on, but there was always one of the guys to hold me there and keep me from looking like a total fool. When 'Don't Cha' is blasted through the speakers, Sierra came running up to me and I finally just let go and we sang it together, giving the guys a show and laughing hysterically. I think every girl ever knows this song, and eventually all the guys left the dance floor to the ladies, making a huge circle to watch our antics. It's the most fun I have had with this many people, ever. I was pretty impressed with Sierra's knowledge of all the rap parts too.

I finally had to step away to get some water and take a break. Sam reluctantly let me go when I promised I would come right back. I was standing at the island in the kitchen, chugging a bottle of water, and heard voices from the back hallway that leads to the garage.

"I just don't know why she wants to keep it a secret. If I was her, I would tell everyone."

"I know, right? There must be something else going on. We'll have to pay really close attention."

Definitely Marnie and Jeanie. I hear footsteps coming towards me, so I scramble back towards the fridge and act like I'm getting something out. They don't even notice me and just keep walking and talking.

"She's probably lying, everyone knows they want their mate. I have heard that all the rumors about them sleeping around are bullshit too. I heard that they are actually waiting to give up their V card to their goddess given mate. Which is totally romantic!" She squeals. "Who knows. They wouldn't all of a sudden decide to hook up with her randomly at a party with the Alpha King here either. No one is dumb enough to believe that," Marnie says. "They've been outside all night. I never saw them leave."

"I don't know. She likes to exaggerate, but would she lie about mates? She's been talking about them being her mates forever," Jeanie asks. "She'd be crushed if she's not the Luna."

"She can't even tell who her mate is for three more years, there's no way." Marnie scoffs. "But I'm not going to stop her from laying claim to them, let her live her fantasy for as long as she can. Cause there is no way she's going to be Luna, she wouldn't be able to handle the job. The Moon Goddess wouldn't make us all suffer like that, she's awful now, can you imagine if she had any real authority?" She giggles, and Jeanie joins in, "We just need to stay on her good side for a few more years, then the truth will come out. She's probably actually mated to some worthless Omega who's abusive. That would be karma, wouldn't it?"

That left me feeling, …I'm not sure actually. I can't believe the people closest to her would talk about her like that, but at the same time, Kaley is a horrible person and clearly still trying to lay claim to the Luna title, clearly spreading lies about her and the twins being together even tonight. I walk outside back to my friends, but I'm not really in the party mood anymore. Every time I hear her mention being with the twins or being Luna, I get an uneasy sick feeling in the pit of my stomach. I go to find the guys to tell them that I am going up to bed, but Sam has other ideas as Just the Way You Are comes on. He grabs Sierra and I and starts serenading the two of us, and all I can do is laugh with her while he tries to dance with both of us awkwardly. The rest of the guys join in our little group and start singing, terribly, to both of us and taking turns to dance with us, very closely and slowly. No one breaks into our little circle, it's sweet and for the first time it leaves me feeling comfortable and safe doing normal teenage things, even in this crowd full of people watching, probably staring at us.

Once the song is over, I break away from Kota and hug each of them, "I need to sleep, I will see you guys in the morning." I hug Sierra a little longer than the rest of them. "Have fun." I wink at her. "If you need to stay tonight you can come cuddle with me."

"Wait. Does that invitation extend to all of us?" Sam asks. I just roll my eyes.

"Hey, wait up, I'll walk you up."

"I battled with about a hundred different people in the last two days, I think I can walk up to my room alone, but thank you, Oliver." I take another step away.

"I'm aware of your capabilities, Bite Size, but my wolf is running circles in my head and giving me a headache at the fact that you are going somewhere without one of us. Especially after the thing with Micah. Can I please just walk with you to shut him up?" He he almost begs.

"Sure, I guess. Does that happen a lot, your wolf being territorial like that?" We start our way to the staircase leading to the second floor.

"Only with you, Bite Size, only with you." He huffs a rare laugh, "And it's crazy, it's like I need to protect you, like my wolf's whole mission is to keep you safe. We haven't even been this protective over a girl we want to hook up with, no offense," he adds quickly at the end, eyes wide, looking terrified that he offended me.

"None taken, and to be honest, I feel the same. You seem to make me calm and centered. I always feel better when I am close to any of you, but each one has a slightly different feel. Is that weird?" I look up at him, and he is smiling, like actually smiling. It is blinding, and jaw dropping. "Oh man! Your mate is in trouble!" I giggle at him.

"What, why?" He sputters and his smile falls; he almost looks like Sam pouting.

"That smile is going to knock her on her ass. I take that back, *you* are going to be in trouble when you find your mate. She is going to lock you up after you throw that smile her way. I thought you were good looking before, but that smile is a whole other level. She's screwed." I laugh again as his grin lights up his whole moody face and he tries to fight it.

I take a look around to make sure no one, mainly Kaley, is looking when I go to punch in the code on the third-floor door. Once Oliver makes sure it is secured behind us, we head up.

"Knock it off, Bite Size, or my ego won't fit through the door." He shoves me in the shoulder with his elbow.

"I'm serious, though. I mean, you're hot just as your broody, silent self, but that smile could probably get you anything you wanted. You should try it on Luna Ava or Martha and see what happens." I laugh out loud this time as we make it to my door. "Thank you for seeing me safely to my door, Oliver, you have done a fabulous job of watching out for me. I hope your wolf calms a bit."

I leaned in to give him a tight hug around the waist. "You are a great friend, and I am very lucky to have you." I rest my cheek on his chest.

He squeezes me back. "Thanks, Sky, that means a lot. Night." He lets me go and steps back, waiting for me to close the door, I guess.

"Night." I close my door and barely get changed and fall into my bed before I am fast asleep.

I wake up to the bright sun streaming through my window and sweating my ass off. What is going on? I try to roll over but there is a weight behind me. I shift forward and that is definitely not a pillow in front of me. I crack my eyes open more to adjust to the light and take a deep breath. Citrus and cinnamon overwhelm my senses. I move to sit up, I really need to go to the bathroom but my legs are completely entwined, I wiggle a little more.

"Tiny, I thought we talked about this, you do not want to move like that this close to us in the morning. Go back to sleep, you have earned a sleep in day," Cam mumbles in front of me, breath fanning my hair.

"I need to pee and you both make that really hard." I laugh at him.

"I'll show you something hard," Kota says low and gravelly into my hair.

"Stop, crazy. Let me up, please," I whine at him. "I promise I will come back and sleep in, just let me pee."

"Fine, you have three minutes before one of us comes in to get you." Kota moves his arm, and I laugh, quickly getting up. I'm not dumb enough to test whether or not he would really come and get me off the toilet.

As I climb over Cam's gigantic body and move to the floor, he does nothing to help, just smiles wide with his eyes closed, I step on something that is definitely not hardwood. I jump, stumble, fall forward and come face to face with Oliver as I belly flop onto his chest. "What the hell?!" I yell as he grunts with my abrupt weight. He coughs out as he stops me from scrambling around on him. "What happened? Are you okay, Sky?" He's on full alert, eyes wide open and body tense as he grabs me by my upper arms, but doesn't move any more than that. Cam turns to look at us from the edge of my bed, but rolls over when he sees me with Oliver. What is going on?!

"What are you doing on my floor?" I push myself up off his chest, but he still has his hands steadying me.

"Couldn't sleep. I just kept getting a weird vibe. This is the only place that made it go away." He closes his eyes and lays his head back down, but not releasing me.

"Huh?!"

He ignores me. "Is there something you needed? Or did you decide you are done snuggling the twins and are ready to share the love?" He wraps his arms around me, smashing my whole body into his chest, and turns on his side.

"Oh no! I have to pee," I say into his chest even though he smells so good. "Let me up before you are the reason I have an accident." He reluctantly lets me go, I scramble away from him and almost trip on my brother's feet at the foot of my bed.

What is going on? I think again. Everything was fine when Oliver and I left them last night. There was no invitation for a slumber party. They aren't here for the fun of it, that much I can feel in my bones. I just don't know why I think that or what could possibly have Oliver on alert next to my bed, my brother on the floor at the foot of my bed, and the twins flanking me. It's almost as if they're waiting for something to come after me. My wolf doesn't think that I am that far off the mark, which has me worried. "What happened last night that made you guys think you all needed to be in here?" I whisper yell at them. Which, of course, gets no reply. They are all happily snoring, with no care in the world. The sinking feeling follows me as I go to the bathroom and on my way back I notice a pile of blankets next to the fireplace. "There's no way," I whisper to myself. I tiptoe over and sure enough, sandy blonde waves and brown straight locks all messed together are tumbling out of the top of the blanket burrito Sam and Sierra are in.

Chapter 30

What in the hell is going on? Why are all my friends in my room? This cannot be comfortable and I don't smell alcohol on them, so I don't think it is a drunken thing, but who knows. I'm too wide awake now to try and wiggle my way between the twins, so I grab Cam's sweatshirt from the floor and head down to see what's for breakfast. I know someone is going to give me a hard time, but I need to try and figure out what the hell is going on. Maybe Kaley became a problem, and they hid out in my room. I feel like I should be more concerned that they were all able to sneak in and I heard nothing. But the 'how' is not as concerning to me as the 'why.'

As I head out, I notice the doors to all the rooms on our floor are closed, even the media room. Weird. The guys never close them unless they are using them. There are a lot of unfamiliar scents up here too, but with the party that's bound to be an after effect. I head down to the second floor and all the guest rooms are closed as well, but there are probably still visiting warriors here surrounding the Alpha King's family. I keep heading down towards the first floor intent on hitting the kitchen and checking in with Luna Ava about the sleeping arrangements. I didn't eat as much as I should have yesterday after the trials. I was too busy talking to everyone and my stomach is mad at me.

As soon as I hit the landing, I'm stopped by a giant of a warrior.

"We are still on lockdown, you need to return to your room." I recognize this guy as one of the warriors from the final phase of trials. He's a big guy, bigger than the Alpha King, my neck hurts from having to look up at him, and I am three steps above him.

"I don't understand, I just came down for breakfast, what happened?" I don't move from my spot, my curiosity getting the better of me.

"We are still on lockdown, you need to return to your room," He repeats.

"Can you tell me when we went on lockdown? I went to bed early last night. The party was still going on when I went up to my room." I point up and behind me in the general vicinity of the third floor door.

"You live here? You're not a guest we detained?" He looks at me with his eyebrow raised and takes in a deep breath. If that clarified anything for him he didn't let on.

"Yes, I live on the third floor." He wants to give me vague answers, I will do the same. I cross my arms, not really to be obstinate, but more visually standing my ground. I wasn't going to be intimidated. "Is anyone else awake? Can I talk to Luna Ava or Alpha Lucas? I don't want to mindlink them if they are sleeping."

"The Alpha King has ordered everyone to stay in their rooms or in their homes for the time being. Please go back to your room."

"Can I at least get some food? You guys did a number on me at trials yesterday and I am starving."

"I will see what I can do, please go upstairs," he growls low and squints his eyes at me like he is trying to remember which wolf I was. Which makes sense considering my size, I don't look like someone who should have been in the trials at all, and I don't remember him at the celebration last night.

"Thank you, Warrior...?" I let the question hang, raising my eyebrows, hoping to get a tidbit of information out of him.

"Osiston Brogan. Go upstairs little one, it's not safe right now." Again, low and growly, like he doesn't want to be heard.

"Why is she walking around and the rest of us are locked in rooms all over the house? Unbelievable! I want to see Cameron and Dakota, this is absurd." My favorite screeching sound comes from above me on the stairs.

I'm still looking at Osiston and we both take a visible, calming breath. He has clearly been dealing with her already this morning. Considering how early it probably is, he has been dealing with her all night. I can't help but smile at him as he rolls his eyes almost imperceptibly.

"You have already been told, *child*, the Alpha King's orders are to remain where you have been placed. We hope to have everyone on their way shortly. The Alpha King, Alpha Lucas, Luna Queen Anne, and Luna Ava will let you know when you can move freely again."

"Well, if she's here, then I can be too," she whines like a four-year-old and begins her stomp down the stairs. I turn and fight an eye roll and a huff.

"Nope! I just had a question, warrior to warrior, about the trials yesterday and since I can't mindlink my buddy Osiston here, I came down to ask." I pat him on the shoulder and he watches the action curiously. He is clearly not a guy people touch without permission. "Now I'm headed back up to wake the guys up. They were all dead to the world when I left them. The party must have gotten wild after I left." I wink at the Warrior who looks a little dumbstruck at my lie, but says nothing.

"Skylar, come find me before we leave, I would love to finish our conversation." His cheek twitches like he wanted to smile, but the act was foreign to him. And how did he know my name? He wasn't a part of the wolves who checked us in and none of the rest of the trainers used our names during the trials.

I nod and turn to walk back up the stairs. "You were put up with Cameron and Dakota?" She takes a deep deliberate inhale. Obviously catching the scent off the sweatshirt to answer her own question. "How did you manage that? I was told no one but warriors were being added to that floor, even when all of the beds had been given out. I know, I was the last to be assigned a spot, and some moron tried to put me on the floor in the formal living room. I had to explain who I was and then move a lesser pack member myself." She sounds almost shocked in her pompous diatribe not like her usual high-pitched voice. I don't think she can ever hide that entitled elitist attitude though.

"Seeing as Skylar is both a warrior and lives in the Packhouse, I see no reason for her to explain the arrangements she has with your Alpha and Luna," Osiston answered before I could. I took another couple of slow steps up the stairs trying to make some distance between her and I before she decided to use her claws against me. But her attention was no longer on me.

Kaley turns to face him fully, throwing a hand on her hip. "And how do you know her name so well, when you call the rest of us child or children? I am going to be the next Luna, you would do well to learn my name, warrior." There's the condescending tone I know.

Osiston stands to his full height, his chest looks even wider like this. Not much scares me, but if he turned that look on me, I would be wetting my pants. "Let's be clear, Luna or not I would still outrank you, so knowing your name is of no priority to me until such time as the Moon Goddess herself decides you are worthy of being a Luna. And even then, you would do well to speak with respect to everyone around you. Next, every one of significance knows Skylar's name because of her efforts in the trials. She has made a name amongst the King's warriors and guards because of her fighting skills, which are unmatched by any other fighter in this pack, and her respectful nature towards everyone in her pack and visiting packs precedes her. You, child, must earn the right to have your name known and more importantly remembered." He stares at Kaley for a moment before his eyes glaze over briefly.

"Skylar, your Luna would like to see you in her room, it will be faster for you to take the elevator from this floor. Nickolas is waiting for you." He moves to step more in front of Kaley to give me space to pass. Once I have rounded the banister and started walking toward the back of the staircase, I hear him finish, "You, child, will be put into the cells if you cannot follow an instruction as simple as 'stay in your room until you are called.' This is your last warning. Move." He didn't yell the last word, but the growl that accompanied it sent a shiver down my spine, there was no denying the menace and power that was rolling off of him.

I got to the elevator and smiled at Nickolas. "Are you going to give me answers, or are you going to be vague like Warrior Osiston? I went to bed early last night, what's going on? I woke up with five boys and my best friend passed out all over my room."

"I can't say much, not here anyway. There was a threat, and we went on lockdown. Anyone that lives inside a mile of the packhouse was escorted home, which was most of the pack members that were still here last night. The rest of the warriors who were still here were divided up into the guest rooms and, as you saw, throughout the packhouse. The guys volunteered to stay in your room and give up their space to the Elite Warriors who are taking shifts to run extra patrols."

"Okay. Well, that is at least more than I got from Warrior Osiston." I shrugged my shoulders and let it go. I figured we were playing it safe for security. I'll get my answers, whatever the Alpha thinks is necessary, in time."

"Someday, you're going to have to tell me how you got him to soften up to you so quickly."

"Huh?" I jerk my face towards him.

"Warrior Brogan. He doesn't usually give his name so quickly, let alone his first name." That was all, no other explanation.

We stand in silence as the elevator rides up to the fourth floor. It's tense, but not uncomfortable. He's on guard and listening to the warriors on patrol checking in or for other instructions, I'm sure. Even my wolf knows something important is going on and is taking in every detail she can. I try to steady my breathing, just like waiting for an opponent to strike in a fight.

Finally, the elevator reaches the top floor and it opens slowly. I feel like time is messing with me with how long it is taking just to get to the Luna and Alpha. All of a sudden, I am engulfed in a hug and blinded by the softest sweater ever. If I could breathe, I would let the Luna keep me wrapped up like this for longer, but I have to tap her shoulder to let her know I need her to loosen her grip on my neck.

"My sweet girl, you're alright!" she whispers out.

"Why wouldn't I be alright? What's going on?"

"The threat we came across last night was not specific, but it was implied that a powerful female was the target. That could be a few different people, the Luna Queen and myself included, but there have been several high-ranking females here over the last few days observing the trials and several in the trials. The Alpha King's guards are running patrols with our warriors to try and find the trail of the messenger, but we haven't heard a thing." She hugs me again.

"I still don't understand what that has to do with me."

"Honey, the threat came right after the warrior trials, and you were the top female. The rest of the ranking females left shortly after the trials were finished yesterday, most can't spend too much time away from their packs. So if the threat wasn't against the Luna queen Queen or myself, we have to assume you would be the next target."

"Is that why Oliver said he got a weird feeling last night? He was on my floor sleeping, said being close was the only thing that made his wolf settle down." She pulled back from our hug and looked at me, a question in her eyes that she didn't voice out loud. "The rest of the guys were sleeping when I left to come down, I didn't get to talk to them." I look around the room, taking in the amount of people here. "Where is the Luna Queen? Shouldn't she be up here, guarded, too?"

"King Reggie felt better keeping her close, his wolf almost took over yesterday after the threat. If Lucas wasn't leading the patrol trying to track the messenger, I would probably be by his side too. He hasn't gone out of mindlink range, though." She smiles at the thought. "He's been checking in every 30 minutes or so."

"What was the threat?" I'm super curious about what has these guys running around in the middle of the night like crazy people.

She closes her eyes and takes a deep breath, like she's deciding how much information to give me. I can see how tense her body is and it's making my wolf and I a little anxious.

"You don't have to say if it bothers you to talk about," I spit out quickly, I don't want to upset her any more than she already is.

"No, sweet girl, it's not that it will upset me, I think it will upset you."

"Huh?! What could have been said in a threat to you or the Luna Queen that would affect me?"

She takes one more deep breath and grabs my hand. I can't tell if she is supporting herself or me with the gesture. "Someone broke through the western border. It's not a far distance over the water to the mainland, but our patrols should have heard a boat coming. The messenger slipped in undetected about 5 miles, left us a package that was clearly supposed to be found quickly and then they disappeared, with no scent or any of the usual signs a tracker would notice left behind. There seems to be no trace of the person or people who left it." She pauses again. She's stalling, but I don't know why and it's making me sick to my stomach. "There was a full search of our territory by all available warriors and while the border patrols are going over every possibility of entry, we are also doing a full investigation on everyone who is here to verify their location at the time of the threat. That is what is taking so long and why everyone is still on lockdown."

"Luna, you are really freaking me out now. I went to bed early, Oliver walked me to my room, but I left early. Am I a suspect? Cause you know I would never do anything to you or Luna Anne…" She grips my hand tighter.

"Shh. Sweet girl." She lifts a hand to cup my face. "It's nothing like that. We know where you were, you are not in trouble, but I do think you might be in danger."

My eyebrows shoot up and the tears pooling behind my eyes slip down my cheeks. "What?!"

Another inhale and then a squeeze of my hand and a soft rub of my cheek with her thumb. "Sweet girl, our warriors found two fingers in a box. They had been frozen and there doesn't seem to be any blood left to use for identification, but we have everyone who could possibly give us answers working on that."

"I still don't understand what this has to do with me." As gruesome as it would be to get cut off fingers delivered, it doesn't sound like something that should have the whole pack in an uproar.

"Both fingers have the mark of a Luna, the one she receives when she accepts her title during the Luna ceremony. Which leads our doctors to believe two Lunas were harmed or killed. The flesh of the fingers appears to have been severed from the body with…" another inhale and exhale, "silver powder. It was burned down to the bone, where there are saw marks. The damage to the skin is the exact same as on your back."

I drop her hand as both of mine fly to my mouth. Someone, or two people were tortured to the point of having fingers removed, slowly, by the burning of silver powder. How long would something like that even take? Hours or days? What would make someone want to hurt another person like that? And why was it brought here? Does someone know about what Kaley has done to me? Is it some kind of sick joke from her? At the thought of her, my mind takes me back to that day and the smell of burning flesh fills my nostrils, the searing pain hits my back like the silver was just applied. My whole body remembers those moments, and everything hurts. I can't move, I'm locked in that memory and can't escape. I glance around and can vaguely see the Luna's mouth moving, but I can't hear a thing she is saying from the blood pounding in my ears. My whole body feels cold and limp, but I am frozen to my spot. I do register a loud noise and then warm hands wrapping around me and tucking my face into a large chest. The warmth surrounds me and feels good, but I can't move, the pain won't leave. My body won't respond to any command I try to give it, I'm a prisoner.

"Bite Size, I need you to breathe for me, please breathe, Bitty. I will punch you if I have to. You are scaring the shit out of us, Skylar. SKY! BREATHE!" I hear the panic in the words, but I can't respond.

Two hands grab my face and cradle it firmly, but gently at the same time. Dark chocolate brown eyes look into mine and the absolute panic there is what catches my attention. Why is he panicked? What did I do to put that look on his face? Oh, Goddess! I put that look on his face! I am the cause of this feeling, this hopelessness and deep bone numbing sorrow. I can't even blink or look away, I'm just lost in the deep warm brown sadness of his eyes.

"Dammit, Bitty!" He he shouts, and I'm confused why he's angry now, but I don't get the chance to think about it before he smashes his lips to mine.

It's as if someone flipped a switch, flooding my senses all at once, sending an electric shock that jolts my lungs awake. I push back and gasp for air, my breath shaky. I glance around the room, still disoriented, but with each deep breath, I begin to focus more clearly on the things around me. It's like someone turned on all of my senses at once sending an electric shock to jumpstart my lungs. I push back again and take a deep, gasping breath in. I look around the room, still confused, but I can actually focus on the things around me the more air I take in. There is a low rumbling growl coming from somewhere near me, and I feel hot all over, like I have been working outside in the middle of a summer day. I remember talking to Luna Ava, then time sort of stopped. I keep turning my head to try and focus on who is in the room with me, then the smell of honey hits my nose, and I turn to face the boy in front of me, still holding my face between his hands, eyes wide and cheeks tear streaked. I let go of his wrists and wiped the tears away. As I do, his hands fall and I notice I am sitting across his lap, his hands are by his sides not touching me at all anymore. When I look back up, he is still staring at me and all I can do is wrap my arms around his shoulders and bury my face in his neck. The growling around me gets louder, but I ignore it. Oliver saved me from myself, he got to me first and I can feel the panic still resonating in him, but I don't think it's worry for me anymore. He's worried about my reaction to what he had to do to snap me out of my shock, about the reaction from the others. Wait, how do I know what he is feeling? I pinch my eyes closed, I don't have time for my squirrel thoughts right now. Oliver is still sitting here like a statue, I can feel the rapid pace of his heart and the tense set of his muscles everywhere I have contact with him.

Chapter 31

"It's okay, I'm okay, we're okay." I just keep whispering the mantra into his neck until he finally wraps his arms around my waist and hugs me back. I have no idea how long we sat like that. Both of us just let the last couple of minutes set in and process.

"That was so fucking scary, Bitty. I have never felt anything like that before," he's talking into my hair and it's so low, it's less than a whisper, but the silence of the room lets me know others are listening in. His arms tighten around me and he takes another shuddering breath.

"How did you get to me so fast? How did you find me? I haven't even been up here that long," I ask, not moving my face from his neck.

"We were actually looking for you, when you never came back from the bathroom. And I got this sharp pain in my chest. It hurt so much I almost collapsed. Then my wolf shouted your name and basically took over my body and brought me up here. Your lips were blue when I got to you, I panicked and didn't know what else to do, you weren't breathing or moving...I'm so sorry." He takes another deep breath, his nose buried in my hair. His body is calming down, but his mind and his emotions are still holding tension I don't understand. He felt my pain. How could he feel my pain? It was the pain of a memory, nothing real. And how did his wolf know where to find me? Too many questions for my brain right now.

"That was scary for more than just the two of you." I notice a voice very close to my back. "What happened?" Cam's deep voice rumbles as he wraps an arm around my waist and tries to pull me into his lap, Oliver loosens his grip, but doesn't let me go right away, a small whimper escaping his lips.

"I squeeze his hand. "I'm okay, not going far." I slide back into Cam's lap, but keep my legs across Oliver's, and he instinctively wraps his hand around my ankle, like it will keep me from disappearing. The rumbling in Cam's chest calms down a little as I get closer to him. That's where the growling sound has been coming from. But, why? Why would he be mad at Oliver for saving me? It's a question for another time. So many questions for later.

"Mom, what happened?" Kota asks as calmly as he possibly can. I can feel the fear radiating off of him too. He comes to sit in front of Cam on the floor. I reach out to play with his hair, knowing he needs contact just like Oliver, Cam and I.

She relays what she was telling me, this obviously wasn't new news to any of the guys and Sierra. They had all been up when everything started to go crazy. She looked in my direction every few seconds like she was waiting for another episode. When she got to the part about the silver, which *was* news to the guys, I scramble back into Oliver's lap, like he's the only one who can battle that demon with me. I straddle his lap, my arms lock around his neck, my face buried in his neck again, his scent seems to be the only thing that is helping me battle the torment of what happened to another wolf and the fact that it might have something to do with me. He just gently rubs my back, not saying anything, conveying everything in his light touches.

"What's the plan, Mom? You and Luna Anne can't just stay holed up forever. And it doesn't seem like we've made much progress with finding the asshole who did this," Kota asks. I don't look up from Oliver's shoulder, I'm really tired all of a sudden.

"I think Lucas and Reggie have what they need for now. Patrols will be increased and a higher security protocol will be in place. Now, please remember, none of the details I have given you have been told to pack members. We have more questions than answers and don't want to incite panic. If you have thoughts about the situation or want to discuss it further, this is the only safe space in the packhouse."

"But, not even our..." Kota starts.

"No, not even your floor can be considered safe yet, and based on Oliver's instincts last night and today the target of the threat is still unclear, and we have to assume all ranked members and future leaders are in danger. Trust his Gamma instincts, they are designed to keep the Luna safe. Just as the Beta's instincts are to keep the Alpha Safe. Brett was a little crazy last night too, he didn't leave my side until I came up here with a full guard. Stick together and none of you are to go anywhere alone. Not even the bathroom at school. Now we are stuck here until Lucas and Reggie return, which will be later this evening. I'm going to bring Xander up and we can all get something to eat, then I imagine all of you could use a nap."

Some of the Omegas bring up food and everything is thoroughly checked before anyone is allowed to eat. I have wanted to be a warrior for as long as I can remember, but this is the first time it has really hit me what that would look like. Fighting is one thing, it's actually the easy part, but the unknown threats, the things that can mess with your mind if you think about them too long. That is something I didn't consider. This invisible threat, no one knows who's the villain, and there is always a villain. Some are just more extreme than others, but you have to watch out for them all, especially when you are responsible for the protection of some of the most important people in your pack.

We all sit on or around the Luna's bed and watch TV, or at least pretend to. She is constantly up walking around, checking in with pack members and giving directions from her own little prison. The warriors watching us are walking around the suite, constantly checking the windows and doors. They are trying to be discreet, but it is really just making me antsy. I don't know how many times I changed positions, but I felt the need to be close to each of my friends. Eventually, I got tired and crawled in between Kota and Cam first, in our usual sandwich position, and I fell asleep immediately.

Their cocoon of warmth and safety allowed the last of my anxiety from the Luna's story to fade and I was able to rest properly. I'm not sure how long I was there, but all of a sudden my body heat kicked in and I had to move before I sweat to death. It was like someone kicked on a space heater in my chest and I was suffocating. I carefully crawled out from their limbs, each wrapped around me like octopus tentacles, and slid to the floor at the end of the bed with Sierra and Sam who were in the middle of some action movie. The sky was growing darker outside, but it couldn't be more than late afternoon. She was sitting in between his legs, so I just lay on my side, using their right thighs as a pillow. Sam casually draped his arm on my side and Sierra started playing with my hair, lulling me back to sleep.

Like before, my body heat raged waking me up from a deep dreamless sleep, but as I tried to move, I realized my body was being trapped by something. Trying not to panic, with everything else going on that's my go-to reaction apparently, I look around and notice I have turned into Sierra with my face buried in her hip. I can still smell Sam, but there is something else, vanilla and spices. Mateo. His strong arm is wrapped around me and has my back pulled tight to his chest. He's using Sierra's leg as a pillow as well. I take another deep breath of their combined scents and feel calmness wash over me, but the heat is going to kill me. I have to move. I dislodge his heavy arm from around me and look around to find Oliver's legs sticking out from the side of the Luna's bed. I crawl over in the darkness, the sliver of moonlight the only thing allowing me to make out their shapes in the still room, to see him lying on his back with his left arm draped over his eyes. This must be his go-to spot for sleeping when a bed isn't an option. I move to his right side, with my head propped on the edge of his pillow, face pressed into his bicep as I wrap both arms around his massive arm, like a child hugging their favorite toy. And again, I drift off.

✦ᐧ⟩⟩⬤⟨⟨ᐧ✦

"Not until she does." The gruff mumble from Oliver alerts me to people talking around me, but I don't move.

"Well, then wake her up, I'm not leaving without her, and by now she's probably starving." Cam's whisper is stern and matter of fact, but at the mention of eating my stomach makes itself known with a loud garbled growl. "See, starving."

"Still, not moving until she does." Oliver's low warning timber makes me smile. "She's probably never slept this long before and needs it."

"You jealous she spent more time with him than you two?" Sam is teasing Cam, but what are they talking about? My brain is still sleep foggy, and I'm having trouble following their line of conversation.

"No!" he said defensively, and a little high pitched, very unlike his usual calm nature, and not in a way that had anyone believing him. "But my wolf won't let me leave without her, and we all need to go downstairs and meet with the Alpha King before they all leave."

I take a deep breath and open my eyes curious enough to want to know what they are talking about. "The Alpha King is leaving, now? Is Xander going with him?" I push up from the floor and feel the tingling pins and needles from my arms waking up. Oliver's arm is heavier than I thought and must have cut off the circulation to my own while I was holding on. I shake them out and wince, trying to speed up the process.

"Of course you get up when we mention Xander!" Kota sounds irritated too. What happened while I was sleeping?

"It's hard to sleep when you guys are arguing right above my head. Are we free to move around the packhouse now? Osiston said they would let us know when we could come out of the lockdown." I stood and stretched. That was some of the best and longest sleep I've had in forever.

"He told you his name?! The rest of us get to call him Warrior or Sir. And, yes, I do have to leave with my father, but we will be in touch. This situation is unusual and until we figure out who the target is or who the intruder is, we will have to keep working together. The castle is only a couple hours from here by car and 45 minutes by boat, so we could be here quickly if you need us."

"You are the second person to ask me about Warrior Osiston's name." I yawn. "Does he really not allow anyone to use it?" Skipping right past the jealousy in Kota's voice. "Do you know when you will be back this way? Or, well, I guess the guys are coming to you this summer for training. So it will probably be after that at the earliest with all of the things going on now. That will be weird to not have any of you around." It finally dawned on me that, at some point they will all be leaving, Sierra included.

"Warrior Brogan, usually goes by his last name, if he lets you call him by a name that is. My father occasionally calls him by his first name, which is the only reason I know it. He really introduced himself with his first name?" He sounds shocked.

I just rolled my eyes and headed toward the elevators. "Can we really go eat? You were right, Cam, I am starving." Cam gives me a little smile at the acknowledgement when I pass him. Everyone shuffles to join me, the elevators ding and we all pile in. Kota pulls me back towards one of the corners and places me directly in front of him, wraps an arm around my waist and locks my back to his chest. Cam stands next to me and grabs my hand, interlocking our fingers. Oliver stands in front of me and Mateo in front of Cam so I am completely boxed in. I'm glad I'm not claustrophobic since I am barely taller than their elbows. I can't see a thing. I resist the urge to roll my eyes and huff, it's a real struggle, though. I am fully capable of protecting myself. The Luna's, who are probably just as equally skilled at fighting, should be the main focus, not me.

When we get to the first floor, there is a steady hum of commotion. Clearly everyone has been released from the lockdown and is in need of a quick meal and to get outside. Our wolves don't like to be cooped up like this. At least we all got to be together, I feel bad for mates who were separated or parents and kids who were separated overnight.

We all grabbed food and headed out back, but instead of going to one of the patio tables, I head straight towards the Luna's garden maze. There aren't any tables back here, but most people won't go back here, and we can get a little freedom from the commotion of the packhouse while still getting to be outside. I head straight toward my shady spot, with the hammock. I'm not dumb enough to sit in the hammock though, knowing the guys are going to want to sit with me and I will not tolerate them breaking my favorite reading spot.

"How long have you been hiding this spot?" Sierra sits on the ground next to me. We all dig in like we haven't eaten in weeks. This might be the equivalent for the guys who are used to full meals all of the time. The never-ending supply of PB and J sandwiches we lived on yesterday were not enough.

"Luna Ava has had it forever, she put the hammock up a few years ago when she kept finding me back here reading." I shrug at her. "It was always a quick place to get away from Dad when he was in a mood." I turned my attention to Xander who followed us in and quickly changed the subject. "When are you guys taking off, I have to make sure I find Warrior Nickolas and Osiston before you all leave."

"Once everyone is done eating, I think. The guys are packing everything up now. Warrior Brogan was asking about you earlier, said you had a conversation to finish." Xander cocked an eyebrow at me, and I just laughed and rolled my eyes. "Are you going to explain, or just leave us all hanging?"

"I can't here, the walls might have ears, but he can tell you on your ride back." I wiggle my own eyebrows at him conspiratorially.

His eyes glaze over for a brief second. "And, on that note, it is time for me to go. Walk me out?" He looks right at me.

"Yeah." I move to stand up and everyone else does the same. I fight another eye roll and move forward to walk by Xander, wondering if they will ever let me be alone with him.

"We are going to have to find a way for you to come out, even if it's with the guys. I know my mother would love to have you and you could see the torture we all go through each summer." He smiles at me.

"That would be amazing, considering you are stealing all of my friends this summer. Even Sierra has to go home at some point." I pretend to pout, trying to give my best Sam impression.

"Well then, we have to make it happen, since we will be the cause for that look." He smiles at me again and it lights up his whole face. I return it easily. I feel like we could be really good friends, if the guys stopped with their interfering jealousy. I'll have to figure out how to give him my information before they leave.

"Little One, you are going to have to explain how you make such good friends and such annoying enemies," Osiston's voice booms at me from the driveway.

"I will when you explain why everyone keeps asking how and why I know your first name."

"Wait! He gave you a nickname too?!" Xander almost shouts.

"That is a good question, and I can only tell you that my wolf decides." Osiston completely ignores Xander.

"What?! What does that even mean?" I'm right in front of him now, straining my neck to look up at him. "And can you squat or sit or something? This is ridiculous."

He chuckles and squats in front of me and we are eye level. "You are special, Little One, I will be seeing you again soon."

"Can I give you something?" I ask, and he looks at me skeptically. "Just give me your phone," I say exasperated, holding out my hand.

He gives it over slowly. I plug in my information, save it, and then flip to Xander's contact and forward him the info. "There, now we can communicate." I'm looking at Osiston, but I'm speaking to Xander as his phone goes off. He looks at the notification and the largest grin splits his face, like a little boy on Christmas morning getting the first glimpse of presents.

Alpha Reggie walks over with Luna Anne. "You really are something special. I can't wait to see what you accomplish." He grips my shoulder in a manly way, and then Luna Anne gives me a hug.

"Keep in touch, sweet girl." She looks over my shoulder and smiles, hugging me one more time and then moving on to the guys, then Alpha Lucas and Luna Ava.

Once everyone is packed up and on their way, we start heading back into the packhouse and an unease sets in my stomach.

Chapter 32

"I really need to run, guys, can we just go to the arena for a little bit? Please? I need a couple of hours, we slept for a whole day." I look at each of them. "You don't all have to come, but I can't go by myself even if you would allow it. Luna Ava said not to do anything alone right now. Please?" I shake my hands out to try and get rid of some of the jitteriness. The closed in feeling is making me anxious. I don't like feeling trapped, even if it's for my own safety.

"Why don't the rest of you run along and Cam and Kota can help me, since she doesn't need all of you to tag along with her. I left a few things up in my room and could use a couple of strong men to help me." Kaley's high-pitched voice cuts through like a dull knife. She's strutting up in what should be a shirt, but she has pulled down and belted to act as a very short dress. "You can both help me gather my things and then escort me to my house." She's smiling at them like a stalker looks at a celebrity. "It will give us some quality time together too." She simpers.

"What could you have possibly brought to the party that would require help from two guys?" Sam asks, not hiding his absolute distaste for her suggestion.

"A girl just needs a strong hand or two, that's all." She waves him away, "And I would really appreciate the help." She flips her hair and flexes her eyes at Sam daring him to contradict her again. The problem is, she doesn't seem to know Sam very well, and he absolutely loves that kind of challenge.

"Oh no, I totally understand, you need a schlep." He looks around and grins wickedly. "Micah!! Hey, Micah, Come here a second!" Sam shouts over the crowd of people hanging outside the packhouse, I'm sure to catch a glimpse of the Alpha King leaving. Almost everyone turns to stare at him.

Micah walks over slowly, eyeing us suspiciously. "What's up, Sam?"

"Kaley here needs some assistance with her things, and you are a perfect man for the job. You know, always wanting to step in and put a *hand on...* I mean, lend a hand to our female pack members. You can follow her up, grab her stuff, and get her settled back at her house, right? Thanks, man!" Sam slaps him on the shoulder, "Appreciate the help. We have our own assignments to get done." Sam turns, wrapping his arm around Sierra, and starts to walk away, not even looking over his shoulder to see who is following. But none of us are dumb enough to stick around and let her try and wiggle her way into our group again.

I told all the guys they didn't have to do any training, but knew they wouldn't be able to sit out either. We did basic cardio, some stretching, which the guys hated, and then strength training in the weight room. I needed to feel like I put my body through something today to get stronger, but I also had two hard days of full battle and I am still recovering from those beat downs. There's nothing like the feeling when your endorphins hit during exercise, though. It's the best kind of high ever, and it makes my muscles hurt a little less.

"Okay, guys, we can go now, we will be back to our regular schedule tomorrow, so let's not overdo it." I laugh at their sweaty faces, look at Sierra then grab her hand and run for it. I have no idea what I was thinking, but for once in my life I went with an instinct to just play, and a game of cat and mouse seems like fun.

We are laughing through the streets, making sure to keep the guys in our sights, but not close enough to catch us. As I run up the steps to the packhouse front door ready to declare myself the winner, I am looking back over my shoulder to make sure I can still see the guys who are kind of running behind us, they have clearly given up on the chase and could have easily caught up a long time ago, when I run smack into someone and and we both go toppling down inside the entryway.

"WHAT THE HELL?! Could you at least watch where you are going? There is no reason to run through the door like a wild animal. This is a formal packhouse and should be treated with respect and dignity."

"I am so sorry, I didn't realize the door was open when..." My words fall short when I look up into the hateful eyes of Kaley. She had already popped back up to her feet elegantly, while I am slowly scraping my heap of a body off the porch. "What are you still doing here? I thought everyone went home." That might be the first time I have questioned her without the presence of a pup getting abused.

"Don't be ridiculous, of course I came back. You don't think you can hog Cameron and Dakota as well as the Alpha Prince, do you, you little skank? You need to get out of the way, there is no reason for any of them to even pretend or entertain the idea of being friends with you, let alone anything more, which is clearly what you are trying to do by leading them all on." She's talking extremely loudly and I'm not sure why. "Won't your boyfriend be upset at all the time you spend with other guys? You must be an expert at all forms of sex to keep them all occupied at the same time. Or maybe you get extra perks with the Alpha by keeping our future leaders satisfied. That's why they moved you in, isn't it?"

"Huh?! What are you talking about?" I'm trying to control my breathing. Did she just ask if I was a sex toy for the twins?

"Why haven't we heard about a boyfriend?" Oliver asks behind me. Kaley looks at me with a triumphant gleam in her eye. "That's something we should probably know about there, Bitty, don't you think?

"What?!" I shriek and turn, "No, I..."

"I think we need to discuss this and make sure we approve of this guy, you know... standards and all of that. Thank you, Kaley, for bringing this to our attention. I'm sure you can see yourself out since you should have left hours ago anyway," Sam chimes in and pushes me past her and further into the packhouse followed by the rest of the guys and Sierra, who shuts the door in her bewildered face.

"We need to find something to occupy that girl, she is exhausting to try and get rid of all the time." Sierra smiles at me. "You okay? She was kind of harsh."

"You don't really have a boyfriend, right?" Kota asks.

"Really? That's what you're worried about? When none of you leave her alone for longer than twenty minutes at a time. Kaley was a bitch to one of your best friends, calls her a slut to her face and in front of as many people as possible. She continues to tell people she's the future Luna; that she's sleeping with the twins exclusively and who knows what else, and you're worried about a boyfriend she fabricated to make Skylar sound like a skank? Sky should be allowed to punch you in the balls as hard as she can for that."

"I'm not punching anyone, right now." I grab Sierra's hand to try and calm her down. "And, no, I don't have a boyfriend. Are you kidding? I wouldn't even know what to do in that situation. I barely talk to you guys, let alone any other guy in the pack. I'm getting some food and heading to my room. I need to get back on track, we still have school and training this week. I need to get caught up." I turn and walk to the kitchen, dragging Sierra behind me, not caring if any of the guys follow.

This whole week has thrown me off my usual track. We've been out of school and I haven't had to deal with Kaley and her minions, everyone visiting has pulled my focus, but now that they are all gone and the dust is settling, my old routine of 'hide from the bitches' will return, and I can only hope I did enough to have the Elite Warriors want me next year.

It's almost as if the kitchen Omegas knew I was coming. A plate was ready for me with a sandwich, chips, veggies, sliced fruit, and a bottle of water. One looked over at me as I came through, nodded her head to the plate, and then winked before going back to her chores.

"Thank you, Lenny! How did you know? This looks amazing!'"

"You always eat a full meal after training. Gotta keep you well fed since you keep those boys of ours in line." She shrugs like it's common knowledge and not a big deal.

"Well, I appreciate it. Thank you so much." I hug her before I grab my things and start to head back out and toward the stairs as the rest of my friends file into the kitchen.

"Hey, Lenny! Can we possibly get a snack too? Smalls totally worked us over and we burned through your amazing cooking from earlier," Kota asks excitedly after seeing my plate.

"All the supplies are right there on the counter for you, boys. Sierra, your plate is right there."

"Wait! You made them plates and not us? I thought we were tight, Lenny!" Sam whines.

"We are, which is why you have access to food right after I just fed half the pack and guests and just finished cleaning everything up. Those two young ladies of yours, however, clean up after themselves and never make me come find my dishes." I giggle at her response. These boys may help with parties, but they clearly don't with the daily chores. She may be an elderly Omega, but she's like a grandma you don't cross at the best of times. I would not want to be on her bad side. She looks like a woman who can use a wooden spoon effectively.

Sierra meets me at the base of the stairs with her plate, giggling as we hear the boys protest Lenny's claims. We head to my room and get started on the work for the next few weeks. I know I'm not behind, but it feels weird to not have a month's worth of assignments basically complete.

For the first time in what feels like forever, but has only actually been about a week, the guys leave us alone. It feels weird to not have their auras and voices filling the room. Once we were done with all of the work we could complete, we headed outside. The day is so nice and I want to soak up the last rays of sun sitting in the hammock and reading quietly. Sierra just laid beside me and dozed.

We only last a few minutes before my distracting thoughts get the best of me. I look over at her lying next to me in the massive hammock. "When do you leave? I actually didn't think about you only being here this year until Xander left today."

"I actually don't know, my parents didn't have an exact return date. Who knows, maybe I can stick around a little while longer." She smiles over at me. "This year has been a blast, and very eventful." She giggles. "I was actually afraid of being bored away from the never-ending business of the Royal Pack. There is always something going on, something that needs attention, some person or pack that needs something. And don't get me started on the morons who think it's a good idea to try and attack and overthrow the Alpha King. But you, my friend, have kept me just as on my toes as any of those people. You are deceiving in your tiny little package." She squints over at me, shielding her eyes from the sun.

"Well, maybe I will get accepted into the Elite Warrior program and I can get out of here and come see your world. That would actually be a fun trade."

"You really have to stop talking about leaving, Bitty." Oliver comes around the corner of the little hedge hiding my hammock, rubbing his chest as he sits down on my side effectively scooching me to the center and almost sending us flying off with the unbalanced weight.

"WHOA SHIT! Sorry!" He yelps and Sierra and I squeal with laughter as he keeps us from toppling to the ground.

Thankfully, he's quick on his feet, literally, and stops the hammock from completely capsizing. He shifts us around so he's lying in between us.

"Why did you change your nickname for Sky? I noticed, before..." Sierra trails off, we are all thinking about how they found me yesterday morning in the Luna's room. "You called her 'Bitty' then too."

"I don't know really. 'Bite Size' was just part of the joke, but we kept it up and since we all started training with her and we all started getting bigger, it dawned on me how little bitty she really is compared to us. So it's something that I have just been thinking in my head, and it came out at that moment." He shrugged. "As much as I want to sit here and chill with you two, we actually can't stay, the Alpha sent me to find you, Bitty. He wants to talk to you about something. Let's go." He moves to get up and almost topples us again. "How do you manage to not look like an idiot getting in and out of this thing?"

"Well, I am about the size of your left leg, so there's that. I'm also just better." I giggle at him, jumping off the hammock sending him and Sierra swinging the other way. She uses the momentum to jump to her feet and the whole thing spins and almost dumps him in the grass. I jump away before he can grab me, trying to think of something to distract him. "Wait, what about Sierra? Luna Ava said not to be alone."

"Never fear, her wolf in shining armor is here!" Sam jumps out from the bushes, causing us all to laugh.

"How long have you had that line in your pocket?" She scoffs at him.

"Long enough, fair maiden. Can I keepest thou company while you lay majestically in the hammock?" He clicks his heels together and bows deeply before grabbing her hand and kissing the back of her knuckles.

"Of course, good sir." Sierra giggles.

"Come on, let's go before they start making out in front of us." Oliver puts his arm around me and leads me out of the little garden.

"Hey! No sex on my hammock!!" I shout over my shoulder only to hear laughter in response. And then Sam's, 'I make no promises,' faintly followed. "Please remind me to sanitize that thing." I look up at Oliver.

"They are probably not the first to bang on the hammock, Bitty." He lifts an eyebrow at me.

"Ugh! I know, but now the thought is in my head and that's not an image I really want when I want to lay there to relax." I scrub my hands over my face. Oliver just laughs at me again.

We make it into the Alpha's office and he's the only person here. I don't know what I expected, but I figured at least Luna Ava would be here.

"Ah, Skylar, grab a seat. Oliver, can you wait outside please, this won't take long."

Oliver is reluctant, which makes me more nervous. I watch him leave slowly, really unsure of what is going on now. "Did...did I do something wrong, sir?" I'm starting to panic a little. I have never been called to see the Alpha before and with everything going on, I hope that I'm not a suspect. I wasn't around when they found the severed fingers and had to lock everyone down. And with no unfamiliar scent leaving the territory they have to think it is someone from this pack. There is no other explanation. Maybe the Luna was just being nice to me yesterday while they eliminated all other options, seeing if I would slip and say something incriminating. Maybe I am the only option left. I can feel my chest starting to heave as I try to control my breathing.

"Child, if you don't shut down your thoughts I will Alpha command you." I bring my unfocused gaze back to him and force myself to look into his face. He is rubbing his temples like he has a migraine. "You are not a suspect, you are not in trouble, but yes— I do think you may have information or might be able to help us with this situation. I have now been given limited details of your situation. I wish you would have come to me, but I also understand why you didn't. As a father, it hurts me to know that's how little you think of all of us fathers because of your personal experience. I know the kind of man your father is for me, my experience is not yours. I will not force you to tell me, but know this, I can and will help you when you are ready to give me your whole story. It does not make you weak to speak out against people who are taking advantage of you or harming you to better their situation." He takes a deep breath before continuing. "As for our most recent incident, you are correct, I think it is someone who is in our pack or on our territory with permission based on the lack of unfamiliar scent. The problem is there was no recent scent to work with. The strongest scent was the patrol wolves that had run in that area about an hour before the package was found. Meaning they are masking it somehow. It didn't occur to me until too late that your unique sense of smell with regards to my sons might be helpful to us in our investigation. I am also aware that my mate and my sons would probably skin me alive for asking you to help since they are all convinced you might have been a target. But, since I am Alpha, I will do what I need to do to protect this pack as I believe you will. So here is my proposition for you—." He takes a deep breath, "I will bring you into this investigation as I see fit. I will not hide it from the Luna, and I will only inform my sons if they ask. I will not lie about your involvement, it just won't be a publicized thing. I will leave it to you if you want to tell the boys of your involvement yourself. Second, I want to know the next time you are harmed at school, no matter how big or little the injury. And before you argue, I have been watching from a distance and knew something was going on, but I couldn't gather enough evidence to do any formal investigation. I still can't, and my wolf and I are not happy about your situation in the slightest."

"I am not tattling every time someone shoves me in the hallway. That does make me look weak, like I can't handle myself."

"Currently, you are not handling yourself. You may be stepping in for lesser or weaker pack members, but you are a punching bag for those who are weak minded. If you were handling yourself, you would treat those bullies the same as you treated your opponents during trials. They wouldn't have years of opportunities to harm you." He squares a look at me, that makes me want to shrink back, but I won't, I won't look weak now that pressure is being put on me.

"I just get in trouble. Even when I only use words to defend myself. The headmaster never believes me and told me if I was in any more fights I would be expelled or at the very least suspended, and I have never actually been caught in a fight." I'm raising my voice, something I normally would never do, especially to our Alpha, but if he is in father mode then I feel justified in reacting like a teenage child. "I can't prove anything, and I can't afford to miss school, especially not now with Elite Warrior training camp on the line. I won't jeopardize my spot, because someone got handsy with me. I will not let anyone take that away from me, I have put up with too much to get to where I'm at." My breathing has picked up and I can feel my chest tightening, tears threatening. "I have to get out of here, I need to find my purpose, my own way. I won't let mindless bullies get in the way of that, they have already taken so many things." The well of tears blurring my vision makes me more angry.

Knock, Knock, Knock. We both turn towards the sound.

The door cracks open. "Bitty, you okay? I'm dying out here, it feels like an asthma attack," Oliver calls in.

I turn to see him grasping the door handle, knuckles white, his other hand on his chest again, and pain in his eyes.

"I'm fine, sorry, Oliver." I take a deep calming breath. I have to remember he is sensitive to my emotions all of a sudden, especially extreme ones. I take another breath and scrub my hands over my face, pushing the sadness into a box in the back of my mind to be dealt with later. Just another reason to keep my emotions in check.

When I look back at the Alpha, he has a curious expression on his face. "How long has he been able to pick up on your emotions like that?"

Chapter 33

"Uh, I'm not really sure. He was able to find me yesterday when the Luna told me about what was in the package, and I was... afraid." I couldn't tell him what really went through my head. "He said he 'felt' it in his chest. And he couldn't sleep the other night after the celebration, that he had a weird vibe and the only thing that made him feel better was sleeping on my floor next to my bed. I mean all the guys were in my room, but the twins were with me in the bed, and he was on the floor next to me. Is that weird?"

"I'm actually not sure, I don't know if I've ever heard anything like it. But another thing and the real reason I brought you in here is the Alpha King, Warrior Nickolas, and Warrior Brogan want you to train with the Elite Warriors. They have extended a formal invitation to me. They want you soon too. I haven't told anyone except the Luna, Kyle, and Brett about this either. Not even your father." He stops and stares at me, letting that information sink in as I just stare at him.

"WHAT!! NO WAY?! ARE YOU SERIOUS? WHEN? HOW? WHAT?!?!" I can't even form a coherent sentence. I am so excited! "AHHH!" I jump up and run around his desk to jump in his arms. He's quick and saw me coming, standing to catch me and wrap me in a hug. I let the small little girl in the back of my head have the fleeting thought that this is what a father should do before I stuff it back down in the darkest corners of my mind. I squeeze the Alpha tighter, hopefully putting all my joy and appreciation into this hug.

"Delta Kyle was not lying when he told you that you went against the most opponents both days. The warriors were trying to see when you would break. You not only didn't break, you outmaneuvered most of the top warriors and the ones who would have eventually worn you down, were properly tired after their session with you. You even gave Xander a concussion that took a few hours to heal from." His chest bounced up and down with a silent chuckle.

I pull back quickly to look in his eyes, to see if he's lying to me. "What? No, I didn't, there's no way. He's an Alpha King, the strongest wolf around. He didn't say anything to me yesterday or today."

"Well, I should say not. I would take that secret to my grave if it were me. But, unfortunately, he chose to challenge you in front of all his trainers, his father, our whole pack, and visiting packs. He's just lucky that no one really knows what his wolf looks like yet, so he can stay somewhat anonymous. His trainers have been giving him a hard time though and will never let him live down getting beat by a female warrior who just learned to shift, is a quarter his size, and weight and three years younger. And you, my dear, beat him, submitted his ass, and now you can choose to let him think you have no idea or rub it in at the perfect moment."

"I really have to process all of that, but when do I get to go for training? I thought they don't take anyone until they've graduated school."

"You are a special case, my dear, not only are you a year ahead on your studies but they have never seen anyone like you and don't want to waste any of that talent. You are correct though, they want to give you a little more time here, so they will come out at the end of the next school year and decide then when you will go, but you *will* go to training." He smiles ear to ear. "I am so proud of you, we all are, I hope you know that."

The tears that have been threatening since I walked in spill and I hug him tight around the waist again. I didn't know how much I really needed to hear that, but the weight that lifts from me as I sob into his shirt tells me and him how much that one little phrase means to me. They are proud of me. The Alpha and

Luna, Gamma Brett and Delta Kyle are proud of me. They see me, my efforts, my accomplishments, my drive. I made someone proud.

The door flies open and bangs on the opposite wall. "Okay, Bitty, I can't handle it anymore, what happened? Cam and Kota are out here asking what's wrong too. You are on some kind of emotional roller coaster, and I'm gonna throw up." Oliver's hand is rubbing his chest again. He does that a lot around me.

"You aren't the only one, I have a massive headache. What did you do to her, Dad?" Cam asks, moving into the room, and close behind me. I can smell the citrus wrap around me like a soft blanket on a chilly night. "Tiny, come here please, my wolf needs a hug from you to know you're okay so he can settle down." I smile into Alpha Lucas' shirt and sniffle in. He squeezes me one more time before loosening his grip.

I turn and hug Cam around the waist. I feel his body relax into mine immediately, then I turn to Oliver who seems to have been on this ride with me the whole time. I rest my forehead on his chest and let him wrap me in a gentle hug. And finally, I move to Kota sitting in the chair I vacated. I sit sideways on his lap and hug him around the neck.

"Do they know?" I ask Alpha Lucas over the mindlink, unsure of whether or not I can say anything.

"No, they don't, but you can choose to tell them or not. It's not a secret you have to keep, but can if you want. They clearly know something is going on with you."

I look up at all of them. This is exciting news for me. Something I have wanted for myself for so long, I don't remember a time not dreaming of this day. I am so excited I don't want to keep it from them. I finally have people to share things like this with, accomplishments that have been in the works for years. I beam at the Alpha then each of my friends. "The Alpha King, Warrior Nickolas, and Warrior Osiston want me to train to be an Elite Warrior." I basically squeal. Kota stiffens under me. Cam grips the edge of his father's desk, knuckles going instantly white, and Oliver's face drops and he sinks to his knees, breathing heavily.

"Bitty, I thought we talked about this." He breathes in deep like it's difficult. "You can't leave. We need you, can't you see that?" It comes out as a pained whisper. Why is he pleading with me? This is good news.

I move to get up, but Kota's iron grip won't let me move an inch. I try again, pushing with my hands this time. He's not looking at me, but at his father, with a glare that would bring a lesser man crumbling down. I reach out to Oliver, wanting to ease his obvious pain. He doesn't move, just stares at me in disbelief.

"I'm not leaving now and it's not forever." I try and reason with them. "It's just training. You guys all know I want to train to be an Elite Warrior, this shouldn't be a shock. They won't even let me start for another year at the earliest, but I didn't want to keep it from you. This is exciting news!" I try to sound cheerful, but their reactions are not what I expected and it's tough to keep up my enthusiasm. "Besides, you are all leaving in a few weeks, even Sierra, you can't be upset that I want to go and become my best self too."

When none of them relax and their sad and angry expressions stay the same, I slump against Kota's chest, feeling angry as my own revelation sinks in. They are all leaving...and leaving me behind. And they are totally okay with that. What hypocrites. They are all going to leave me here, alone, while they go off and learn how to do a job that the Moon Goddess designed for them, but they want to keep me here under lock and key like a fragile flower and go off to have fun and adventures. They are no better than my dad with his baby factory thoughts.

I can feel the tears burning the back of my eyes again, and normally, I would blink them away or run and hide so they won't see them, but the more I think about the injustice of their motives, the more the angry tears build, and I eventually just let them fall. I don't sob, I'm not wracked with heartbreak, I'm furious. Angry tears just fall at the revelation that they want me stuck here, with no ambitions of my own, only what they allow. Just continue on the well-worn path that they are comfortable with, caged like a pretty bird only for display, never allowed to spread her wings and see what she is capable of. I am the pack trophy to show off as a party trick when other high-ranking wolves come to visit. The freakshow that they can use to make the pack look better.

I stare at the window, letting my dark thoughts spiral, a strong longing to be in the forest outside hitting me, feeling the walls closing in on me suddenly. My body starts to shake with the anger coursing through me, boiling in my veins. I push at Kota's arms again, the steel embrace keeping me firmly in place.

"Move your arms, Dakota, and let me up before I break them." I say it as calmly as possible through clenched teeth, but the anger is definitely there.

He hesitates for just a moment before he snaps out of whatever trance he's locked in with his father and slowly loosens his arms. "We need to talk about this, Smalls, you can't just leave us to go off on your own, it's not safe."

"NO!" I stand up, breaking his hold on me with more force than was probably necessary. I kind of hope I leave a mark for at least a little while. Alphas heal quickly and that was nothing really, but I can wish in my anger. I back toward the door like a caged animal ready to strike. "You all can talk about this. Talk about how to wrap your tiny minds around this." I point at the three of them. "When the Alpha King calls for me...I will go. Until then keep your distance, all of you. No more nicknames, no more slumber parties and hanging out. I am not your playtoy or your property. I am a warrior of this pack and will be treated as such. My name is Skylar and you will use only that. You are all leaving for training, leaving me behind, it's bullshit to think that I can't do the same! You are no friends of mine if you can't see what I truly want for my life and be supportive. You are a bunch of hypocrites." I don't raise my voice or yell at them, just state the facts.

"I will not stay here, caged and restricted. I will leave at the first opportunity, and you may or may not be told about it if this is how you are going to react." I change my focus to the Alpha. ""Alpha, may I use your gym? The Luna does not want us to go out alone, and I respect that, but I don't want any of these guys near me right now, and I have some anger to work out." My whole body is still shaking in anger, and I need to desperately release the energy before I shift in the middle of this office. My wolf is just as pissed as I am. She's ready to bang their heads together.

"Yes, sweetheart, use it as long as you need, I will send Brett and Kyle down to check in in a little while, you may need sparring partners." I nod my head and turn to leave. "Stay put." The Alpha aura was strong and suffocating, it had me stutter in my steps until I realized he was giving me the space from them that I needed. "Would you like me to send Sierra down in a little while as well?"

"That's fine, thank you, Alpha," I say over my shoulder. I can't bear to look any of them in the eye. I won't feel bad about this.

As soon as I am through the door the explosion of arguments from all three of them make me flinch. They can't be that angry about me leaving. It's not their decision, it's mine. And just the thought of them feeling so entitled makes the lava in my veins run even hotter.

Gamma Brett is waiting for me in the hallway, his blank expression tells me, he has been told of the situation, and he turns as soon as he sees me and walks to the stairway that leads down to the cells and the Alpha's personal weight room.

He can't always get to the gym that is attached to the main arena, and frankly, probably can't get a workout in if he does go. There is always someone who wants to talk to him or ask a favor of him, so he had a portion of the old cells turned into a gym with weights, hanging bags, and a large area for sparring.

Gamma Brett lets me in with his code. "Do you want me to wrap your hands? The Alpha had a brand-new bag hung that could use some breaking in." Like father, like son, I guess. That thought just adds fuel to my flames. He gives me a little smirk. Now I know he's aware of the whole situation and wants me to burn some of the energy before offering himself as a partner to spar with. At least he appreciates my strength and skill level.

"Yes please," is all I say as he walks me over to the storage rack that seems to have everything I might need to burn off the negative energy I have aimed at my friends right now. He takes my hands like Oliver has done so many times and gently wraps each of my fingers, making sure the straps are secure.

Once he is done, he steps back towards the door and takes the position of a sentinel on guard. No words or eye contact needed, just my protector so I can disengage and fully let loose without having to spare energy on the world falling apart around me.

I let the world fall away. No friends, no limitations, no bullies, no one to answer to, just me and the bag in front of me. Every possible emotion I have pent up inside goes into each and every hit. Every kick more lethal than the last. I lose all sense of time and feeling. All the negative thoughts swirling in my head are released into the bag. Everything my father has ever spit out at me, every insult and false accusation from Kaley and her minions, all the self-doubt that has pushed me to be better each and every day. I heard a crack a while ago, but I don't stop to check for breaks in my hand. The pain just fuels the anger more. Pain is a weakness, and I am tired of feeling weak, being treated like I am weak, seen as being weak. Even my wolf is giving me space. She hates that we are fighting with the guys, she wants her pack, needs them, but she has always understood what I want and need. She hates being stifled by them too. She will not fight me when I choose to leave and further my training. Whether my mate is here or not this is a decision I have to be able to make. Training has really been the only thing I have ever had control over, that will not change now. I will never let anyone take this physical release from me. It's my bliss, my zen, the happy place that is attributed to no one other than me. I want to push and see what I am really made of. I know I'm not the best based on how I did in the trials. I want to be THE best, not just the best here in this pack. I want to be tried and tested, battle-worn with experiences I will never get being stuck here, so I can come home and pass on the knowledge to future generations.

When all of my limbs are numb, and I can't even lift my arms to throw punches, I sit in front of the new bag and just stare at the hole I produced. The bowels of stuffing and sand spilling out onto the floor in front of me. I don't even know when it broke. I just stare and cry, let the emotional exhaustion take over, and a sick, twisted part of me hopes they feel it. Feel it to their core and it brings them to their knees. I want them to feel the pain and heartache, confusion, anger, determination, all of it. A lot that they have contributed to, unconscious or not for my whole life.

At some point, the weariness must have taken over, because the next thing I know, my eyes are fluttering open to the sounds of voices. Angry, but whispering voices. I strain to listen while I take in my surroundings.

Chapter 34

"She has broken every bone in both her hands…"

White walls, my bedroom walls are white, right?

"How is that even possible, she wasn't down there that long?"

These sheets are scratchy, definitely not mine.

"She punched a hole straight into the brand-new bag! It's one hundred percent possible."

I don't recognize the smell, I'm not in one of the guys' rooms either. I wish these people would shut up, I'm exhausted and I'm sore from trials.

"There are stress fractures in both forearms and in her lower legs that have already begun to heal. She is severely malnourished too, but that is probably a result of her level of training and participating in the trials and not replenishing properly. And don't get me started on the list of old injuries that were never treated properly before she got her wolf."

I try to move my arms to sit up. "Ugh!" Everything hurts, what the hell happened? Even my hair hurts.

"I hear her, please, can I go in?" I know that voice. Luna Ava.

"Yes, Luna, but only you. We don't want to overwhelm her with too many people, she clearly has had plenty to deal with. It took 2 of us over an hour to catalog all of her previous injuries."

What are they talking about? Who are they talking about?

"What the hell is beeping?" My sandpaper dry mouth croaks. "Can someone turn that off?" I mumble out as my eyes attempt to focus.

"Oh, sweet girl." She breathes out. "You're awake. You have no idea how happy I am to see those gray eyes." I blink again as I concentrate on Luna Ava walking over and grabbing my hand. I wince at the gentle touch and she quickly drops my hand.

"What happened? Where am I?" I grumble.

"We had to bring you in when you passed out in the gym, and Brett couldn't get you to wake up."

"Where is here?" I can feel my heart rate rising at the thought.

"You're in the pack hospital, sweetheart. Why didn't you tell me how bad it was?" she's whispering as she moves closer, tears filling her eyes.

"How bad what was?" I try to play dumb, but my slow brain is starting to connect the dots of the conversation that was going on out in the hall.

"You said the bullying wasn't that bad and you could handle it."

Something in me snapped. "The beatings? The torture? Who cares? No one gives a shit or it would have stopped. No one in our school cares about helping anyone else, they only care about their own status and personal well-being. They all just keep their heads down and don't make waves, because being an inconvenience is punishable. People look the other way when students are missing from classes, they don't bat an eye when injuries, that have nothing to do with training, show up. Why would anyone tell, when there is no one who will listen?" I know she means well, and she is not the real target for my anger, but she is here, and she asked. I hope my voice is loud enough for the jackasses in the hall to hear through the crack in the door.

"We do care, there is just..."

"Nothing to go on? No proof? Concrete evidence?" I raise my eyebrows at her, trying to keep my voice level, and she looks ashamed. "Those excuses are just more proof that not every voice is listened to with the same level of interest, if you aren't deemed important, then no one takes a second look. The only important people are the future ranked leaders, just so you are aware." I sit up gingerly, and start to pull the I.V. out of my arm, wincing at the pain from the needle and all the bones still healing in my hands. Then I start peeling all the sticky pads off the various parts of my body as the monitors scream in protest. The doctor and a nurse rush in, looking horrified.

"You can't leave, we need to get you healthy and strong." The nurse pleads trying to grab my arm. I slide off the bed, too quick for her.

"Please come sit back down, we will make arrangements for you to be moved back to your room at the packhouse if you don't want to stay here." The doctor whimpers as Luna Ava reaches for me, looking like she wants to cry.

"NO!" I shout, letting my wolf add her growl for effect.

She flinches back, and I briefly feel bad for being so nasty to her. She only wants to help, but I shake it off. I walk to the chair that has my dirty, blood-stained clothes and drop the hospital gown, not caring who sees my scars anymore. If they want to care for me they can see me as I am, and learn to do it without looking at me like I am broken or with pity. I despise pity, hate it with every fiber of my being. I dress slowly, keeping every sound of pain stuffed deep in my chest. I know it's only punishing me to not ask for help, but this is how it has always been for me, and they should see that too since we are airing out all of my dark secrets. No one has ever been there to mop up the mess before, why start now? I turn towards her when I am finally done.

"I'm going to the Beta house, to my isolated room where no one bothers me or cares about what I am doing. I'm going back to having freedom and control without having to check in every three seconds. Or having people follow me and force me to do things differently without a second thought, or even just asking if I'm alright with the change, assuming they know what's best for me. You think you can make me healthy? I wouldn't even *know* what that is." I seethe, on a roll now, letting all my unfiltered anger spill. It hurts to move, but my hands are gesturing wildly. "I am broken beyond repair, and I have been surviving that way for as long as I can remember. You heard the doc, irreparable damage has been done. There is nothing you can fix. Cause even on my worst day I still perform better than everyone in that hallway pretending to care about me," I jab my finger at the door, "while overlooking every red flag that has ever been wrong with me. I will heal myself, by myself, it just works better that way. I'm sorry, Luna, I just can't do this anymore, it hurts too much." I let my voice trail off, I can feel more tears wanting to spill.

I take a deep breath and channel the anger, stuffing the sadness. My voice is raspy and my throat hurts, but I continue to speak. "Maybe somewhere everyone holds onto a soft spot for the small, spare Beta. The one her father can't even stand to look at or be around, who *TOLD* the principal and teachers to punish her more because she is unworthy and could use the lesson in humility. I don't want love that comes from feeling bad for my situation. This is me, damaged and messed up, love me like this or not at all. I can't change for everyone else anymore." I turn my back on her and walk toward the treatment room door and find all of my so-called friends and family huddled red-eyed and grief stricken. Their eyes widen at the gruesome sight of me. I can feel my ponytail hanging lopsided on my head, stringy, loose pieces are stuck to my neck and face. I didn't see a mirror, but their reactions tell me enough. Even my dad had the decency to show up and feign a look of shame. I just roll my eyes and walk past everyone down the hallway and out the door.

I run all the way back to my house, pain shooting up my legs, not noticing or caring if people were staring at me. I let myself in the back door like always and walk the silent halls to the staircase leading to my former prison. I ascend slowly, everything about this feels wrong, but so does the thought of going to my room at the packhouse. I don't belong here, it doesn't fit anymore. Like clothes that are just too small, no longer comfortable and easy, but suffocating and tight. I agree with my wolf, the packhouse is home now, but I just can't be around the guys or even Sierra right now.

I make it into my room and head straight for the shower to get rid of the evidence of my self destruction. I don't cry though, which is something new for me. I'm not sure if I am just all cried out or if the anger has finally replaced the sadness.

I climb out, dry off and get dressed. The first thing I need to do is figure out how long I have been at the hospital and see if I have missed any school. All my stuff is in my room at the packhouse. Just another thing I'm going to have to deal with later. I leave my door locked and head out the window, just like old times. I can't believe it's been almost a year since I have had to sneak out. I don't need anyone scenting me come and go. I head straight for school taking the well worn long way through the woods. Sneaking in a back entrance that I broke a couple years ago so I had a quick escape in or out if I needed it. And I used it for both on a regular basis.

Now, who to talk to to get caught up on the day? Doc. T. is a no go. The pack doctor is just going to send me back to the hospital and almost guaranteed to call Luna Ava. The only other person who doesn't completely hate me is Mr. Lyons the history teacher. He is old and could care less about pack drama. The hallways are empty and I think it's too early for lunches. I take all the paths that I know are blindspots for the security cameras. That will be one of the first things I fix when I get back from training, but for now I'm going to use them to my advantage. I peak around corners like a criminal trying to make it to the classroom and not get caught sneaking into school.

I get about five feet from his door when a hand grabs my wrist. I instinctively twist and take a defensive stance ready for an attack.

"Relax! It's just me." Sierra whisper yells, dodging my fist as it comes flying at her face. "I told the guys you would show up here, they didn't believe me. They are all still camped at your house trying to figure out how to get you to come out and reason with you."

I go to open my mouth to argue, but she puts her whole hand on my mouth, stopping any protest.

"Stop! I don't want to hear it and I'm not here to fight. I am not your enemy and no matter how stupid the guys are, neither are they. That's all I am going to say about it now though. You are not going to avoid me and I will not force you to be around the guys, cause whatever this is," she gestures at all of me, "It's bigger than any of us thought. Your trauma runs deep and you are the only person who can get yourself past that since you won't let anyone in far enough to help." She's not hiding her irritation with me, "Now, It's Monday and we have about eight minutes before the bell will ring for second period. I already went to the packhouse and grabbed your stuff and I stopped at your locker and got everything you usually have for all classes before lunch. I talked to the school counselor and I have been moved into all of your classes, that way neither of us are alone per Luna Ava's request. The guys might catch on by lunch, so I will switch everything out for you and we can make a better plan for tomorrow, cause this hiding shit isn't going to fly past today." With that she handed me my overly stuffed backpack and started to walk off.

"Sierra, I'm not going to come between you and the guys, I won't make you choose. But I just can't..."

"Stop. I told you I'm not talking about them today. You are my concern right now. I had to watch your basically dead body, covered in blood, being carried out of the basement. I watched Gamma Brett *run* with you to the pack hospital, barely breathing. I can't feel your emotions like Oliver and apparently the twins, I don't know where your mind is at, but that was the scariest fucking thing I have ever had to go through. I will be angry with you later, now is not the time. And we do care, I care, but I can't help if you keep things from me. I didn't realize getting out of here was life or death for you, but that's how bad it is, isn't it? You will die if you don't get out of here." Tears are rolling down her cheeks now. I just step up to her and pull her in for a hug. This is what I didn't want, my needs are affecting others. This is why I feel stuck. She's right I need to go, but I don't want anyone else to hurt because of my decisions. I'm going to follow her lead; I'm not going to think about it. We are here, right now, and she is on my side, apparently, no matter what I do or say.

We both take a big breath in and sigh out, silently agreeing to just get through today. We walk off to second period and she fills me in on everything that happened while I was in the hospital.

We made it through the day uneventfully, the guys never showed up or chose to stay far away. She even helped me come up with a reasonable excuse for missing the first class. I was at the pack hospital for a training injury. Mostly the truth so I don't feel bad about the lie and it could be verified by Doc. T. if anyone really wants to question it. I have been getting a lot of looks from people today, but no one approaches and that suits me and my mood towards my peers in general. When the day is done she grabs a bag packed with food from Lenny and helps me sneak into my room. When I try to question it she looks at me like I am a moron.

"It's so you don't have to leave. Lenny was not happy to hear you are malnourished. She's taking that personally. I will leave you alone tonight, but only on the promise that you don't shut me out and you had better meet me for breakfast at the diner tomorrow." I get a full on finger point in my face until I agree, even though it's the last place I want to be. She only stayed for a little while after that. Sam started blowing up her phone and I kept reminding her that I wasn't going to come between her friendships even though mine were imploding around me.

"What do you want me to say to them? You know they are going to smell you on me and ask questions."

"Just tell them that you were right and I did show up at school. You understand me better than they do." I shrug. She just rolls her eyes, but doesn't argue either.

"Do I really have to go out the window?" She grimaces.

"I don't want them to know how I come and go even if they are playing at being guards at my door. They can't know you were here. So yes, out the window it is."

"You know they will still probably smell my scent right?"

"Don't care, now go before he comes searching for you here."

I sit on my bed in the quiet and finished the little homework I had left, then laid down to read a book in the silence of my childhood bedroom. I was bored and reading the same line for the third time when an all pack mindlink comes through.

*"**All pack members 18 and older, with their wolf, will begin running patrol shifts effective immediately. We have a potential threat on our hands and our leadership council has decided training for all is vital for pack safety. You will get your patrol time at your regularly scheduled***"*

training session in two days. Any students, this will not affect your studies." Alpha Lucas closes the mindlink to the pack.

"That's strange, I thought he wasn't going to say anything to the pack until he actually had something to tell." My wolf questions.

"Maybe news from the Alpha King set him off. We aren't in the pack house so we aren't privileged to that info."

"Or he just thinks it's a good idea to be prepared. I mean, it's the reason we train pups so early, isn't it?" She has a point.

"I guess we'll find out in a couple days. Are you sure you're okay with this? Being away from the guys and all. You are getting so strong, I don't want the separation to harm you too."

"I have a feeling it will be alright and we are still close enough that I can talk to their wolves, they really aren't that far away. That's enough for now. When you all are done being over-emotional humans let me know and we'll set things right."

I just roll my eyes. *"Goodnight."*

"Goodnight. Luna Ava said to tell you to sleep well, and your room will always be available and waiting for you." I smile, she's giving me space but not really.

Chapter 35

I get up early the next day feeling a little better. My stomach is still in knots at the thought of staying away from the guys, like I'm physically not well, but I push past that so I can focus on getting out of here and following through on my life plans. I force myself to eat a few of the protein bars I stashed along with a bottle of water. There is nothing left of the dinner Lenny sent with Sierra.

Mateo and Oliver stayed by my door last night. They might have even slept against it with how strong their scents were wafting through the gap. I will say the scent was calming and I had a deep dreamless sleep. They get points for perseverance that's for sure, but I have to keep my mind on my goal. My goal is to get trained to be the best warrior I can be for my pack. I can't let my, as my wolf calls them, 'human emotions' get in the way of that. I can feel it in my bones, that I need to go do this, more than I need them by my side at this moment.

I pack a bag with a change of clothes so I don't have to leave the training arena after we are done. I'll shower and change there, again like old times. As soon as I have everything I will need for the day, I head out my trusty window, making sure to take a good look around to make sure the coast is clear. They aren't stupid and will figure out what I'm doing sooner rather than later. But I will use my advantage for now.

I know Sierra said I was her priority, but she may think telling the guys I can sneak out would be helping me. So I am treating everything as if I can only trust myself and my wolf implicitly. I make it out okay and head toward the diner,

Sierra meets me outside and we head to a table in the complete opposite corner of where the guys normally go. A fact Martha is quick to point out.

"We just needed some girl time and didn't want them hounding us about being here without them. So we'd rather leave our scents way over here and hope they don't notice if they do come in." Sierra says easily with a bright smile and I don't know if Martha buys it or just decides to go with it. She brings everything out a little while later in to go containers and gives us a wink. We both look at each other and back to her in silent question.

"Luna Ava gave me a heads up and you have about three minutes to clear out. Enjoy your day ladies!" She waves. She is way too cheerful about this sneaking around thing than she should be.

"Wait! How much do we owe you?" I ask, confused.

"I told you. You eat for free! I haven't had this much fun in so long. The looks on those boys' faces when they think they know what's what and either of you put them in their places is so entertaining, it's worth it. Now go out the back I think." She winks again and we laugh as we take off.

When we get to the training arena a note on the outside gate says training has been postponed today while the warriors are in planning meetings so we head off to find a place to eat our breakfast in peace while we wait for school to start.

We are not as lucky in our avoidance tactics at school. The guys stalk the halls in all their broody glory, snapping at anyone who gets in their way. They catch up with us and walk wordlessly to each class we have together and manage, somehow, to be even angrier when they realize that Sierra is no longer in their classes if I'm not. We don't approach the subject of why none of us are talking and I only interact if and when absolutely required for class.

Sierra and I are leaving English, one of the few classes the guys aren't in. "I officially hate you for how smart you are, just so you are aware." She rubs her forehead dramatically. "How do you even understand what she is saying? It's English, it's not supposed to be that hard." Sierra groans. "You are going to have to do my homework for the rest of the year if I stay in that class. I'm pretty sure that one is for advanced seniors. Give me science anything any day, you can keep the endless writing and grammar."

I giggle at her, but my amusement doesn't last long as we walk towards the lunchroom. Sam walks straight to us, but doesn't make eye contact with me. Until this week I didn't know his face could make a frown. He's doing a great impression of Oliver right now.

"We need to report to dad after school, all warriors eighteen and older with their wolves are going to start running patrols. He wants to pair underage warriors with seasoned warriors so we can all learn the routes and procedures. Ride with us or don't, it's up to you, but we're all going to the same place." Sam huffs, still not looking at me, before turning silently to head off to get lunch.

The rest of the guys stand hovering in the hallway a little longer staring at us. I'm not sure what they're looking for, but it's not long before they all walk away as well.

"Well they must really be pissed at me if Sam is the one giving the cold shoulder. You should go sit with them, you both do not deserve to be caught up in the BS between the twins, Oliver and I. I swear I will be okay on my own for a little bit. I promise I will even sit close enough for you to keep an eye on me." I shove Sierra, who's staring longingly at Sam's retreating back.

I walk away, not waiting for her to respond, to a corner table no one is occupying, my appetite is lost after realizing what my behavior is doing to my friends' relationship. This time I can't just give in when they say sorry though. Their opinion won't change, but neither will mine.

It's nice and quiet over here. Most people don't like it because it is tucked into a corner, you can't see a portion of the lunch room and, more importantly, you can't be seen. I have Sierra in my sights, which means she can see me, so I'm *technically* not alone. I pull out a book from our strategies class. We are working through wars that happened in the last hundred years and analyzing why they started in the first place, what ultimately ended them and how each side was either successful or failed. Our teacher also posed the question of should they have started in the first place? It's super fascinating.

I was so caught up in a war that Alpha King Reggie's grandfather fought in, I didn't see my brother sneak up on me. Another downside to this corner is the AC unit blowing across my head making me upwind, I didn't smell him coming up behind me.

"You need to see this from our side, Shorty. We can't protect you if you go away and we don't know who you'll be with or what they are going to do with you and that scares the shit out of all of us."

I don't look up from my book. "I will accept your position…" He takes a deep breath in, sighs it out loudly and relaxes next to me, but I'm not finished. "When you all accept my position. You do not *NEED* to protect me. I'm sure in our short time spent together you have all at least figured that out. As far as who I will be hanging around with, get over yourselves." I scoff, rolling my eyes at him. "Do I need to remind you that until Sierra came, none of you gave two shits what happened to me, or who I was with. So find a new excuse for your tantrum. Just because you care now doesn't change that. I am doing my best to not hold it against you, but it's hard when your archaic misogynistic sides come out in all their flying colors." I look back down.

"That's not fair, you never said anything, never asked for help, never complained. Had you said something we would have stepped in sooner."

I take my own deep calming breath, and grip my book tightly. I cannot lose my temper here. I stare at the wall. "Did you just say it's my fault that dad treated me the way he did? Pawned me off on a nanny who wasn't allowed to do more than feed me and get me to school. Or that getting bullied is my fault?" I turn angry eyes slowly to him. "What happens to me now, I will fully own, it is my choice to take the burdens of those younger and weaker than me, but not originally. You did not take notice then and I won't let you put that blame on me." I am full on glaring. "I'm not going to let you make me feel guilty for how you feel now."

"That's not what I said, and you know it."

"That's exactly what you just said!" I screech. I clear my throat and quiet my voice getting control of my temper. "At least I know how you really feel. It won't matter how many times I beat you and the guys, you all think you are better than me and that I need you and can't survive life without you. Thank you for clarifying Mateo, excuse me, I have class to get to." I shove everything in my bag and get up to leave. I haul ass, not waiting for anyone to catch up with me.

I get to our Health and Healing class and make my way to the back of the room aiming for the corner, hoping that people will sit around me and none of them can come near me. I'm not lucky enough though, no one is going to mess with the guys looking the way they do when they come in the room. Sierra sits next to me, Oliver in front of me, Mateo diagonal, and Sam, Kota and Cam finish out the back row next to Sierra. Again we all only speak when necessary, but you can cut the tension in the room with a knife. If this keeps up, I may go to the Luna and see if I can just finish my classes remotely. This is ridiculous.

We play the rest of our day the same. Sierra and I trying to hold awkward, mundane conversations while the guys listen in, but pretend not to pay any attention to us. As I put my books away at the end of this mind-numbingly long day, Sierra waits on me. We decided to walk over to check in with Delta Kyle, Kaley walks straight up to me and goes to slam my locker shut. This time I don't let her. My reactions are fast and I'm done with her bullshit as much as the guys'. I catch the edge of the locker and push it back open. She stumbles a little as I glare at her. I won't do anything here at school, my conditioning still won't let me retaliate against her here, but I'm not going to let her walk all over me anymore either.

She lets out a little squeak before she composes herself again. "Whatever you did to piss off our future Alphas, you need to fix now! Your stupid childish games are making life hard for the rest of us. Apologize, grovel, kiss their feet or whatever they want and make this better. They have been yelling and growling at people all day. You even have them raising their voices at me, which is unacceptable!"

"I don't see how my relationship with any of them is any of your business. And I will not take responsibility for whatever stupidity of yours that got you yelled at." I said without looking at her and finished what I was doing, then closed my locker and turned to walk in the opposite direction, Sierra close behind.

"How dare you turn your back on your future Luna and speak to her like that!" She grabs my shoulder to spin me around. But before I can do anything a shout from down the hallway stops everyone.

"TAKE YOUR HANDS OFF HER!" A loud growl resonates the hallway. Oh goody, just another incident where Mateo thinks he needs to step in for me.

"And stop talking in third person, it's weird." Sierra adds under her breath. Kaley either doesn't hear or chooses to ignore it, and doesn't take her hand off my shoulder. It takes all my patience to not rip her fingers off me.

"I was just explaining that she needs to be more kind to her future Luna. Her childish behavior is going to get her into more trouble, and I think there has been enough of that, don't you, Skylar? I mean you have spent more time in the principal's office than in class. And she is constantly distracting you all which is unacceptable as well. We can't have an unruly student running a muck."

The guys all look at me. It's actually not true, but I come and go from classes as I need to because I am so far ahead and I am only in one class with her, so she wouldn't actually know if I'm in class or not. I spent a ton of time there last year though, due to her antics, but she conveniently left that part out. I choose not to answer, they want to think and act for me, I'm not going to stop them. They can prove how well they know me by choosing to believe her accusations or not. I cross my arms and look defiantly at everyone daring the guys to choose, Kaley or me.

As predicted, none of them say anything. They are not supporting me or her, which hurts just as bad as if they would have taken her side. At least then I would know where I stand. Based on the look on her face, she thinks that they agree with her. They just showed both of us they think of us as equals or at the very least are chickenshit and don't want to look like they are taking sides which solidifies my belief in my true place in their life. I roll my eyes and turn to walk away.

"We're going to be late to meet Delta Kyle." I say over my shoulder to no one in particular. "Are we walking together or not?"

I don't get an answer as Kaley grabs their attention again. "Should Marnie, Jeanie and I meet you at the packhouse Saturday for the ball or are you boys going to come and pick us up? I'm sure Daddy can arrange a car to take us all, that probably would be best to really showcase our arrival."

I roll my eyes again and start walking faster. As often as they have told Sierra and I that they have shut those three down, clearly they aren't doing a good enough job. I don't want to hear their lameass answers, diplomatic and vague replies are clearly not working, not if there is any opening for interpretation. Those three girls only hear what they want, I'm over the back and forth and passive aggressive tiptoeing around her. They are going to have to learn to make solid decisions, even if they make some people mad. That's part of being a leader, do what's right and best for the majority, not everyone will be happy about it. Make decisions and deal with the outcome that plays out.

Sierra and I walk into the training grounds surrounded by a bunch of our peers. Delta Kyle is at the front of the group ready to give instructions.

"We are going to be pairing you up with a current patrol warrior. This will allow us to give our warriors much needed rest and you all a chance to learn tracking and surveillance skills. For those of you still in school, we have done our best to not interfere with that, but you may need to arrive late or leave early. We have already spoken to your teachers if that is the case and only those who are excelling in their studies will get that privilege. Patrol is not an excuse to be lazy, your homework and classwork is still expected to be complete and on time. As we are almost into the summer, we will rotate the patrols and your partners on a monthly basis. That will also allow us to account for those of you traveling for training and school outside the pack. If you have questions, ask your warrior partner first then come find me. The list is on the training announcement board. Take a good look, some of you start training tonight."

There was no direct dismissal from him, but we all took our cue to line up and see when our shift was. Waiting in comfortable silence, the guys roll in looking, if it was possible, more irritated than they have been all day. They head over to Delta Kyle and talk to him briefly before turning around to leave again, with no notice of Sierra or I.

Sierra huffs. "Just go with them." I say trying not to sound defeated. "You need to spend time with Sam. This whole situation is stupid and neither of you should be caught up in it. I will have Delta Kyle take me back to my house." Knowing the argument that is about to come out of her mouth.

"They will kill me once they find out I left you here alone, even if it is with the Delta. I'm not dealing with that. I will just meet up with him in a little bit... After I make sure you get home and can tell them that I honestly did." I rolled my eyes at her, but I'm done arguing, this protection detail is getting tiresome.

"Fine, let's get our assignments and then you can go console your suddenly moody boyfriend." I try to lighten the mood.

"Not my boyfriend, my mate is the only one that will get any kind of title." She smiles and winks at me.

"Whatever you say." I smile back at her.

It doesn't take long for us to get to the front of the line. "They split us up, how dare they?" Sierra lets out mock indignation. "At least I don't have to get up in the middle of the night. You have fun with that."

"You act like I don't do that already. I have to report at 4 which is my usual time to get up, the only problem is I will miss morning training."

"I'm sure that was by design, based on the last couple of days with the guys. Don't think any of this has gone unnoticed by all your parents. I think they are hoping the separation will be beneficial for you all to at least concentrate on what you are supposed to be doing. I don't know if you noticed, but none of us are in your group time."

I had noticed and unfortunately I felt a surge of excitement to do something without them, followed by a sense of sadness followed by guilt at not being disappointed. I didn't say any of that though. "Let's go to the Beta house, so you can give your not-boyfriend some attention."

We start walking. "Not home?" She asks cautiously.

"No, it's never been home, it's the Beta's house, which is currently my father and then will be my brother and his family. The woods are my home, even the room Luna Ava gave me at the packhouse is more home than what I grew up in. It just doesn't feel right to go to the packhouse right now. I need that separation. I have to figure out what to do with myself when all six of you leave this summer anyway, might as well get used to it now."

"So this might get me in trouble, but what about the dance this weekend?" She cringes at me.

"What about it?"

"You're still coming right? You promised to go with me since it will be my first and probably my last. But I wasn't sure how you felt now that things are also...strained..." She trailed off, but I understand what she is asking me.

"I will go with you and for you. You have been an amazing friend to me and don't deserve all the crap you've been thrown in the middle of. I will be on my best behavior with the guys and I promise to not start any fights with them. I will not hesitate to finish a fight or leave if they start shit though." I giggle at her, and just to make her day I add, "I will even let you do whatever you want with my hair and make-up."

"YES! This is why I love you!"

We made it to my father's house in record time and headed towards the back after checking thoroughly that the guys weren't lingering. Once I was safely inside I waved Sierra off to go meet up with Sam at the packhouse.

I did all my usual things, homework, shower, read and then lay on my bed and stared at the ceiling. Not being able to train alone was awful. Sometime after the sun went down, there's a knock on my door. As usual, I don't answer.

"Skylar? Sky, I have food out here. I know you didn't eat lunch and I have no idea if you've eaten today or not. The doc gave a specific diet for you. I have to go run my patrol shift. I guess I'll see you at school tomorrow when you're done with yours. I love you. I hope you know that." I heard Mateo sigh then retreating footsteps.

A single tear escaped. Deep down I know they all care and this is punishing everyone, but I can't back down, I need to get out of here and the sooner the better. I know I am not weak or useless, but that little voice in the back of my head that sounds suspiciously like Kaley or my father likes to tell me otherwise. I just feel the absolute need to prove myself and my worth. No amount of words from them will make me believe I am good enough until I do.

I finally conceded and went to the door and grabbed the food he brought up after I was completely sure he and everyone else was out of my house. I eat slowly, not hungry, but I am tired of hearing how small I am from too much training and not eating enough. I leave the empty dishes outside my door, to show him I took the offering and appreciate the gesture.

Chapter 36

After the most fitful sleep, I get up groggily. I am so tired I forgot to use the window and head to my patrol spot using the front door. I bump into a solid mass as I walk down the sidewalk lost in my thoughts.

"Whoa there Smalls," a throat clears as I get my bearings, "I mean Skylar." Cam lets go of me as quickly as he grabbed me. He tries for a smile, but it doesn't reach his eyes. "You headed for patrol?" I nod my head and look away. I can't take the look in his sad green eyes. "Do you want me to walk…" He gestures back over his shoulder. "Uh, nevermind. Okay…I'll see you at school later. Training isn't going to be the same without you, you know."

"I agree." I give a small smile, but can't look him in the eye. "I'll see you later." I move around him and do my best to hold it together, I miss them. I knew I would, but this sucks so much more than I thought. I hurry faster to meet up with Gamma Brett, I really need a distraction now.

Breaking out into a run I take in the different shades of greens and browns of the forest and the earthy smell that always calms my nerves. I arrive too quickly to the patrol cabin where everyone checks in before their shift starts. A full ten minutes before Gamma Brett gives me time to school my emotions.

"I should have known you'd get here before us." He smiles at me and I return it before it hits me.

"Who's us?" I look at him confused.

"We came across an issue yesterday and had to reorganize some of the groups. We figured with your background and level of training it wouldn't be a problem to double up." He shifts and Marnie is behind him looking worse for wear. Her hair is in a tangled mess on top of her head, her eye make-up is smeared and her well chosen outfit looks like she put it on in a hurry and maybe in the dark. The bright colors clash with the muted tones of the forest and aren't something you want to wear out in the woods, unless you want to be spotted...by the enemy.

"What the fuck?" I ask my wolf

"You're asking me? I was going to say the same thing. Watch your back, we don't know why she was put with you. It could be an honest pairing and Gamma Brett honestly thinks you won't need as much or any help so he can focus on her... Or it's a set up to spy on you for Kaley. She's not supposed to be here, she doesn't have her wolf yet."

"I thought that's what the Alpha said the other day." I close my eyes and take a deep breath.

"So what do you want us to do first?" I ask Gamma Brett, completely ignoring Marnie's presence. She can't cause trouble if I don't talk to her.

"We are going to run the perimeter, in human form since Marnie can't shift yet, and that will give me a chance to show you ladies the things we are looking for while we are on patrol. The pattern we run is similar to what you were talking about with the Alpha King the other night, Skylar..."

Marnie lets out a little squeak interrupting him. "You got to talk to the Alpha King?" She asks breathily, eyes wide at the thought.

So much for not talking to her. "Uh, yeah. He stayed at the pack house so we had a couple interactions." I keep my information brief and Gamma Brett looks at me with an eyebrow raised. I usually like to talk about strategy, what he doesn't understand is I like talking with people who understand what I'm talking about. Marnie is not one of those people. I can at least say she shows up to training and does parts of the workouts, mostly stretching to get attention from guys when she's bent over suggestively, but there is no reason for her to be out here with us, she doesn't like training, she doesn't like to get dirty and she can't shift yet. Maybe that's why she is with Gamma Brett and I. If something happens we can protect her and defend together, rather than her being a liability that would get everyone killed.

"Like I was saying," Brett continues, "we will run one of seven different patterns that surround and cross the territory. It keeps the patrol schedules less predictable and we focus on the pack territory as a whole, not just the perimeter."

He leads us to start jogging our portion of the perimeter, passing other teams on the way. Gamma Brett is keeping up a hushed commentary of what to look for without stopping our movement, giving us insights to basic tracking. Things I've studied in strategy and battle classes, but it is nice to put it to practical use.

"We are accomplishing a few things by patrolling. One is to scent the area so outside wolves know where the territory begins. Our situation is unique because we are surrounded by water on three sides. Land based packs define their territory by scenting. There are several small islands between us and the mainland and the mountains that run through the center of our area give us a good vantage point, but you can never be too careful. The mainland is only about a thirty to forty minute boat ride away on this side of our territory and not all the islands from here to there are inhabited, several are considered part of the National park our territory is on and can't be built on. That doesn't stop people from using them as pit stops on the way to us. The second reason is having teams overlap doesn't give intruders much opportunity to pass through our patrol lines undetected. We are also looking for any disturbance in the foliage. There aren't many small animals that stay here since wolves are predators and they naturally steer clear, so broken branches and leaves could mean a wolf passed through. Pups also can smell the stronger scent here and know that this is the end of the territory and their boundary, it helps keep them safe if they wander off."

We made it a whole 45 minutes before Marnie starts asking when we are done and whining about leg cramps, being hungry, and thirsty. It's not even five in the morning yet and we all run a five hour shift. There are four hours to go. I will strangle her myself if she whines the rest of the time.

"I didn't think we would be running the whole time or I would never have signed up to do this. And when I was told the Gamma would be my partner, I thought they meant Oliver." She pouted with her lip out, not looking at either of us.

"What exactly did you think 'patrol' was? What did you think you were going to be doing out here with Oliver? We're here to protect our pack from unwanted intruders, what about that information was misleading?" I can't help asking. Gamma Brett has to stifle a laugh.

"For sure not this. I thought we would be cuddled up monitoring some screens attached to security cameras or something. Kaley's dad said Jeanie and I would be safer with Mateo or Oliver and he would make sure we were all paired up with the best and the men would do the real work, we were just here to observe."

I turn to Gamma Brett, "I didn't realize we signed up for this, I thought everyone with a wolf had to run patrols. And since when can we make requests on assignments?" I look back at Marnie. "And what is this crap about the men doing the real work? You weren't planning to be helpful at all?" She winces a little and I look back at Gamma Brett.

He gave me that dad look that says I am really close to crossing some line, but I also wasn't too far off the mark of annoying situations. Which means one of the twins was probably going to have to deal with Kaley in their group and my brother probably got Jeanie in his. I can't believe they are putting our pack in danger just to try and spend time with the guys. Don't they know how serious this actually is?

"At least you know you are paired up with the literal best. Skylar has beaten out everyone in every test we have done so far, so Cunningham wasn't wrong. We still have time, quite a bit actually, so you are going to have to figure out how to suck it up today, because we are in the middle of a shift and can't take you back. None of us can be out here on our own, not even me. We always team up just in case. I will mention to the Delta, who is coordinating the rotations, of your misinformation."

With that he turns around and continues jogging. I guess it was a good enough answer for her, she didn't bring it up the rest of the time.

⊹)⟩●⟨(⊹

That was the second most torturous experience of my life. Marnie even kind of tried, and it was terrible. She stopped complaining after Gamma Brett told her to suck it up, but she progressively got slower as the time went on and Brett had to call for another team to come in early to pick up the slack. I am actually embarrassed that, as a team, we couldn't get her to move faster without literally carrying her the whole time. And that was never going to happen.

I head straight to the Beta house after to take a quick shower and get to school. I know Luna Ava said not to be alone, but the walk to and from patrol is pleasantly quiet and drama free. I feel like I can breathe for the first time in a long time. I walk up to my house and see Sam on my porch, casually waiting. At least the scowl is gone, hopefully meaning that he was able to spend some quality time with Sierra and therefore less angry and short tempered. He stands when he notices me, walks straight over and locks me in a huge hug, pinning my arms to my sides.

"I'm sorry, I didn't know how bad it was for you here. Don't be mad at Sierra for telling me, she needed to vent as much as I did. I won't stop you from leaving or tell you you can't go. You're not wrong, we all get to come and go as we please and you feel stuck and we made you feel more trapped. You do make us better though and we are afraid you won't ever come home once you get away." He word vomited all over me. Then as an afterthought asks, "How was your training?" He gives me a knowing look before letting a huge smile break out over his face.

"It sucked as much as you think it did. What happened? How did they weasel their way into rotations? Who got stuck with the other two?" There is no need to specify who we were talking about.

"Sierra got Jeanie and I got Kaley. Neither were happy with the pairings and I'm sure my dad will hear about it from my uncle. But my uncle also can't come right out and say he's trying to force Kaley on Cam and Kota, even though everyone sees that's what he's doing. My dad isn't stupid and this is actually a serious situation that my uncle thinks is a game he can use to play matchmaker by forced proximity."

"I forget that you and Kaley are cousins. That's so weird to process. Hold that thought though, I need to shower and I assume you are my escort to school?" I don't let him answer, "Give me ten minutes." I start to move past him but he grabs my arm.

"Here, Luna Ava wanted me to bring you this and said 'come home as soon as you're ready.' She probably figures you don't have anything left here." He holds out a bag I didn't even notice before.

She's not wrong. My hasty escape to my childhood prison did not involve bringing supplies, like multiple changes of clothes.

I take the bag and just nod my head before running up the stairs two at a time. I am done in record time and have to laugh at what Luna Ava packed. She knew who I would forgive or, at least talk to, first and who I would need more time to earn a second chance. She must have come into my room and taken the little I do have so I had no choice but to wear what she packed me. Although, there is no other scent but mine. Sneaky, meddling woman. I'll have to ask her about that.

At least she packed my own underwear, bra and jeans, but she gave me Oliver's tank top, a t-shirt of Kota's and Cam's sweatshirt. And they all smell like she pulled them off their bodies just before she packed them. I roll my eyes while I roll up the sleeves on the sweatshirt and head outside. I have to tuck the hem of the shirt into my pants too since it goes all the way to my knees, this takes the fashion term 'oversized' way too far. I give Sam a serious look.

Chapter 37

"Hey, don't shoot the messenger. You will notice your brother and I didn't contribute to the cause." He waves up and down my outfit.

"That doesn't mean you didn't help with the removal of my other options." I say as we start toward the school, clearly neither of us are in a hurry to get there, we're already late, the teachers stopped caring when I come and go. They also probably notice there are less incidents when I'm not there. And he's the future Delta, primary schooling is just a formality. He hands me a granola bar and water bottle, I just roll my eyes and laugh. He and Mateo are taking the malnutrition diagnosis to heart. What they don't know, is I've gone longer on less food. But that is not something I am going to tell them after all of this crap.

"So while we are talking about being your escort..."

"How did you make that jump from Luna Ava's choice of my outfit?" I almost screech.

"Don't change the subject! You are still going to the ball with us right? You can't go alone, none of us can, it's not safe for so many reasons." He laughs darkly an shudders. "Plus now that you have been officially recruited by the Alpha King you may not get to go to another one."

"I guess." I shrug, taking a bite of the dry bar. "With everything else going on, the Mating Ball just seems stupid, especially for me. I'm only eighteen, still super awkward around anyone who isn't you guys and Sierra and I can't dance. I can't even find my mate for three more years. Our elders are lazy and it seems like many of them are just using the ball to try and force chosen mates to heighten status or as political strategy. I wouldn't want to be in any of your positions, at all, basically paraded around like cattle at an auction."

"You're no different really, are you?" He looks at me sideways

"What do you mean?"

"They way your dad talks, that's basically what you are being set up for too. So a guy can level up his rank or you can get chosen by an Alpha or, I guess, some higher rank from the Alpha King's guys since you clearly have *ALL* of their attention now." He wiggles his eyebrows at me. I roll mine back at him.

"I guess I never really saw myself in that position before, my brother is the Beta, not me. I'm just a warrior. It's all I have ever wanted to be, it's all I'm good at."

"You have never been *just a warrior*, but that is why you need to give us a little slack when we have a less than pleasant reaction to other guys around you. You honestly have no idea how others see you and that is great, because your ego will never be your downfall. But, it's also dangerous because it makes it too easy for someone to take advantage of you. And yes, jealousy is a part of it, but none of the other guys will ever admit *that* to your face." He gives me a sheepish grin and I giggle a real laugh for the first time in days.

"Even Xander, the Alpha Prince?" I sass, completely joking.

"Especially him. He probably has more girls thrown at him in an hour than the twins do weekly." He grimaces. "That sounded awful, but it's the truth. Here, he sought you out, not the other way around. And, you didn't fawn over him like every other girl here, you treated him like a person not a prize or trophy. You also completely kicked his ass. He probably fell in love with you the minute you knocked him out."

"You guys don't like it when girls throw themselves at you?" I am not touching the comment about Xander. "The way you all fill your social calendar would suggest otherwise."

"Don't get me wrong the sex is always fun, but they all want more, the status, the money, they want to be trophy mates, and our jobs, including our mates', is a ton of work. None of them know what the job is or that there is work involved with the title. We keep to ourselves for a reason, even when we are out with other kids. It's not an elitist thing, it's a self preservation thing, but no one gets that if they don't have to live it. And it's not just the girls, their parents throw them at us as well, whether the girl is willing or not. Kind of like your dad."

"I guess. Speaking of my dad, let's get into class before the principal tells him I'm skipping or something else that will get me punished."

"I don't think that is anything you have to worry about ever again. After you called every single one of us out in the hospital, everyone took notice. We all know your schedule, your grades, all your efforts, academically, at least." I cringe and rub my forehead. Probably not my finest moment and I could have been more tactful in my delivery, but the words needed to be said and more importantly heard.

We walk in silence into school, but don't get further than my locker before Kaley comes up to me with Jeanie and Marnie in tow.

"What took you so long to get back? And why are you dressed like that?" She sniffs, "Where did you get Cam's shirt? He never lets me wear his sweatshirts. I demand you hand over my boyfriend's shirt now!" She raises her high-pitched voice. "And I will be letting my father know that you aren't taking the responsibility of getting back to school in a timely manner seriously after your shift." I look at the hand she has held out to me, like I really would pull off Cam's shirt and give it to her.

"The Luna chose her outfit after her patrols this morning. If you have a problem, you can take it directly to her. As for arrival times, we are well within our allotted return times, I should know, I wrote them. Speaking of, how were your shifts ladies? I hope all of your requests were met and satisfactory since you were all so eager to join even though you aren't qualified yet and don't participate regularly in any type of training that would prepare you for a situation like patrols." Sam finishes sweetly next to me. Something is brewing in his eyes and I'm here for it.

Both Marnie and Jeanie mumble unintelligible things, not looking at either of us. Marnie still looks as tired as she did when she got to me this morning. But, she appears slightly more put together now. I bet she isn't allowed in Kaley's presence without checking off certain boxes on her personal 'must look this way' list. Early doesn't suit her at all, I almost feel bad she was forced into this with false advertising and promises. Maybe she'll drop it and put me out of my misery."

"There was a misunderstanding with our shifts. Daddy will fix it before the end of the day today." Kaley flips her hair over her shoulder. "We won't need to actually learn any of that stuff anyway, I don't know why we were lumped in with the rest of the help." She waves a dismissive hand and I take in a breath calming my temper.

"I don't really consider myself 'the help,' thanks. And your schedules are set for the rest of the month. There is no changing them, regardless of what my uncle thinks he can get away with. Welcome to natural consequences. The task of arranging them has been left to me," he gestures at himself, "and considering you couldn't be bothered to show up for your assigned shift on time or complete the whole thing you will not be given any special favors. I suggest you start wrapping your head around having to actually work for a change. Your daddy's time of fixing things for you is coming to an end." Sam's voice is uncharacteristically hard. He looks Kaley dead in the eyes and for a brief second I see a flash of something like fear cross her features. "Oh and Sky, I will need your report on Marnie by the end of the day, we are evaluating all of the new patrol recruits, remind me to tell Sierra when we get to class. She has to do Jeanie's report as well. They, at least, showed up." He glances at them, then at me, then he wraps an arm around my shoulder, guiding me away from that potential train wreck.

"What do you mean report? They are just as new as we are!" Jeannie shouts, finding her voice.

"Sierra and Skylar have been working with leadership and patrols for some time, you have not. You are not the same." Sam throws over his shoulder.

"You do realize the target you put on our backs right? I don't know how the family stuff works, but they are going to make Sierra's and my life a living hell."

"Let's be honest, you can take them all blindfolded with one arm tied behind your back, but at least you would have a reason to fight back. I also believe you are currently working your way through hell, I don't think any of them could actually make what you are going through worse. She can't get to you as easily, and she knows, or at least grasps, what you mean to us. She's not dumb enough to go after you again." He raises his eyebrows letting me know he and Sierra discussed me at length.

+)❭●❬(+

I found that making up with, or I guess, acknowledging Mateo and Sam was more punishment for the other three than ignoring them all. I have never heard more growls and incoherent mumbling from any of them before. I'm still not saying much to anyone, they all have to figure out I'm not a china doll, but that won't be a reality until we are all in an actual situation that involves me saving myself and not needing them in the slightest.

I still chose the corner table at lunch. It's safe enough and separated. I have to figure out this balance between socializing and having personal space. It feels like I went from one end of the spectrum to the other and then back again. The pendulum gives me a headache.

I'm completely lost in my own thoughts when a flash of yellow sits down beside me, Marnie, followed by Jeanie on my other side in bright blue and they both lean into me, looking around skittish like they don't want to get caught talking to me.

"We cannot fail the patrol thingy. What do we need to do? Today was awful, but I can't have a bad report and if Kaley's dad can't rig it for us, you have to help us." Marnie's eyes look almost wild in her real panic as she wraps a taloned hand around my forearm.

"Umm."

"Please? We know we are terrible and we are the last people that you should help, but we can't fail again. My mom said she would send me to another pack if I do." Jeanie pants at me. "We don't even care about Kaley, she set us up."

"I guess, I could give you some pointers, but it's really hard since you guys don't actually participate in regular workouts. Your conditioning isn't where it should be."

"We will literally do anything." Marnie flashes her hopeful, crazy-looking smile at me. "Like show you how to dress better to get guys to notice you or how to get them excited and do whatever you want or show you the best way to go down on..."

"NOPE! Nope, nope, nope." I wave my hands, "Stop right there. I have no idea what your skills are, but I want none of that. Make sure you get a good night's rest, drink water and eat well today. That should help with the fatigue I saw in Marnie this morning. Wear dark colors, the idea is to not be seen in that situation. And show up and participate in training every day. After that it's about being consistent in your training. You need your cardio and strength to get through this." This is so weird, I have no idea what to make of this situation at all. I'm talking fast, I want them to get away from me as much as they want to run.

"Okay, Thanks!" They say together, popping up from the seats next to me and leaving just as quickly as they came.

"What was that all about?" Oliver's timber growls behind me. I stiffen, but don't look up.

I can't deny the calm that washes over me as he comes closer, and of course the irritation that follows at the realization. I inhale, taking in the honey scent, resisting the urge to roll my eyes and turn to him. It's so strange that such a sweet smell comes from such a menacing person. If I didn't know him, I wouldn't want to cross his path on a good day with the way he schools his face into an indifferent mask that borderlines on hostility to everyone but his closest friends.

"Sam told them that Sierra and I were evaluating their performances during patrols and they came to ask for help. I guess they are worried about failing if Kaley's dad can't rig anything in their favor. They've probably never had to truly work for something before" I shrug, turning to put my book back in my bag.

"Huh." He stands quietly behind me, then huffs before speaking again. "You need to eat something, you are not gaining weight fast enough. No skipping meals, ever." He slides a tray with a sandwich, chips, veggies, fruit and water on it towards me, then turns and just leaves.

I blink, take another deep breath and try to remember that he is taking care of me in his own caveman way. It's a sign of him trying to mend fences that he came over in the first place and as much as I want to throw it away to show I am still angry with them all, I don't. I am hungry and the doc said I wasn't eating enough for my activity level, so I eat everything, quickly, then get up to throw my stuff out and head to our next class without a backward glance. The presence of six bodies behind me tells me I have a full entourage this time.

Chapter 38

The next couple days are more of the same mundane routine, but I really don't mind routine. Sometimes with all the chaos, having expected things happen the way they are supposed to is calming and reassuring. Marnie took my advice and while she isn't any better, she isn't as big of a pain as she was on day one and she seems to be really trying. Sierra said something similar about Jeanie Friday morning.

"So after training tomorrow morning we are getting ready in the Luna's suite for the mating ball. You have zero choices in this matter and I don't want to hear about it. We also have to be ready by 5pm because Martha wants to see us at the diner first before we head over to the ball." Sierra looks over at me like I might explode at her for telling me what our plans are for this stupid dance. The casual way she just throws more things we have to do before actually attending the ball is wearing my nerves though. She has talked of nothing else all day and I don't think we have discussed the same thing twice as we walk between classes. I am also doing the mental math and do not understand the amount of time she has allotted to get ready either.

I made my peace with attending the stupid ball with her and the guys and I have determined myself to have a good time, even if it is for Sierra's sake alone. I can see her almost vibrating with excitement about the whole ordeal. We have one more class for the day and then I can get to the gym. It has become a necessity since I started running patrols. Sam, Mateo and Sierra have been taking turns 'hanging' out with me there. After what happened last time no one, including

Luna Ava and Delta Kyle trust me in there by myself. None of us really talk, just work. The twins and Oliver have yet to take their turn though and I can't decide if I am more happy or disappointed in the amount of space they are giving me.

Tonight is Sierra's turn, she asked if we could use the packhouse gym for convenience, and the topic returned to the ball. This time we are discussing the after party that seems to be happening at the packhouse. We, apparently, have to have a different outfit for this party than the dresses we are wearing to the dance.

"The Luna has us covered though. She told me this morning that our 'after-dresses' will be hanging in your room and we should be able to quickly do a wardrobe change before anyone notices we're missing." She keeps rambling as my eyebrows rise farther into my hairline and I am momentarily stuck mid squat.

"Are you serious? I am already wearing one dress that you chose for me. Why does there have to be a second monkey suit?"

"First, monkey suits are for the boys. Second, I don't argue with the Luna." She giggles at me and I can't help but crack a smile, knowing full well there wasn't a fight at all.

I just roll my eyes and get back to my leg workout. An hour later, my newly imposed time limit, Sierra and I emerge from the dungeon of the packhouse to find all the guys conveniently hanging around the island of the kitchen as we come out. Sam and Mateo make eye contact and give me a half smile, the other three just stare, no expression on their faces. Oliver slides a shaker to me, full of a dense brownish concoction, without a word or a second glance then heads out of the room. A few minutes later I hear the soft whoosh and snick of the front door opening and closing.

"He had to get to his patrol shift." Sam says by way of an explanation. "He said you still need to put some meat on your bones. Well he said a lot more, but that was the jist if it."

I take the shake rolling my eyes and head upstairs. I don't bother going back to the Beta house tonight, I have an early morning, and I am going to need plenty of rest to deal with these assholes all day tomorrow. For the first time in a long time, Sierra doesn't follow me. Maybe she thinks I'm safe here in the confines of the packhouse. And since there is no other babysitter following me, everyone else is in agreement that I'm not a flight risk here and need to be monitored.

I shower and spread out my books to make sure that I am as far ahead as I can be on my work, since I know I won't be getting anything done this weekend before going to bed.

I woke up early, well, my usual time and was both relieved and lonely finding my room completely empty of my friends. The revolving door of protectors the last few weeks with everything going on meant there was a constant presence, whether outside my door at the Beta house or camped on the sizable couch that showed up in my packhouse bedroom after the threat was delivered last week and everyone stayed with me.

I'm still trying to wrap my emotions around my friend's behavior. They know very well that I am a great fighter, but treat me like a porcelain doll. They claim to trust me, but have secret conversations without me over their mindlink. I know they care for me, but the looks of fear and uncertainty thrown my way make me anxious.

I get ready quickly and head down to grab a bite to eat before my patrol shift starts. I'm met with Gamma Brett and Oliver standing at the island having a low, heated conversation that quickly stops once they notice my presence. Oliver hands me another shake but turns to walk away without even a glance. I reach for his arm as he walks by me. He stops but doesn't turn his head.

"Thank you." I whisper, indicating the shake.

He takes a deep shuddering breath, then steps out of my grasp and heads for the stairs, clearly just off his shift. I take my own calming breath before turning to Gamma Brett who just watched the whole situation in silence.

"Ready?" Is all he asks. And I nod in response.

If that interaction is any indication of how tonight is going to be, then I may skip out on the ball all together. Sierra would understand, hopefully. Especially if the twins are similar.

Patrols were the same. We have found nothing out of the ordinary along the coastlines and the doubled up patrols across the isthmus that connects our territory to the mainland. Everything and everyone that comes and goes is now thoroughly checked and vetted before coming onto our territory.

I think best when I run, and I have found that even actively participating in patrols and concentrating on what we are being taught, my brain processes information so much better and I have come up with a theory as to why we haven't found anything yet, but the threat wasn't clear and there wasn't any indication that whoever sent it would be back. I just don't understand what the severed fingers mean and what is the significance of the silver?

"What are you thinking about so hard over there?" Gamma Brett asks, a little amusement in his tone.

"Theories."

"Really? Care to share?"

"Not sure they are worth sharing, honestly. Just jumbled thoughts. Probably things everyone else has already thought of and planned for."

I don't know why I am being so vague. It's weird talking to him when normally I would be hashing my ideas out with the guys. They are my equals. Maybe the Luna or Delta Kyle, but just because they have seen me grow over the last year and inserted themselves in my business. I'm just a kid to Gamma Brett, we don't chat and shoot the shit. He's more than likely just asking to help me learn a lesson of some kind, like any trainer, giving me prompts to help me come to the conclusions his team probably already has, especially when it comes to the Luna's safety. As her Gamma, he is almost as protective as the Alpha is.

"You know you can talk to me right? Or Kyle or Gwen or Ava. You seem to have shut everyone out, not just the boys. And just to be clear, I agree with you. Maybe not your way of going about this whole thing, but what I understand of your motives."

I take a deep breath, knowing he's right, but too stubborn to admit it out loud. I ignore the comment about my choices.

"I don't think we are going to see anything else until after the guys leave for training. Even with all the extra lessons and patrols, we are losing five of our best fighters when they head to the Royal Pack. Whoever is behind this has to be waiting for something. That's the next big transition for the pack, it's logical to assume something will happen then. But I also feel like it's too obvious at the same time. Maybe tonight at the mating ball? There are a ton of people from other packs that are here, maybe then? But I'm sure that you have all thought that through and taken precautions on top of all the inspections of outsiders coming in, otherwise we wouldn't be having it at all. Unless you're using the ball as bait to get the culprits out into the open. Which is sketchy by the way." I side eye him, he smiles the same smirk Oliver gives out occasionally. *"And what is so special about the two fingers that were sent and the silver powder that was clearly the weapon. Luna Ava didn't say if there was a note or any other message with them. I feel like there are a lot of holes in this mystery. It kind of makes my brain hurt."*

I snort an unamused laugh and get a strange look from Marnie. She must have just realized she's being left out of the conversation.

"You know it's not fair to give inside information to her just because she's the favorite and can shift and mindlink right?"

"I wouldn't dream of doing that, besides..." He switches from speaking to mind linking. *"I have the ability to link both of you even though you cannot respond Marnie. Please be careful of your accusations before you start letting them fly out of your mouth without any real thought."* Gamma Brett links both of us. Her eyes go wide. I don't think she has ever been called out like that before, so used to getting away with flippant comments. He was far more calm than I would have been after days of her frustratingly holding us back. She's trying, but it's not any less frustrating, she's slow and loud and distracting in the worst possible way. "Sky to answer your question, we have started to think of those possibilities and work through them, and no, we would not use anyone as bait unknowingly.

Marnie's eyes go wide at the mention of people being used as 'bait.' I nod and we continue. Marnie makes no more comments or even asks what my question was.

The only good thing is her and Jeanie at least took my notes seriously and they have actually started participating in training, but they are years behind, which is painful for everyone involved.

The five hour shifts are only slightly less painful than the first day with her, and to think, I have three more weeks of this rotation. I'm so overjoyed, ugh!

We head back to the patrol cabin and check out before we all go our separate ways. I head off to Saturday morning training with the pups. They should actually be close to wrapping the first session up with the younger kids when I get there. It feels like forever since I have seen these kids, with the trials and the lockdown and can't wait to catch up with them. I didn't realize how much I would miss training with them. Getting to see their excited faces when they finally master something they have been working on forever.

When I walk into the arena, training is in full effect and for the first time ever, I just stop to watch the beauty that is my pack. Each of the guys and Sierra have taken a group and they appear to be teaching release techniques for close combat. Everyone is sweaty and red-faced, but happy and engaged.

"Sky! Sky! Come look. I did it!!" Brandon, a very hyper eight year old that reminds me of Sam when he was little, shouts at me as he barrels into the side of my leg, breaking me out of my thoughts.

"What did you do?!" I ask excitedly as he grabs my hand and I can't help but be drawn in by his enthusiasm. I let him drag me across the field, we are both smiling and laughing and I am so caught up I don't realize who he is dragging me to. Until I'm thrown straight into a solid wall of muscle. I bounce and strong hands keep me from embarrassing myself by falling on my butt in front of all these kids.

A sharp intake of Citrus lets me know exactly who saved my dignity. I look up at Cam's face and give him a small smile. This is only the second one on one contact we've had in days and I have to admit, it's also the first time I have felt any sense of calm since our fight. I shamelessly take another deep inhale of his scent closing my eyes to savor the peace that washes over me. The rumbling chuckle in his chest lets me know the action didn't go unnoticed.

"The feeling is mutual, Tiny, I mean Skylar."

Every fiber of my being wants to tell him it's okay to call me by the pet name, but thank the Goddess that my brain is in charge. I just nod and then clear my throat.

"Umm, Brandon said he had something to show me." I look down at the boy still attached to my hand, looking up at us, completely oblivious to the moment that just passed.

"Yes! I totally took Alpha Cam down! It was the greatest thing EVER!" Brandon has a crazed look, pumping his fists and his whole body is vibrating with excitement. I am fighting to hold back my laugh.

"Oh, really? I would like to see that. It's not everyday you get a chance to beat an Alpha." I giggle and wink at Cam who has an unreadable expression on his face.

"Alright little man, it sounds like you want a challenge and I don't know how I feel about you taking my girl's attention or holding her hand. I might not play fair now."

Brandon's eyes go wide and he looks at his hand in mine and jumps back like I electrocuted him. "I'm sorry Alpha, that's not what I meant at all. I just wanted Sky to watch, you know, since she's been teaching us and all, and..."

"Brandon, relax, he was just teasing." I try to calm the rambling boy down.

"Was I though? If I'm not allowed to touch you, no one else is." Cam mindlinks me.

My jaw drops open, but Cam just turns around. "Come on Brandon, let's show your fearless leader what you can do." Cam walks off with Brandon, and I am speechless.

As soon as my brain checks in and I realize I should be moving, a massive arm wraps around my shoulder.

"It's only fair that I get to be close too, even if it's a minute. Yes, I'm jealous that an eight year old was holding your hand and from watching my brother hold you." Dakota mindlinks me, but doesn't look at me, just propels us forward where Cam and Brandon are setting up to spar. He doesn't release me like I thought he would though, just leaves his arm loosely draped over my shoulder.

"Alright little man, let's see what you got." Cam taunts Brandon who doesn't seem phased at all. He's bouncing around like a heavy weight boxer getting ready to start a fight.

They get into position and Cam grabs Brandon like they were practicing before, but instead of letting Brandon win the fight quickly, Cam puts more resistance on him and makes it more difficult for Brandon to break the hold. Brandon tries the release again and again, finally on the fourth attempt Cam lets him break the hold.

"Awe man, that was way harder this time. Did you just go easy on me to make me feel better the first time?" Brandon almost looks defeated. I move to go to him and try to help him understand that Cam is making him better this way, but Kota grabs my arm, holding me in place.

"I would never do that to you little man. The first time was to show you how getting out of the hold works, then we keep working on it so the move is in your muscle memory no matter the situation, then as you get better, we make it harder and harder to break so you're always learning. Besides, I couldn't let you make me look weak in front of the girls." He wiggles his eyebrows at Brandon whose smile lights up his whole face, making me smile too.

A low rumbling huff comes from the other side of the sparring circle. I look up sharply to see Oliver staring daggers at me with a scowl on his face. He rolls his eyes and turns to walk away.

He doesn't get far before we hear, "Oh Goddess there you are! I have been looking for you everywhere. The Luna wasn't sure where all of you were. Of course you are working with these sweet little pups, it's so great how you spend your spare time with them. I just wanted to make sure that you boys left on time to get ready to take us to the mating ball. We have to be right on time for the grand entrance. I heard that Alpha Prince Alexander was coming too since he became such good friends with you all during the trial, so we for sure can't be late." Kaley's high pitched tone came at us from the entrance of the arena. She is talking animatedly with her hands like a fairy in a movie.

"What are you talking about?" Sam asks coming up next to me. "We have plenty of time, two more training sessions and none of us are taking you anywhere. I know that we all made that perfectly clear. We are going as a group." He points generally to the guys, Sierra and I. "And just to be one hundred percent clear that does not include yourself, Marnie or Jeanie. Please stop trying to force the issue or change our minds."

Kaley's face went more crimson than I have ever seen it before, but I'm not sure if it was from anger or embarrassment at this going down with an audience.

"My father said Cameron and Dakota will be escorting me, Mateo will be escorting Jeanie and Oliver will be escorting Marnie. I have no reason to think otherwise. He set everything up and I expect you all to pick us up on time so we can make our entrance properly as the future leaders of this pack." She raises her chin to Sam as if she is giving a command.

"I suggest you watch your tone to your future leaders." Oliver emphasizes the word 'leaders.' "Your father is not a leader in any way shape or form, and therefore has no control over us or really anything in this pack. As you have been told on more than enough occasions, we are going as a group." He gestures to the guys around the sparring circle again for emphasis. "The future Alphas, Betas, Gammas and Delta. You are none of those things. Do not expect any of us to show up to escort you anywhere. None of us can sense our mate, so this ball is nothing more than an end of year dance and formality for any of us. There is no reason to make such a big deal out of it. If you choose to attend we might see you later." He turns and heads towards the entrance to the arena without a glance back at any of us.

I did not miss the plurals of 'Beta' and 'Gamma' including Sierra and I by our ranks. My heart stings watching him go, he's still angry at me for wanting to leave and not listening to his pleas to stay. I take a deep breath and roll my eyes inwardly. He has to let me go. I can't be stifled here.

Before Kaley can say anything else Delta Kyle comes up and claps his hands. "You all did very well today, we will see you next weekend. Make sure you work on everything that you learned so you can come back stronger next week. The Luna would like a word with you all so I am going to take the rest of the training for today." He doesn't even spare Kaley a glance.

"Awe man! I was totally going to whoop you this time too." Brandon stomps the ground.

"There's always next time, little man." Cam pats him on the shoulder.

I turn out of Dakota's grasp. "I'm just going to grab my things then I will be on my way, you guys don't have to wait, I'll catch up." I head swiftly towards the locker area.

I don't have anything to grab, I just really don't want to walk with them. There's still a huge tension between all of us and I'm not sure how to get past it. I guess I'll have to figure it out soon if I want to hang out with all of them for the rest of the night though.

I fiddle around in the girls locker room for about ten minutes and figure they should be gone by now and if they aren't I will just have to deal with them walking me to the packhouse. As I go to grab the door it comes flying open and the momentum I wasn't expecting knocks me on my butt. Before I know what is happening I see a fist flying towards my head and then everything goes black.

Chapter 39

Plink Drip. Plink Drip. Plink Drip. Plink Drip.

"Ugh." What is that sound? And why does my head hurt so badly? Where am I? I try to open my eyes, but they feel like they are being weighed down by something. I move my eyeballs around behind my eyelids really slowly and then try opening again. This time I get light through just a sliver of an opening in my eyelids, but everything is fuzzy. I blink some more willing something to come into focus.

Plink Drip. Plink Drip. Plink Drip. Plink Drip.

I squeeze my eyes shut, which actually hurts, then crack them open again and get enough body awareness to shift my head toward the sound that's like nails on a chalkboard in this otherwise silent space. Finally I can see it. One of the faucets in the communal showers is dripping, I'm still in the locker room. Why was I in the locker room? The obnoxious sound is coming from the water hitting the metal soap shelf and then the drain and sending chills up my spine. I slowly move my head forward, why am I so slow and groggy? Even thinking is hard. I don't think I am standing, but I don't think I'm on the floor either. Huh.

I can't see and I don't think I can move, what can I do? I need to focus. I can smell...maybe. I try to inhale. "Umph, uhh." Shit that hurts. My chest is on fire now, for sure broken ribs. I try again more slowly this time, expecting the pain. Blood. All I smell is blood. My blood to be exact, and a lot of it. What the fuck is going on?

"It's about time you stupid, interfering bitch. It took far too long for you to come out of that. They didn't even hit that hard or give you that much sedative. You are as weak as you look." A flash of light goes off near me, making me flinch. I didn't realize there was anyone here with me. I wonder if my nose is broken, maybe that's why I can only smell my own blood.

I know the voice though. Kaley. This cannot be good. I do a physical check while she yammers on about me being pitiful and useless. Nothing original in her string of insults. I can't move my toes, but I think I can feel them. My knees hurt which unfortunately is a good and bad sign, I have some sort of use of my legs, but not much. I can't tell if my shirt is wet or if I am bleeding, maybe both, but something is for sure not right on my torso, I can't feel my fingers, and my shoulders are burning. Probably from being tied up or dragged around, but I don't have the body control to even look at myself yet. This may be worse than the whipping.

I try to say something, but it feels like someone dumped a bucket of sand into my mouth and throat and as I flex the muscles in my face I know there must be some spectacular bruising and broken bones. It hurts to move my tongue inside my mouth.

"Don't bother with your smartass remarks. I'm just here to tell you to stay away from the twins, permanently. They are mine and I will not have you getting in the way any longer." A kick to my stomach makes me choke on the little air I can take in. I am for sure not laying down. "Stop annoying them." Kick to my side. "Stop distracting them." Kick to my other side. At least two people are helping her. "And stop trying to force yourself on them." Slap. A warm sensation flows down my lips. "They. Are. Mine." She punctuates each word. I try to focus on where I hear her voice. She isn't close enough to be the one inflicting my torture. Punch. This one right across my face including the broken cheekbone. I think I lost a tooth with that one and I can't stifle a small whimper this time.

"UGH! Watch where you are flicking her nasty skank blood. I have to be presentable for Cameron and Dakota at the mating ball. I'm tired of you getting attention you don't deserve." Punch. "Having access and time with the Alpha and Luna that should be mine." Kick. "You should not be the favorite, you worthless spare beta, I should be. They are all just taking pity on you since not even your dad wants you." Slap. "Get it through your head now. I. Will. Be. Luna. And there's nothing you can do to stop me." A sharp pain pierces my thigh. I felt it again and again in both legs and then dragged up my arms. I can barely breathe, I can't scream, the searing pain is so bad I want to throw up, just like when... When she used the silver powder on me. Oh shit, she's going to really kill me with silver this time!

I can't call for help, or even beg her to stop, I *am* weak. I would beg for her to stop if I could. I can't feel my wolf because of the silver and whatever else has me disoriented. I just keep shouting in my head hoping someone can hear my stifled cry for help. I don't focus on one person, I shout out to the whole pack, praying someone can hear me. Maybe Oliver and the twins can feel my agony, anything to stop this. But, maybe they can't since there is probably wolfsbane blocking my connection. Maybe my wolf is the only connection I have to them. Maybe she's the reason we are so close with them. It's not because of me, she's the one that is special. I am still just the unwanted spare. I can hear muffled conversation around me, but I can't make anything out through the blinding pain.

My head is whipped back and someone has a firm grip on my hair. My body makes an involuntary noise of agony. I still can't see anyone, but I can feel several of the tiny baby hairs pulling from my scalp, making my eyes water. Then the unmistakable sound of scissors cutting slowly, deliberately slowly. Snip, snip, snip, snip, before my head falls forward unexpectedly lighter, and freshly cut, short, loose strands fall into my eyes and poke at my face. She cut off my hair?! What is wrong with her? I'm already beaten to the point of not being recognizable.

"There, now even if you do heal, you will look terrible and none of the guys will want to look at you or to be seen with you. Make sure she's out until after the ball is over, preferably for a day or two. That should give me plenty of time with the Alphas. And if I see you anywhere near them after this, Skank, I will make sure you don't survive the next round. There are plenty of wolves willing to help me get rid of worthless trash like you. If you can survive this you should scurry away like the vermin you are." The unmistakable sound of heels clicking on the tile floor of the locker room retreat behind me. Punches and kicks rain all over my body again. A few more to my face tell me this is probably why I can't see, my eyes are swollen almost completely shut.

I just keep chanting 'please help me" in my head over and over again as my cries of pain go ignored. I can't move my arms or legs. Maybe I'm bound, maybe they're broken, who knows. I knew that there was a target on my back when the guys said they were taking Sierra and I to this stupid ball and hanging out with us, but I didn't think this was going to be the result. I hope Sierra isn't locked somewhere going through the same torture. I can feel the warm stream of tears running down my deformed face. I can't believe this is how I am going to leave this world, there's no way I will make it to a next time. Drugged and beaten in the locker room of my favorite place. The arena, my true home. The place that allowed me to feel normal and part of this pack, with a purpose. This is where I am going to take my last breath. I guess it could be worse. I am home. I just wish I would have been able to fight for my life, not trussed up like a pig for slaughter.

The light is starting to fade and it has gotten more quiet, but maybe I just can't hear anymore. I'm making out less and less colors in front of me. I didn't get to say goodbye to my wolf or the kids, that would have been nice. And Brandon really wanted to show off with Cam. I bet it would have been really cute watching him go up against the future Alpha again, so serious and determined he could win. And Cam would have played along, even just for a bit. Dakota would have been standing by to give Brandon pointers on how to beat his brother. I can picture the sparkle in his eye. Sam would have been talking smack to Cam about having to go up against a kid to look good and Mateo and Oliver would be standing watch to make sure nothing went wrong. Always the protectors.

I wish I would have been able to see Oliver's smile one more time. I hate that my last thought of him is going to be that moody scowl of his walking away from me angry and resentful. My brother finally got to see the real me and was proud. I wish I could have been more for him. Stronger, by his side. Not weak, needing his protection all of the time. I love you guys.

I take a deep, slow breath. It hurts so bad, I let out a strangled cry. But, I guess I really don't need to anymore do I? Breathing makes my whole chest sear right now. It really would just be better to stop. I'm tired.

BANG!

My ears are assaulted by sounds. It's so noisy. What happened to the quiet crushing me? Can't I just die in peace?

Firms hands. My head is floppy. I don't like all the moving, it hurts so bad. Leave me alone already! But my mouth won't say anything. What's happening? Everything is throbbing. I think someone is talking, but it sounds like we're under water.

"Oh...Don't. Wake Up. Keep... Open."

What? Don't do what? Keep what open? I can't open anything. I'm so confused, is someone talking to me? I just want to die in peace.

"Breathe, Skylar! I need you to open your eyes sweetheart. Let me know you can hear me. I know it's hard, there's a lot of silver and wolfsbane in your system, I can smell it all over you, but I need you to keep fighting it." I know that voice, it's deep and stern, but comforting. Who's voice is that? Why do they want me to fight? I just want to go to the Moon Goddess in peace.

"Mmmm." It's all I can manage to whimper out, my eyelids don't want to move from this kind of open position.

"She's still with us! We have to move fast. Sky try and stay with me, keep trying to talk to me."

"Who y..?" I think that was a whole thought, did I say it or think it? My mouth is swollen and puffy. I think I am floating now, cold air hits my skin and a breeze is blowing over me, cooling me down. I didn't know I was hot until right this second. "Mmm hod." I slur.

"Your body is trying to burn off the silver in your bloodstream. Don't worry we'll get you fixed up. She was left to die down there, but why? There was no scent but hers and there's no way only one person pulled this off in the time they had to get to her." I still can't place that deep voice, but I should know it. It's familiar and makes me feel safe. I don't want to feel safe though. I'm done with this bullshit. I want to go home to the Goddess.

My head starts to hurt, like a blinding migraine coming on. I groan out the pain, but my body can't move to curl in on itself or wrap my arms over my head to try and soothe it. I am completely numb, and yet, everything hurts at the same time. A squeal of pain leaves my lips and I can feel tears trickle down my deformed face.

"I know, I'm sorry."

"Let me die." I whisper the first coherent thought yet.

"Never." A growl comes out. This time the voice that was so comforting was scary, menacing.

I take another painfully shallow breath. The next thing I know is darkness.

Chapter 40
Bonus

Thank you for reading Book 1 in the Blood & Bond Series!

So you all know I can't go a whole book without giving you some of the research and tidbits I have for this part of the story. If you have been with me from the beginning you know I love a good Pinterest board and I love when things have layers and meanings.

I work really hard to have a meaning or purpose to all the things that I write and this book is no different. Not counting this bonus section, this book has 39 chapters.

The Kickstarter for this book went live on 8/8/2025, the Lion's Gate Portal, which also happened during a full moon. If that doesn't say 'launch my were-wolf series,' I don't know what does. In numerology double eight = infinity and abundance, so it's branded as a door (portal) to set intentions and "call in" big goals. And together we hit big goals!

Thirty-nine is a multiple of three — to be exact, 3 × 13 — which means it carries the vibrational energy of *three* in its very bones. Three is the number of balance and completion: past–present–future, birth–life–death, mind–body–spirit, beginning-middle-end. In magic, three is the smallest number that creates a pattern — the point where chaos finds structure. You all know I like my chaos and a whole lot of patterns.

The other factor of thirty-nine, thirteen, is no wallflower either. It's the number of lunar cycles in a year, the sacred rhythm that witches have followed for centuries. Thirteen can be a number of rebellion and renewal, the moment you step outside the ordinary and into the unknown. When multiplied by three, it becomes a force that strengthens cycles and repeats them with purpose. Skylar and I have both stepped WAY out of out comfort zones here and it has been an amazing ride so far.

Numerologists often say thirty-nine represents the completion of a cycle and the preparation for a new one. It's the transitional space, not the doorway itself, but the threshold where you take your breath before stepping through. In storytelling, it's the penultimate moment before the finale. In life, it's the space between who you were and who you're about to become. This book is all about Skylar's initial thrust into the transformation of who she is meant to be. The number three is an amplifier, a progression that hints that every cycle of life you complete makes you stronger for the next one. I feel like this is also my personal push through the door of my writing. We are here and never going back!

In the next installment of Sky's story, we get to see her cross the threshold into a new life, new challenges, new friends, and a new location for it all.

Chapter 41
Kickstarter Backer's Page

Hey Backers!

Wow. Just... wow. You guys are amazing. I can't believe you believed in *Unbreakable* enough to help me get this project off the ground! Every pledge, every share, every message of encouragement reminded me that this story isn't just mine—it's ours.

This page is for you—the top-tier backers who made this dream possible. You're the real MVPs, the ones who saw potential, got excited, and jumped in to help. I am beyond grateful, and I hope you love seeing the world of *Unbreakable* come alive as much as I loved creating it.

Thank you for making magic happen with me!

On 8/8/2025 we launched a Kickstarter campaign for the first physical publication of this series. Here are some of the ***Amazing*** people who believed in me from the get-go.

Natasha Keeler – Sandra Ibañez – Mary Melissa – Fuzzy Reads

Melissa Blazer – Camy Jo Weber – Jade Mandiville – Amanda Hobbs

Alichia Brown – Daisy Graham – Newvine Family – Peter Mihelich

Katlyn Pecora – Janet Perry – Stephanie Benson – Tracy Winters

Borrada Z. – Pamela Brown – Martha Willis – Josephine Carroll

Charlotte Best – Shaey T – Ashleigh Staples – Alexis Garnett

Bryana – J.E. Varilek – Dayna – Dominique R. Fontaine

www.ingramcontent.com/pod-product-compliance
Lightning Source LLC
Chambersburg PA
CBHW040330020826
48978CB00013BC/1006